Praise for the novel

"A lovely story spanning all the emotions—from a woman's worst moment to her self-reflection and growth to, ultimately, the perfect love."
—Lori Foster, *New York Times* bestselling author, on *The Runaway Bride of Blossom Branch*

"Maynard delivers in spades." —*LifetimeTV.com*

"[Janice Maynard is] sensual, sassy and emotionally riveting!"
—*Thoughts of a Blonde*

"An engaging, sexy story set in a charming small Southern town readers will want to visit again and again."
—JoAnn Ross, *New York Times* bestselling author of *Forever in Honeymoon Harbor*, on *The Runaway Bride of Blossom Branch*

"*The Runaway Bride of Blossom Branch* is a delightful romance with well-drawn characters and a lovely setting. Janice Maynard writes with tenderness and heart. I can't wait for another visit to Blossom Branch!"
—RaeAnne Thayne, *New York Times* bestselling author

"[Maynard] never disappoints." —*Romance, Jane and Louis*

Also by Janice Maynard

The Runaway Bride of Blossom Branch

Look for Janice Maynard's next Blossom Branch novel
available soon from Canary Street Press.

For additional books by Janice Maynard,
visit her website, janicemaynard.com.

ONE
Sweet
Southern
SUMMER

JANICE MAYNARD

CANARY STREET PRESS

CANARY STREET PRESS™

Recycling programs for this product may not exist in your area.

ISBN-13: 978-1-335-52306-8

One Sweet Southern Summer
Copyright © 2024 by Janice Maynard

Maybe My Baby
Copyright © 2024 by Janice Maynard

For questions and comments about the quality of this book, please contact us at CustomerService@Harlequin.com.

TM is a trademark of Harlequin Enterprises ULC.

Canary Street Press
22 Adelaide St. West, 41st Floor
Toronto, Ontario M5H 4E3, Canada
CanaryStPress.com

Printed in U.S.A.

CONTENTS

ONE
SWEET
SOUTHERN
SUMMER

ONE

"HAVE I MADE A TERRIBLE MISTAKE?"

Leah Marks leaned on a fence railing that still smelled of new wood and tried to ignore the panicked butterflies whirling in her chest. In the distance, middle schoolers crisscrossed the newly sodded lawn, finding their quarters and laughing excitedly. Or at least most of them were enthusiastic. She had already spotted a few loners who arrived with either sulky or wary expressions.

Three years ago, her great-aunt Trudie, wealthy and childless, had left Leah a charming bungalow in the town of Blossom Branch, Georgia, along with this fifty acres of land farther out from town that encompassed a healthy peach orchard and the remnants of a summer camp from the 1970s. Plus an embarrassing amount of cash.

Leah's aunt hadn't particularly liked children as far as Leah could tell. So the inheritance had come as a complete surprise.

A letter from the grave had expressed Trudie's desire for Leah to *make her mark on the world.*

Even as a young woman, Leah understood the implication. Her parents' marriage was very conventional, with her mother accommodating her father's wants and needs, sometimes at the expense of her own. Leah's brothers were showered with encouragement to try new things, take risks, reach for the stars.

Leah was a shy, bookish, introverted kid growing up. The only things she had been encouraged to do were to be quiet and polite and make good grades. Sports were never suggested, and since Leah had always seen herself as being on the clumsy and gawky side, she certainly never wanted to sign up for volleyball or soccer. She'd tried dance camp for a time, and after that, one brief, embarrassing summer of gymnastics, but for the most part, *risk*—physical or otherwise—was not something to be embraced as a female in the Marks family.

Even more recently, with her degrees in hand, she had struggled to know where she wanted to live, what she wanted to do, how she might stand out as an adult woman *not* in the shadow of her male siblings.

Then came Aunt Trudie's unexpected gift. It had been a watershed moment. A wake-up call. A dogged insistence from a remarkable woman who had never allowed herself to be sidelined that Leah should *do something.*

Even with the inheritance and Trudie's posthumous urging, it had taken time to settle on a project. Her mother had wanted her to put Aunt Trudie's gift in a college fund for Leah's theoretical future offspring, managing to point out more than once that her daughter needed to get "out there" and find a man. Her father had urged her to sell the valuable property and invest the cash. But Leah had been drawn to the idea of summer camp. Why, she wasn't sure. *She* had certainly never been to camp as a child.

But this land was hers. *Hers.* She would never forget the first day she walked the property after the lawyer's call. Something about the romantic aroma of peach trees heavy with fruit, the thick summer air, and the zip of dragonflies over a mysterious pond had been exhilarating and empowering. Endless conversations with her two best friends had brought Leah to this pivotal moment today.

She had been blessed by her aunt's gift, and now she wanted to share her good fortune. While doing an internship at an alternative school during her senior year in college, she had seen enough of other families' pain in the world to know the money would feel like a burden unless she spent it well.

Establishing a nonprofit, renovating the camp, and funding a program for troubled young teens had seemed like a great way to pay it forward and put her psychology degrees to good use. But now that the twenty middle schoolers had arrived from Atlanta—her very first campers—she felt out of her depth.

Her best friend Cate mimicked Leah's pose and looked out across the corral that would facilitate equine therapy. "Of course you're not making a mistake. Don't be silly. Your counselors are highly trained adults with backgrounds in trauma and addiction. You've turned this camp into a showplace. These kids are extremely lucky to be here."

Cate's words didn't entirely erase the queasy feeling in Leah's stomach. Now that the day had come, the risks—both financial and emotional—seemed startlingly real. The whole reason she had gone into psychology in the first place was because she wanted to help people, but that was easier said than done.

The gentle I-told-you-sos from her family would be endless if this camp failed. They didn't *want* her to fail. They loved her. Truly they did. She knew that. But none of them *expected* her to succeed.

Just once in her life she would like to surprise them.

Having Cate as an unofficial adviser on this project had been a welcome support. Leah's gorgeous blonde friend was as talented as she was beautiful. Cate did volunteer work with Atlanta's High Museum of Art as a facilitator with kids from high-poverty areas of the city, in a program that offered a chance to understand and appreciate great paintings and sculptures. The campers who arrived barely an hour ago had been selected via those contacts.

Despite Cate's knowledge and input, Leah knew that a residential camp was a far cry from two-hour classes at a museum. Leah would be feeding these kids, housing them, keeping them clean and safe, entertaining them. The list was endless.

"What if I fail?" Leah said, wiping beads of sweat from her forehead. The day was wicked hot. She had spoken aloud, but mostly to herself.

Cate turned to face her. "Why would you think that?"

"I don't know." But Leah *did* know. She'd spent her whole life in the shadow of three overachieving older brothers. Though her family loved her, they thought a woman's primary goal should be to settle down and start a family, even if she worked full time outside the home.

"I can stay the night," Cate said. "It's not a problem."

"Thank you, but no. I'll be fine." Leah had hired two capable and highly credentialed camp directors. She didn't have to *run* the camp, but at day's end, she was in charge, and she would be staying on-site any time camp was in session.

Cate eyed her sympathetically. "It's normal to be nervous in the face of a big undertaking."

Leah winced. "Like a wedding?" she asked dryly. "Or is that joke too soon?"

Her friend smiled, but for a moment a flutter of *something* flitted through her eyes. A year ago, almost to the day, Cate had stood in front of twelve hundred people in a beautiful Atlanta church and instead of getting married, had been dumped by her fiancé.

Leah couldn't imagine surviving that kind of humiliation.

But Cate had come out of the ordeal stronger, happier, and still as generous with her time. Years ago, her friendship with Leah at the University of Georgia had given a painfully shy Leah the chance to bloom. Leah owed her so much. Their friendship had deepened exponentially in the years since.

Cate sighed. "Jason did the right thing. Maybe his timing sucked, but what happened that day was for the best."

"And now you have Harry."

"I do." Cate chuckled. "Can you keep a secret?"

"I think you know I can."

"Harry and I got married when we were in Antigua this spring." Cate glowed. "I couldn't face the thought of another traditional wedding after everything that happened. But we're going to try getting pregnant, and I wanted to be married first."

Leah hugged her. "Congratulations. That's wonderful. And so romantic."

"Thanks."

"When will you break the news to everyone else?"

"We're planning a reception later in the summer. I'll keep you posted."

Leah glanced at her watch. "You should probably go," she said, disguising her unease. "Don't want to get caught in rush hour traffic."

"You're right."

Leah walked her to the car. "Thank you for everything you've done, Cate. Working with social services. Identifying and screening our campers. You've been a godsend."

"I was happy to help, but this is all you, Leah. You had a dream, and you made it happen. Your family will be very proud and impressed. Wait and see."

At 3:00 a.m. Leah smelled smoke. Almost simultaneously, the fire alarm went off. And her phone dinged with a text. Fire in kitchen/dining hall. Already called 911. Looks like all kids are accounted for...

That was Jim. He and Peg were social workers in their forties who believed, like Leah, that summer camp with kids in need would be fun and rewarding. They, along with two other residential counselors, slept in the cabins with the children.

Leah trusted Jim and Peg implicitly, but until she could see for herself that the campers were safe, her heart wouldn't stop pounding.

There was no time to change clothes. She threw on a button-up shirt over the tank she was wearing. Her thin knit sleep pants would have to do. A pair of Crocs were the closest thing at hand. She shoved her feet into them and ran out the door.

The main house, the owner's lodge, was the structure nearest the front of the property. The large building that housed food prep and dining areas—in addition to the office—sat farther back. The two dormitory-style cabins were fifty yards away.

Given Jim's text, there was little reason to think any of her campers were in danger, but Leah hustled anyway, her heart in her throat. As soon as she rounded the corner of her house, she heard sirens, and she could see the blaze at the back of the kitchen.

A heavy rain shower earlier in the day had left the air humid and heavy. She had to step carefully to avoid mud puddles where the new grass hadn't taken hold sufficiently.

And now, smoke.

Though her instinct was to check out the fire, she headed for the camper cabins instead. Jim met her out front, his expression grim in the illumination of a security light. "Peg is making sure they're all back in their beds, even if they don't sleep for now."

"All twenty there?"

"Yep. But you're not going to like this. I'm almost a hundred percent sure Benjamin started the fire."

Her heart sank. Benjamin had arrived at camp angry and

sullen. Apparently, nothing had improved. "Why do you think that?" she asked.

"He reeks of smoke, far more than he should to have been so far away. And he gave me a nasty, snarky grin when I was counting heads."

"Damn," she said glumly.

"Yep." He rubbed his chin. "What do you want to do, boss?"

"Are they safe to stay where they are?"

"Should be. I'll get a second opinion from the fire and rescue folks. But we'll need breakfast in about four hours."

"Do you have a suggestion?"

"I think everybody should get more sleep when things settle down. Peg offered to drive into town and grab a simple meal at the grocery store. Cereal, orange juice, milk…whatever we need."

"But we have all that," Leah said, mentally counting the dollars and cents.

"Not if the fire smolders for a few hours."

"Ugh." She rubbed two fingers in the center of her forehead where a headache brewed. "Okay. That's our plan, then. Both cabins have porches. We can always eat there if we have to…" She inhaled. "You and Peg stay with the kids. I'm going to check in with the firemen."

"Got it."

Jim walked away, and Leah turned toward the dining hall. Flames no longer jumped in the sky. Now, a plume of smoke rose from the back of the building.

She headed in that direction and immediately saw a tall man in full gear approaching her, a frown on his face.

"Don't come any closer," he said. "Are you in charge here?"

Something about his stance made her legs shaky. "I am."

"Was anyone in this structure when the fire started?"

"Not that I'm aware. We've accounted for all our campers and staff."

"And you are?"

She stuck out her hand. "Leah Marks. I own the place."

The fireman held up his gloved fingers. "No offense, ma'am, but you don't want to touch me."

"Oh." Her face burned. It was hard to tell what he looked like underneath the helmet and heavy coat, but what she could see of his face was masculine and striking. His voice was deep and commanding.

She felt the need to back up, but when she did, her right foot hit a slick spot and she went down hard, flailing her arms, landing on her right hip and elbow, and twisting her ankle badly. Pain shot through her body, even as mud covered her from shoulder to toe.

Embarrassment made her even clumsier as she tried to roll over and get up. But Mr. Hot-and-Sexy fireman was already squatting to help her. When he pulled off one glove, the touch of his warm hand on hers was shocking.

"Did you break anything?" he asked, the words sharp with concern.

"No," she said, not bothering to hide her exasperation but trying to ignore the zing of attraction. "I'm *twenty*-six not eighty-six. I can handle the occasional bounce." Best not to mention the ankle.

"Even young people break bones." Without asking, the fireman scooped her into his arms and stood.

Leah squawked, mortified. "Put me down," she demanded. "I'm too heavy." She'd been struggling to lose the same fifteen pounds forever.

The man ignored her. "We train for this all the time. Quit wiggling." He strode across the lawn to the front of her house. "That mud will harden and get nasty. You probably ought to get in the shower ASAP."

"Are you sure you don't want to carry me in there?" Leah was trying to be sarcastic about his take-charge attitude. But instead, the words came out sounding like an invitation. *Oh, Lordy.*

Her rescuer froze, his foot on the bottom step of her porch. Leah's face flamed.

He set her carefully on her feet and stepped away. "I've got to check on my men," he said. "I'll be back. Don't go near the fire." Then he paused and rubbed his bare thumb across her cheekbone, examining the dollop of mud he collected with a rueful grin. "Might need two showers," he said, chuckling. Then he turned and strode across the lawn.

Leah limped inside, strangled with humiliation, even more so when she confronted her bathroom mirror. It was a big mirror. Too big. In one glance she saw her mud-soaked head and face and everything else. Surely she had imagined the awareness between her and the big, bossy fireman.

The clothes were probably a total loss. She turned on the shower and grimaced as she stripped to her bare skin and took the fastest shower on record. The worst part was shampooing her shoulder-length hair. It was hard to tell if she was getting all the mud out. Her natural color was not far off mud-brown, so maybe it didn't matter.

When she was dry except for her damp, thick waves, she found real clothes, dressed, and went back outside. On the far horizon, a faint glow reminded her that dawn was approaching. She and her staff were going into the first full day of camp sleep deprived.

Fortunately, her roster of college-aged junior counselors would show up around eight. She didn't have enough cabins yet for them to stay on-site. That was next on the list. The twenty-somethings had been trained to lead crafts and games and adventure activities like swimming and kayaking and scaling the modest climbing wall. Even a ropes course when it was finished, hopefully by the end of the week.

Ideally, the campers were supposed to take turns serving

meals and cleaning up afterward. Team building and developing a strong work ethic were core parts of the camp philosophy. Those responsibilities would have to be put on hold until the dining hall was cleared for use. Leah had hired a trio of local women as cooks. She'd already sent texts waving them off for this morning.

The two cabins where campers slept were dark. Hopefully, exhaustion had overtaken adrenaline. She didn't want to bother anyone if they were all knocked out. So she backtracked until she could see inside the eating area.

There was no glass in the windows. Nothing was winterized. Just screens and ceiling fans. During a Georgia summer, there would be really hot days. But they would all adjust. A hundred years ago, children in this rural area would have played outside from dawn until dusk.

Leah had enjoyed just such an idyllic childhood in Blossom Branch. Cate had, too, though she and Leah hadn't run in the same circles back then.

A deep voice made her jump. "I told you to stay away," the voice said, clearly irritated.

It was the bossy fireman. Leah turned, wrapping her arms around her waist. He had lifted the visor on his helmet, so she could see his face now. His extremely handsome face. She ground her teeth. "This is *my* camp," she said. "What's the status?"

"The fire is out. I'm going to hang around for a few hours to make sure nothing reignites. But I have bad news, Ms. Marks."

She eyed him morosely. "Other than the fact my brand-new kitchen is a mess?"

He ignored her sarcasm. "We found evidence of arson. The sheriff is on his way. I imagine he'll want to interview your campers when they wake up."

Leah's heart sank. "You should know something. My kids, twenty of them, have a history of behavior problems. And they've faced all kinds of difficult home situations. Poverty, foster care, abuse—you name it. So we were bound to have challenges. I just didn't expect something so big, and not in the first twenty-four hours."

"Do you have any idea who might have started the fire?"

"Possibly. One of my two senior staff members told me Benjamin smelled strongly of smoke. He's in therapy for anger issues. But I don't want to press charges. We'll deal with it here. Jim and Peg are highly trained social workers."

"It may not be up to you. Arson is a felony."

"But he's only thirteen!" Tears pricked her eyes. Things were unraveling. This wasn't how she had envisioned starting the summer.

"May I ask you a question?" the fireman said.

Leah wiped the back of her hand over her eyes. "Yes."

"Are you one of those rich, do-gooder types who thinks she can save the world?"

Her spine stiffened. "Do you know how incredibly offensive that question is? I'm not rich."

"This camp would say otherwise."

"I have no plans to save the world, Mr....?"

"Carter. Lucas Carter."

"Of the Plains, Georgia, Carters?"

He snorted. "Hardly. I'm not from around here. And don't think I can't tell when a woman changes the subject."

"Let's circle back to the kitchen. How bad is it?"

"Could be worse." He shrugged. "You can pay industrial cleaners. It looks like the fire was set in a metal trash can with a wad of kitchen towels. The flames went high enough to involve the back corner of the building, but only a small section of the roof. From my perspective, it shouldn't be more than replacing one or two walls and some plywood and shingles. Assuming the electrical passes inspection from water damage. That's not my area of expertise."

"Awesome." She laid the sarcasm on thick, but he didn't seem to notice. He was big and tall and uber masculine, and she was positive no one ever expected him to fail at *anything*. "Excuse me," she said, turning to head back to the house since he wasn't letting her near the dining hall.

"Why are you limping?"

The sharp question made her wince inwardly. "I'm not."

"Bullshit." He scooped her up—*again*—and carried her like he had before. "You hurt your ankle when you fell. Why didn't you say something?"

"You're supposed to be taking care of the *fire*, not me," she said, shoving her hair out of her face. Even though he reeked of smoke, there was nothing off-putting about him. Quite the opposite. The fact that he wasn't even breathing hard made her quiver. Pure animal attraction, that's all. Prehistoric biology, from a time when women needed a mate who was strong and capable.

But Leah Marks was a twenty-first century woman. She didn't need to be rescued or protected. Proving it to herself and her family might be an uphill battle, especially at moments like this.

Her knight in sooty armor strode up her porch steps and deposited her in a rocking chair. The darkness evaporated with each passing moment. Somewhere, a rooster crowed. The sun was itching to come up. "I don't have time for this," she said. "My campers will be awake soon."

Lucas ignored her protests. He removed his helmet and shrugged out of his heavy jacket. Then he crouched in front of her. "Let me see that ankle." When he rolled her pant leg to her knee, she swallowed hard.

His hands on her leg were uncomfortably personal. Had she shaved last night?

"It's swollen," he said bluntly. "You shouldn't be walking on it."

"Fine," she huffed. "I'll find a crutch somewhere."

He looked up at her. "I know you're in the middle of a crisis, but it won't help matters if you mess up your mobility. I'm serious."

His gentle smile disarmed much of her frustration. Did he always get so involved at the scene of a fire, or was he taking an unusual personal interest in her?

His dark hair, darker than hers, was rumpled from his helmet. Streaks of soot on his face mingled with sweat. But none of that disguised the fact that Lucas Carter was a very beautiful man. Classic features. Strong jaw. And piercing eyes that appeared to be a mix of dark green and gold. Still not enough light to tell for sure.

Without his coat, she could see the long-sleeved white T-shirt he wore. It clung to his damp body, revealing broad shoulders, a muscular chest, and his flat belly. The suspenders were a whimsical touch.

Leah had never really been into the strong, physical type. Her few boyfriends had been more cerebral. Lucas Carter might have a 160 IQ, but that was never going to be the first thing a woman noticed about him.

"Thank you for your concern," she said. "But I really do need to check on my staff and kids." Suddenly, she remembered that she *did* have crutches, one anyway. It was in her closet waiting to be used for a simulation game with the campers.

When she said as much, Lucas rose to his feet. "Tell me where, and I'll get it." He stepped out of his boots and stared at her. "Leah?"

"My bedroom closet," she muttered. "Far left corner of the house."

"Be right back."

The thought of Lucas Carter rummaging through her things— made her uneasy. She was not a neat freak. Was he in there judging her?

He returned in less than five minutes, crutch in hand. "This will work," he said.

"Good."

He frowned when he saw her standing beside the rocking chair. "I need to wrap your ankle in an elastic bandage. The EMTs are gone, but I think we have a kit on the truck."

"No," Leah said. And then more forcefully. "No. Thank you. I'll take care of that later. Don't you need to get back to the fire station?"

Lucas stared at her. His intense stare made her shiver inside. "My shift ended at six. I told the guys I'd linger here for a few hours and check for hot spots. They're about to head out."

"I see. Are you normally so altruistic with your free time?"

"Somebody needed to do it. I figured I could nap in this rocking chair if necessary. Besides, I like the view."

His devilish gaze was definitely flirtatious. *Oh, gosh.* Her mouth went dry.

She avoided staring into his eyes, though it wasn't easy. "Help yourself," she croaked. "I have work to do. Please tell your crew thanks for getting here so quickly."

Even with the crutch slowing her down, Leah hustled down the steps and across the lawn before he could stop her.

Jim and Peg were standing outside the cabins, yawning, when Leah walked up. "How did the rest of the night go?" she asked.

"They're all still sleeping." Jim chuckled. "Nothing like a middle-of-the-night emergency to wear them out."

Peg adjusted her hot-pink glasses frames and cocked her head. "What happened to you?"

"Fell in the yard. It's nothing."

"And how bad was the fire?"

"No one will let me back there to look for myself, but apparently, it's not as awful as it could have been. I'll start calling contractors before lunch. But we have a problem."

"Oh?" Both of her employees looked resigned.

Leah shook her head slowly. "You were right, Jim. They suspect arson. So we'll be dealing with law enforcement today. But I won't press charges."

He sighed. "I'll do a preemptive session with Benjamin. If I get him to confess and be ready before the arson investigator gets here, it will be much better."

Leah and Peg exchanged a glance. Jim was good at his job, but would Benjamin shut down to save his skin?

Peg motioned toward her car parked nearby. "I've already been to the grocery store. I got bananas and juice. Plus some yummy pastries from the bakery. It will seem like a treat, though we'll be sitting everywhere to eat it."

"Thanks for doing that. Even if we can't get back in the kitchen immediately, I'll have someone clean the dining area, so we'll at least be able to sit down for meals. Maybe the ladies will be willing to cook things at home and bring them out here for this week."

Jim smiled. He was short and stocky with a heavy beard and kind eyes. "We'll make it work. Not to worry, Leah."

"I don't know what I would do without both of you," she said. "Thanks."

"So who told you about the arson?"

Peg's innocent question made Leah blush. Maybe Peg and Jim wouldn't notice. The sun was just now peeking over the horizon. "The fireman in charge. He came up to the house to update me. Apparently, he's hanging around for a bit in case there are hot spots."

"That's impressive," Jim said. "Especially for a small town."

Leah had cast her net wide during the interview process. Jim was from Baton Rouge, Louisiana, and Peg from Roanoke, Virginia. Neither of them had been in the Blossom Branch area for more than a couple of weeks, so they hadn't yet had time to absorb the nuances of small town life.

"Well," she said, "Blossom Branch has always been that kind of community. People helping people and going the extra mile."

She glanced at her watch. "If you guys have breakfast covered, I think I'll start making phone calls."

Jim waved a hand. "Go do what you have to do. Besides, the rest of the staff should be here at eight. The bulk of our schedule will be intact. Today is swimming and kickball and crafts."

"Good luck."

Peg grinned. "You, too. Sorry we're off on such a rough foot. But things will get better, Leah. Don't worry. We've got your back."

"Thanks, you two." She glanced up at her house. No sign of the bossy but intriguing Lucas. If the fire was out, there was no reason she couldn't take a look. Carefully, of course.

She had been so excited about this first week of camp. Now, it was hard not to let depression take hold. For months she had believed this was the path she was supposed to take with her life and her windfall.

Had she been completely wrong?

She hobbled around the dining hall to the back, frustrated with the crutch and her ankle. The closer she got to where the fire had blazed, the stronger the smoke stench was. Wrinkling her nose, she tiptoed around a wet spot and peered in the window.

TWO

"BUSTED." LUCAS DIDN'T FEEL A HINT OF REMORSE when Leah Marks whirled around and stared at him with a guilty expression.

"I thought you were taking a nap," she said.

When she turned so fast, she nearly got herself twisted up in the crutch. He sighed. "You don't take direction well, do you?"

Her brown-eyed gaze narrowed. "Not from men with God complexes. The fire is out, Mr. Carter. I'm in no danger."

"And if the roof caves in?"

"You told me the damage isn't all that bad."

He ground his teeth. "If I take you inside and let you see, will you promise not to come back until it's safe?"

She gnawed her lower lip. "And when will that be?"

He shrugged. "When I say so."

"Fine," she said stiffly. "You have my word."

He stepped past her and opened the back door to the kitchen. He was accustomed to scenes of destruction; Leah wasn't.

Her eyes welled with tears. "You call this a small fire?"

He nodded slowly, hovering close enough to catch her if the crutch slipped on something. "It looks worse than it is. A lot of what you see is cosmetic damage. The metal trash bin contained most of the blaze. If whoever did this really wanted to burn down the building, it could have been much worse."

"Swell," Leah muttered.

He grinned at her. "We'll have you up and running in no time. One of my buddies is a contractor. I've already called him. He'll be out here at eleven, and I made him promise to give you a friends and family discount."

The woman at his side scowled. "Do you have a girlfriend or a wife?"

He stared, confused. "No. Why?"

"If you did, I was going to send her a sympathy card. Did it ever occur to you that I might want to handle my own repairs?"

"But you don't need to…" He held out his hands. "You have your hands full with camp, and I have the contacts to make this cleanup easier and quicker. I'm trying to help you."

"Without asking," she said flatly.

Her unappreciative attitude nicked his pride. "Fine. I'll wave him off."

Leah lifted her chin. "Oh, no. You've set everything in motion. I'd be stupid to turn down help. But in the future, I'd at least like to be dialed in when you make your grand gestures."

"Sarcasm?"

"For sure."

Her scowl didn't faze him. From the moment he'd scooped her out of the mud, he'd been fascinated with this small, curvy woman. He was usually good at first impressions. Unless he was way off base, this determined female had a heart full of love and compassion and a genuine need to make the world a better place. "I'm sorry," he said. "Duly noted." He needed to work on a charm offensive. He had ruffled her feathers without meaning to…

His apology softened her body language. She sighed and took visual stock of the damage. He could almost see the wheels turning in her head. The woman barely looked old enough to have a cocktail.

"How long do you think it will take to get us back up and running?" she asked.

"Jeff will be able to tell you. And it will be a legit date, not one of those sliding things. He's a pro. Honest as the day is long."

"That's comforting."

"Do you have good insurance?"

"Yes. But a high deductible. Trying to balance the budget has been tricky. I want to spend the bulk of my dollars on staff. These kids need so much support and love."

"How did you end up doing this?" He was genuinely curious.

Leah smiled faintly, still taking in the soot and smoke and water. She wrinkled her nose, perhaps bothered by inhaling the acrid air. "I'd be happy to tell you, but aren't you hot in those pants?"

He blinked. "Um, yes."

His new friend turned red as a Georgia tomato. "Oh, shoot, that came out wrong," she said, visibly mortified. "What I meant was, you said you're hanging around for a few hours. Do you have clothes to change into? Do you want a shower and a meal?"

"Both would be great. I thought maybe I could wash up in one of the bunkhouses?" He made it a question.

Leah shook her head slowly. "The kids just arrived. I don't want to mess with their routine. You're welcome to use my bathroom. I'm not the world's greatest cook, but I can do bacon and eggs."

"That sounds wonderful," he said. Truthfully, if he had gone back into town, he would probably have grabbed a fast-food breakfast, showered at home, and crashed for a few hours. He'd been awake a long time, but he wasn't about to turn down Leah's offer.

Getting to know her was a far better alternative than anything else on his schedule. Besides, seeing her campers brought back a host of memories he needed to sift through. He'd seen and experienced a lot of tough stuff as a kid. His life had been filled with roadblocks and difficulties. Knowing that someone like Leah cared about the troubled or forgotten children of the world touched him deeply.

Despite her earlier embarrassment, she was all business when she took him back to her home and played hostess. The owner/director's house as she called it had clearly undergone recent renovation. Though the style and layout were 1970s era, the kitchen and bathroom were completely updated.

Lucas had grabbed his duffel bag from the truck. He always carried a shaving kit and a set of clean gear. Nothing fancy. Jeans. A cotton shirt. Underwear, socks, and athletic shoes. Sometimes he liked to hit the gym when his shift ended. It wasn't always easy to go straight into sleep mode after working a fire.

Some rescue workers he knew were undeniable adrenaline junkies. Not Lucas. He did the job because it made a difference in a community, and he was good at it. Usually, he worked for a time and moved on. Some might say he had a restless soul. It was nothing as poetic as that. He simply wasn't the kind of man to settle in one place forever. In fact, his stint in Blossom Branch was the closest he had come to putting down roots.

Sometimes that realization bothered him. Other days he managed to ignore it.

Right now, remaining in Blossom Branch for a little longer held a new appeal.

Standing in Leah's shower made it impossible not to think

about her. His prickly new friend was a conundrum. She said she wasn't rich, but how else did she afford this project?

She was maybe five foot four. Barely. Curved in all the right places. Her brown hair and brown eyes gave her the kind of beauty that some men overlooked. Not flashy, but oh, so appealing.

When he'd picked her up both times, he'd enjoyed an armful of 100 percent femininity. Soft and sweet smelling, even though his nose had been full of smoke.

When she wasn't being angry with him, he'd thought for a moment she might have felt the same kick of attraction that was riding him this very moment. He'd better get himself under control, or he'd risk losing the chance to connect with her.

She already thought he was arrogant and bossy. Maybe it was time to show her he could be house-trained. At least temporarily.

He finished his shower and dried himself on a lavender towel. It was fluffy and plush and smelled like fabric softener. Despite his best intentions, the mental image of Leah Marks standing naked in this bathroom made him hard.

It had been too long since he'd been with a woman. The very brief, mostly sex-oriented relationships he'd enjoyed as a younger man had started to pall in recent years. His bones creaked sometimes, and he wasn't quite as quick to scale a ladder.

He'd begun to think about the future.

Even though he still scored at the top of the charts on his fitness evals, he was thirty-three years old. Sex with strangers was not something he enjoyed anymore.

Was that pathetic, or did it show personal growth?

He snickered at himself in the mirror as he slicked back his wet hair with two hands. After stuffing everything in his bag, he picked up his heavy, smoke-laden pants with two fingers and carried them out to the front porch. His jacket, boots, and helmet were still out there.

Unfortunately, he hadn't wanted to strip down completely, or he would never have brought *any* of his professional gear into Leah's house.

He left his bag by the front door and went in search of his hostess. "Something smells great," he said as he strode into the kitchen.

When she looked up and smiled, he felt it in his chest. *Uh-oh.* Sexual compatibility was one thing. A woman who had forever written in her eyes was something else entirely.

"Just in time," she said. "Do you want coffee or juice or both?"

He sat down meekly, trying to look the opposite of arrogant and bossy, whatever that was. "Both would be nice."

Leah poured his coffee in a large blue mug that held at least sixteen ounces. She raised an eyebrow when he dumped in four spoonfuls of sugar. "I don't drink soda," he said. "This is my vice." He cupped his hands around the stoneware and inhaled the scent of good coffee. When he took a sip, he sighed. "This is great."

"I made plenty," she said.

Moments later, she sat a plate in front of him. Scrambled eggs, crisp bacon, and whole wheat toast. "Thank you, Leah. This is the best breakfast I've had in weeks."

She brought her plate to the table and sat down opposite him. "Do you have the same schedule all the time?"

He swallowed a bite of eggs. "Right now, I'm doing four twelve-hour overnight shifts. Then I'm off for three days. When I go back after that, I'll do four 6:00 a.m. to 6:00 p.m. shifts."

"That must be hard."

"You get used to it."

They ate in silence for several minutes. But it was comfortable. Nice.

Leah shot him a sideways glance. "You don't have a Georgia accent. And you said you're not from around here. When did you end up in Blossom Branch?"

Was she really interested in him, or was this polite chitchat? Clearly, she wasn't a woman he had picked up at a bar for a one-night stand. If he was imagining Leah as a potential lover, she would expect more than pheromones.

Because her appealing personality and cute feistiness drew him in, he found himself being more forthcoming than usual.

"About six months ago. Moved here from Nashville. But I've lived all over. I was born in upstate New York. Grew up in foster care—the good kind, not the nightmares they make movies about. When I turned eighteen, I took advantage of financial aid and a government program and went to college. Earned a degree in criminal justice. Started traveling."

She stared at him, her eyes wide. "No high-powered job?"

"Not then. I'd work at a restaurant for a month, pocket the tips, and keep going. I had nothing and no one to tie me down. It was great. I saw a huge part of the country."

Her smile was wry. "I'm jealous, I think. The riskiest thing I've ever tackled is this camp. So how did you become a firefighter?"

He watched her weigh him up, clearly trying to decide if they could be friends.

"When I made it as far as Jackson, Wyoming, the fire department had a couple of openings. I was tired of waiting tables, and I was ready to stop wandering, so I went through training and interviews, and snagged a job. I decided I liked the camaraderie in the fire hall."

"Have you ever been in serious danger?"

That was genuine concern he saw in her wide brown eyes. Despite himself, he was beguiled and tempted. A woman with a big heart who was worried about *him*? That made him feel *something*. Something a little too intimate and sweet for his peace of mind,

"A few times. Comes with the territory. But enough about me. You promised to tell me about the camp."

She tucked her hair behind her ear. "What do you want to know?"

Leah Marks had an air of caution about her, as if she was guarding someone. Herself? Where did that come from?

"Start from the beginning," he said.

"Yes, sir!" She saluted, clearly mocking his command.

He couldn't help himself. He was used to being in charge. If Leah Marks didn't like that, he might have to temper his tone.

"Well," she said, "that would start with my great-aunt, Thelma Gertrude Marks, my grandmother's much older sister. Fifteen years older, to be exact. Because she was widowed in her twenties, she became an influential businesswoman in Blossom Branch years before it was commonly accepted for women to have careers."

"What did she do?"

"A little of everything. She and her late husband owned peach orchards all over the state of Georgia. At one time, she operated a general store. By the time I was born, Aunt Trudie had sold off a lot of her orchards and put all her money in the bank. I didn't know her very well at all. She was eccentric and reclusive in her old age. Because she'd never had children, and because I was the only girl in our family, she left everything to me when she died three years ago."

"Everything?"

"A house in town. The remnants of a camp from the 1970s, which became this one. A fifty-acre peach orchard. Don't ask me why she owned a derelict camp. My guess is that it and the orchard were something she purchased in one big lot. Maybe she had plans to raze the camp and expand the orchard. Who knows? The money was put in trust until I turned twenty-five."

"Were you tempted to spend it all on travel and cars and clothes?"

"You're teasing me," she said, laughing.

"Maybe. But my question stands."

Leah took both their plates to the sink and rinsed them. "I bought myself a diamond tennis bracelet. And I paid off my car. Other than that, I left the money alone. After a lot of soul-searching in the last two years, I came up with the idea to resurrect Camp Willow Pond. My friend, Cate, volunteers with at-risk kids in Atlanta. She helped me work with social services to identify campers who could benefit from our program."

"That's pretty impressive, you know."

Her smile glowed. "I've never done anything like this. I don't know if it will work long-term, but I'm excited."

"You should be." He rolled his shoulders. "We got off to a rocky start, I think. You want to do things your own way, and I get that. Let's call a truce. I'll try not to be bossy and maybe you can let me offer a hand when you need one."

The pink in her cheeks deepened. "I'd like that, Lucas. Thank you." They exchanged cell numbers and discussed a few more details about the fire damage. He paused, feeling the food in his stomach do an odd flip-flop. "Will you have dinner with me Friday night?"

Leah's reaction to his impulsive invitation was unexpected. Her expression shut down. She avoided his gaze.

"That's very kind of you," she said, the words prim. "But I have my hands full right now, as you can see. I do appreciate the invitation."

He felt his face get hot. Maybe he was spoiled, but he couldn't remember the last time a woman turned down a simple dinner invitation from him.

He stood abruptly. "Thank you for the shower and the meal. I need to check on your camp kitchen. See if everything is still okay."

"How will you get back to town?"

"One of my guys can come pick me up."

"I could take you."

Her comment was so obviously reluctant he was insulted. "No need. Good luck with your repairs. I'll see myself out."

When Leah heard the front door slam, she sat down at the table and put her head in her hands. She hadn't handled that well at all. Lucas had been interested in her, but she had shut him down. Why?

Maybe because he wasn't her type. The man's physicality was intimidating. She wasn't used to dating someone with so much natural masculinity.

Lucas was young and ripped and not the kind of man to be easily managed. A relationship with him would be a huge risk. She had enough on her plate right now. Right? She had to be sensible.

He'd flirted with her on and off for hours. But she hadn't thought he was serious. Even in a town as small as Blossom Branch, a guy like him could have his pick of women.

She had seen the shock in his eyes when she said no. And yes, she was embarrassed. But it was for the best.

Then why did she feel so glum?

After tidying up the kitchen, she went in search of Jim and Peg. The junior counselors were in full swing with the day's activities. Jim and Peg had come up with workable plans for lunch and dinner.

"I'm meeting with a contractor at eleven," Leah said. "Hopefully, I can give you some answers after that. But we'll have to cover meal planning for this week at least. I've looked at the forecast. It's not supposed to rain, so that's in our favor."

Jim nodded. "I've already spoken with Benjamin. He clammed up at first, but finally told me what happened. He's apologized to me, but I told him he needs to make things right with you, too. Have you heard from the sheriff?"

"Not yet. I'll let you know."

After that, it was almost time to meet the contractor. Lucas's friend had sent her a text confirming their appointment. She abandoned her crutch. Her ankle was feeling better, and the swelling was minimal.

Inside the kitchen, her mood plummeted further. Everything here had been so clean and new and appealing. Now, it was a sodden mess.

A knock had her turning around. The door was open, but the man rapped his knuckles on the wall. "Hi," she said. "You must be Jeff?"

He stepped gingerly into the kitchen and shook her hand. "Jeff Grainger. I'm really sorry about your fire, Ms. Marks."

"Call me Leah, please. And thank you so much for coming out so quickly."

The tall, lanky man grinned. "When Luscious Lucas speaks, we all jump."

She lifted her eyebrows. "*Luscious* Lucas?"

"That's what the boys at the fire hall call him. Not to his face, of course. They have the utmost respect for their fire chief."

"He's the boss?" Leah was shocked. "He never mentioned that."

"Well, he is. Blossom Branch stole him from Nashville. He and I have been friends for years. Went to college together. I suggested he apply for the opening."

"I see. And *Luscious*?"

Jeff grinned. "You saw him. The man's a walking, talking Greek god. Us mere mortals have to rib him to keep his ego in check."

"Ah." There was so much more on that subject she wanted to explore, but she couldn't waste the contractor's time. "Lucas seemed to think this damage is *minor*. I want to hear what you think."

"Sure." For the next several minutes she shadowed him as he took photographs and jotted notes. Then they went outside and did the same thing.

When he was done, he stared at the building, his brow furrowed. "Lucas is right. The damage is minimal. Doesn't mean the supplies won't be expensive."

"Everything is these days. I understand."

"Give me until this evening to work up a quote for you. Obviously, the cleaning has to be done before my crew can start." He pulled a business card from his pocket. "These folks are top-notch if you want to try them."

"Thanks," Leah said.

"I'll be in touch."

Jeff had barely driven away when the sheriff showed up with an arson investigator in tow, a woman with clipped speech and a no-nonsense air about her. After the two of them examined the kitchen, Leah escorted the couple up to the house and offered them snacks.

"I'll go get the young man we think is responsible," Leah said. "But to be clear, I won't be pressing charges. He's young and afraid and has no support system at home. That's why he's here at camp in the first place."

She sent Jim a text. By the time she walked down toward the bunkhouse, she saw the two males approaching her. Benjamin looked terrified.

"I'm sorry, Ms. Marks," he blurted out. "I don't know why I did it."

She kept her expression neutral. "Do you *want* to go back to Atlanta?"

"No, ma'am," he said. "No, ma'am. I think I like it here."

"I'm glad." She shot Jim a wry look and then touched Benjamin on the shoulder. "The sheriff will ask you questions. Be sure to tell the truth. Jim and I will be there with you. I'm not going to send you to jail. But we have to get past this."

He nodded, his small, wiry body tense. "Okay."

In the end, the interview was difficult, but not traumatic. The sheriff and the investigator each spoke, outlining the gravity of the situation. Benjamin said his piece. The young teen was put on probation, though Leah suspected the consequence was a *scared straight* tactic rather than anything official.

When the patrol car headed back to town, Leah and Jim and Benjamin sat on the edge of her porch and exhaled a collective sigh of relief. She patted the young teen on the back. "You did fine. It's over now. Why don't you go meet up with your group? I think they're at the pool, right?"

Jim stood, exhaustion marking his face. "Or they may be at lunch. I'll walk him down there."

When she was alone, Leah stretched her arms toward the sky, wondering if the entire summer was going to be so hard. She had expected this new endeavor to stretch her capabilities and hopefully build her confidence. But what if running the camp was going to be *too* hard? What if she had jumped in the deep end too fast?

She pulled her phone out of her pocket and scrolled through her contacts. Lucas had taken her phone and created an entry with his info. The words and numbers didn't come close to explaining who he was.

Luscious Lucas? Good Lord, no wonder she felt intimidated by him. Even his own crew recognized his stunning physical attributes…enough to kid about it. Leah had a decent self-concept. She fretted about her weight sometimes, but so did a lot of women. Considering that one of her two best friends was a literal beauty queen and the other, Gabby, was tall and slender with glossy dark hair and incredible skin, it was a wonder Leah felt attractive at all.

She was solidly average. Fortunately, that had never kept her up at night. And she wasn't as shy as she used to be.

Still, she felt conflicted about how things had ended up. Lucas probably asked out a dozen women every month. He wouldn't have been hurt by her refusal. But dating him might have been fun.

He had dealt with the fire crisis, and he had sent Jeff her way. She was thankful for his help. Even if socializing with the hunky fire chief wasn't a sensible option, an independent woman always paid her tab, emotional or otherwise.

Reluctantly, she pulled up an empty text and debated what to say...

Lucas—This is Leah. Thanks again for sending Jeff my way. He was very helpful. I'm sorry if I seemed ungrateful earlier...your team did a great job.

She hit send and immediately felt dumb. Her info was in his phone. He'd made sure of that. So of course, he knew who was texting him.

Oh, well, perhaps that was going to be her MO with Luscious Lucas. Feeling dumb. Then again, maybe she wouldn't run into him all that often. She would be spending most of her nights at camp during the summer. Lucas worked in town.

That thought deposited a leaden feeling of disappointment in her stomach. She liked him. Even if he did have a slight problem with bossing her around. To be fair, he probably bossed everyone.

It occurred to her that she needed something for lunch if she was going to keep running around this afternoon. After she fixed herself a peanut butter and jelly sandwich, cut up an apple, and sat down at the table, she glanced through her paper planner, wondering how long the kitchen would be out of commission.

Her campers were all going to stay for twelve days each session. Arriving on Sunday evening and departing on the second Friday. Then, Leah's staff would have more than a week off to regroup and recharge before the cycle started over again. Four sessions total. On the calendar, an eleven-week stretch.

That agenda was the most they could handle and still fit

around the school schedule in Atlanta. Even then, she'd had to pay attention to which counties started when and stagger them. When she was consulting experts and creating a program, everyone had agreed that a single week wasn't enough to build community and have time for small group counseling and all the fun things Leah wanted to include.

This summer would be the test case.

She desperately needed to succeed. Not only did she want her family to see that she had skills and hopes and dreams, she also envisioned more options for next summer and the one after that. When she thought about the possibilities for expanding, she felt both giddy with excitement and a little overwhelmed.

One thing at a time.

After finishing her simple meal and tidying the kitchen, she glanced at her phone. No reply from Lucas. She was feeling gloomy about that until she realized he was likely sleeping. Unfortunately, he was probably going to be short on sleep today since he'd lingered to have breakfast and a shower.

She could swear she noticed his masculine scent in her bathroom. Was that possible? If anything, he should have smelled of smoke.

But in her mind, every time she thought about his tousled hair, green-gold eyes, and soot-stained face, all she could remember was the aroma of pine and the way an ordinary white T-shirt stretched across rippled abs...

THREE

LUCAS SLID INTO A BOOTH AT THE PEACH CRUMBLE and ordered the blue plate special—meat loaf and two sides with freshly made yeast rolls.

Jeff joined him moments later and requested the same.

His buddy glanced at the iced tea Lucas was drinking. "No beer?"

"I have to work at six. Remember?"

"Oh, yeah. I forgot. That's why we're eating with the senior citizen crowd."

Lucas grinned. He'd spent a large portion of the last half dozen years eating and sleeping at odd times. He didn't mind. His body always adjusted.

Jeff leaned back in the booth and sighed. "What a Monday."

"Tell me about it," Lucas muttered. He was still trying to form a reply to Leah's text.

He'd been sleeping great when his phone dinged. His own fault. He'd forgotten to put it on *do not disturb*. Reading Leah's text—even though it had been completely impersonal—had jerked him awake and reminded him why he was uneasy in his own skin.

He liked her, damn it. A lot. Clearly, the feeling wasn't mutual.

When the food arrived, both men dug in. They worked hard and played hard. The home-style cooking at this cozy Blossom Branch diner was the best food either of them enjoyed all week. But Lucas couldn't help remembering the bacon and eggs and coffee and big brown eyes that had lodged in his psyche.

Jeff poked at his meat loaf. It was a huge serving. "I met your new friend today," he said. "She's cute."

Lucas bristled inwardly. "She's not exactly my friend," he said. "I don't think she likes me very much."

"Why the hell not? You're the knight on the white horse charging in to save her."

"She didn't see it that way." Lucas finished his tea. "Never mind that. Tell me what you think of her kitchen repair."

"If I can round up a crew who will commit to working Thursday, Friday, and Saturday—maybe even Sunday if we have to—I think we might be able to get them back in that building by next Monday."

"Really? I'm impressed."

"I may have to scoot a few projects around, but hers is important. Those kids need structure. I really admire what she's doing out there. But that's assuming she can get the heavy cleaning done in the next two days."

"She made quite an impression on you," Lucas said, his jaw tight.

Jeff cocked his head. "You have a problem with that? Like maybe you've already staked a claim?"

"Of course not. Men don't stake claims these days, haven't you heard? Women don't like being treated like gold mines."

"Very funny." Jeff glanced at his watch and stood. "I've got another estimate to do before dark. We still on for poker Friday night?"

"Wouldn't miss it." Belatedly, he realized he had asked Leah to dinner on a poker night. But it didn't matter. She'd turned him down.

Lucas finished the last of his meal leisurely after Jeff headed out. No point in returning home. He could go straight from here to the fire hall.

For the dozenth time, he glanced at his phone. Leah had texted him at one thirty this afternoon. He still hadn't answered.

What was there to say?

With a sigh, he pecked out Not a problem...

His response seemed brusque. That was the trouble with texting. Tone of voice was impossible to convey.

Ten minutes later, he picked up the phone again. He told himself to let it go, but his fingers had a mind of their own.

I've been thinking. If it works with your curriculum, I'd be happy to come out to camp and teach some fire safety stuff to your kids. Just let me know. I'm off Friday and Saturday this week...

After hitting send, he put a fist to his forehead. Why hadn't he left well enough alone? Why spend more time chasing a woman who didn't want to be caught?

Because Leah was special. It was that simple. Her heart and her curvy body made him want her to an uncomfortable degree. It wasn't a kind of one-and-done lust. He had a desire to dig deeper. Really know her.

But apparently, Leah didn't feel that way about him.

He wasn't a Neanderthal. He respected women and did his best not to be a jerk. Leah Marks had turned down his dinner invitation without hesitation. No point making both of them uncomfortable.

It made sense. Leah was focused on her fledgling camp.

She'd showed him the beautiful new sign: Camp Willow Pond. Handling all the details and putting out fires—literally—was going to keep her busy for weeks to come. The *why* of her refusal wasn't as important as the fact that he had to accept it and move on.

His twelve-hour shift was busier than normal. A guy burning brush on a too-windy day. Inspecting smoke alarms at a new apartment complex. Rewriting a section of the employee manual to include new female employees.

The list was endless. But he liked the hectic schedule. Made the hours pass quickly.

Occasionally, he had personnel problems. One guy who showed up late. Another who called in sick far too often. Lucas dealt with it.

His crew was like family. As the boss, he recognized there were boundaries he had to keep in place. But he erred on the side of caring. He had grown up with families who took him in and nurtured him. If Lucas could be that support for his fellow firefighters, that's what he was going to do.

The following morning when he clocked out just after six, his mind went to Leah and the camp. The kids at Camp Willow Pond this week were kids like he'd been. That woman was more than a pretty face. She was *real*. Somewhere between those two facts, Lucas found himself caught in a web of wondering.

Was Leah as genuine as she seemed? Was the camp going to matter in the lives of kids year after year? Why did he care if he was eventually going to leave Blossom Branch? There was no reason for the fire chief to check out yesterday's fire. Plus Leah had never answered his text. The message was clear.

He needed to stay in his lane.

When he made it home, he was tired enough to sleep. But he dreamed. Explicit dreams involving a faceless woman.

At three he was up and energized. Five times he told himself to stay put. But curiosity and a certain something had him picking up his car keys.

He had time for a quick drive before work.

The camp wasn't far outside of town. Fifteen minutes at the most. The June day was idyllic. Though he had lived all over the country, semirural Georgia was beginning to feel like home, which was odd, because he'd never had a true home.

He knew the summer heat and humidity were going to be a bitch, but last winter when he'd been able to go for a run wearing only shorts and a T-shirt, he'd decided he was willing to take the trade-off.

Still, weather wasn't enough to make him stay or make him go.

When he drove through the camp gates and parked beside Leah's house, he saw a buzz of activity at the dining hall—three vans from the cleaning company Jeff had recommended. Good. That meant Jeff and his guys might be able to start Thursday after all. Lucas thought about taking a peek, but he didn't want to get in the way.

What he *really* wanted was to see Leah Marks.

But should he wander unannounced around the property? Probably not.

While he was deciding what to do, he saw movement in the distance. The door to one of the dormitories opened and a familiar figure walked out, clipboard in hand.

Her head was down as she scribbled something.

Lucas saw the exact moment she spotted him. Her steps faltered, and she stopped dead in her tracks. He lifted his arm and waved, just to see what she would do.

The woman had guts. She could have veered in another direction and pretended not to see him. But she didn't. After three or four seconds, she continued striding up the lawn.

Though she was neither short nor tall, the woman had legs that were long and shapely. She wore a turquoise Camp Willow

Pond T-shirt knotted at her waist and cutoff denim shorts. Were those back in style? He didn't keep up with women's fashions.

In style or not, Leah wore those Daisy Dukes like a runway model.

To be fair, her frayed-hem shorts were several inches longer than Daisy's. There was nothing at all suggestive about them. But Lucas was in the throes of a powerful attraction, and all he could think about was getting cozy with Leah on a bale of hay.

He had to clear his throat and count to a hundred while she covered the distance between them or risk embarrassing himself.

When she was close enough for conversation, her smile was pleasant. "I didn't expect to see you today."

"You never answered my text about the fire safety session," he said. He rubbed his chin. "I thought I should make sure everything is okay out here."

She seemed puzzled. "Why wouldn't it be? And yes, Saturday will be great for your talk. I'm sorry I forgot to answer your text. Things have been hectic."

"I understand."

When she took off her sunglasses, he could see those beautiful brown eyes. Chocolate was one of his weaknesses, whether at the candy store or in the shade of a woman's irises. This close, he could see that Leah's had tiny sparkles of gold. Her hair did, too, now that he noticed. The sun caught random strands and lit them up.

Her skin was the color of the magnolia blossoms on the tree in his front yard. Her lips were pink and glossy. And her breasts…

She interrupted his appreciative assessment. "Are you here for a reason, *Chief* Carter?"

"I thought we agreed you'd call me Lucas."

"We didn't *agree* on anything," she said, her gaze cooling. "Besides, you never told me you were actually the *fire chief*. I'm sure that requires a level of deference from your constituents."

She was deliberately trying to wind him up. And it was working. Though possibly not in the way she intended.

"I'd like you to call me Lucas," he said quietly. "All my friends do."

"We're not friends," she pointed out. "We only met Monday morning."

"We *could* be friends," he said.

"Sure, Lucas. But I have a million things to do in the meantime, and although I'm super grateful you kept my dining hall from burning down, I'm really busy."

Nothing ventured, nothing gained.

"Are you interested in hanging out with me?" he asked. "I felt a spark yesterday when we met. I'm curious to see if it's one-sided."

Her mouth dropped open, and her face turned red. "It definitely is. One-sided that is. You and I have nothing in common."

"What does that have to do with sexual attraction?"

She gathered her composure and stared at him. "I don't have time for sexual attraction. Not at all. You're welcome to check back in September."

Interesting. She wasn't *denying* anything.

"Here's the deal," he said. "I had a hard time sleeping today. I kept wondering what it would be like to kiss you."

Her gaze narrowed. Heated. "Maybe I wondered that same thing. But we're adults. We know how to put our responsibilities ahead of our needs."

Bingo. She had admitted what he wanted to hear.

He assumed his meekest, most nonthreatening expression. "It would be a generous act of community service on your part to help both of us figure it out. You know. One way or the other."

She took a step in his direction. Her chest rose and fell. "Figure out what?" Her gaze landed on his lips.

"What a kiss would be like."

"You're delusional," she said, frowning at him again, though she stepped even closer. "Or you must have inhaled too much smoke on the job. I'm not going to kiss you right in the middle of camp where impressionable young teens might see us."

"On your porch, then?"

She sputtered, putting two hands flat on his chest and pushing half-heartedly. "Go away. I don't have time to kiss you."

Leah's fingertips tingled where they pressed against Lucas's warm chest. Even through a layer of fabric. Touching him was a mistake. It made her want more.

She took a deep breath. "One kiss," she said, hearing her abrupt about-face and hoping he didn't know her knees had turned to Jell-O. "In my living room. To satisfy our curiosity. You have to be at work soon. I can't linger."

He stared at her so hard a shiver ran up her spine. But he didn't say a word.

She gulped. "I think you've made a mistake, Lucas. I'm not one of those women with whom hot guys have one-night stands."

"I'm not a hot guy," he protested. "I'm ordinary."

"Nice try."

His jaw clenched visibly. "I like you a lot, Leah. I thought you felt the chemistry, too."

"I'm sure *Luscious Lucas* has chemistry with any number of women."

He blinked in shock. "Where did you hear that?"

"Your nickname? From Jeff."

"The guy who used to be my best friend," he groused. "Maybe my buddy Jeff was trying to cut me out. Look," he said. "It's just a stupid joke. I'm the boss. They need to rag on me. Stick it to the man. You know."

Her expression gentled. "It's okay. Really it is. If I had time to date—and I don't," she said quickly. "I suppose you and I could have a nice friendly dinner. But you should definitely find someone more in your...*genre*."

"What the hell does that mean?"

She pursed her lips. "*The studly fireman and the blonde bombshell.* I'm sure there's a movie like that on some late-night cable channel. I'm not your type. You're not my type. I'm guessing you typically go out with women who are free to play around."

His eyebrows went up. "Are you in a relationship?"

"No. But camp is my focus right now."

"Twenty-four seven?" He seemed skeptical.

"Sometimes, yes."

"Fine," he said.

She nodded. "Fine."

The flash of disappointment in her stomach made her feel off-kilter. Surely she was doing the right thing. Or was she choosing—like so many times in her life—to avoid risk?

He folded his arms across his chest, unmoving.

Her cheeks felt hot. "I don't understand this fixation you have with kissing me."

"I carried you in my arms, Leah."

"Yes, you did." And she remembered every nuance of that first encounter. "Okay," she said in a rush before she could change her mind. "One kiss and then you go."

Shock flickered across his face, especially when she reached out and took him by the wrist.

Step by step, she led him toward her house, around the corner, up the front steps, and right inside.

He didn't say a word. But a huge burst of heat shimmered between them.

When she closed the door and locked it, he twitched the drapes closed. "Protecting your reputation," he said solemnly.

She nodded, her gaze focused on his face. Her entire body shivered. Never had she done something so *forward* with a man.

Taking what she wanted. Being brave. Throwing caution to the wind.

"Leah?"

"Hmm?"

He took the clipboard out of her hands and tossed it on the sofa. "You don't have to do this if you don't want to. I can live with the disappointment."

"It's okay," she whispered. "Anything to get rid of you."

She was teasing, and he must have known that. But he winced theatrically. "Now you're just being mean." He stepped in front of her and slid his hands under her hair, cupping her head in his fingers and tracing the line of her jaw with his thumbs. "I'm not interested in a one-night stand. I want to get to know you," he muttered.

Her whole body was taut. Trembling with anticipation. In fact, she couldn't remember ever feeling this level of wanting.

She managed a shaky laugh. "This seems like a good start." When she put her arms around him, she slid her fingertips inside the waistband of his jeans right at the back.

He rested his forehead against hers. "Leah," he murmured. And then he kissed her.

There were only so many ways two people could press their mouths together. It was a basic human contact. Leah had kissed and been kissed enough times to know the good and the bad. But nothing like this.

Lucas's firm lips and coaxing caress were disarming and addictive.

She couldn't help the embarrassing noise at the back of her throat when he slid his tongue deeper and dragged her tight against his chest. *Sweet heaven.*

She was over her head in no time. Lucas had been right about one thing. There *was* a spark.

When his watch alarm dinged, they both groaned.

He pulled back and wiped a hand over his face. "Sorry. I

set a reminder every time my shift alters. I don't ever want to be late."

"I suppose you should go," she whispered. She exhaled, a shaky breath that did nothing to settle her emotions. "Is that what you call a spark?" she asked, searching his face.

"No," he said flatly. "That was a four-alarm fire."

Leah spent the seventy-plus hours after Lucas's visit walking around like a zombie. A good zombie. One who could pass for human.

She dealt with each of her responsibilities efficiently and thoroughly. With Jim and Peg and her junior staff, she was supportive, cheerful, and upbeat. But inside, she was a jangled mess of uncertainty.

The fact that Lucas Carter was a good kisser didn't surprise her. A man with his looks and physical prowess must have practiced a lot. Probably since he was the age of her current campers.

What gave her sleepless nights was the way *she*, Leah, had responded to Lucas. Like she had been without food and water on a desert island for weeks and months, and Lucas showed up to restore her to life.

She didn't have time for life restoration. She was smack in the middle of an ambitious and risky project. Starting a new camp. From scratch. And it was *hard*. Did Lucas think she would simply drop everything to fool around with him?

Surely not. He had a job that was as demanding as hers. Or at least close.

But the real reason his kisses had overwhelmed her was that she was scared.

She'd spent her entire life standing in the wings. Not a wall-flower exactly, but certainly not the star of the show.

It wasn't false modesty to say Lucas was out of her league. She didn't want to let herself believe he was serious about the two of them having something. A spark? She snorted inwardly.

She'd had a crush on her family's mailman once upon a time. That was a spark.

This thing with Lucas was terrifying and risky in the extreme. The last thing she wanted was to embarrass herself. If he was hoping for a temporary, lighthearted romp, he was out of luck.

The only way to deal with this at all was to stop thinking about him. Period. That would be a challenge, but she was going to try.

She knew she was kidding herself, but fortunately, camp kept her plenty busy.

Amazingly, the industrial cleaning team finished their work in the promised two-day window. No more water, no more soot residue. Everything back to normal. Sort of...

The faint lingering odor of smoke would dissipate gradually. In that instance, they were lucky. Because the building was screened-in, there was plenty of airflow.

Once the cleaners moved out, Jeff's crew had been able to start Thursday morning. The sound of ripping drywall and electric saws permeated the camp. But not in a bad way. The campers were excited about the prospect of eating regular camp food at tables and not sitting on the ground.

Picnics were fun occasionally, but restoring order would mean that mealtimes could be easier and less chaotic.

Leah was rethinking her decision about having two-week sessions. The work was hard, and she didn't want to burn out her staff. The long break before the next group arrived was something to look forward to, but that was still a week away.

Friday afternoons at three had been designated as free time. Given the needs of her campers, it was risky. Most of them thrived on structure. So this first block from 3:00 to 5:00 p.m. was an experiment.

When small groups ended and everyone scattered to pick their own amusements, Leah kept watch outside to observe the changeover. So far, so good.

Moments later, she saw one of the female campers approach her. Alaina was fourteen, very overweight, and had a deceptively angelic face, with blond hair, blue eyes, and a dimple in her right cheek. She had spent most of the past school year under at-home suspension. Multiple offenses.

Her first infraction was vaping in the girls' bathroom.

After that, it was hacking the library computer and sending porn site links to everyone in her homeroom.

But the last straw as far as her principal was concerned was Alaina bringing her mom's handgun to school in a backpack.

The girl never took it out. Had no intention of threatening anyone. But she had bragged about having a pistol, and that information inevitably made it back to the powers that be in the front office.

When Alaina was expelled in April, her mother had contacted social services and asked for help.

Everything Alaina had done was a cry for attention. She was too smart for her own good and too bruised by life to handle this awkward age.

Her smile was tentative. "Hey, Miss Leah. I checked with Miss Peg. She said I could talk to you during free time. If you're cool with it."

Leah smiled warmly, ignoring her ever-burgeoning to-do list. "Of course. Would you like to sit by the pond?"

They snagged two Adirondack chairs and pulled them at right angles beneath the shade of a large mimosa tree. A trio of startled frogs leapt from their lily pads and disappeared beneath the water. Once Leah was off her feet, she exhaled, taking in the idyllic scene and relishing the chance to be still for a moment.

Poor Alaina was nervous. She tugged at her khaki shorts and picked at her purple nail polish.

Leah knew the pain of being fourteen and uncomfortable in her own skin. But at least she'd had the support of a stable home life.

"How are you liking camp so far?" she asked, keeping her tone casual.

Alaina shrugged. "It's dope. I wish I could stay all summer."

The unspoken subtext hurt Leah's heart. "Well, you have another whole week. Have you made any friends?" There were ten girls in the cabin. Small groups of five rotated for various activities. And the sets of five would change for week two.

"Not really." Another shrug. "The young ones are dumb."

Leah winced inwardly. She had kept the camp's age range from twelve to fifteen for that exact reason. But even the narrower spread was magnified in middle school. The oldest campers would start high school in the fall.

"Well," she said. "They'll be looking to you as a leader."

Alaina rolled her eyes. "Right…"

Leah let it slide. "What has been your favorite activity so far? Swimming?" That was usually the most anticipated hour of the day.

"Are you shittin' me?" The child curled her lip. "I'm fat, Miss Leah. Putting on that stupid swimsuit is torture. I wear my T-shirt over it, but it don't help much."

Leah's heart sank. She remembered far too well what it felt like to be Alaina's age. The uncertainty. The lack of confidence. The desperate desire for a tiny, society-pleasing body instead of appreciating her own.

It was painful.

FOUR

LEAH MANAGED NOT TO REACT OUTWARDLY. AND SHE decided to ignore the profanity. She was walking a minefield, but she refused to lie.

"May I tell you something personal, Alaina?"

Another shrug. "Sure."

Leah chose her words carefully. "When I was in sixth grade, my mom bought me a pair of knit pants, leggings really. They were the 'in' thing that year. All the popular girls wore them. But that was the same time I was going through puberty. I was *filling out*…everywhere. My legs, my bottom, my breasts. I didn't know how to live in that new body."

"So what did ya do?"

"There wasn't much I *could* do. But I thought those leggings were going to make me look like all the other girls."

"And they didn't?"

Even now, Leah could remember the humiliation. "No. They didn't. A boy in my class called me *Lumpy Leah* when we were in the lunch line. I wanted to die. A lot of my classmates heard him and snickered. Lucky for me, the teacher put a stop to it, but it was too late. I already felt lumpy."

"That sucks."

"Yes. These may not be easy years for you, Alaina. The only way to navigate them is to concentrate on your passions and to be kind, even when other people aren't."

"So you're not going to tell me to lose weight?"

Leah smiled ruefully. "No. You could lose forty pounds, and you would probably still feel like the same girl inside. If you want to try out some healthier habits, any of us can help you with that. But as far as feeling good about yourself? That starts in the brain."

Alaina scrunched up her face. "I read the camp brochure online. You've got two of those psychology degrees, right?"

"Yes." Leah wasn't sure where this was headed.

"So you're trying some of that fancy mumbo jumbo on me?"

"Not at all. It's plain science. The only person who can make us feel good about ourselves is *us*. Compliments and all that stuff are nice, but until a woman feels her own worth, she can't be completely happy." Leah believed what she was saying. But perhaps she needed to listen to her own advice. Especially when it came to her relationship with Lucas.

They sat in silence for a few minutes. Alaina stared out across the pond, clearly digesting what Leah had said.

Finally, the girl spoke again. "You got a boyfriend, Ms. L?"

Immediately, Leah flashed on Lucas's cocky, sexy smile. Her stomach curled. "No. I don't."

"You ever had one? Serious, I mean?"

It hurt to see the child's naked yearning.

"Yes. My senior year in college."

"So what happened? You're not married or nothin'."

"No. Never have been. We broke up in May that year."

"How come?"

"I had been spinning this crazy fantasy where he was going to propose to me at graduation. But those daydreams were all in *my* head. The engagement plans were never anything he was interested in. Some guys really are different from girls, Alaina."

"'Cause they want to hump anything that moves?"

Maybe she was savvier than Leah thought. She smothered her smile. "I guess you could put it that way. Some guys focus on sex, yes. Many people, a lot of women—but not all—enjoy sex *more* within the security of a relationship. They *like* sex. Just as much as guys do. But…"

"But we don't get bossed around by our dicks."

"Alaina!"

"Sorry," the girl muttered. "My bad."

It was all Leah could do not to burst out laughing. She bit down hard on her lower lip and sighed. "You aren't wrong, but let's watch the language."

"Yes, ma'am." Alaina drummed her fingers on the arms of the chair. "So how do I know what my passions are? I'm just a kid."

Leah glanced at her watch, feeling torn. Was she the best person to give this young woman/child advice? Years of schooling and two degrees, and yet Leah had still struggled to find her path. Honestly, she couldn't say with 100 percent certainty that she was even *on* the path. She hoped she was, but the fire had shaken her. "Let's circle back to that…okay? Maybe tomorrow afternoon? I need to check in with the guys doing the repairs on the kitchen. They're about to leave."

"I understand." Alaina stood. "Thanks for talkin' to me."

Leah smiled. "It was my pleasure."

The young girl headed back toward the cabins, and Leah went to find Jeff. When she reached the dining hall, she was astonished to see how much he and his crew had accomplished. Yesterday, the men had rebuilt one corner section of the roof and covered it with new shingles. Today, they had ripped out more than half of the Sheetrock and started over with fresh materials. The room wasn't back to normal, but it was a million times better than the wreck she had examined Monday with Lucas.

Jeff was on a ladder cleaning a light fixture.

She put her hands on her hips and looked up at him. "You're a miracle worker," she said. "I'm so grateful, Jeff."

He climbed down the ladder and wiped his hands on a rag. "My guys are top-notch. And honestly, we're really impressed with what you're doing here. We wanted to get your kids back where they belong as soon as we can."

"So what comes next?"

"We'll finish up tomorrow morning and start the painting. Then we'll lay the new tile. Any last bits can be tweaked Sunday afternoon."

"I'll pay the overtime," she said. "I don't want your business to take a hit on this."

"I have a better idea," he said, smiling. "How about you and I grab dinner one night? And maybe a movie afterward?"

"Well, I..." She stuttered, suddenly feeling like she was in one of those hidden camera shows.

Jeff's happy expression faded away. "Aw, man. Lucas already has you tied up, right?" His dismay was clear.

The *tied up* thing made her thoughts go in an entirely inappropriate direction. "No," she said carefully. "No one has me tied up. I'll tell you what I told him. I don't have time for a social life this summer. But thanks for the invitation."

"I hope I didn't offend you," he said, looking uneasy.

"Of course not. I'll see you tomorrow, Jeff."

She headed back to her house, needing a moment of peace and quiet. Often this week she had eaten with the campers, mostly to support the counselors. It hadn't been easy for the adults doing meals with no dining hall.

Right now, she was bone-deep tired, in part because she had lain awake for the last three nights wrestling with her attraction to Lucas Carter.

She hadn't been out with any men at all in the last eighteen months. Too much going on. In fact, she hadn't even had a date for Cate's wedding. Which was just as well. That day had ended terribly.

Had she given up on love? Sometimes she thought it was more trouble than it was worth. Cate and Jason had nearly made a huge mistake. Leah's own limited experience with committed relationships was disappointing at best.

And now she was suddenly attracted to a funny, handsome man at a moment when she had virtually no time for a personal life. She wasn't a workaholic. But because this camp was so new, she had to be very involved.

Talk about bad timing…

She snorted out loud as she poured herself half a glass of Chablis. The bottle had been in her fridge for at least a month. It tasted like it had bits of cork in it, but she didn't care. After she drained the questionable alcohol, she flopped on her back on the sofa and put an arm across her face.

Two men in one week had asked her out. What did that mean? Was she excreting pheromones that said she was fertile and available? If so, it was completely unconscious. Or maybe it was something else.

She had gained confidence in the last two years, particularly recently. Though she was worried about the camp's success, she was proud of the careful planning and dreaming that had gone into Camp Willow Pond. In some exciting moments, she realized that her opportunities were endless. She was doing a good job, and she was in charge.

Maybe men liked that.

Maybe she was finally discovering her own worth…

Lucas Carter was in a bad mood. Really bad. That admission coming from a generally sunny-tempered guy was enough to stop him in his tracks.

Leah Marks had never given him the specific instructions for teaching her campers about fire safety. Instead, she had passed him off to someone named Jim.

Jim seemed like a perfectly nice dude, and Jim had been more than happy to line up a session with Lucas on Saturday, but Lucas had planned on interacting with Leah.

Because this whole endeavor had gone sideways, Lucas was now using one of his days off to do a good deed, with no assurance of impressing Leah.

He knew he should be happy to educate kids under any circumstances, and he was. But the Leah thing had promised to be a nice bonus.

It was all probably his own fault.

Lucas might have spooked her with that kiss.

Not because the kiss was bad, but because it was so damn good. He was 99 percent sure Leah thought it was amazing, too. But that last 1 percent had him sweating and uncertain.

He'd never felt more unsure of a romantic or sexual encounter.

As far as he could tell, Leah didn't realize how sexy she was, how appealing. She was focused on her admirable project, and according to her, she didn't have time to indulge her personal wishes.

That meant it was up to him to 1) help her create some time, and 2) help her identify every one of those wishes.

When he pulled through the camp gates, the view felt familiar already. Lucas liked that feeling. He parked beside Leah's house, mostly because he didn't know where official visitors were supposed to park, but also because he was hoping to catch a glimpse of her.

He saw that Jeff's crew was still working at the dining hall judging by the three vans parked there.

Jim had explained the schedule while asking if Lucas would be willing to do the fire safety spiel three more times this summer. Lucas had agreed. And he now knew Leah would have an entire eight-day stretch in between sessions. Promising. Very promising.

Unfortunately, it was Jim—not Leah—who came out to meet him.

Jim stuck out his hand. "Chief Carter. It's a pleasure."

"Please call me Lucas. Where are we going to do this program?"

"In the future, we'll be in the dining hall, but for this afternoon we're gathering the kids at the amphitheater."

"And how many of them are there?"

"Ten girls and ten boys. Ages twelve to fifteen. Middle schoolers are a tough audience. I hope you brought your A game."

"I'll do my best." Despite his furtive glances right and left, Lucas saw no sign of the camp's owner. "Will Ms. Marks be joining us?"

Jim's grin said he knew exactly what Lucas was thinking. "Probably. She had a Zoom meeting with her camping certification board. It should be over soon."

Lucas nodded like it was no big deal.

Seeing the campers took him right back to his foster care days. He'd had the same defiant posture, the same need to prove himself when he was their age. They were more than kids but not yet adults, and clearly they had issues, or they wouldn't be here.

He took his place in the center of the semicircle and smiled. "Hey, guys. Have you had a good week?"

A tepid response told him to abandon that tactic.

He had a canned speech prepared, but he decided to take questions. "So tell me what you want to know…"

After a long pause, a skinny, tall boy in the second row of benches raised his hand. "Have you ever found a dead body in a house and had to carry it out?"

The gruesome subject took Lucas off guard. "Um, no. Thank

goodness. But a lot of pets, unfortunately. While we're on this subject, I want you all to know a very important point about fire danger. The majority of deaths in house fires result from smoke inhalation."

A redheaded girl spoke up. "Then how do *you* breathe?"

"We use oxygen masks. With our helmets and suits, we can stay inside a burning building longer…but not forever."

One of the older boys entered the conversation. "Why did you want to be a fireman?"

"Well, I like helping people. And I like the fact that I have to stay physically fit to do my job. We have benchmarks we need to meet to stay certified. Blossom Branch has a paid fire department, but there are hundreds of volunteer fire units all over the country. Each one is different."

He paused. When no more hands went up, he continued. "Does anyone know what your first line of defense is in a fire situation?"

"Smoke alarms." Half a dozen kids shouted it at once.

"Exactly right. And if your home doesn't have them—or they're old or nonfunctional—call your local fire department. I promise they'll help. Lots of towns give away smoke detectors for free once a year, especially during Fire Safety Month in October. It's that important."

He'd been concentrating on his young audience. For the first time, he realized Leah had joined the group. She was standing to his far right at the edge of the amphitheater, arms crossed, watching him.

"What about you, Ms. Marks? What else do you think these kids need to know?"

She gave him a look…a faint smile that was for the kids' benefit, not his. He'd bet his life on it.

"They should know how quickly you and your team responded to the 911 call and how hard you worked to put out the kitchen fire at the dining hall. It could easily have been much worse."

"We don't need your gratitude. It's our job. But thanks." He noticed she didn't mention the arson. Lucas had followed up with the fire inspector. Lucas knew the kid's name who did the deed. And because he had a description, he also had a good idea which camper was involved. The boy in the green shirt had barely looked at Lucas the whole time he'd been speaking.

Jim stepped forward. "Let's all thank Fire Chief Lucas for sharing his time with us."

After a smattering of applause, the counselors led the kids away.

Lucas walked to where Leah stood. Her gaze was wary. "Thanks for doing this," she said.

"No problem." She wasn't wearing those frayed denim shorts today. Too bad. Instead, she was in a yellow top and khaki skirt, very professional. Probably because of her Zoom meeting.

Her legs were still bare in deference to the heat.

He cocked his head, trying to determine if he had a shot. "How about dinner tonight? You must be getting tired of camp food."

"I'm busy," she said. Her tone wasn't rude. More like something she had programmed herself to say.

He shook his head slowly. "When we first met, you told me you own this camp. And I know you hired capable people to run it. It's Saturday night. What could it hurt to be gone for a couple of hours? What could possibly happen?"

She raised her eyebrows. "Oh, I don't know. Maybe another arson event. Or some kid with a meltdown. A nasty thunderstorm."

He glanced at the sky. The heat was oppressive late in the day. The conditions were right for a pop-up storm. But that was hit or miss.

"If anything happens," he said, "I could have you back here in twenty minutes. Please, Leah. Have dinner with me."

Leah knew when she was beat. Lucas Carter was extremely persuasive. And since she was inclined to *be* convinced, his job wasn't very hard. "Okay," she said. "I suppose it couldn't hurt."

Lucas's grin was wry. "Don't get *too* excited," he said. "I might start to think you actually like me."

"Ha." She studied him carefully, trying to analyze what it was about his vibe that made her stomach trembly and her legs weak. Today he wore faded denim jeans with cowboy boots and an olive Henley. With the shirtsleeves pushed to his elbows, she could see his tanned, muscular forearms.

Cowboy boots were ubiquitous in Georgia. Nothing about Lucas's appearance was out of place. Even so, he made an impact. He was tall, at least six-three. His innate air of command didn't bother her, so long as he refrained from bossing her around.

"Do I need to change?" she asked.

"Nope. I thought we'd grab something at The Peach Pit. Saturday nights are double-decker burgers with José's homemade chips and salsa. Is that okay with you? You're not a vegan, are you?" he asked, looking slightly alarmed.

"Would that be a deal breaker?"

Lucas stared at her, his gaze settling on her mouth. "Nope. Not at all. As long as you don't ask me to eat kale."

"Duly noted. And the menu sounds good."

The Peach Pit was Blossom Branch's most famous watering hole. It had been around since the 1950s with updates along the way. Everyone from college kids to older couples liked the atmosphere. Over the course of a year, the proprietor's choice of bands offered something for everybody.

As they walked back up to Leah's house, she expected to see a dusty pickup truck. Maybe a flashy Camaro. But Lucas's vehicle of choice surprised her. It was a sleek, sporty sedan from one of the prestige automakers.

She stopped short. "Wow. That's a beautiful car." It was an eye-catching shade of midnight blue.

"Thanks." Lucas ran his hand along the hood, almost like she imagined he might caress a woman's hip. "I'm pretty frugal overall," he said. "But cars are my weakness. I've spent a lot of time on the open road, so I like to drive in comfort."

After Leah went inside for a moment to get her purse and a light sweater in case the air-conditioning was too cold, Lucas helped her into the car. The leather seats were soft and smooth and smelled new.

"How long have you had this?" she asked.

"Two years. But I like to keep her clean and neat. No eating cream horns in Bessie."

"Bessie?"

Lucas turned the key. The engine was a quiet, powerful purr. "One of my early foster mothers was named Bessie. She used to let me sit on a stool and help her cook. I can still remember the way her kitchen smelled. Warm and happy. That's the way this car makes me feel."

Leah didn't know how to respond to that. He had just shared something very personal with her, but he did it so casually, she didn't know if she was allowed to ask questions, especially since he turned on the radio afterward. Maybe he regretted his candid reply.

The Peach Pit was hopping on a Saturday night. Even though the place didn't take reservations, Lucas had somehow snagged a table in a back corner. It was far enough away to be somewhat private, but close enough for a good view of the band.

"How did you manage this?" she asked.

His grin was boyish. "There are a few perks to being fire chief."

"Ah."

Leah decided this wasn't a bad place to hang out with Luscious Lucas. It was loud and crowded, so there would be no awkward moments.

She might even have fun…if she still remembered how. For a long time now, her only focus had been proving she could get the camp up and running. Relaxing seemed like a foreign concept.

After consulting her, Lucas ordered for the two of them. She ate healthy most of the time—and obviously he did, too, or he wouldn't look like he did—but the juicy burgers and chips and salsa were delicious.

Lucas laughed when she had to ask for extra napkins. "I take it you're enjoying the food?"

"Oh my gosh," she said. "I haven't had anything this good in ages."

He sobered as she wiped her chin. "I've always liked women with healthy appetites. I like *you*, Leah."

When he leaned across the table and touched her hand, she tugged it back. "Don't," she said. "We're here as friends."

He frowned. "Friends as a starting point to something else?"

"No." She sighed. "I told you, Lucas. This isn't going to work. I thought you were offering dinner. Nothing more."

"I'm not dead. You're a very appealing woman."

"I have a healthy self-concept. But I'm also a realist. You said it yourself. You've traveled and lived all over. From that, I can extrapolate that you've been with a lot of women. No judgment," she said hurriedly. "But I don't do one-night stands, and you're not a guy who does permanent. So why complicate things?"

His scowl was dark. "If that's how you feel, why the hell did you agree to come with me this evening?"

She shrugged. "I was hungry. And the burgers here are to die for. Plus I love your car. And I was tired of spending every waking moment with middle schoolers this week. You were my ticket out."

He sat back in his chair and shook his head ruefully. "You're hell on a guy's self-esteem, Ms. Marks."

"Give me a break," she said. "You have the ego of an alpha male in a complicated escape room."

"That's oddly specific."

"I was a psychology major. We learned all about men like you."

"Not to pick apart your analogy, but I think what you're doing is called *generalizing*. Isn't that a big no-no, Ms. Psychologist?"

She wrinkled her nose. "Touché. But the point is, I'm not the kind of female who gravitates toward the alpha male. I might admire you. And even enjoy your company. But in a relationship, I would be overwhelmed by you."

"You're being ridiculous."

"Maybe so."

"How many men have you dated, Leah?"

"The number doesn't matter. I learned from my failures."

"I can't believe that. Any man would be an idiot to walk away from you."

"You talk a good game, but you can't speak for the entire male sex. I was almost engaged once. Unfortunately, I found out that all those *happily-ever-after* vibes were only in my head. He simply liked having a girlfriend for regular sex."

"And how long ago was that?"

"Does it matter?"

"I think it might."

"Five years," she said.

"So you were still a kid."

"I was twenty-one. Almost twenty-two. Old enough to know better."

"Are you the same person you were then?"

Leah thought about it. "No. Thank goodness. But I haven't seen anything in the intervening years to change my mind. I'll find somebody one day. A guy who shares my values and goals and dreams for the future. Until then, I'm happy to be single."

"And celibate?"

She blushed. "Women don't need a man for orgasms."

"Technically, that's true. But don't you want somebody who will burn for you? A guy who will adore you?"

Unwittingly, Lucas had hit on her secret fantasy. But that's all it was. A fantasy.

Leah stared at him, managing not to blush further. She *wanted* to believe there was a perfect match for her out there somewhere, but she wasn't sure such a thing—such a man—existed. "You're talking about a soulmate. Those relationships are few and far between. It's hard to find the right person, harder still to keep the magic alive."

"But possible?"

Leah shrugged. "I don't know. What do *you* think?" Did she really need to hear his thoughts on such a dangerous subject?

For once, Lucas was silent. He finished his beer along with the last handful of chips in the napkin-lined wicker basket. Finally, he lifted his head and stared at her.

"I'd like to propose an experiment."

FIVE

LUCAS WASN'T SURE AT WHAT POINT HE'D LOST THE THREAD of where he *thought* they were headed. But it had become clear to him that Leah Marks was not going to end up in his bed anytime soon. Maybe not ever.

The disappointment he felt was considerable.

Finding a woman to sleep with wasn't a problem.

Finding a woman who interested him was far more difficult.

He grinned inwardly at the look of suspicion on Leah's face. If he was in her shoes, he'd be suspicious, too.

She eyed him warily. "Experiment?"

"Maybe that's too official. Let's call it an idea."

"I'm listening."

"I like you. You like me. Hanging out together is fun. Why don't we take sex off the table while you're tied up with camp. We'll be friends getting to know each other."

"What's the catch?"

"No catch," he said. "I'd like to know you better. And maybe

I can convince you that I enjoy your company for other than carnal reasons."

Her gaze narrowed. Soft pink lips pursed in a disapproving line. "And when camp is over?"

"If we're still getting to know each other and having fun, maybe we'll circle back to the sex question."

"It's a long summer. That's ridiculous." Her fair skin was naturally pale, but now even the tint of blush pink was gone. Her brown eyes rounded in what might be shock or indignation or maybe stunned interest.

"Not at all. I'm going to prove to you that a guy can enjoy a woman's company even platonically. We'll have ground rules, of course."

"Ground rules?" Leah parroted the words, her gaze locked on his.

"No touching below the waist. No complete nudity. Kissing is fine. And you have to believe me when I pay you compliments."

She sat back in her chair, glaring at him. The pink cheeks returned. "That's absurd."

"Not at all. I want you to trust me." Even if they never ended up in bed together, he was interested in her. The no-sex thing would be a pisser, but he could handle it if he had to…

"And if you get bored before my camp season is over?"

He cocked his head. "Now why would I get bored?"

"Oh, I don't know. Maybe because I'm too busy to pander to your ego. Or because you'll meet some other woman who isn't picky about one-night stands."

"Won't happen. Besides, my ego isn't as inflated as you seem to think. I have plenty of faults. I proudly acknowledge each and every one."

Finally, her body language relaxed. "You're a weird man. In a nice way," she said hurriedly.

"I've been called worse. Would you like to dance?"

His abrupt segue seemed to confuse her. "Dance? Oh, no. I don't dance. No rhythm at all. I once fell off a balance beam that was three inches from the floor. Broke my collarbone. The only sport I'm decent at is bowling."

He stood up and held out his hand. "I won't let you fall, I swear. This is a slow song. You won't even *break* a sweat."

"Very funny." Her hesitation lasted forever. But finally, she stood and put her hand in his. "You won't be so jolly when I stomp on your toes."

Lucas didn't know why he was trying so hard to make her comfortable with him. He was competitive by nature. He liked to win. But an uneasy feeling in the pit of his stomach told him this thing with Leah was much more than wanting what he couldn't have. He was confused about his own motives. He wanted Leah Marks in his bed. But even with sex off the table, he still had the urge to keep her close, to coax her into trusting him and having fun with him.

She fit into his embrace perfectly. He folded her against his chest and sighed, tangling his fingers in her soft, silky hair where it tumbled past her shoulders. Her scent was light and appealing, a mix of floral and citrus.

The music was familiar, but he couldn't pick out the words, because all his attention was focused on this first big step with the standoffish Leah Marks.

Early on in his chosen career, he had learned that a fire could smolder unnoticed in the walls of a house for hours, maybe days. He was convinced that the fire between him and the woman in his arms was real. And that Leah sensed its presence, just as he did.

What remained to be seen was whether the fire would prove to be destructive or if it might instead be warm and seductive and ultimately life-giving. He'd never belonged anywhere. Not really. Once he left childhood behind, he'd told himself that belonging was an illusion. And that was okay. He liked his life.

Being with Leah, though, gave him a tantalizing feeling there might be something more. Unsettling perhaps, but true.

At last, the dance ended. Her yawn told him it was time to get her home.

"Sorry," she said sheepishly as they returned to their table. "Camp starts early."

He lifted his hand to summon the waitress for their bill. "You don't have to apologize to me. I work tough hours all the time. I get it."

On the drive home, Leah was quiet. Was she thinking about his proposition? He hoped so. He couldn't ignore his fascination with her. This summer would seem like an eternity, but Leah was worth it, even if only as a friend.

When they reached the camp, he parked beside the welcome sign, not in sight of the camp.

Leah turned to look at him. "Tonight was nice. I like you, Lucas. You're sweet and sexy, and Blossom Branch is lucky to have you."

"I'm not sweet," he muttered.

"Well, let's put it this way. You make me feel safe."

He frowned. "And that's a good thing?"

She cupped his cheek in one hand, leaning closer. "It is," she whispered.

All his noble intentions went up in smoke. He pulled her close and slanted his mouth over hers. "I like kissing you," he muttered. She tasted like coffee and strawberry cake.

Lust drove him hard, but he ignored it. Instead, he focused on an unexpected wave of tenderness, a little shocked he was able to do so. Leah was the kind of woman who valued tenderness. He had seen it in her interactions with campers. And though the softness in her personality was not a sign of weakness, he knew she would want a man who understood her need to be seen as more than a female body.

Turns out, that wasn't so hard. They barely knew each other, but already he wanted to be a hero for her. He wanted to see approval in those gorgeous eyes. He wanted to make her happy. His stomach curled with a sudden jolt of anxiety. He might be a fireman, but he wasn't destined to be any woman's hero. Not for the long term. "Tell me to stop, Leah," he begged.

Things were heating up too fast.

She traced his ears with her fingertips. "I don't want to stop, Lucas. This is nice."

The way she kissed him back was adorably teasing and hell on his better nature. When her tongue made a tentative foray, he groaned and shook. He knew she wasn't a virgin. She was a grown woman in her twenties. But he had promised her sex was off the table for now. He would have to rein in his libido and muster up some self-control.

It took all he had to release her and settle back in his seat. "You're a firecracker."

"No, I'm not."

He couldn't tell if she was insulted or merely disbelieving. "Apparently, you don't see yourself the way I do. Let's do dinner again. Tomorrow night."

She winced. "Sorry. It's the camp talent show. I have to be there. Monday is movie night. I could slip away then."

"I work until six that day. And I don't always finish right on the dot. What if we eat on our own and I'll pick you up at seven thirty to go bowling?"

"Do you know *how* to bowl? I can't imagine you in rented shoes."

"Don't need them," he said smugly. "I have my own. And a ball, too. The fire station guys in Nashville were part of a league with other first responders. We played at least twice a month. Though in all fairness, I might be rusty. Haven't touched a bowling ball since I moved to Blossom Branch."

"Then we're on," she said. "You'll like the Spare Peach. It has *atmosphere*."

"Is that good or bad?"

She grinned, brushing the hair from his forehead. "You'll have to wait and see."

Lucky for Lucas, not much was burning down in the forty-eight hours after he dropped Leah off at camp. His concentration was shot. He had promised her they were getting to know each other, and he was serious about that. But nothing said he had to say no if *she* initiated sex.

That prospect kept him going. After a quick shower and a cheese sandwich Monday evening, he threw his stuff in the trunk and jumped behind the wheel. Blossom Branch was quieter than normal, given that it was a weeknight.

One of the first things he noticed when moving here was the way all the merchants had joined in to promote a town theme. There was the pizza joint, Peach-aria, The Peach Pit, and an ice cream shop called Peaches and Cream. The list went on and on.

The Spare Peach was a particularly clever one. Their logo was a woven bushel basket resting on its side with a single peach inside.

When he picked up Leah, she came bouncing out of the house with her hair in a ponytail. Her skinny jeans showed off every fabulous curve. A deep turquoise polo shirt clung to her generous breasts.

Suddenly, he realized the *just friends* thing was suicide. How was he going to spend time with her and keep to the script?

They didn't talk much until they arrived at the bowling alley. Leah didn't have her own equipment, so he paid for her shoes while she picked out a ball.

She grinned at him when they sat down at lane seven. "Lucky seven," she said.

He didn't feel lucky at all. He was like a condemned man who could see and smell a feast but knew he would never taste it.

Leah insisted he go first. Once the game began, his competitive instincts kicked in. Leah was good. Really good. She threw perfect strikes in the first three frames. But after that, she missed a split spare. It rattled her confidence. Slowly but surely, Lucas narrowed the gap in their scores.

At the end of the ninth frame—in which neither of them had a strike *or* a spare—Leah was at 203. Lucas at 201.

They hadn't talked about anything personal during the game. The bowling alley was loud. There was barely enough time to sit down between frames with only the two of them playing. The game went fast.

"I have an idea," he said, trying to look innocent. "How about a bet? If I beat you, we'll go back to my place and watch a movie."

Leah shook her head slowly and rolled her eyes. "I may not have as much sexual experience as Luscious Lucas, but even *I* know that *watch a movie* is code for making out."

He chuckled. "So you think you'll lose? Is that it?"

She lifted her chin. "Of course not. I'm the better bowler. Anybody can see that."

"Then why not take the bet?"

He was teasing her, taunting her. Wondering if she would play along.

Leah chewed her bottom lip. "I'm not going to lose," she said. "Okay."

She lifted her chin. "I'll take your stupid bet."

His sex twitched in his jeans. There were definite suggestive overtones in their banter. He was going to win this game or die trying.

Leah waved her hand. "You're up, stud."

"I know that." His palms were damp. He used the powder pack and picked up his ball. For a moment, all the sounds around him faded away. He existed in a cocoon of silence. All he could hear was the beating of his own heart. Leah made no move to distract him.

He hefted the ball, positioned his foot on the line, walked forward, and released. His form was smooth as butter. The swirly patterned green-and-gold ball went flying down the center of the lane and hit exactly in the pocket, just to the right side of the center pin.

Strike!

Behind him, Leah shrieked, jumping up and down. "Go, Lucas."

She still thought she had him beat. He could see it on her face.

His score stood at 211 now. Because he had bowled a strike in the final frame, he was entitled to two more balls. If he could make both tries strikes, he was convinced he could win. But he got overconfident. His next ball knocked down only eight pins.

He kept his smile. Last ball. The most he could hope for now was a 221. If he got both pins. It wasn't a split. But there was air between them.

His brain did the calculations. His gut told him to go for it. He rolled.

He picked off the one on the right, but not the other.

Final score—220.

"Congratulations," Leah said with a smug smile. She kissed his cheek. "You did great."

And then she was at the line. He sat in the chair by the electronic scoring pad and tried not to stare at her ass. That would only make things worse.

Her first ball was a textbook strike. Her form was spot on, her confidence unassailable. When she turned around and smiled at him, he wanted to throw her over his shoulder and march right out of that damn bowling alley.

She already had 213 points. No way for her to lose now. He was statistically screwed. Any high school kid with a lick of skill could knock down most of the pins, even if it wasn't a strike.

Leah lined up her shot, took a deep breath, and swung the

ball. But somehow, she slipped. Her right ankle—the same one she had twisted the day of the fire—gave out for a second. She stumbled, caught herself. But it was too late.

Gutter ball...

Lucas jumped to his feet, dismayed. "Are you okay?"

Leah whirled around, eyes blazing, ponytail bouncing. She held out her hand to stop him. "I'm fine," she said. "Sit. Down."

In that moment, he realized his fragile Southern flower was every bit as competitive as he was. Though she looked soft and cuddly and utterly feminine, she had a core of steel.

All ten pins still stood. This was Leah's last chance.

He watched her gather herself. He saw her wince when she put pressure on her right foot. Nothing he could say would stop her.

She was slower this time, more tentative. And her release was awkward because she was favoring her wonky ankle.

It wasn't a strike. The pins wobbled and went down slowly, one tumbling into the next. But when the dust settled, there was only one pin standing.

Leah had bested him, 222 to 220.

He was beset by the oddest mix of feelings. He hated to lose. Always had. And this meant he had lost the bet. No cozy cuddle at his house with Leah.

But the one notion that drowned out all others was how proud he was of her, and how impressed by her talent and determination.

As she limped back to the chairs, he stood and high-fived her. "Nicely done, Ms. Marks. I've been beaten by a pro."

She sat down and rubbed her ankle. "I haven't scored that high in ages. We're well-matched."

He sat beside her and pulled her leg across his lap. "Let me see what you've done to it."

Her skin was soft, her anklebone delicate. A bit of bruising lingered from the week before, but no real swelling.

"See," Leah said breathlessly. "I'm fine."

"Maybe."

She rested her head against his shoulder. "I'm not in the mood for a movie, but do you want to go back to your place and talk?"

Leah wasn't stupid. When Lucas's whole body tensed, she could read his mind. He had lost the bet. He knew they weren't going to jump into anything physical. But no matter what he'd said about being friends, he clearly didn't want to talk.

How else was she going to get to know him? So far, each of their dates had occurred in loud, crowded, public places. Leah had enjoyed both outings. But she was curious about Lucas, and she needed the two of them to get past the superficial and into deep waters.

Even if they never slept together, she admired him and wanted to know him, really know him. About all she had so far was a fireman raised in foster care who liked nice cars.

That left a million unanswered questions.

"Never mind," she said quickly. "I should get back to camp anyway. It's late."

Lucas's expression was hard to read. Closed off. Remote.

"We can go to my house," he said. "Do you like popcorn?"

"Doesn't everyone?" She grinned at him, trying to ignore the fact that his finger lingered on her ankle, sparking heat up and down her leg.

"Okay then," he said.

When she eased her leg off his lap and set her foot on the floor, she realized it was time to change shoes. Neither of them had mentioned playing a second game. She wasn't sure her heart could take the excitement.

Besides, Lucas had to be at work at six in the morning. Even camp wouldn't be rousing at that hour.

After she put on clean socks and her sneakers, she put her ball on the rack and carried her shoes back to the counter. Lucas was stowing his gear back in his fancy bag.

When they stepped outside, the humidity was shocking. The bowling alley kept its thermostats set to arctic chill.

"Are you serious?" Lucas asked as he opened the car door and waited for her to get in.

"About what?"

He slid behind the wheel. "About going to my place."

"Oh. Well, given our agreement, it might not be fair to you. I know guys *feel* things. I wouldn't want to torture you."

In the illumination from the security light in the center of the parking lot, she saw his lips twitch. "I'm not seventeen," he said. "I think I can keep from pouncing on you."

"Well in that case, yes."

Lucas's apartment was modern and not particularly attractive. In fact, it looked exactly like the kind of temporary place a bachelor would choose.

The most interesting item in his living room was a fancy fish tank.

"This is cool," she said, bending to look more closely.

Lucas locked the door and tossed his keys on the counter. "I love dogs, but my schedule makes it tough to have pets. We do have a cat at the fire station, a communal feline if you will. The guys named her Inferno."

Leah laughed. "Sounds scary."

Lucas shoved his hands in his pockets. "Do you really want popcorn?"

"If it's not too much trouble."

He shot her a dark, wry look. "I have a microwave. I think we're good."

His living room was compact but comfy. A large masculine sofa sat at right angles to a matching overstuffed chair. Leah took the chair.

Lucas joined her five minutes later with two bowls of popcorn and two bottled Cokes. He set Leah's share in front of her on the coffee table. "Dig in. There's more in the kitchen."

She ate a couple of bites and set the bowl aside, choosing to drink her Coke instead. Her throat was tight, making it hard to swallow.

An uncomfortable silence reigned. She didn't want this to sound like an inquisition, but she didn't know how to start.

Lucas made it easy for her in the end. He sighed. "Okay. What do you want to know?"

"Any subjects off-limits?"

He froze, his bottle halfway to his lips. "I'll let you know if one comes up."

His dry response told her he was not an open book.

"Well," she said slowly. "You mentioned foster care. How old were you when you went there, and what happened to your parents?"

A shadow slid across his face. Maybe he didn't even realize. But Leah saw it.

Lucas shrugged. "I was an infant. Left on the doorstep of the Catholic church in our town. They turned me over to social services. Very dramatic."

She stared at him, trying to process what he wasn't saying. "So why weren't you adopted? I thought that was the problem with foster care. The older kids get passed by because everyone wants babies."

He looked down at his bowl of popcorn, taking the time to pick out a handful of burnt kernels. "My parents didn't sign away their rights. I was *Lucas—middle name Carter*—with no surname. The note they left—with their first names only—said they would come back to get me," he said. "I was never eligible for adoption."

"Oh, Lucas." Who would be so callous and cruel? She hated his parents already.

"It was all good," he said, giving her a smile that was unconvincing. "I had great foster families. Honestly."

She bristled. "How many foster families?" In eighteen years, what could the number have been?

His jaw worked. "Does it matter?"

SIX

HIS REPLY ECHOED SOMETHING LEAH HAD SAID TO him when they talked about her failed "almost" engagement. "Yes," she said. "I think it does."

For a long moment, she thought he wasn't going to answer her. Or maybe he was going to lie. But at last, he shot her a dark, unreadable look. "Twenty-seven foster homes. The shortest was four weeks, the longest four years."

Her jaw dropped. Her stomach clenched. She would never come close to knowing this man, really knowing him, unless she understood how the first eighteen years of his life had shaped him. He didn't want sympathy. That was clear.

She was attracted to him, sure. But now, another feeling crept in. Compassion. Caring. In the same way she wanted to help her campers, she now yearned to make up for everything Lucas had missed out on as a child.

"Did you try to find them when you turned eighteen?" she asked.

Lucas knew who she was talking about. "No," he said bluntly. "Why did it matter? If they didn't care enough to let me be adopted, I sure as hell didn't want any contact. My eighteenth birthday freed me. From then on, I was the master of my own destiny. *I* took charge of my life. Me. No one else."

It was a lot to process. Not long after she met him, Lucas had told her he was a foster kid. He wasn't trying to hide anything. But his open cheerful personality might be concealing some heavy stuff in his psyche.

"And you turned out great," she said. "Except for the arrogant, bossy side."

His grin was genuine this time. "Sorry, Leah. I'm used to being in charge. If you sometimes get caught in the crossfire, I apologize in advance."

"Got it." She picked up the popcorn bowl and tried to make herself eat. But she still felt queasy. A baby. A toddler. A first grader. A boy nobody wanted permanently. His life must have been incredibly painful.

Lucas leaned forward. "My turn."

"Oh, goody," she said, grimacing.

He laughed at her. "I already know you're an heiress."

"I'm not an heiress," she said. "That's dumb." She winced inwardly at the differences in their realities. She'd been surrounded by immediate family and even a great-aunt who cared enough to leave Leah an inheritance. No wonder he had initially been suspicious that she was a rich do-gooder.

"Call it what you want," he said, laughing. "Now tell me about *your* family."

She chose her words carefully. "Unlike you, I was very lucky. My childhood was super conventional. My dad is a successful dentist. In fact, he has three offices and clinics spread around the area. His base is in Gainesville. My mother was a stay-at-home mom in the early years and later his receptionist."

"Siblings?"

"Three. I'm the baby of four. My brothers set the bar high. The oldest, Craig, is a pediatrician in Atlanta. My middle brother, Martin, is an up-and-coming actor on the West Coast. And the one closest to me, Keith, is an agricultural missionary in Sudan."

Lucas blinked and rubbed his chin. "Wow. I don't know who to feel sorry for. You…or me."

"Well, I wouldn't put it exactly that way, but yes. I've spent a lifetime trying to measure up."

"Which is why Camp Willow Pond is so important to you."

She stared at him in surprise. He had cut to the heart of the matter easily. "Yes. I know it sounds like a cliché, but for once in my life, I'd like my parents to be proud of me. I was an average student, a below average athlete. And I'm a failure when it comes to finding a man and producing grandchildren for them."

"No pressure." His smile was sympathetic. "Poor Leah. Good thing you have me in your corner. I happen to think you're amazing."

"Do you really mean that? Or is it a line you use to get girls out of their undies?"

He raised an eyebrow. "Careful, Ms. Marks. If we're going to impress your parents, you can't say things like that."

"*We're* not going to do anything," she said. The thought of introducing Lucas to her parents made her shudder. Her mother would be hearing wedding bells before the night was over.

"I'm an asset," he insisted.

"We'll see…" It was the universal answer for *over my dead body*.

Lucas sat back, laced his hands over his flat belly, and propped his feet on the coffee table. "So a doctor, an actor, and a missionary. Sounds like the beginning of a bad joke."

"It's no joke," she said glumly. "And I haven't told you the most embarrassing part."

"I'm all ears."

Leah could have skipped this sidebar. But he might as well

know. "My mother is gorgeous. In fact, she was a beauty queen back in the day. She's slender and blonde and looks fifteen years younger than she really is. My brothers—all three of them—take after her. They've been fending off female admirers since they were still in kindergarten."

He frowned. "And this affects you how?"

She stuck out her chin. "I look like my maternal great-grandfather, Hiram. He was a forbidding old codger. Everyone was afraid of him. I have the same coloring, the same sharp nose. It's not easy being the ugly duckling in a house full of swans. Even my dad is very handsome."

"Does this explanation somehow imply that you are not attractive?"

"You don't have to pretend, Lucas. I know I'm not ugly. But I'm never going to be the kind of woman men spot in a crowd."

"That's true," he said. "I thought the same thing when I met you. Your beauty is more subtle. Like a deep, mysterious, peat-stained pond in the winter. But your kind of beauty will last a lifetime, long after the flashier birds have lost their feathers."

She gaped at him. Poetry from a fireman. Who knew? The fact that he hadn't tried to convince her she was a ten instead of a solid six point five made her believe his words were sincere.

"Thank you," she said stiffly. "Can we change the subject now?"

"Sure." He glanced at his watch. "What time do you need to get in bed?"

Her throat flushed. She felt the heat roll upward from her chest. Hearing Lucas say the word *bed* was unsettling.

It was almost ten o'clock. "Probably now," she said. She had enjoyed herself tonight. In fact, she didn't want it to end. But *she* was the one who had insisted she didn't have time for a dalliance—even if the thought of *dallying* with Lucas Carter made her want to be wild and irresponsible.

She stood and carried her popcorn bowl and Coke bottle to

the kitchen. When she turned around, Lucas was on her heels. She practically bumped into him.

Without a word, he set his things on the counter and put his hands on her shoulders. "For the record," he muttered. "You are *exactly* my type. I've wanted you from the first moment I touched you."

She stared up at him, trying to read the secrets in his eyes. Never had she wanted a man more. Never had caring seemed so dangerous. Weren't there a million reasons to put an end to this? Or was that the old, risk-averse Leah trying to keep her life on an even keel?

There was something to be said for boring and safe. But was that what she really desired as a woman? She had branched out in a big way for her professional career and dreams. Didn't she deserve the same risk and reward for her personal life? "I want you, too, Lucas," she said. "But…"

Before she could finish that thought, he had her pressed up against the refrigerator kissing her slowly. Thoroughly. His hips moved restlessly against hers. His erection was impossible to miss. But he abided by the rules. No touching below the waist. No complete nudity.

In her addled brain, Leah came to a hazy conclusion. Nothing was stopping her from touching Lucas. She slid her hands under his shirt, palms flat, and found warm smooth skin over a hard, muscled belly.

Oh, my…

Lucas shuddered, murmured her name, and gripped her arms.

"I like touching you," she said.

"Ditto." The hoarse word boosted her confidence.

She knew she was skating a thin, dangerous line. If she really didn't want to fool around with Lucas Carter, she needed to walk out of this house. Right now.

Reluctantly, she stepped back. It took several seconds for

Lucas to realize she was trying to slip out of his embrace. When he did, he released her immediately.

"Leah?" Consternation marked his face.

"I need to go home," she said simply. "Thanks for bowling with me. And for the popcorn. It was a fun evening."

He touched her cheek. Barely a brush of his fingers. "What's wrong?"

She stared at him. It was like looking at the sun. He was literally the most beautiful man she had ever seen. And she wanted so much more than his friendship. All she had to do was tell him that. End their silly platonic agreement.

But she had a camp to run...with big responsibilities. These next ten weeks were the most important ones of her adult life. It wasn't as simple as making her parents proud of her. She carried the hopes and dreams of eighty kids in her hands. For some of them, Camp Willow Pond might be a turning point. Something that would change their lives forever.

Jumping into a physical relationship with Lucas seemed selfish, no matter how wonderful he was. If she slept with him— even once—he would take over her world. Not on purpose. And not with any arrogance on his part. But because she would be wallowing in the delicious novelty of being with a man who made her body sing with pleasure.

It seemed pretentious to say all that to Lucas, so she just smiled. "It's getting late."

He seemed confused, but he reached for his keys and walked her out to his car. The radio broke the silence. Thankfully, the trip was short.

This time, Lucas didn't stop at the sign.

When he pulled up in front of her house, she opened the car door quickly and jumped out. "Bye, Lucas," she said.

He stepped out of the car, too. But he didn't try to follow her. Even so, his deep voice carried on the night air. "Don't be afraid of us, Leah. Please."

She stopped at the top of the stairs and turned back. There was no moon. He stood in the shadows. "I'm not scared of you," she said.

"But?"

"But nothing. You're a nice man. I'll see you around."

Lucas was stymied. He'd never wanted a woman he couldn't have. Was that hubris? Probably. But it was the truth.

Which meant he didn't know how to handle his feelings for Leah Marks. She liked him. Their attraction was mutual. He'd bet his life on that.

Even so, she was focused on making her camp a success. He admired her dedication. He even understood it. But he was selfish enough to hope she would find time for him. He didn't want to wait almost three months for a chance with her.

It made sense that Leah's focus was on the camp. She had poured time and money and energy into her endeavor. She cared deeply about the first group of young teens who had come to Camp Willow Pond. And she would continue to care about the ones who followed.

What would it be like to have all that passionate, loving care focused on him? The idea was both appealing and uncomfortable. Leah didn't do anything by half measures. If she chose to be with Lucas, she would give a lot and expect a lot from a relationship.

Was he ready for that?

He'd never *belonged* to anyone. Long ago, he had learned that he was good on his own. He had friends, of course. And work colleagues. But at the end of the day, he was unfettered. Free to come and go. Or free even to leave for good.

He knew in his gut that Leah would neither like nor accept that.

So was it better to settle for friendship with her? Safer?

Fortunately, work kept him busy for the next few days. A

couple of his crew were out sick with a stomach bug. The station alarm rang for two house fires in one day, which was unusual for a town the size of Blossom Branch. And Lucas realized he had slipped up and missed a date for CPR recertification.

He handled it all. Barely. When he clocked out at 6:15 p.m. Thursday evening, he went home, ate a sandwich, and crashed hard.

Friday dawned bright and beautiful…and with it, the knowledge that Leah's first group of campers would be heading home this afternoon. Leaving Leah—and her staff—with a much-needed eight-day break.

He told himself Leah needed space. He told himself he ought to go fishing to clear his head. But after lunch, he climbed in his car and headed out to camp. She had mentioned at one point that the closing "ceremonies" would take place at 2:00 p.m.

Lucas wanted to be there.

When he arrived, campers were gathering in the open area between the dining hall and Leah's house. Chairs had been dragged outside. It was a warm day, but cloudy. Lucas spotted Jim and went to say hello.

Jim saw him and lifted a hand. "Well, we made it through the first session," he said.

Lucas grinned. "I'm guessing you're ready for some R and R."

"The kids are great, but it's pretty much a twenty-four seven proposition."

Lucas admired the man. Jim and Peg and the other two residential counselors had worked nonstop for these kids. Leah paid her senior staff very well, but even so, this kind of thing was a calling.

Jim frowned suddenly. "I don't see Benjamin."

The arson kid. "I remember him. Did the rest of camp go okay after the fire?"

"Yes. But he's supposed to be out here with the others. Will you come with me to find him?"

Lucas frowned. "Why me?"

"We have stringent guidelines about no adult ever being alone with a single kid. It's a safety thing to prevent abuse. We all abide by those rules. But we need to hurry so he won't miss anything."

"Sure," Lucas said.

The two of them set out at a fast clip in the direction of the dorms. Jim whispered an explanation to Peg as they hurried past. She nodded.

The boys' cabin was dark and quiet, everybody outside. All the suitcases and duffel bags sat neatly packed at the end of each bed ready to be loaded onto buses.

In the far corner of the room, a small figure huddled against the wall, head bowed. Jim took the lead. Lucas followed him but stopped a few feet behind.

Jim spoke in a calm voice. "Benjamin? Buddy? They're getting ready to start the camp closing. It's fun. You don't want to miss it."

Benjamin straightened, but he blanched when he saw the fire chief. "I don't care," he said. His habitual insolence was there in his voice, but it was muted, as if Benjamin had lost the will to fight.

Jim sat down on the opposite end of the bed. "What's going on?"

"I don't want to go back to Atlanta." The kid was a scrappy thirteen-year-old. But in this moment, he was a scared child.

Jim grimaced and shot Lucas a look. "Benjamin lives in foster care. He hasn't always had the best experiences."

Lucas stiffened, wondering if he was being set up. Had Leah told Jim about Lucas's past? He had to know. "Jim," he said, "do you know how I grew up?"

Jim frowned as if to say, *what the hell does it matter?* Lucas realized from the other man's response that this situation was a sad coincidence.

Lucas inhaled sharply, knowing he couldn't walk away. He tapped Jim on the shoulder. "May I?"

Jim seemed befuddled, but he swapped places with Lucas.

Benjamin watched the whole thing, eyes wide.

Lucas smiled at him. "I know you set the fire. And I know why."

"You do?" The kid's expression was a mix of horror and curiosity.

"Yep." Lucas sighed. "I spent the first eighteen years of my life as a foster kid. I know what it feels like to have someone else plan every moment of your day. It drives you crazy, and then sometimes you explode. I'm guessing you didn't have a choice about coming to camp, did you?"

The boy chewed his lip. "No, sir."

"That's what I thought. Here's the thing, though. It *will* end. You'll get to be an adult. And in some ways, you'll find out that's scary as hell. But you'll be free. What you need to do in the meantime is start dreaming some dreams. Keep yourself out of trouble."

Benjamin had his eyes locked on Lucas's face. "Is that what you did?"

"You bet your ass. I figured out that if I kept my nose clean, I had a little more freedom. When I turned eighteen, I decided I wanted a college degree. There are need-based scholarships for people like you and me, especially if you're willing to have work study jobs. For the first time, I met guys in the dorm and in my classes who were like real brothers. I got an education. I learned skills. Now, I make the life I want. You can, too."

Benjamin pouted. "Five years is a long time."

Lucas smiled. "If it's okay with Mr. Jim, I'll get you some stamped envelopes, Benjamin, with my address. You can write to me anytime, and I swear I'll answer." Lucas felt an ache in his chest, wishing he'd had a mentor in his own life when he was a teenager.

Jim nodded. "That sounds great. But we've got to go, bud. Come on."

Leah stepped around the corner of the building, out of sight of the three males, and dabbed her eyes. She'd been standing just outside the door, listening in case Jim needed backup. But instead, it was Lucas who had saved the day.

He had spoken from the heart, and Benjamin had responded.

She hadn't even known Lucas was coming to the closing ceremonies.

When she first saw him get out of his car earlier, her heart practically jumped out of her chest. Four nights had passed since their bowling date. Four nights where she tossed and turned, wondering why she had turned down the chance to be intimate with this incredible, complicated man.

She had always dreamed of settling down with a man who would give her children and that coveted white picket fence. But did it have to be now? There was nothing permanent on the horizon with Lucas. That much was clear. She understood him more than he knew. He was the proverbial rolling stone that gathered no moss. Was that a reason to miss out on a wonderful relationship? He was special. One in a million. He was generous and dedicated to helping people. He was sexy and funny, and she knew he cared about her.

But could she—should she—jump into a physical relationship knowing it would never be what she ultimately wanted?

Unfortunately, there was no time for introspection or decision-making. Camp closing was about to start.

Jim played the role of emcee. Skits were first. Two by the college-age counselors, then two written and produced by the campers themselves, with help, of course.

Next, one of the junior counselors—who was a music major

at Emory University—led the group in singing several of the camp songs they had all learned that week.

After that, three kids volunteered to get up and say what they liked best about Camp Willow Pond.

Then Leah had to take the mic. She was nervous. And surprisingly emotional. Having Lucas there to hear everything she said made it worse.

She cleared her throat. "You guys may not know it, but you will always be very special to me. Because you're my first group of campers at Camp Willow Pond."

Applause broke out, led by the counselors, but including the kids.

When the noise died down, she continued. "There are so many people to thank, but some of them are not here. We have dozens of folks, mostly in Atlanta, who believe in you and want you to have a great life. Their donations helped fund the camp and make it possible for each of you to come. I hope you've had a wonderful time here. I know I speak for all my staff when I say that we love each one of you, and we've loved getting to know you. I hope in the fall we can have a one-day camp reunion where you and anyone you want to bring can come back for games and food and just to enjoy the time together. We'll keep you posted on that."

When she fell silent, Jim rescued her. "Three cheers for Ms. Leah!" After an enthusiastic response from the crowd, Jim said, "Buses load in exactly one hour. But first we have hand-cranked homemade peach ice cream and pound cake for everyone. Enjoy yourselves."

Leah watched, misty-eyed, as campers and counselors ran to get in line.

This was what she had strived for…this warm, joyful celebration of what it meant to be a kid. A kid with hopes and dreams.

She had only been able to give them two weeks. It wasn't enough to make up for everything they had lost before coming to Camp Willow Pond. But she hoped it would be enough to give them a reason to fight the forces that would drag them down.

Peg put an arm around her waist. "Well, boss, you did it. You made your dream come true. You should be darned proud. These kids will never forget the two weeks they've spent here."

"Thank you, Peg." The other woman was only sixteen or seventeen years older than Leah, but Leah relished her support.

Suddenly, Lucas appeared, his smile warm. "This is a redletter day. You ladies hit it out of the park."

Peg chuckled. "Thanks. I'll leave you two to catch up. I promised Jim I'd get ice cream for both of us…in case they run out when the kids start demanding seconds."

An awkward silence bloomed amid the chaos. Lucas shoved his hands in his pockets. "This was a great way to end camp."

Leah shifted from one foot to the other, suddenly remembering how tired she was. She yawned. "I didn't sleep at all last night worrying about everything."

"And now you can breathe a sigh of relief."

She rolled her eyes. "At least until next Sunday night."

He tucked an errant strand of hair behind her ear. "That's nine whole days away. And besides, you love it," he said.

Leah smiled, turning to look out across the lawn where kids and counselors swarmed. "I do," she said. "I wasn't sure in the beginning, but I do." She shook her head slowly. "Maybe I sound like that rich do-gooder you don't like, but it's so rewarding to see these kids happy, even if it's just for the moment. Honestly, this afternoon is the first time I've been sure I did the right thing. I think I've found my calling. Is that too dramatic?"

He surveyed the chaos and smiled. "Not dramatic at all. You were born to do this, Ms. Leah Marks. Thelma Gertrude would be happy today, too."

Leah cocked her head and stared at him. "I didn't know you were coming today."

He shrugged. "Neither did I."

"Why did you?"

His gaze heated. "Why do you think?"

Now her throat was dry.

Fortunately, she didn't have to answer that loaded question, because Jim appeared, holding two bowls. "Enjoy," he said. And then he disappeared into the crowd again.

Lucas took a big bite. "Holy hell," he said. "This is the best stuff I've ever tasted."

Leah nodded. "It's my grandmother's secret recipe. I've always thought it tasted like summer and love."

"You're not wrong." When they finished, Lucas took their paper bowls and tossed them in a large trash can. "How about I treat you to dinner tonight?"

Her heart raced. "That sounds wonderful, but I'm going to be toast when this is all over. Can I have a rain check?"

"Counterproposal. What if you take a nap on my sofa while I grill steaks? You won't have to lift a finger. Let me pamper you. I think you deserve it after the last twelve days and nights."

"That's very tempting." Leah debated his offer. She didn't have any groceries in her house. And the cooks had cleaned and shut down the kitchen after lunch. "I accept," she said. "But I don't know what time we'll be finished here."

His smile was brilliant. It made her knees weak. "I'm in no rush."

As it turned out, both she and Lucas were dragged into the fray immediately. Loading twenty kids onto a bus and making sure nothing was left in the cabins was like herding cats.

Some of the junior counselors were riding back to Atlanta on the luggage bus as well. Some had their own cars. Jim and Peg were to ride on the bus with the kids. After all the campers were picked up, Leah's two senior staff would take an Uber back to Blossom Branch. Like Lucas, they lived in rented apartments.

When the last vehicle exited the camp, the silence was deafening.

Leah heard birds singing. The farmer across the highway was mowing his field with a tractor. Cows mooed in the distance. The sun had come out, and the top of her head was hot. "What time is it?" she asked. She had been dead to the world when the alarm went off that morning. Her sleepless night had caught up with her just before dawn.

"Four forty-five. Do you have to do anything else before we go?"

She handed him a master key. "Do you mind double-checking all the doors at the cabins and dining hall? They should be locked already, but one more peek won't hurt. I'll change clothes and be ready when you get back."

Leah paused to watch him walk away before making her way up the low rise to her house. She knew all the camp doors were fine. Jim had made sure of that. But Leah needed a moment to regroup. First, she put a small suitcase in her car.

During the afternoon, she'd been wearing shorts and a camp T-shirt. Now she took a two-minute shower and changed into jeans and a ruffled sleeveless top in pink and lime green. She had redone her toes a couple of days ago, so she opted for the comfort of slip-on sandals in cotton-candy pink.

When Lucas knocked on her front door, she let him in. "I'm almost done," she said. Without making a big deal about it, she set the thermostat where she needed it and closed all the shades to keep the house cool. Then she picked up her keys. "I'll follow you into town."

"No way." He frowned at her. "I don't want you driving out here later—alone—after dark. Especially with Jim and Peg and the others gone."

Leah slung her purse over her shoulder. "I'm not coming back," she said calmly. "I only stay here when camp is in session. When I leave your house, I'm going home." She was excited about that. It would be wonderful to unwind.

"Home?" He parroted the word, his expression comical. "What do you mean, *home*?"

She sighed. "It's not a secret. I told you days ago. My Aunt Trudie left me a house in town."

"I do sort of remember that," he said. "But I assumed you were either renting it out or else it was a run-down dump."

Leah laughed ruefully. "I can assure you, it's not a dump. My aunt had exquisite taste. The house was built in 1915. It's one of the premier examples of historic architecture in Blossom Branch."

"Wait a minute," he said. "What's the address?"

"Seventeen thirty-two Begonia Lane."

His eyes rounded. "I've passed that place a hundred times. It's a beauty."

"Thank you. I'm lucky to have it." Now he was probably making assumptions again. Judging. Assuming. The rich do-gooder thing.

"And you walked away from a house like that to live at camp?"

"Not permanently," she said, grinning. "I'm going to sleep in my Blossom Branch house tonight."

SEVEN

EVERY TIME LUCAS THOUGHT HE HAD A HANDLE ON who Leah Marks was, she surprised him again. He glanced in the rearview mirror and saw her following him at a distance. This wasn't how he'd seen the evening playing out.

He'd been straight with her. His plan had been to pamper her, not seduce her. But he had anticipated driving her back out to camp later, maybe being invited inside. Possibly enjoying a good-night kiss.

He shifted restlessly in his seat. He wasn't accustomed to denying himself physical satisfaction. Most women chased him, not the other way around. It had been like that since he was in junior high. And though he would never admit it in a million years, that early attention had made him feel weird.

He'd liked it. Sure. What teenage boy wouldn't? Thank God he'd been smart enough not to get anyone pregnant. But eventually, he'd begun to feel as if he was being used. As if there was nothing more to him than a pair of broad shoulders and set of green eyes that brought the girls running.

Not once had any of those teenage females given any indication they were interested in his brain. Or his plans for the future.

He'd been a trophy. At the time, he had wondered more than once if his foster care status made him unsuitable as a long-term boyfriend. He couldn't ever remember being invited home to meet a girl's family.

Often, those trysts—some of them no more than heavy petting—had been secretive meetings behind bleachers and in the custodian's closet.

He'd been a guilty secret.

Sometimes that had been a problem with his foster families. And sometimes he'd been blamed or punished for things he didn't do.

The unfairness of it all had left him cynical and untrusting as a teenager.

Even now, the memories left a bad taste in his mouth.

Those same memories had shaped his interactions with adult women. He never gave much of himself at all. He was polite. And honorable. But he walked away first.

It was stupid to be controlled by the past. He was no longer at the mercy of other people. He had shaped his own life.

Dealing with Leah, however, felt like unfamiliar territory.

She parked her car behind his in the driveway. When she got out, smiling, he was waiting for her. Something kicked in his chest, stealing his breath. This moment felt important. Leah was entering his home. Taking one more step into his life.

He should be worried about that. It wasn't his way. But the quiet pleasure remained. "Come on in," he said, sliding his fingers through her hair where it bounced on her shoulders. "Mi casa es su casa."

She laughed. "Your Spanish accent is terrible, but I appreciate the hospitality."

Inside, he grabbed a pillow and a soft blanket out of the hall closet and ushered Leah toward the sofa. He cupped her face in his hands. "I was serious," he said. "You told me you didn't sleep last night. So relax. Take a nap."

The mauve shadows beneath her eyes betrayed her exhaustion. "Are you sure? I'd be happy to help with dinner."

He kissed her forehead, inhaling her now familiar scent. "I'm used to being on my own. I've got this. You close your eyes and have sweet dreams."

It was a sign of how much this first camp session had taken out of her that she didn't argue with him. After kicking off her shoes, she sat down on his comfy couch, stretched out with her head on his pillow, and smiled at him as he covered her up. "Thank you," she said. "All I need is twenty minutes and I'll be good as new."

An hour and a half later when he peeked into the living room, his guest was still out cold. The meal was ready. Steak and colorful veggie skewers. He always threw multiple things on the grill at once so he would have healthy alternatives to fast food and wouldn't have to cook again for several days. Tonight, he'd also added baked potatoes...and a store-bought key lime pie for dessert.

He took a few quiet steps in Leah's direction, watching her sleep and feeling the oddest mix of anticipation and regret.

In his gut, he knew that being her lover would be an incredible experience. Without question. But if he let the relationship progress that far, was intimacy with her going to tie him up in knots? Make him do things he wasn't ready for?

She had said it herself. She came from very conventional circumstances. A family intact. A small-town, storybook childhood. Leah belonged in Blossom Branch.

By the time she finished college, she'd been convinced her boyfriend was going to propose. That's what some young women who were brought up in sheltered, stable families expected. And maybe in a lot of cases, that's what they got.

Despite Leah's disappointment five or six years ago, he knew she likely still harbored those same dreams. But Lucas couldn't be the hero in that scenario. He wouldn't.

He hated the idea of breaking her heart. One man had done that to her already.

Was it possible to reach for what he wanted in the short term without hurting her? Since becoming an adult and achieving his independence, he had always pursued his goals with dogged determination. Rarely had he let anyone—or anything—deter him.

He wouldn't lie to Leah. He wouldn't make promises he couldn't keep.

Would that be enough to win her trust?

Carefully, he sat down on the coffee table, his knees brushing the sofa. He touched her arm. "Leah? Wake up, sweetheart."

Long lashes fluttered and rose. She'd had her hand tucked beneath her cheek. Her chocolate gaze was hazy. "Lucas?"

"Dinner's ready," he said, watching the sleepy confusion clear from her eyes.

She sat straight up, visibly alarmed. "Dinner? What time is it?"

Before he could say a word, she glanced at her watch and groaned. Then she put both hands over her face. "I'm so embarrassed," she said. "Why didn't you wake me up? Did I drool?"

He grinned. "I didn't wake you up because you obviously needed the sleep. And no. You didn't drool."

She swung her feet to the floor and straightened her shirt. The sleep crease on her cheek was adorable. "I am so sorry. I was supposed to help."

"I didn't need help," he said. "I've been on my own a long time. Under those circumstances, a guy learns to be self-sufficient, or he goes without."

"I see." His answer seemed to bother her.

"Are you hungry?" he asked. "I made plenty of everything."

Leah sniffed the air. "It smells amazing." She met his gaze, this time with a shy duck of her head.

He hadn't meant to kiss her right now but seeing her all rumpled and drowsy reminded him too much of what it might be like to wake up beside her after a round of wild sex.

"Appetizers first," he said gruffly. He leaned forward and touched his lips to hers, tangling his hands in her hair and anchoring her head. When Leah made a soft muffled noise, he let the kiss go deeper. With his tongue, he stroked her mouth, mirroring what he wanted desperately to do with both of them naked.

"I could eat you up, Leah Marks," he muttered. "You're like a delicious pastry, layered…decadent."

She put her hands on his shoulders. Then she changed her mind, leaned closer, and wrapped her arms around his neck. "You're a great kisser," she whispered. When she kissed him back eagerly, he blacked out for a moment. The roar of lust filled his head, blinding him.

When had he ever wanted a woman this intensely?

Carefully, he peeled her arms away and set her against the back of the sofa. "Food's getting cold," he said, the words hoarse.

Leah's lips were rosy where he had bitten them gently. There was a mark on the side of her neck as well. Her expression reflected confusion. As if aliens had snatched her away and then dropped her back into reality. "Of course," she said.

And then he saw it. The hurt. In her eyes. She didn't understand him. Already he had hurt her without meaning to in the least. *Damn* it.

"Leah…" He scrubbed his hands over his face. "Surely you know I didn't want to stop kissing you."

"You didn't?"

He could see the doubt in her gaze.

"No," he said bluntly. "I didn't. But I made a promise to you. We took sex off the table. This is the getting-to-know-you phase. Remember? So I have to keep some boundaries. You're an endless temptation."

She blinked, then frowned. "I am?"

"Come on, woman." He made himself take her by the hand, even if touching her shredded the fragile hold he had on his hunger. As he drew her to her feet, he managed a smile. "I've cooked several steaks from medium rare to well done. You can have your pick."

Discussing the menu felt bizarre under the circumstances.

Leah was in his apartment, steps away from his bedroom. All he had to do was walk her back there. He was almost certain she would let him.

Doggedly, he tried to breathe in and breathe out.

Somehow, they made it to the kitchen. Gradually, he found control. The rote motions of getting plates down, shutting off the grill, and serving the food helped center him.

He didn't let Leah help. He couldn't risk bumping into her. She made him weak with her lush breasts and voluptuous body.

Leah sat meekly at his table, her gaze locked on him, following his every move.

That regard made him itchy. Was she even a fraction as turned on as he was?

Her cheeks were flushed, but that could be from sleeping. Besides, she was so naturally fair, any little emotion might bring color to her face.

At last, everything was on the table, including water glasses. He didn't offer her wine. Alcohol lowered inhibitions. He needed *somebody* to be clearheaded and in control.

It certainly wasn't him. Even though he was stone-cold sober.

A few minutes were consumed with buttering potatoes and cutting meat. Leah had settled on a small serving of medium rib eye and one of the skewers.

"These veggies are delish," she said.

He nodded. "One of my favorite things about living out in

the country. If I'm not working, I try to hit up the Blossom Branch Farmer's Market once a week during the summer." Leah's delighted smile made him frown. "What?" he demanded.

She shook her head slowly, still grinning. "I'm having a hard time adjusting to this domestic side of you. I think I love it."

"There's nothing domestic about it. Men like to eat good food. Even if I were married, I wouldn't expect my wife to be a culinary goddess. I'd want her to save her energy for other things."

Leah's eyes went wide. "Oh."

He chuckled. "You're such a baby. You blush if I even mention sex."

"I'm not a baby," she said, her voice even. "And you know it. You're only trying to pretend I am, so you and I won't do something reckless."

Lucas gulped inwardly. She'd pegged his motivations neatly. "I'm never reckless," he lied. "I'm a highly trained professional."

"Right." She rolled her eyes at him. "So tell me about Jeff," she said.

The change of topic caught him off guard. "Jeff?"

"Jeff Grainger. The man you referred to as your best friend? You don't have many close people in your life, so I'm curious."

Lucas shrugged. "As I was finishing high school, my social worker liked me and offered to reach out to a few of her contacts down south. I was happy to get away from New York winters. Jeff and I met the first week of classes at the University of Tennessee. I was working three different jobs. Jeff was a naive kid from a small rural town. I had come out of the foster system in New York State with a ton of need-based scholarships and a chip on my shoulder. We banded together to keep from drowning. Been friends ever since."

"That's nice." She wrinkled her nose. "In the spirit of full disclosure, I should tell you he asked me out."

Lucas flinched. For a moment, something hot and dangerous flared in his chest. "He did?"

Leah nodded slowly. "Yes. But I told him the same thing I told you. That I don't have time for a social life this summer. The difference is, Jeff is a gentleman. He accepted my explanation. Unlike you, who never takes no for an answer."

"I go after what I want. That's not a bad thing, is it?" He stared at her, still feeling an illusory threat. He was honest enough to admit to himself that Jeff was a better match for Leah than he was.

Didn't matter. Leah was *his*, no matter how illogical the conclusion. And it *was* illogical. They were friends. He wanted to have her in his bed. Eventually. He cared about her. But that was as far as it went. That was as far as it *could* go.

His buddy Jeff belonged in Leah's world. Lucas had never belonged anywhere.

"Jeff and I have never squabbled over the same woman," he said, the words flat.

"Delightful. Chivalry is alive and well in Blossom Branch."

"Would you like some pie?" He didn't want to talk about Jeff. Nor did he want to think about how Jeff might move in on Leah when Lucas was unable to give her what she wanted. Or needed.

Or when Lucas moved to another town in another state.

Her smile was wistful. "No, thank you. I shouldn't."

"Shouldn't? I'm confused. Why?"

Her eyes flashed. "I don't need the calories. And thank you for making me say it out loud."

"Oh," he said. Her face had turned a rosy shade of pink. "Your body is perfect, Leah. Why would you deny yourself the pleasures of pie?"

A hint of vulnerability surfaced in pools of brown. "For the same reason I haven't slept with you. Some things are enjoyable in the short term, but we pay the price afterward." Her scowl took him aback.

"I don't like the sound of that."

She carried her plate to the sink. "I should go," she said.

He had embarrassed her. Maybe he *was* a jackass. Or at the very least clueless.

"Please don't go," he said. She was standing motionless at the counter, her back to him. "I have a confession to make," he said gruffly.

She turned to face him, wrapping her arms around her waist in a protective posture. "Do tell."

He shrugged. "I put in for several vacation days, and I also switched schedules around. I'm off from work all eight days until your next camp starts."

Leah stared at Lucas in shock. Had she misunderstood him?

"Why would you do that?" she asked, flattered, confused, and mildly exasperated. "I told you I have a very busy few weeks ahead of me." Did he really want to be with her that much? As a friend? Not a lover? Or did he hope to wear her down? Surely Lucas didn't really believe they could be all chummy for eight days and avoid falling into his bed or hers.

In her experience, most men preferred convenient sex. If a woman was too difficult, they moved on to greener pastures. What was he really thinking?

He shrugged, his gaze guarded. "You're very busy. I like being with you. I decided to clear the decks so I'm available whenever you are this week."

"But I..." She stopped, not sure what she wanted to say to him. This whole situation was confusing. For several years now, she had wanted to find a man to share her life with. Occasionally she heard that annoying biological clock. A decade ago, a younger, more naive Leah had assumed she would be married by now with a wonderful husband, a cozy home, and perhaps a baby on the way.

Now suddenly, fate had dropped Lucas at her feet. The timing was off. He almost certainly was the *wrong* man. But maybe she needed to reframe her needs.

Perhaps she didn't have to have a soulmate at this point in her life. Maybe Lucas was her *right now* man. Fun. Not too serious. Great in bed.

Of course, she hadn't tested out that last part, but she had a strong hunch he knew how to satisfy a woman.

She shifted from one foot to the other, feeling her body warm. The kitchen was air-conditioned, as was the rest of the apartment, but she felt hot, her forehead damp.

Lucas had worn crisp khaki shorts today with a casual button-down shirt in navy and citrus. The shirt was untucked. His legs were bare. Earlier, he had kicked off his leather deck shoes. He looked like a man settled in for a cold beer and a football game.

Yet he had cooked dinner for her. And he had let her find sleep when she needed it so badly.

She shivered inwardly, assessing her options.

Before she could land anywhere, Lucas took her by the hand. "Let's go in the living room and relax," he said.

She allowed him to pull her along behind him until they reached that big, comfy sofa. He tossed the blanket and pillow aside and sat down, settling Leah beside him. "Here's the thing, Leah…"

"Yes?" She half turned so she could see his face.

His expression was intent. "You can't work every minute of every day. It's not healthy."

"That's very true," she said solemnly.

"I'd like to propose an outing for tomorrow evening. What if we get dressed up and go eat somewhere fancy in Atlanta? White linen tablecloths. Maybe a strolling violinist. An edgy restaurant on the top floor of a downtown office building with 360-degree views of the city. Fresh flowers on the table. Candlelight. What do you say?"

What he described sounded amazing. "I'm sorry," she said wistfully. "I can't."

His expression morphed from cajoling to incredulous to frustrated. "Why not?"

She sighed. "All my brothers are in town—in Atlanta, I mean. They and my mom and dad and my sister-in-law are coming to Blossom Branch tomorrow evening to have dinner with me. I'm doing the meal."

"I thought you said you're not much of a cook."

"I'm not. But my friend, Marisa, is a caterer. She'll prepare the various dishes, bring them to my house, and transfer it all to pots and pans on the stove and in the oven so it looks like I made everything myself."

Lucas stared at her. The small crease between his eyebrows said he was puzzled. "Why on earth would you go to so much trouble? Surely they know this first session of camp has been a huge undertaking."

"Maybe they do. But they don't care. What I do at camp isn't important to them. No one thought I should open a camp at all. On the other hand, me being a consummate Southern hostess is expected. My mother holds a high regard for women who entertain well. Hospitality is a Southern thing. If you knew my family, you would understand. Trust me. This is the best way. The only way."

"I could help you fix a meal," he said. "With both of us, it couldn't be too bad."

His offer touched her. "Thank you, but I've already ordered all the food."

"I see."

A heartbeat of silence. Then another. She grimaced. "I'd like to invite you, but..." Lucas's jaw thrust forward. "But what?"

She should have been prepared for that question. Yet she wasn't.

When she hesitated, Lucas's masculine, sharp-cut cheekbones flushed a dull red. "Are you ashamed to be seen with me, Leah? Is that it?"

"Of course not," she muttered.

He didn't look convinced. In fact, he ran both hands through his hair, leaving the strands rumpled. "I'll admit I was a liability as a teenage boy," he said, "but I cleaned up my act. I've been impressing mothers and grandmothers for over a decade now."

"Please understand," she said urgently. "I don't need you to impress *anybody*. If you were there tomorrow night...well...there would be questions. I would hate that, and it wouldn't be much fun for you either. Sort of like a root canal without anesthetic."

"You're exaggerating," he said, the words flat.

"Maybe. But my siblings and my parents can be a bit much when they all get together. I'm used to it. You're not."

"What about the one sister-in-law? How does she survive?"

"My oldest brother, the doctor, has practically achieved sainthood, so by default, his wife is beloved. Plus she's trying to get pregnant, so no one bothers her."

"Are you not allowed to have friends?"

"If you're talking about men, not really." Leah managed a laugh. "I've had a few casual relationships since college. The longest of those was eight weeks. I don't think I'm cut out for twenty-first-century dating. I never know what men expect. Are all first dates now supposed to end up between the sheets? Or is it the whole sex-on-the-third-date thing? Who knows?"

Lucas's rigid shoulders finally relaxed. He rubbed his thumb over her cheekbone. "Poor Leah."

She grimaced. "I'm trying to spare you, I swear."

"I can handle myself. Don't you worry."

"Let me ask you a question," she said impulsively.

"Okay." His gaze was wary.

"Have you ever come close to getting married?"

His eyes went wide. "Lord, no."

Leah nodded slowly. "That's what I thought."

He linked his hand with hers. "I'm gonna be as honest as I know how, Leah. I'm not a minivan and making-babies kind of guy. I saw too much of the tough side of marriage while I was growing up in all those foster homes. I'm not even sure romantic love exists. I always shoot straight with my sexual partners. Fun and games, yes. Happily-ever-after, no."

Leah's heart pinched. She honestly didn't know what to do. Lucas was amazing. Fun and interesting, and he made her happy when he was around. Still, if there was no future for them, was it fair to anyone to introduce him to her family? "I appreciate your candor. But I need a little time to decide if I'm willing to have a public friendship with the fire chief. Blossom Branch is a small, gossipy town. Wonderful, yes. But certainly not very private."

"I'd like to help you with that decision."

She saw the hunger in his eyes. An answering heat flared in her midsection every time he got close to her. Her response was inevitable, prompted by an irresistible combination—his masculine scent. His honed body. The fascinating color of his eyes—sometimes they were the sunlit green of summer moss, at others more amber. Then there was the man himself. The more she knew of him, the more she respected and admired his code of honor.

Despite a very hard life, he wasn't bitter. He was generous. His strength was available for healing a troubled boy. His job took him into danger for the sake of others. His team looked up to him. His best friend cared enough to coax him to Blossom Branch. So far, the worst Leah could say about Lucas Carter was that he was a tad arrogant and infuriatingly bossy.

Could she be his friend—and maybe soon his lover—without letting it destroy her? Establishing Camp Willow Pond was the most exciting and rewarding thing she had ever tackled. Even after the first two-week session, success wasn't a given. She had a long way to go. Shouldn't she focus all her energies on her *job*? Would Lucas distract her too much? Would a broken heart taint her summer?

Lucas waited patiently as her brain raced. But his body was tense, poised to do whatever she asked.

"Yes," she said quietly.

His gaze narrowed, sweeping from her eyes to her breasts and back again. "Yes, what?"

"You can help me make up my mind."

Shock held him immobile for a split second. Then his expression gentled. "I won't encourage you to do anything you don't want to, Ms. Marks. Your virtue is safe, remember?"

She leaned into him, resting her cheek over the spot on his chest where his heart thundered. "And if I don't want it to be?"

He pulled back, his expression serious. "You'll have to be the one to ask. You'll have to set the limits. I care about you. I won't seduce you, Leah. But for the record, I'm entirely open to *being* seduced."

"That's fair." She listened to the steady thump of his heartbeat. "Are you into baseball?"

Lucas chuckled. "Not sure where this is going, but yes. I enjoy the game."

She toyed with one of his shirt buttons. "Around here in Blossom Branch, we're mostly Braves fans. From way back."

"I know, believe me. Jeff took me to a game at the new stadium when I first moved here. What does that have to do with us, Leah?"

She chewed her lip, still picking at his button with her fingernail. "I know we're both grown-ass adults. But for tonight, I'd like to try for second base."

"But no further."

"Correct."

"I can handle it if you can," he said, tracing the shell of her ear with his tongue and making her shiver.

For a panicked moment, Leah wondered if this was wise. This was a huge step for her. Playing with fire.

Opening Camp Willow Pond had been and still was a huge risk. Intimacy with Lucas might be riskier still. But she had come too far to back out now. Not because of Lucas. He would stop at any point.

Leah, however, was mesmerized by the possibility of making love to Lucas Carter. She'd never been with anyone like him.

His confidence might be brash and cocky, but it wasn't repulsive. If anything, she found it comforting to know that even if *she* lost her way, Lucas would steer them both where they wanted to go.

She sat back and looked at him, lifting her chin because he was so tall. "Kiss me."

His eyes glittered. "Yes, ma'am."

Expectation was a funny thing. She'd pictured him laying one on her. A hard, possessive, carnal kiss.

Lucas did the opposite. He waited.

The anticipation was excruciating.

He tucked her hair behind her ears and used his teeth to nuzzle the skin just below, his breath hot on her sensitive flesh. "Is this going to be our fourth kiss?"

"Um…" Leah barely registered the question. Her senses were on overload. "Maybe. I don't know."

Lucas sat back and shook his head, manufacturing a hangdog expression. "I must be doing something wrong if you don't remember every single one."

She stared at him, frowning. "The only thing you're doing wrong is torturing me."

He threw his head back and laughed. Then his gaze settled on her lips, making her heart race. His eyes were dark green now. "We don't know each other well enough yet for those kind of sex games, Leah. Give it time."

EIGHT

THE LOOK ON HER FACE WAS PRICELESS.

Shock. Interest. Need.

Lucas was on the verge of exploding. Every cliché he could imagine. Fireworks going off. Champagne corks popping. Pipes bursting.

He wasn't going slow solely for Leah's benefit. The pace was designed to give him breathing room. His mind raced. He wanted to be the man Leah needed. It was important that he do the right thing for both of them.

Obviously, her innocence wasn't physical. He understood that. But there was something about her, something sweet and earnest that tugged at him inexorably. He wanted to protect her and ravish her at the same time.

The two opposing forces threatened to tear him apart.

"Maybe *you* should kiss *me*," he said gruffly. The words came out of nowhere, surprising even him. He hadn't known what he was going to say. But it made sense. When Leah felt comfortable and in charge, she was not so nervous.

She nodded slowly. Her throat moved when she swallowed. "Okay."

Lucas rested his hands on his thighs, but he couldn't unclench his fists. His body vibrated with his need for her. The intensity of that yearning rattled him.

In his experience, sex was fun and easy. This thing with Leah was so much more than physical. She delighted him in every way. Her open heart and generous spirit. The connection between them was visceral. Complicated. And perhaps it threatened his peace of mind in a way that was alarming.

Maybe he should end this before he did something he would regret. "Leah," he said impulsively, "I think—"

She put her hand over his mouth, a faint, teasing smile tipping up the corners of her eminently kissable pink lips. "No talking. I need to concentrate."

"You do?"

"Yes." She cupped his face in her hands, testing the stubble she found there. "You've been with a lot of women. I need to bring my A game."

"I can't remember a single one." It was true. His world had narrowed to one woman and this oddly pure and desperate moment.

Leah pulled his head down toward hers and slanted her mouth over his.

Somebody groaned. Him? Her?

His heart slammed against his ribs. His erection was painful. One gentle, puritanical kiss and he was lost in lust. But not raw lust. This roiling need he felt had been refined by fire. Fire had brought them together. Fire had sparked between them from the beginning. Now, fire might consume them.

"Touch me," she begged.

"I don't think I can." He could barely force the words from

his tight throat. Maybe his vocal cords were paralyzed. "I can see third base from here." He tried to make a joke of it, but he had never felt less amused.

Leah deepened the kiss, her tongue stroking his.

He found her breasts. Her thin cotton top and the bra he couldn't see were no match for his nimble fingers. When he found a tight nipple, he squeezed it.

The woman in his arms moaned, a sound that ratcheted his hunger until he shook with it.

He kissed her back, taking what he wanted and knowing it wasn't enough.

Never had he been so torn between his body and his brain.

He wasn't an animal. He knew his limits. Leah wasn't sure of him. He could understand that. Asking her to take a chance on him with no promises was unfair.

For a split second, he flashed back to being fifteen years old and horny all the time. One of his foster mothers had loved historical romance. Lucas had sneaked one of her books and read it under the covers at night with a flashlight.

He had learned the word *rake*, a man who used women with no regard for their well-being. A man for whom physical pleasure was the only goal.

The adolescent Lucas had understood the driving need to be with a woman. But he also understood the power dynamic.

Leah was no eighteenth century, well-bred virgin.

But maybe she was the modern equivalent.

Lots of women enjoyed purely recreational sex. It was no big thing.

Yet in this moment, Lucas knew he didn't want to be one of Leah's regrets.

He grabbed her wrists in his hands and pulled them away from his face. "I think that's enough."

She blinked, her gaze hazy, her lips shiny and swollen from his kisses. "Is it?"

He stood and put the room between them. "Yeah. I thought I could handle second base, but you do something to me, Leah. Something blistering and unexpected. We need to stop while we can."

Her eyes cleared. All the pleasure faded from her expression, replaced by what looked like hurt masquerading as cynicism.

Leah stood as well. She shoved her hands in the pockets of her jeans and glared at him. "I'm supposed to believe that kissing me drives you so wild with lust that you can't control yourself? Give me a break, Lucas. You've been around the block a dozen times in a dozen different towns. I'm not buying it."

"It's true." He felt odd. This wasn't a situation he had ever experienced. "I think I should walk you to your car."

"Sure," she said, her jaw clenched. "I didn't want to stay here anyway."

Outside, the muggy June night did nothing to clear his head. The heavy, moist air made him think of hot, tangled sheets and screwing.

He cleared his throat. "May I please come to dinner tomorrow night? I want to meet your family as your friend. I'd like to support you, because I can see this family visit is stressing you out and making you doubt yourself."

"Why come?" she shot back. "We're not sleeping together. We haven't even seen each other naked. Besides, there won't be enough food."

He managed a smile despite his turbulent mood. "Liar. I've watched you at camp. You plan for every eventuality. And then some."

She opened her car door and tossed her purse on the front seat. "Fine," she said, huffy and adorable. "But you'll be sorry."

"I'll take my chances." He wanted a good-night kiss, but it was smarter to go without. Those earlier kisses had shown him his limits. Soft, sweet Leah was gone. This woman looked like she would rather castrate him.

She didn't even bother to say goodbye.

He watched her pull out of his driveway, move slowly down the street, and disappear around the corner into darkness.

Saturday morning, Leah slid into a booth at the Peach Crumble and smiled when Cate joined her moments later. Unfortunately, Gabby was tied up with a weekend seminar out of town. "How are things at the store?" Leah asked.

Cate owned a delightful gift shop on the town quad—in sight of the iconic Blossom Branch gazebo, and perfectly situated to entice tourists and locals alike through the doors. Her younger sister, Becca, currently managed the business. Cate popped in and out from Atlanta several times a month.

Becca and Cate's relationship had been rocky during Becca's adolescent years, but now the sisters were closer than ever.

Leah envied them. Brothers were fine, but she had always wanted a sister.

Cate dabbed her forehead with a paper napkin from the metal dispenser on the table. "It's hot as a jungle out there. Other than that, the shop is great. In fact, I may have to order more inventory before the Fourth of July. Things are flying off the shelves."

"That's great."

"What's wrong?" Cate said, zoning in on her companion's dull tone.

"I didn't sleep much last night," Leah admitted. Her head throbbed.

"You look like hell."

"Gee, thanks."

"You know what I mean. Those purple shadows under your eyes are dreadful. Is it your folks coming tonight that has you rattled?"

"Partly." Cate was well-acquainted with Leah's family.

"And what's the other part?"

They had to pause any serious discussion for a moment while the waitress took their orders. When the young woman walked away, Cate repeated her question. "What's the other part? Is it camp? I thought this first session was a success."

"It's not camp."

"Then what?"

Leah lowered her voice, feeling remarkably self-conscious and exposed. How many people in this little diner *knew* Lucas Carter? Probably a lot. "I've met somebody," she whispered.

Cate screeched, in no way picking up the vibe that Leah didn't want to make a big deal about this. "It's about time," she said, practically bouncing in her seat. Cate was blissfully happy in the romance department and wanted all her friends to have the same good fortune. "Tell me about him."

"Well, you remember the fire at camp?"

Cate frowned. "Duh. I was about to drive down here that night. You scared me to death when you texted."

"Everything turned out fine. The repairs were finished in record time. It's all good."

"But?"

"The fire chief was part of the crew that night. He…uh… he and I hit it off." Leah put her head in her hands. "Oh, gosh. I sound like a spinster in an old musical."

Cate's eyes rounded. "I've never seen you like this. Not even back in college when——"

Leah held up her hand. "I know what happened back in college. I've moved on."

The waitress dropped off two iced teas and two side salads.

When the woman departed, Cate leaned forward. "Details…" she demanded.

At least this time, she lowered her voice.

Leah drank half of her tea. Now *she* was sweating. "He wants to sleep with me," she muttered.

"Is that a problem? What, you don't like him as much as he likes you?"

"I think you're missing the point. This is more about lust than liking."

Cate grinned. "Can't it be both?"

"I don't know. Lucas is willing to wait on the physical part until we've known each other longer. But I'm not sure I want to wait. What if I make a mistake?"

Finally, Leah's misery got through. Cate frowned, her protective instincts obviously kicking into gear. In college, she had mother-henned half a dozen girls, especially Leah and their friend, Gabby. The three women were all from Blossom Branch, but their families hadn't intersected socially when the girls were kids. It was only at the University of Georgia—and particularly as sorority sisters in Zeta Zeta Pi—that the three women became close.

Gabby had come from very modest circumstances. Leah had suffered from damaged self-esteem. Cate had been their champion. Cate had turned a ho-hum college experience into a wonderful adventure.

Cate reached a hand across the table and touched Leah's arm briefly. "I think your recent dry spell is like falling off a horse. You need to get back in the saddle."

"That's a terrible analogy." Leah picked at her iceberg lettuce and found a carrot. "I *want* everything," she said. "But it's complicated."

"Always is…" Cate's gaze was measured. "What aren't you telling me?"

"It already feels like Lucas and I have been friends forever. I'm *comfortable* with him, and that's an awesome feeling. But at the same time, he ties me up in knots. Does that even make sense? He asked if he could come to dinner with my family tonight, and I said yes."

"Wow. That was fast. I don't know what to say. Obviously, he's smitten."

"Oh, no," Leah said. "There's no smiting. He's only curious because I've told him about my brothers and my parents and my lowly place in the hierarchy."

"Boyfriends never want to meet the family...unless they're serious."

"Wrong again. Lucas isn't like other guys. He's refreshingly honest. He's already told me flat out that he doesn't do mini-vans or making babies and that he doesn't want to get married."

"But *you* do, Leah. You always have." Cate had eaten only half of her salad, but she pushed the bowl aside, all her attention focused on Leah. "Most men think like Lucas in the beginning. He'll come around."

Leah shook her head slowly. "No. He had a tough life growing up in foster care. He's cynical about love and romance and happily-ever-afters."

"But he wants to have sex with you."

"He claims I drive him wild with lust," Leah said. "It's ridiculous."

"How so?"

Leah sighed. "His nickname at the fire hall is Luscious Lucas. He's gorgeous, Cate. On a scale of one to ten, he's a solid thirteen. Think of every leading man in Hollywood you love to watch on the screen. He's that and more."

Cate shook her head slowly. "You're my dearest friend, but damn, Leah. You need to wake up and realize you have it all. You're cute and smart and funny. I know Larry the turd messed you up in college. And your family has spent a lifetime making you feel small. But none of that is the truth about you. Here's a great guy telling you flat out he wants you. If you feel the same, go for it."

"I tried that, Cate. Last night. He...well, he..."

"He what?"

"He quit kissing me. Said we had to stop. I think he thinks I'm not ready."

Cate grinned. "Sounds like he knows you pretty well. What's your biggest risk in sleeping with him?"

"Maybe I'm bad in bed?"

"If you're naked and available, I guarantee he'll have no complaints."

"I suppose."

"Listen. You have a lot on your plate. Four sessions of camp. This dinner with your family. Lucas was probably trying to be a gentleman."

"And that's a good thing?"

They both laughed.

Cate squeezed Leah's hand. "Don't worry so much about when it's going to happen. Enjoy his company. Listen to your heart. When it's time, everything will work out."

The food arrived, and both women dug in. Cate's baked cod and farm-fresh green beans looked healthy and wonderful. Leah had gone the comfort food route. Meat loaf and mashed potatoes.

They decided against dessert, but lingered, having another glass of tea and catching up. Both of their lives had become increasingly busy. They had made a pact to maintain their close relationship because it was so important. Leah relied on Cate as a sounding board. And she felt the same about Gabby. Cate and Jason's aborted wedding had been hard on everyone, but thankfully that was in the past.

At last, Cate was the one to look uncomfortable. "I want to ask you a question," she said.

"Okay. Shoot."

"Do you know if I did something to upset Gabby? I've spent months trying to line up a lunch date with her. But she's either too busy to see me or we settle on a time, and then she has to back out at the last minute."

Gabby was the third point in their friendship triangle. A good triangle. Ever since freshman year in college when they bonded over being out of their element and homesick for Blossom Branch, the three women had been tight.

Gabby had been enormously helpful in overseeing the camp's finances and making budget suggestions. She was a workaholic at times, but given her upbringing, that wasn't surprising. Gabby needed financial security.

"I can't imagine why Gabby would be upset with you," Leah said. "She's probably just super stressed. That girl is driven. Four promotions in five years. It's crazy."

Cate gnawed her bottom lip. "That's true. But do you remember when the three of us met for lunch after the wedding?"

"Not to be too technical, but there *was* no wedding."

"Fair point." Cate winced. "Well, anyway...you know the day I mean?"

"Yes. It was awkward, Cate. Neither Gabby nor I knew what to say to you. We felt terrible."

"You were there. And you were supportive. That's what counted. But that's the first time I remember Gabby acting weird with me. And she rushed back to the office. Ever since then, it's been the same. I get her attention for five minutes, and then she's gone again. Am I being paranoid?"

"Probably. I ran into her in town at the grocery store about a month ago. Maybe her mom's not doing well. She depends on Gabby a lot."

"True." Cate glanced at her watch. "Oh, shoot. Forget about me obsessing over nothing. We've got to head over to your place and get busy."

Fifteen minutes later, they were standing in Leah's kitchen.

Cate looked around with envy. "I forget how much I love this house. It's absolutely perfect."

"Thanks," Leah said. "The cleaning ladies were here right before camp started. But I had to open all the windows this morning, because the house had a closed-up smell. I've got the air-conditioning on now. And I'm going to light a candle or two."

"I didn't notice a thing when I walked in. Except how beautiful it is. Okay, girl. Let's get this done."

Cate had come to help Leah set the table and have everything ready when the caterer arrived later. Aunt Trudie's large rectangular cherry dining table seated eight comfortably. Leah had invited Cate to the dinner, but she and Harry had symphony tickets for the Saturday evening performance. As it turned out, Lucas would be rounding out the numbers.

It wasn't even. Three women and five men. But this was a family gathering, not a fancy society event. It would do.

While Cate ironed an ecru linen-and-lace tablecloth, Leah brought out all the china. The cherry hutch matched the table and was built into one corner of the room.

When Aunt Trudie died, Leah had wondered what she would do with all the beautiful antique dinnerware and linens. Gradually, she had made the decision to use and enjoy them. Otherwise, they would be worthless to anyone.

Once the table was set, both women stepped back and looked at it with a critical eye. The florist had delivered a beautiful, appropriately low arrangement of purple, yellow, and white Dutch iris. Aunt Trudie's ivory dinner plates had gold trim that was timeless.

Leah couldn't help feeling the contrast between camp and this house. Her campers *and* Lucas had certainly never experienced this kind of elegant meal, at least as children. Would seeing all the *fuss* make Lucas revisit his rich, do-gooder assessment of Leah?

"Well," she said, chewing her thumbnail. "What do you think?"

Cate nodded. "It's perfect. In every detail. Very impressive."

Leah shrugged. "My brothers probably won't even appreciate the fancy stuff."

"But your mom will," Cate said, her warm gaze filled with understanding. "That's what matters, right?"

"Yes." Leah sighed. "I'm headed toward thirty and still trying to please her."

"You don't have to explain yourself to me. Mom and I butted heads over eighty percent of the wedding details. Different tastes. Different generations. I love her, but she drove me crazy. And then it was all for nothing."

"I'm so sorry that happened to you, Cate. Are you truly over it?"

Cate grimaced. "Is one ever truly over getting jilted at the altar? But yeah. I'm fine. Jason's timing could have been better. Still, he saved us from making a big mistake."

"And Harry?" Harry had rescued Cate when her wedding day imploded. He had given her a place to hide out until she could handle the grief and bewilderment.

Cate's smile was smug. "Harry is freaking fabulous. I adore him."

"And vice versa." Leah had seen the two of them together on more than one occasion in the past year. Seeing the way Harry looked at Cate made Leah ache. Would she ever have a relationship like that?

"I should head back to Atlanta," Cate said. "Unless you need me for something else."

Leah smothered the urge to beg her to stay. Not only was her family a handful, but tonight, Leah had Lucas to deal with as well. Was she regretting the fact that he was coming? Her feelings were mixed. After that kiss, she hadn't known what to say. "You go," she said. "We're all good here. Thanks for everything you did."

Cate hugged her. "Happy to help. And just so you know, I won't wait forever to meet this Lucas person."

When the door closed, Leah took a deep breath and ran to

her bedroom. She had barely enough time to change and maybe indulge in a tiny panic attack.

She made a face at herself in the mirror. It was just one dinner. How bad could it be? Her father would drone on about the dental practice. Her brothers would tease her. And her mother would offer a plethora of small suggestions on how to improve for the next dinner. No surprises there. Besides, Leah loved her family, and they hadn't all been in the same room since last Christmas.

Tonight, everyone had agreed to *dress* for dinner. Leah's sleeveless knee-length black sheath was simple but elegant. Her black designer flats were blinged-out with tiny black rhinestones around the edges. She tucked her hair up in a loose chignon and added the dangly diamond earrings her parents had given her for college graduation.

Makeup didn't take much time at all. Mascara, a dash of eyeliner. A hint of blush, and some pinky-neutral long-wear lipstick.

At the second glance in the mirror, a different woman stared back at her. This woman looked confident and stylish.

But it might be a lie. She wasn't sure how she felt. Oddly enough, she was more worried about Lucas than her opinionated family. That must mean *something*.

Her heart stopped when the doorbell rang. In the next second, she realized it was Marisa Evans with the food. The caterer's white van was parked out front with the *Peaches To-Go* logo on the side panel and on the back with a phone number.

Marisa started unloading trays and waved Leah off when she tried to help. "Nope. I got this. Don't want to mess up your clothes."

In less than twenty minutes, the two women had transferred the food into Leah's oven to stay warm. Leah had all her great-aunt's serving pieces ready, waiting to be filled at the appropriate time.

Marisa consulted a list from her pocket. "Okay. You've got the chicken cordon bleu. Brussels sprouts with bacon crumbles and diced apples. Long grain and wild rice. Yeast rolls, and the apple pies for dessert. Can you think of anything else?"

Leah laughed. "I hope not. They're all going to fall into a food coma. Everything looks amazing. Thanks, Marisa."

"Happy to do it. Tell your friends."

"I will. How's the business going?"

Twenty-five-year-old Marisa was tall, blonde, and lean... with a girl-next-door vibe. She had gone to culinary school in Atlanta on a scholarship and come home to Blossom Branch, hoping to supply a niche in the market. Blossom Branch had restaurants and fast food, but until Marisa returned, no catering companies at all.

The other woman leaned against the door frame, her posture betraying exhaustion. "Everything is going great. In fact, I'm overwhelmed. I think I'm at the point where I need to hire staff. But I don't have the time to find them or train them. It's a catch-22. And I feel like I can't turn down jobs because I want to grow."

"Does the term *burnout* mean anything to you?" Leah asked with a grin. "I know something about the subject. Getting Camp Willow Pond up and running has required a lot of long days and weeks and months."

"I hear you, believe me. But starting a small business is brutal. The bank is always breathing down my neck. Food prices are getting higher all the time. And my van has broken down twice in three months. Sometimes I wonder if I've bitten off more than I can chew."

Leah laughed. "My grandmother used to say that to me all the time."

"And was she right?" Marisa grimaced.

"I hate to say it, but yes. More often that I want to admit.

What about getting a high school kid who needs volunteer time? You know, an apprenticeship."

"I'm afraid the hours wouldn't be steady enough to really help."

"True."

Marisa glanced at her watch. "Oh, shoot. I've got to go. Let me know how the evening turns out."

Leah grimaced. "I hope there's nothing to tell. They eat. They drink. They go home."

"Is that likely?"

"Probably not, but I'm trying to be positive."

NINE

LUCAS KNOCKED ON LEAH'S FRONT DOOR, FEELING oddly unsettled. Her impressive house was two stories tall with an attic on top. The steeply pitched rooflines and dormer windows gave it a whimsical charm. White trim accented traditional brick.

He'd dealt with enough incident reports on some of the older Blossom Branch structures to spot that the windows were original to the house. The slightly wavy glass was a dead giveaway. The wraparound porch and hanging baskets of petunias completed the picture. The house was perfect.

It was also an example of why he and Leah were never likely to understand each other. Her family might not be wealthy by today's standards, but they had enough money for an older single woman to bequeath this valuable and impressive property to Leah.

This place shouted *home* in every possible way. Leah would glow amid this perfection. The ambiance echoed her quiet beauty. It was uniquely her. The charming house and the intriguing woman belonged together.

He adjusted his navy-patterned silk tie, wondering if neckwear had been necessary. His charcoal sport coat and navy dress pants were like new. He'd bought them last year to wear to a funeral.

The conservative mode of dress didn't suit his personality, but he wanted to honor Leah's commitment to this family evening.

He might not *be* family, but anything he could do to make Leah comfortable and offer her his support tonight would be worth it.

The door swung open without warning. Leah stood there staring at him, eyes wide. Her black dress showcased beautiful legs and emphasized her lush curves. "Lucas," she said. "You look amazing."

Her warm smile melted his misgivings. "Not too much?"

"Oh, no. My family will be spiffy. The boys like to outdo each other when it comes to fashion."

"Even the missionary?"

Leah laughed. "Him, too. But only when he's in the States of course. They'll be jealous of your *fire chief* status. I grew up in a house of alpha males. Everything is a competition." She stepped back to let him enter. "Would you like something to drink?"

"No, thanks." He paused, wanting her to believe him. "You look stunning." He leaned in for a quick kiss. "That dress gives a man wicked ideas. And with your hair up, your neck is biteable."

She blushed predictably. "Is that a word?"

"It is now." He reined in his impulse to devour her. "I came early to see if I could help you."

"Where's your car?" She peeked over his shoulder.

"I wasn't sure how many vehicles your family would be bringing, so I found a spot down the street."

"Oh."

"How soon will they be here?" he asked.

"Mom texted from the car. They're running late. It will be another twenty minutes."

"Is the food all set?"

Leah frowned. "Yes, why?"

He took a deep breath. "Because I want to kiss you again, and you'll need time for repairs."

Thick, beautiful lashes flew up. Her pupils dilated. The tip of her tongue came out to wet her lips. He saw a ripple in her throat as she swallowed. "What a lovely idea."

He tried to rein himself in. This was not the time for a full-out assault on the castle walls. But his hands shook. "Come here, Leah. Let me taste you."

When she instantly obeyed his coaxing plea, his sex went rock hard and his brain turned to mush. He took her narrow, fragile wrists in his two big hands and lifted her arms over her head. "You can't touch me right now," he said. "My self-control is iffy. I don't want them to walk in and see me doing something naughty to you."

Her little gasp echoed in his head. He backed her against the wall beside a huge grandfather clock that was probably worth ten grand and moved his mouth over hers. Leah tasted like the sin one of his foster mothers used to warn him about.

"Lucas..." She breathed his name in a tone that made him shiver.

He told himself nothing was going to happen. They were about to be interrupted by six full-grown adults expecting to be fed and entertained.

But his body had a different agenda. "I love the way you fit against me," he said. "We'd be perfect in bed."

She had closed her eyes, but now they opened slowly. "Would we?" she asked, her tone diffident. "I don't think I'm very good at it."

He kissed her again, feeling the way her breasts nestled against his rib cage. "Impossible, Leah. You're the sexiest woman I've ever met, and you're not even naked. My brain may explode when I see you the first time."

"You're just horny," she said. "Maybe you need to forget about me and get laid. I hear the guys at the fire hall have a posse of groupies."

"First of all, that's dumb gossip. And secondly, yeah…I'm horny. But only for you. So deal with it, babe."

She laughed softly and nibbled on his bottom lip. "No one has ever called me babe."

"Did I insult you? I'm sorry."

"I like it," she said. She kissed him again, sliding her tongue into his mouth and making a little whimpering noise that drove him wild. "What time is it?" she asked, the words barely a whisper.

He glanced at his watch. *Damn.* "Too late," he grumbled.

When he released her, Leah touched her hair self-consciously. "I need to disappear for a minute. If the doorbell rings, *don't* answer it."

"I'd like to see your bedroom," he said, trying to look innocent.

"No," she said firmly. But her blush deepened.

He had barely cooled his heels five minutes when she was back. Her hair was perfect. In fact, everything about her was perfect. No sign that she'd been fooling around only moments before.

"That was fast," he said.

"I didn't have much choice." She took a deep breath. "I need to check on the food. You can help put ice in glasses."

"No wine?" he asked.

"My brothers enjoy wine. But my dad's brother is an alcoholic, so when we have family gatherings, Daddy insists on iced tea. He's always been afraid that one of us might follow in Uncle Ernie's footsteps."

The kitchen was small but nice. Lucas eyed it with interest. The room was homey yet sophisticated if such a combination was possible. "Did you do the updates?" he asked, noticing the porcelain farm sink and the top-of-the-line appliances.

Leah opened the oven, stirred something, and turned around. "With help from a designer," she said. "It was a challenge. I didn't want to alter the original footprint of the house, so we had to narrow our search to items that would fit. I only finished everything a month ago. My family hasn't seen it yet."

"Were your brothers upset that your aunt left everything to you?"

Leah leaned against the sink. "If they were, they didn't say so. I think Aunt Trudie witnessed and understood the family dynamic and wanted me to stand up for myself. In fact, she told me that once when I was fourteen. She was a little fierce and scary. I'm guessing she saw the inheritance as a way for me to break free and be my own person."

"And has it worked?"

"Baby steps, Lucas. I'm not there yet. After dinner tonight you can tell me what you think...as an outside observer."

At the front of the house, the doorbell rang.

Leah paled, wiping her hands on her hips. "Here goes."

Lucas followed her to the foyer but hung back, interested to see how things unfolded.

Leah's mom entered first and hugged her daughter. "Hello, sweetheart. You look pale. Did you sleep well last night?"

After that, it was like a dam broke. Large, good-looking men poured through the door, one by one, into the house. Also, a woman who clearly belonged with the older brother. The last to enter was Leah's father. He was tall and distinguished with silver hair and a deep voice.

The brothers were all different, but clearly related.

Because the house was old-fashioned, the small adjacent sitting room was not suitable for so many people to gather and converse. Leah smiled. "Why don't you guys take a seat in the dining room, and I'll get the meal started?" Lucas wondered if he was the only one who spotted the strain behind the smile. She hesitated. "This is my friend Lucas Carter. He's the local fire chief here in Blossom Branch. Lucas has been a big help out at camp."

Lucas shook hands all around while Leah escaped to the kitchen. That hadn't been his plan. He had wanted to help her. Get his hands dirty. Take some of the load off those feminine shoulders.

But instead, he found himself at the table being grilled.

First off, it was the doctor sibling. "So tell me, Lucas," he said. "Why a firefighter? Are you an adrenaline junkie?"

There was an edge to the question, but Lucas wouldn't let this guy bait him. "No," he said calmly. "I got my degree in criminal justice. Then after traveling—crisscrossing the country for a few years—I decided I liked the camaraderie of fire halls. The physical demands keep me in shape, and the job is a direct way to help people." He grimaced. "Maybe that sounds sappy."

"Not at all," Mrs. Marks said. But she was sizing him up, that much was clear.

The actor, Martin, was next. "You ever been to California?" he asked.

"Several times," Lucas said. "It's gorgeous, no doubt about that. But I love the pace in small Southern towns. Blossom Branch is a great place to live."

Leah's dad shot him a measured glance. "Where are your people from, son?"

Lucas stiffened, debating how to answer.

At that exact moment, Leah sailed into the room in full mama bear mode. "Leave him alone, Daddy. Lucas has lived all over. Dinner's ready. I'll serve the plates and bring them out. Lucas, will you help me?"

In the kitchen, Lucas seized the moment of privacy. He touched Leah's arm. "I don't need you to fight my battles."

"I warned you how it would be." Her grin was wry.

"They seem nice enough. Strong personalities, every one. Except maybe your sister-in-law. She watches the action from the sidelines."

"True." Leah surprised him by lifting his hand to her lips for a soft kiss. "We'd better get the food in there," she said. "Before my brothers get grumpy with empty stomachs. I can't blame them. I'm hungry, too."

After that, there was no chance for intimate conversation. By the time the whole group was seated and served, Lucas saw immediately that the meal was going to be noisy and entertaining. The group of seven knew each other well. And apparently, each one played a role.

The doctor brother, as Leah had mentioned, was revered. Lucas didn't know if that was a typical first-child thing or not. But Craig Marks was a brilliant man with a biting wit. His quiet wife adored him, judging by the way she looked at him when he was talking.

Leah's parents were the glue that held this group together. They were well-read, sophisticated, and surprisingly opinionated.

Martin, the actor, liked to play the clown. He was funny and charming. He amused the group with his anecdotes about seeing famous people at the grocery store. From what Lucas could discern, the guy was making headway with auditions and bit parts.

Keith was the moral compass of the family and clearly Leah's favorite. He related stories about Sudan that were both heart-wrenching and hopeful.

But what struck Lucas by the end of the first hour was how they all talked *around* Leah. Almost as if she were invisible. He frowned inwardly, trying to figure it out. He'd assumed that Leah was sort of exaggerating about her place in the family. But now, he was beginning to see that it was true.

Not one of them asked about the first two-week session of camp.

Not one of them complimented the meal.

Finally, he decided he'd had enough of seeing his wonderful Leah sidelined. "Have any of you been out to the camp yet? Leah has created an amazing environment for nurturing kids, especially the ones who face challenges in their lives."

All conversation halted. Silence held for the beat of four seconds, maybe five. Leah shot him a look that promised retribution later. Her expression confused him. Didn't she *want* to show her family she was doing something remarkable? He'd thought her desire to be accepted and valued was part of the struggle.

Craig broke the uncomfortable pause. "I confess, work keeps me tied to Atlanta. But I'm sure the place is great."

Martin nodded. "I've been on the West Coast until yesterday, but I checked out the website."

Kevin frowned. "I've worried that it's a lot for Leah to handle. But I guess she's hired good staff, right, sis?"

"Yes," Leah muttered. "Let's change the subject."

Her father's face reflected some strong emotion Lucas couldn't place. "I wasn't happy to hear about the *fire* in the pages of the *Blossom Branch Register*. I would assume my own daughter might have given me a heads-up."

"Sorry, Daddy," Leah said. "Things have been hectic."

Mrs. Marks suddenly put two and two together. "Is that how you met your young man, Leah? Because of the fire at camp?"

Leah's face was pink now. "He's not my young man. We're friends, that's all. But yes. Lucas and his crew responded to the 911 call. It was such a relief. They had the fire out in no time, and the repairs were minimal."

Lucas raised an eyebrow as he suddenly processed what Leah's father had said. "Blossom Branch still has a newspaper? I guess it's online?"

Dr. Marks set down his fork. "Online yes, but it also has several hundred print subscribers. Tradition is important in this town, Chief Carter. A lot of the newcomers flock here for the peace and quiet. But we also reflect solid family continuity. That's attractive to some people."

Lucas wondered if those words were a thinly veiled warning. "I understand from Leah that she's the only one of your family who actually lives here."

Dr. Marks blinked. Perhaps he was accustomed to people accepting his pronouncements at face value. "Well," he said, "when my wife and I invested in our first dental clinic, Blossom Branch was much smaller. We needed an area with a bigger client base. But we kept our house here until Leah finished high school. I commuted to work."

Leah stood up abruptly. "Lucas, will you help me in the kitchen again?" She glanced at her family. "I'll bring dessert in here. You guys relax."

Once Lucas and Leah were in the kitchen with the door closed, the conversation in the dining room escalated. Lucas could tell it had nothing to do with Leah. He heard an argument about a movie. That exchange segued into a heated back and forth about the baseball season.

Lucas stretched and ran his hands through his hair. "What do I need to do?"

Leah glared at him. "Not talk, for one thing."

"What the hell does that mean? You want me to sit there in silence?"

"What I want is for you to quit trying to *save* me. You promised to rein in your bossy side. Our family dynamic may be challenging, but I can *handle* it. I've been handling it just fine for almost thirty years."

"No offense, babe, but lying about who cooked the dinner would say otherwise."

Her face turned red. "Now you're just being mean."

He snorted. "Am I? They should be *interested* in you, Leah. But they're all a little self-centered. Maybe not Keith, but you know what I mean."

"It's okay," she said. "I'm the baby girl nobody planned on arriving in the mix. Probably an accident of menopause. But they do love me, Lucas. It's just that the boys are more interesting."

"Bullshit," he said, not bothering to rein in his heated tone. "You're every bit as accomplished and notable as they are."

She shook her head, frowning. "I don't like tooting my own horn. The others are all extroverts. They think big and talk big. I was mostly content to sit in the background growing up, but now I'm not. I want Camp Willow Pond to show them there's more to me than being a mouse. That's my dream. I don't want to risk bragging too soon about something that might fail. It may not make sense to you, but that's how I feel."

"This conversation isn't over," he insisted. "Nevertheless, they're all waiting on dessert."

As Leah scooped out servings of apple pie, Lucas topped them with generous helpings of ice cream. Then they carried the bowls into the dining room.

When everyone's mouths were full and the noise level dropped, Lucas made a snap decision and addressed the table. "It won't get dark for another hour and a half. Since none of you have seen Willow Pond, why don't we all load up and head out there for a quick tour?"

After a split second of silence, Craig waved his spoon. "I'm in. Don't know when I'll have a chance to get back to Blossom Branch, so carpe diem and all that."

Martin and Keith nodded. "Us, too."

Leah's parents seemed more hesitant, but they agreed. Her father spoke pedantically. "But remember, I have clinic in the morning, so we can't linger."

Leah's expression was a combination of distress and conciliation. "I won't take the time to load the dishwasher, Daddy. I'll put the dishes in a sink of soapy water and deal with it when we get back."

Lucas stood and began picking up empty plates and bowls.

Leah and her mother helped. In the kitchen, Mrs. Marks smiled at her daughter. "Everything was delicious, honey. But you don't have even a dab of leftovers. Those boys can put away a lot of calories."

Leah dried her hands on a dish towel and faced her parent. "It's fine. I won't need to make room in the fridge this way." She paused and shot a look at Lucas—one he couldn't read.

What was she up to now?

"Mom, I have a confession to make," she said.

"Oh?"

"Lucas called me out on something, so I'll be honest. I didn't cook any of this. A friend of mine has a catering business. She brought everything here and we transferred it to my dishes and pots and pans. I wanted you to be proud of me. The truth is, though, I'm not great in the kitchen, and the first two-week session of camp wiped me out. I'm sorry I let you think I did all the work."

Mrs. Marks cocked her head, her smile fading. "I'm sorry you felt the need to fib about something so simple. I hope you know I'm always proud of you. Besides, your cooking will improve. At your age, I wasn't that great in the kitchen either. You have time, Leah. One day you're going to be a great wife and mother. And for the record, I *sometimes* use a catering service."

Lucas was aghast. Leah was up against far more than he had realized. Expectations. Sexist, outdated expectations, at that.

He gave her mom a hard look. "Camp is Leah's responsibility right now. She doesn't need to be Superwoman."

Mrs. Marks hugged her daughter, avoiding a reply to his pointed comment. "We certainly appreciated your invitation to host tonight, Leah. It was lovely to have the family together again." She glanced at Lucas. "Now that we're all spread out, I don't get my chicks back in the nest very often."

Lucas smiled. "I can understand why. It must be nice to have Leah and Craig close."

Leah's mother seemed taken aback. As if she had never thought of it that way. Or maybe because she had concentrated more on Craig and his wife and the possibility of a grandchild than what her youngest child and only daughter was up to…

"We should go," Leah said. "I'm sure Daddy's getting impatient."

The Marks crew had all come in one large, high-end van. It technically had room for two more, but Lucas shook his head. "We don't want to crowd anyone. Leah and I will take my car. Give me a minute to circle around the block. Then you guys can follow us."

Leah didn't say a word as they walked the short distance to his car. He opened the passenger door, waited for her to be seated, and rounded the car to hop behind the wheel. The street was one-way, so he circled the block and pulled up beside Leah's family. With a wave of his hand, they were off.

It took him five whole minutes to realize Leah was pissed. She stared straight ahead, her hands clenched in her lap.

He sighed. "What's wrong? I thought you'd be pleased that all your family will get to see the camp at once."

"But it didn't occur to you to ask my opinion, did it?"

"The time was right. They were all in Blossom Branch tonight. What could be better? I wanted them to see how incredible you are. How much you've accomplished."

"*I* wasn't ready yet." Her jaw jutted. "And that's not what they'll see. Everyone will pick away at it. Pointing out flaws. Telling me what I *should* have done. The camp is *my* baby, Lucas. Now you've ruined everything."

His temper flared. Her lack of appreciation for his support stung. "Well, it's too late now, so we'll make the best of it."

"Fine," she muttered.

"Fine."

The icy silence continued all the way to camp.

It was sad to see camp so empty after the vibrant atmosphere he had witnessed in the last two weeks. When everyone piled out, Lucas didn't say a word. Leah smiled at her family. "I guess we'll start with my house."

The tour was quick. He lingered at the back of the group as she showed them the sleeping cabins. After that, they moved en masse to the cafeteria/kitchen/office area. Leah had been right about one thing. There were plenty of opinions thrown around. Except for her sister-in-law, every member of Leah's family had a suggestion for improvement. Almost as if she was a child who needed guidance.

Her father insisted on seeing where the fire had happened. Lucas was happy to determine that it was almost impossible to separate the repairs from the original materials. Jeff and his team had done a great job.

Next was the pool, the fire circle, the ropes course, the pond, and the corral. When everyone asked about horses, Leah explained they were rented once per camp session and brought out on those two days from a nearby stable.

Toward the end, everyone broke up and wandered back to places that had caught their attention. Lucas found himself standing beside Leah's middle brother. Martin leaned his elbows on the corral railing and shook his head slowly. "I feel like the odd man out," he said quietly. "Craig and Kevin and now even Leah are saving the world. But what am I doing? Trying to break into show business." He grimaced. "Sometimes I feel like I should find another path. A better path."

Lucas hefted himself upward and perched on the top rail. Now he could see almost the entire camp. It struck him that Martin's words echoed Leah's feelings about not fitting in...not measuring up. Maybe even *normal* families screwed up their kids to some degree. "I think you're wrong," he said quietly. "Life is hard. The world can be a cold, difficult place. People need entertainment and joy in their lives. Laughter. Escapism. When I was a thirteen-year-old kid, I teetered on the edge of serious trouble.

Could have gone either way. I started doing odd jobs so I could afford one movie ticket every weekend, plus snacks of course. Movies were a way I could steady myself...step outside my skin. Figure out who I wanted to be. Don't discount what you do."

Martin was silent for several minutes, watching his family move around the camp. "And are you trouble for my little sister?"

Lucas hadn't expected the direct challenge. "I don't want to be. She told you the truth. We're friends. That may be all it ever is."

"You strike me as the kind of dude who's man enough to change her mind."

"Maybe." Lucas shrugged. He wasn't ready to go into all the reasons why he and Leah were a bad match. Martin would find out soon enough.

Martin bumped Lucas's shoe with his fist. "We'd better catch up to the others. Mom and Dad aren't night owls. They'll want to get their jammies on soon."

"Sure."

By the time everyone had gathered around the two vehicles, the sun had dropped below the horizon. Dr. Marks spoke to his daughter, his face more relaxed than it had been at dinner. "I like it, Lee-Lee. Maybe I could come once each session and give the kids dental exams. Would that be helpful?"

Lucas smothered a grin. The stunned look on Leah's face was worth having to facing her anger in the car earlier.

From where he was standing, the family visit had been a success.

Unfortunately, he and Leah didn't always see eye to eye.

TEN

LEAH COULDN'T DECIDE WHAT SHOCKED HER MORE—
hearing her father use her old childhood nickname—or his offer
of free dental care for her kids.

"That would be awesome, Dad. Thank you."

Her mother hugged her. "We need to get home. But I'm glad
we did the tour. You're doing a great thing, baby girl."

Suddenly, there was a flurry of hugs and laughter. Moments
later, the van pulled away.

Leah turned to face Lucas. "I hate it when bossy, infuriat-
ing men are right."

He gave her a rueful smile. "I shouldn't have sprung it on you."

"Correct." She went to him and slid her arms around his
waist. "Thank you, Lucas. I was afraid the camp wasn't ready
for outside eyes. Or that I wasn't ready. It means the world to
me that they all got to see camp."

"Were you ever going to invite them?"

She sighed and rested her cheek against his chest. "I don't know. Sometime. Next summer maybe."

He laughed. "I hadn't pegged you as a procrastinator."

"You'd be surprised."

He pulled her tightly against him, making her shiver. The summer night still glowed at the horizon, but it was hard to see his face with the gloaming fading into dark. The air was thick and heavy. Leah's forehead was damp.

Lucas pulled the pins from her hair and tucked them in his pocket. Then he slid his fingers against her scalp, fluffing out the strands. "I love your hair," he said.

She laughed softly. "And I love your gorgeous jaw and the way you smell like lime and evergreen forests and temptation."

He threw up his hands. "Me?" he huffed. "Temptation? Pot. Kettle."

"Come home with me," she said quietly, feeling her nerves settle. She had faced her family. Shown them the fruit of her dreams. They had all offered unsolicited advice and a few veiled criticisms, but nothing awful. Though Lucas's invitation to her brothers and parents had seemed risky and terrifying, it had turned out pretty well. Her ego had received a much-needed boost.

She was turning into the Leah she wanted to be. Capable. Confident. Happy.

The only other big decision she faced right now was whether or not to move forward with the man in her life. As it turned out, the choice wasn't hard at all.

He went still. "I have to go home with you, babe. You came in my car."

"That's not what I mean, and you know it. I want you to stay the night."

"Why now?" He cupped her face in his hands.

"You took vacation days for me. That's sweet."

"I'm *not* sweet." He pretended to bristle.

No. He was physically and mentally tough. He cared about people. He was exasperating and sometimes overbearing, but she wanted him more than she had ever wanted anything or anyone.

She put her hands on his wrists. "Kiss me, Lucas."

"Don't have to ask me twice," he muttered. His lips found hers. Claimed hers. His kisses had a focused passion that melted her core and ignited her need. She surrendered to the moment, to the inevitability of this relationship, whatever it turned out to be. They were standing only yards away from where she had fallen in the mud, twisted her ankle, and been rescued by a big, macho fireman in full gear.

As if he had read her mind, Lucas scooped her into his arms. "What are you doing?" she asked, the words breathless.

He nuzzled her nose with his. "Taking you home."

When he deposited her in the passenger seat, he stole one more kiss. Leah was dizzy, torn between excitement and anxiety. She didn't want to disappoint Lucas. She didn't want to disappoint herself.

Tonight was a huge step.

Phrasing it that way in her head made all the jitters come back. Stealing her peace, her certainty. If she could have made love to him at the camp director's house, it would have been immediate and easy—both of them caught up in the moment.

This drive back to town, though not far, gave her too much time to think.

Lucas turned on the radio, so maybe he didn't want to talk. Before getting in the car, he had removed his tie and sport coat and tossed them in the back seat. He'd also rolled up the sleeves of his crisp dress shirt.

His hands on the wheel looked masculine and strong. Everything about him telegraphed confidence. How had a boy from such humble beginnings learned to be so comfortable in his own skin?

They stopped briefly at Lucas's apartment for him to throw a few things in a bag. Leah stayed in the car, trying not to hyperventilate. He was a pro at these kinds of casual relationships. She wasn't.

With her family long gone, Lucas was free to use Leah's driveway. But in a flash, she knew what that would look like to her neighbors. "Let's pull around back," she said, "and you can park in the carport. It's a double. My car is there, too, because my tiny garage is full of remodeling debris."

Lucas did as she asked, but he gave her a teasing glance. "Trying to hide me, Leah?"

"Yes," she said baldly. "I don't like being the subject of gossip."

"Fair enough." He carefully parked his car beside hers, shut off the engine, and turned sideways, resting one arm across the steering wheel. "We don't have to do this if you've changed your mind."

"I haven't," she said firmly. "I *want* you to spend the night."

"Good," he said gruffly. He pulled her close in the dark. Now that they were behind the house, there was not even a streetlight to offer illumination. She felt his fingers trace her ears and tug gently at the diamonds in her lobes. "I can't wait to undress you," he said. "I've imagined you naked a hundred times."

Leah winced. "You may be disappointed. I haven't seen the inside of a gym in two years, and I have a weakness for cinnamon sugar doughnuts."

"Stop that," he said sharply. "Don't put yourself down. You're a stunning woman, Leah. In every way. You have a big heart and a gorgeous smile, and you make me wild with lust."

The sincerity in his words warmed her—starting deep in her heart and spreading outward to every corner of her body. Lucas *wanted* her. *Her*, not some random woman in a bar. She sucked in a deep breath. Wrapping her arms around his neck, she found his mouth with hers. "I want you more than the pony I asked for on my thirteenth birthday."

He laughed, but when she kissed him, he went rigid for five seconds, maybe ten. Then he dragged her even more tightly against his cotton-clad chest and kissed her back. It was wonderful. Every amazing fantasy she'd had about getting close to him was true. He was hard and warm, and he smelled delicious. If they had been out at camp, she would have climbed across his lap then and there.

Instead, she opened her car door. "We're wasting time," she said, panting.

"I'm following you," he said, heat in his voice.

For a split second as she unlocked the back door and they went inside, she remembered all the dirty dishes in the kitchen. Facing them in the morning would be a nasty chore. But she didn't care.

She took Lucas by the hand. "I have three bedrooms upstairs, but mine is on this level."

"Good," he said.

She led him down the hall and flipped on the light. "The bed is a queen, not a king. But this room used to have two twins, so we'll call that progress."

Lucas looked around with interest. Leah's bedroom was restful and appealing, much like its owner. The walls were painted a delicate shade of pink, almost like the inside of a seashell. Her furniture, presumably her aunt's antiques, was the kind that was expensive and had been well cared for.

But honestly, the only thing Lucas really cared about was the bed. It was covered with a dozen pillows and a quilt that looked to be a priceless heirloom.

When he turned around, Leah had her back up against the door, her arms crossed around her waist. Her gaze was wary.

"I like it," he said. "It suits you."

When he took a step in her direction, her lashes flew wide, and her gaze radiated alarm. "Do you want the first shower?" she asked.

He stopped, sensing her unease. "We could share."

No teasing on his part. Just an honest suggestion that made his sex ache.

Leah shook her head. "The bathroom's too small." She seemed relieved to have a rebuttal. "You go ahead. There are fresh towels in the linen closet."

He frowned. "I get the feeling you'd like me to leave," he said bluntly.

"Oh, no." Tears welled in her eyes but didn't fall. "I don't, I swear. I'm just..." She bit her lip, clearly searching for an adjective.

"Shy?" he asked, feeling tenderness mix with the driving need in his gut.

She nodded, her expression filled with self-disgust. "Yes. And I hate it. I've always wanted to be more like my friends Cate and Gabby. I freeze up in social situations. I'll probably turn into one of those old cat ladies who die buried beneath stacks of newspapers and magazines and no one finds them for days."

Lucas stared at her. He opened his mouth and closed it when he realized he didn't know what to say. A friend of his who joined the navy had learned how to dismantle and remove mines in waterways. It was a difficult and dangerous job. Now, seeing Leah's fidgety nerves made him think tonight was something of a similar task. "We can go as slow as you want, Leah," he said, groaning inwardly. It had been years since he had indulged in nothing more than heavy petting. But for this woman, he would do it willingly.

When she didn't say a word, he continued.

"You don't own a cat," he pointed out. "And I happen to know you're supersmart. Otherwise, you couldn't have pulled off starting a camp." He paused. "I cleaned up before I got dressed to come over here for dinner. You probably did, too. So if it's the prospect of you and me taking a shower—alone or together—that's making you nervous, why don't we just sit on the bed and make out?"

She chewed her lip. Because he had taken her hair down earlier, the long, thick coils fell around her shoulders like waves of dark bourbon. "Could we turn off the lights?" she said.

He shook his head slowly. "No. I want to see you, Leah. I want to see all of you. But I'm willing to settle for what you want to give."

"We don't need the lights on," she said, her expression haunted.

"I think we do. I want you to see how excited I am. How you turn me on."

Color flooded her cheeks. "I'll take your word for it," she muttered.

He closed the small distance between them and took her hands in his. "Come on, sweet girl. Let's do something naughty." He pulled her across the room. They both took off their shoes. He ran his thumb down her soft cheek. "This is a beautiful quilt. I'm going to fold it up and get it out of the way. Then we can sit up against the headboard or get comfy on our backs. Your choice."

She couldn't quite meet his gaze. "I'd like to be comfortable."

He had a feeling her statement possessed multiple layered meanings, but in the short term it meant stretching out with Leah beside him. Her breathing was jerky, and one of her hands clenched the thin blanket and sheets as if bracing for an earthquake.

He turned on his side. "Look at me, Leah."

She mirrored his pose and rested her head on her hand. "I'm looking."

"Why don't you unbutton my shirt?"

"Happy to," she said. Her relief was palpable as she handled the job like a pro. He frowned inwardly, trying to puzzle it out. But when he felt her cool hands on his hot skin, several circuits in his brain misfired. She whispered his name as she ran her hands over his bare chest. "It's like a solid wall," she said. She thumped him with her fist. "Look. Nothing moves."

"Very funny." He shrugged out of the shirt completely. "Let me kiss you now."

She came willingly, melting against him, tangling her tongue with his, and moaning in a way that made the hair on his arms stand up. Leah Marks was so damn hot, and she had no clue.

He fisted his hand in her hair, holding her lightly, but worried that she might run. Carefully, he reached behind her and started lowering the zipper on her dress.

Leah froze and scooted back. "Please," she muttered.

He frowned. "Please, what?"

"The overhead light is too bright. Can we use a lamp instead?"

"If that's what you want." He didn't think the wattage above them was particularly harsh, but if the bedside lamp made Leah happier, he was all for it.

He rolled to his feet and crossed the room, hitting the switch beside the door. The room plunged into darkness. Carefully, he felt his way back to the bed. He sat down on the side of the mattress and reached for the lamp.

When he clicked it on, he glanced over his shoulder. "Better?"

Leah nodded. "Yes."

Suddenly, he knew he had to ask one important question. "Do you trust me, Leah?"

When she hesitated, he was honestly shocked. "Yes," she said.

"But you had to think about it." He couldn't entirely disguise his frustration.

"Lucas…" She trailed off, her face reflecting the same emotions he felt. "We barely know each other. It's asking a lot."

"Just because one man didn't live up to his promises doesn't mean we're all like that."

"Larry," she said. "His name was Larry. And either he was a great actor, or I was hopelessly naive, or both, but I believed him when he said things to me in bed." A wry grin lifted her lips. "My friend, Cate, calls him *Larry, the turd*."

"I'm glad I don't know the guy. But I wouldn't mind meeting him in a dark alley if he's responsible for making you doubt yourself."

"I'm an adult," Leah said. "I hope I've learned from my mistakes *and* my successes. But sex is a whole other thing."

"Maybe you should give us a chance."

"I'm trying…"

Lucas took her hand. "Stand up for me, Leah. I want to unwrap you like a present. And I swear I will never say anything to you that isn't the unvarnished truth."

Her gaze locked with his. "Okay."

She scooted off the bed and stood in front of him.

"Turn around and hold up your hair," he said quietly.

She nodded slowly.

When he reached for her zipper…again…he realized his hands were shaking. In a split second of clarity, he understood that everything he wanted amounted to nothing if Leah wasn't happy. He lowered the tab slowly, revealing, inch by inch, the curve of her spine and her beautiful soft skin.

"Damn," he said.

She turned her head, her expression alarmed. "What?"

He kissed her shoulder. "I wish you could see this view." After sliding the dress off her shoulders and down to her knees, he held the dark fabric as Leah stepped free.

Now Leah stood in a sheer black bra and matching bikini undies. He unfastened her bra, removed it, put his hands on her hips, and turned her slowly. She was curvy in a way that was intensely appealing…no hard angles. No visible bones.

He looked up at her. "Do you know what you do to me?" She frowned. "No."

"Are you trying to suck in your stomach?"

"Does it matter?" she snapped. "I don't have rock-hard fireman abs."

He kissed her belly, stroked her hips. "Don't ever change a thing," he muttered, teasing her navel with his tongue. "You are exquisite." Because he sensed she was still not entirely comfortable, he lifted his head and stared at her breasts. They were full and round with pale brown nipples.

He put a thumb on each sensitive tip and caressed her.

Leah sucked in a sharp breath and groaned. When he palmed her breasts and squeezed them, she wrapped her arms around his neck and rested her chin on his head. "This might be more fun if you were naked, too," she whispered.

Lucas buried his face in the valley between two lush, erotic mounds. He inhaled Leah's now-familiar scent. Something light and flowery. "Yes," he croaked, barely able to get the word out.

He stood and picked her up, holding her against his chest and feeling his heart jerk and thud with his need to be inside her. When he laid her on the sheets, she stretched her arms over her head and looked at him with a tiny smile that drove him mad. Clumsily, he removed his pants and boxers and socks, pausing only to take several condom packets from his pocket and toss them on the bedside table.

Then he was down beside her, drawing her into his arms and feeling the oddest mixture of white-hot arousal and aching tenderness.

Leah was so unguarded, so open, so easily bruised. Her emotions were written on her face. If she couldn't protect herself, he had to be the one to do it. She was taking a risky step, and she knew it. It shamed him that he had told her about his rules for sex. Why had he been such an ass? Couldn't he have kept that for later?

But he'd wanted to be honest.

And now here they were, Leah offering up her body and her trust while Lucas had no clue what he was doing.

He shoved the unwanted introspection aside and kissed her nose. Then with one hand, he removed her panties. His excitement turned to shock. His eyes rounded. "Leah?" Her mound was waxed clean except for a tiny heart-shaped fluff of dark hair.

Her cheeks went pink. "Cate talked me into it. We were having a girls' spa day. She's been trying to get me back out into the dating world again."

His gut clenched. No man was going to see this but him. *No man.* Later, he would poke at that raging certainty, but for now, he stroked the tiny, alluring shape. "I like it," he said gruffly. "Very sexy and unexpected. Kind of like you."

She raised up on her elbows. "What does that mean?"

"Exactly what I said. Sometimes I think I know who you are, but there's a new Leah around every corner. You keep me guessing."

She cocked her head. "I don't know why you think that. I've made it clear I think you're a hottie. And a very decent man."

He winced. "When I'm touching your naked lady parts, I'd rather not hear the 'd' word. I want to know I arouse you."

Her lips quirked. "Maybe I'm one of those weird women who gets turned on by decency. Did you ever think about that?"

Lucas smiled. He was charmed and touched amid his arousal. Had he ever met anyone like her? He cleared his throat. "I want to make love to you, Leah. But you call the shots. You have to be sure."

She moved restlessly. "Now," she said. "Now."

After that, there was no more talking. Lucas couldn't decide where to start. Her body was a feast. He wanted to take his time. Because those gorgeous breasts were calling to him, he worshipped them—licking and squeezing until Leah panted and squirmed.

He understood. It was all he could do not to pounce and take without an ounce of finesse. Though he considered himself a generous lover, right now he felt like a rank amateur.

When he kissed her some more, unable to get enough of her sweet taste, Leah kissed him back eagerly, but she pinched his butt hard. "Enough foreplay. You're killing me. I want you, Lucas."

He didn't need a second invitation. Leaving her even for a moment was difficult. But he dealt with the necessary protection and then rolled back to her, loving the way her beautiful hair fanned out across the pillow in messy abandon. It made her look even more intensely sexy and feminine.

"I've wanted to do this since the first day I met you," he said.

She cupped his face with her hand.

He turned his head and kissed her palm.

Later they would be inventive. Right now, all he could think about was entering her. The prospect made his forehead damp and his stomach tighten in anticipation.

"Ready?" he asked.

"Yes."

He positioned the head of his erection and pushed, watching her face to see if she stayed with him.

For the first three seconds, her gaze locked with his. But maybe it was too much, or she was too shy, because her eyelids drifted shut as he surged deeper.

The sensation was indescribable. The sex felt new and different. A jolt of something uncomfortable joined the mix. A feeling of possession. Leah was his. As of this moment and from now on. He hadn't meant to stake a claim. This was supposed to be fun and light and recreational.

They had both agreed.

So why did he feel a desperate need to claim her?

Leah's body was soft and supple. When she wrapped her legs

around his waist and hooked her heels at his back, the angle changed. He was deep now, committed.

The urge to come was almost impossible to control. But he wasn't going to be fast off the mark like a hormonal adolescent. His breathing was harsh, his pulse rapid.

He kissed her, feeling desperate and weird. "Are you with me, babe?"

"Yes," she said politely, her gaze dreamy.

That wasn't exactly what he meant. When she kissed him back, her lips coaxing and eager, he lost it. With a groan of incredulity, he withdrew and slammed into her, his reality exploding in pleasure so intense he saw tiny yellow spots dancing behind his eyelids.

When he returned from his out-of-body experience, he took a moment to relish the feel of her soft frame cushioning his. He buried his face in the curve of her neck and swallowed hard. "You didn't come, did you?"

"No." She moved restlessly. "But it's okay. I told you I wasn't very good at this. You were amazing."

He couldn't decide whether to laugh or cry. Leah Marks was a babe in the woods. "No," he said flatly. "I wasn't. No man worth his salt takes what he wants and leaves his woman unfulfilled. I didn't mean to be so selfish. And I have no excuse except that I've dreamed of this moment, and when I touched you, everything went way too fast." He reared up on his elbows. "We're not done here."

She grimaced. "Maybe you should go home, and we'll try again another time. It's been a long day. I'm wiped out."

Lucas eased out of her, dealt with the condom, then lay back down and pulled her into his arms. "I'm sorry, Leah. I'm the one who sucks, not you."

"It's okay...really. I'd like to go to sleep now."

"Does that mean I can still stay?"

"Um...no...I'm sorry."

He could tell she was embarrassed, and that made him angry...at himself. He'd handled the situation badly. But he was determined to fix this. "I'll go," he said. "But first I want to give you a back rub. Your family ties you up in knots, don't they?"

"Yes." Her tone was resigned. "That's nothing new. I'm fine, Lucas. We can talk tomorrow."

"Roll over." He helped. When she was on her tummy with her face to the side on her pillow and her arms tucked under it, he put his hands on her shoulders. The back rub had been a pretext, an excuse to give him more time with her. But wow, she was tight. He found a knot and dug his thumb into it.

"Ouch," she said. "That hurts."

"I think it's supposed to." He backed off on the pressure a little bit. Gradually, he worked his way from one side of her back to the other, finding problem areas and doing his best to loosen the kinked muscles.

"Poor baby," he crooned. "You have way too much on these beautiful shoulders. Let Dr. Lucas make you feel better."

ELEVEN

LEAH FOUND HERSELF HOVERING SOMEWHERE BE-
tween heaven and hell. She was completely mortified at what
had happened—or hadn't happened—between her and Lucas.
She had been so tense in the beginning. Just when she had
begun to relax and enjoy herself, it was all over.

And now, Lucas had turned her whole body into warm gooey
pleasure with his talented hands. Her muscles were lax and
loose. He was a magician.

Something else was happening, too. Her body began climbing a sharp, steep journey to arousal. Between her legs, she was
damp and needy.

Even the accidental brush of Lucas's fingers on the back of
her neck made her shudder and shiver.

If he would just leave, she could take matters into her own
hands.

But the man was stubborn.

"I think that's enough," she said. Her voice was embarrassingly weak and shaky. "My back is much better."

Other parts of her, not so much. But he didn't need to know that.

Lucas slid an arm beneath her and turned her over. She found it hard to meet his gaze when she was hovering on the verge of a climax. "I'd rather not get dressed," she said. "You can see yourself out."

She looked at the ceiling, the bathroom door…anywhere but at his face.

Lucas took her chin in his hand. His expression was intense, predatory. "You can't be shy with me now, Leah. Not after I've felt your body take mine in and hold me and steal every last one of my brain cells."

"Um…"

He spread her legs and sprawled between them, resting his cheek on her hipbone. "Now for the rest of the massage."

When he touched the tiny, sensitive bundle of nerves that controlled her orgasm, her hips came off the bed. *Oh, no.* This was worse than what happened before. He was going to see her face, witness her total loss of control.

She put her hand over his. "This isn't necessary, Lucas. There's nothing to prove. I'll sleep with you again, I swear."

His smile was curiously sweet as he looked up at her from his provocative position between her thighs. "Relax, Leah. Close your eyes. Will you please let me pleasure you?"

She did close her eyes, but only because she was too flustered to watch. "Yes," she whispered. "You can try."

She hovered in a giddy place between embarrassment and arousal. But soon, the pleasure built so quickly, she was dazzled, uprooted from reality. His fingers on and in her sex were sure and firm, setting up a rhythm that had her sobbing his name as she came endlessly, her body pummeled by wave after wave of shivering delight.

It was a giddy, fizzy explosion of excess. Somewhere in the

middle of it, she forgot to be bashful with Lucas Carter. In the end she was limp and satiated, and when she finally met his gaze, she wasn't embarrassed at all.

She tried to catch her breath, but there was no oxygen to be found. "Wow," she said.

He scooted up beside her and kissed her. Then he took her hand and wrapped it around his erection. "See what you do to me? I wasn't lying about that, Leah."

Exploring his body would have been difficult an hour ago, but she was replete now, chill. Comfortable for the moment with the naked man in her bed. She stroked him gently, then more surely when he closed his eyes and breathed harshly.

"Lucas?" she asked softly.

He didn't look at her. "Don't stop, babe."

"Do you have more condoms?"

Now, he eyed her warily. "Yeah."

"Then quit wasting time, big guy."

Relief flooded his face. He moved in an instant, took care of business, and came back to her so fast she was stunned. "You ready?"

When he touched her intimately, her body quivered, despite her recent orgasm. "Oh, yes," she said.

"Keep your eyes open when I take you," he muttered, the words hoarse.

It was hard to do, but she managed. They were so close she could see his pupils dilate when he filled her. He withdrew and surged hard again.

Leah had just come. This was for him. Or so she told herself.

But two minutes in, she was right there in the middle of the party. The shock of it had her wiggling beneath him, trying to drive her partner deeper.

This time, she was only seconds behind him. The way he held her so tightly as he found his release made her fly. For one perfect moment, she felt as if the two of them were a unit, a team, a couple.

When she listened to the narration in her head—really heard and absorbed it—she was horrified. No way was she going to make this mistake again. Great sex was great in and of itself. But it was no predictor of future bliss.

She gave herself one last moment to pretend Lucas was her forever guy, and then she pulled herself together, scooted out from under him, and smiled. "I'm going to take a shower before I fall asleep."

He was half-comatose already. "Come back." He tried to grab her wrist, but she eluded him.

"I won't be long."

When she returned to her room fifteen minutes later, she was warm and clean. She paused in the doorway, taking in the sight of Lucas in the middle of her mattress. The bulk of the covers were a twisted mess at the foot of the bed. The top sheet covered him from his waist down. Those beautiful shoulders and his sleekly muscled back were on display.

Her heart clenched hard as she realized how dangerous *he* was and how vulnerable *she* was. Many single women her age enjoyed having fun, casual sex. Leah had never been able to do that. She tended to lead with her optimistic spirit and to believe in happy endings when the story hadn't even been written yet.

So much in her life had changed. She was growing, learning, maturing. Starting Camp Willow Pond wasn't the same as having a baby, but she had birthed something special. She was proud of what she had accomplished and elated that her family might be seeing her in a new light after all these years.

But romance? Even if she had moved past the heartache caused by Larry the turd, she still wanted a long-lasting relationship. A man who would choose her and put her first.

Lucas—by his own admission—wasn't it.

Somehow, she had to keep him at an emotional distance. If

she wanted to enjoy his body and his considerable skill in the bedroom, she *had* to build a wall around her heart. To protect herself would mean deliberately creating a buffer in their relationship.

It wouldn't be easy. Lucas tended to make real connections with people, at least on a social level. His relaxed personality and charm were probably a product of having to live in so many different homes growing up. She had certainly been drawn in quickly.

Even with the excuse of camp keeping her busy, Lucas had coaxed her first into friendship and now something deeper. Not out of any malice or manipulation on his part, but because he was the kind of person people liked to be around.

Pretending she was in it for the orgasms would not be easy. Dishonesty didn't fit in with her desire to grow and mature and find value and reward in all parts of her life. How could she pretend she didn't want a man who would "nest" with her? Pretend her work was so fulfilling she had no desire to settle down and have babies? Pretend that love wasn't important?

Maybe she had been pretending for the last few years. Pretending she was happy on her own. But now, Lucas's advent into her life had shown her what she really wanted.

She padded quietly toward the bed feeling the smooth hardwood beneath her bare feet, inhaling the unmistakable male scent of her visitor, a masculine fragrance she had already memorized.

He never moved when she straightened the covers. But as she lifted all the layers and climbed in beside him, he wrapped one strong arm around her and dragged her against his chest, spooning her from behind.

"You were gone too long," he muttered, clearly only half awake.

She curled her fingers with his and lifted his hand to her lips, kissing his knuckles. "Shh. I'm here now."

★ ★ ★

Leah's first thought when she awoke and saw dawn peeking through her window shades was disappointment. Last night when she snuggled with Lucas, drowsy and happy, she had wanted to savor those moments and hold on to them, because she had a strong hunch they were ephemeral.

But she must have fallen asleep almost instantly.

She couldn't reach her phone. A peek at the clock beside her bed told her it was only six. Neither she nor Lucas had any pressing to-do list today—if you didn't count wrangling the mess in the kitchen. Maybe morning sex might be on the agenda. She sighed with pleasure and closed her eyes.

Unfortunately, reality intruded rudely an hour later when Lucas's phone rang at seven and woke them both. He reached for it groggily, answered, and frowned. "When?" he asked. And after a moment—"I'll be there before eight."

Her heart sank. "What's going on?"

He sat up and ran his hands through his hair. "I have to go in and cover for one of my guys. His wife is pregnant. Wasn't due for another month. She went into labor last night, and it looks like today is it." He slid the sheet aside and ran his hand from her waist to her hip. "I'm sorry, Leah."

She managed a smile. "That's the trouble with being the boss."

His wry grin was rueful. "Yeah. I told you I had cleared the week, but this may mean I'm back on the schedule."

"I understand." She did understand, but that didn't make the sad feeling any less painful. "Go," she said. "Do what you have to do."

He stared at her, his gaze heating. "I want you again. Last night was only a taste of what's to come. Always assuming you feel the same way. I *shouldn't* assume..." he said, grinning.

Leah laughed softly. "I think you can *assume* I'm on the same page. Last night was wonderful. And fun." She made herself touch his arm lightly, even though her heart clenched with pain. This was the perfect opportunity to convince him she didn't expect a grand romance. "We're both busy people, but I'm sure we can line up our schedules occasionally. Don't worry about it."

A frown gathered between his brows. "It's a little more important than that."

"Sure," she said. "Now go. Something might start burning down."

There was nothing like antique plates in cold, dirty water to make a woman come firmly back down to earth. It took Leah two and a half hours to get her house in order.

She drew the line at laundering the linens. On this occasion, she would bundle them up for a run to the dry cleaners. Her time was valuable.

The day dragged on after that. She didn't expect to hear from Lucas since he was at work. But what would happen when he got off at six this evening?

It occurred to her he might ask to come over to her house again.

She wasn't sure how she felt about that.

There was no question she wanted to be with him again. Intimately. But tonight was too soon. She needed some temporary breathing room.

Because she was so conflicted, she came up with an escape plan. She called Gabby in Atlanta. They hadn't seen each other in weeks, though they texted frequently. Her friend answered on the second ring.

"Hey, Leah. How's camp?"

"Well, we survived the first session. The kids went home Friday night. Now I have a few days to breathe before the next group. Any chance I could come see you and spend the night tonight? I have a couple of appointments tomorrow, but I also need to talk to you about something."

"Just you?" There was an odd note in Gabby's voice.

"Yeah. Just me."

"That would be fun," Gabby said. "I might even be able to take off a half day tomorrow afternoon."

"You?" Leah teased. "Ms. Workaholic?"

Gabby laughed. "For you, Leah, anything."

They talked for a few more minutes, and then Leah hung up and started packing an overnight bag. It would be good to see Gabby. Leah really did have business in the city, but she couldn't kid herself. The real reason she was escaping Blossom Branch was that she didn't want to see Lucas yet.

Yesterday and last night had shaken her. She believed he found her attractive. And she was confident he would never lie to her. That much, she had learned about him already.

But was she honestly going to be satisfied with a relationship that was nothing more than sex? Or sex and friendship?

Wouldn't she always be wondering if she could change him? That was a surefire way to court heartbreak.

With so many big questions to answer, it seemed wise to take things slowly.

She wasn't a naive college kid anymore. She had faced disappointments and challenges. Aunt Trudie's bequest had given Leah choices, but it had also forced her to look for meaning and purpose. Camp Willow Pond was more than a job. It was her calling...at least for now.

No matter how hard she tried, she couldn't see how Lucas might fit into the big picture. Not with what he had told her about himself.

Did life ever get easier than this? Professional struggles? Personal doubts?

She was growing and changing and finding strengths she never knew she had. But it was hard. So hard. Occasionally, she remembered being an unnoticed mouse and wished for the good old days. She paused in front of the bedroom mirror and made a face at herself.

She couldn't have it both ways.

The drive from Blossom Branch to Atlanta on a Sunday afternoon was an easy one. *Hotlanta* was never without traffic, but Leah had no problems making it into town.

Gabby lived in an older apartment complex with lots of trees and a wide variety of residents both ethnically and socioeconomically. Leah's successful friend could certainly afford to move somewhere far posher, but Gabby enjoyed her little nest.

Leah parked in a visitor spot, grabbed her bag and purse, and locked the car. It was a perfect summer evening. Lots of tenants were outside. Kids playing kickball. Old men discussing politics. Teenagers washing cars.

Gabby's two-bedroom apartment was on the top floor. Leah decided to climb the stairs for exercise. If she was going to get naked with Lucas Carter on a regular basis, it wouldn't hurt to tone up a few areas.

She was huffing and puffing when Gabby answered the doorbell. Gabby raised an eyebrow. "Come on in. Why is your face all red?"

"I'll tell you later." Leah set her things down and hugged her friend. "You look amazing."

It was true. Gabby was five foot ten and slender. Her chin length black hair was striking against her magnolia skin. Gray eyes and smoky lashes gave her a dramatic beauty that was at direct odds with her personality.

Gabby was smart, practical, and not given to flights of fancy.

She was also the kind of woman who got hit on by the opposite sex frequently. To Leah's knowledge, her friend had dated over the years but had never let any man too close. Gabby was self-contained and self-sufficient. Her confidence was remarkable given her severely impoverished childhood. That same poise and certainty were things Leah had always envied.

Suddenly, Leah realized the apartment smelled great. "You cooked?" she said. "I told you I wanted to take you out, my treat."

Gabby waved a hand. "It's hard to cook for one, so I rarely take the time or make the effort. Your visit inspired me. Come sit down. All I need to do is pour the wine and get out the salad."

Leah's friend had prepared homemade lasagna. The aroma alone was probably fattening. Plus there was garlic bread.

When they were seated, Leah took a bite and groaned. "This is incredible. I don't know how one woman can be good at everything, but you are."

Gabby's smile was wry. "I'm definitely not, but thanks. So tell me what's up with you. What are these meetings tomorrow?"

"I've been talking with a foundation that gives money to operations like mine. I emailed one of their staff this afternoon to see if she's free tomorrow. She's going to give me pointers on how to write my grant proposal. After that, I'm hoping to track down a couple of good used vans. There are days when I'd like to take the campers into Blossom Branch for special occasions, but the camp doesn't own anything big enough. I rent the school buses that transport them to and from Atlanta."

Gabby stood, went to a small desk, and rummaged in the drawer. "Here," she said. "This guy has a dealership that does a fair amount of charitable stuff. Tell him I sent you, and he'll give you a decent price."

"You dated him?" Leah took the card and glanced at the name.

"Yes."

"And?"

Gabby shrugged. "And nothing. He's a very nice man. But he was ready to get married and have babies. I wasn't."

Inwardly, Leah flinched. Gabby was so sure of her choices.

"Do you ever look back and second-guess those kinds of decisions?"

"Not really. My life has always been focused on work...out of necessity. Not much room for fooling around with dumb rabbit trails." She paused. "Why do I feel like I'm being grilled? We've been friends forever, Leah. What could you possibly want to know about me after all this time?"

"I want to know how you understand men. How you deal with them." Leah blurted out the words, her pride less important than getting help with her current problem.

Gabby drained her wineglass and sat back in her chair. "I see." She cocked her head and studied Leah's face. "I thought you've been living like a nun for the past few years. What happened? Who is this man who has you in a tizzy?"

"I'm not in a tizzy," Leah protested.

Her friend's smile was equal parts teasing and warm concern. "You walked up several flights of stairs a little while ago. *Something's* going on."

Leah didn't really want to spill all the details, but she needed Gabby's perspective. Gabby was one of her two very best friends. Cate was aglow with Harry and relationship perfection. Today, Leah needed a more rational and unbiased view.

"I met someone," she said. "He likes having sex with me, but it's only temporary. He knows that. I know that."

"So, what's the problem? And PS, kudos for getting back out there."

"Thanks. I think." Leah paused, searching for the right words. "You know how I am. I tend to romanticize guys. You've always been cynical about the male sex. How can I be more like you, so Lucas doesn't break my heart?"

Gabby blinked. "I think I've been insulted."

"Not at all," Leah said urgently. "You have the ability to see through a man's BS. And you have this princess-in-the-tower thing going on that keeps men at a distance and at the same time makes them determined to have you. Teach me how to be a hard-ass instead of a marshmallow."

"You're not a marshmallow, hon. Maybe too trusting sometimes. But that's not a crime. We all love your generous heart."

"That's not what I asked. How can I have sex with Lucas and not fall in love with him?"

Gabby drummed her fingers on the table. "I don't think this is a quick fix. Did you bring comfy shoes?"

"Yes."

"Then why don't we change and go for a walk?"

"That sounds great."

Fifteen minutes later the two of them exited the apartment and joined the group of Atlantans enjoying a balmy summer evening. Leah was happy in Blossom Branch—and at the camp—but sometimes she missed the energy of her big city. It was nice to be back, even if for only one night.

For a little while, they chatted about random topics as they walked. Leah's family dinner. Gabby's recent business conference in Miami. Finally, Leah stopped in the middle of the sidewalk. "So if it's not a quick fix, at least tell me *something*."

Gabby's expression was hard to read. She shook her head slowly. "I'm no relationship guru. In case it escaped your notice, I don't have a single meaningful relationship under my belt. It scares me to let down my guard. What you see as confidence with men is the opposite. I don't know what the hell I'm doing in that department."

"But what about sex? And companionship?"

"As long as I have batteries, I'm good. I'd love to have a dog, but I work too much. Fortunately, I enjoy my own company, so I get by."

Leah frowned. "But I thought you had slept with a lot of guys."

"What makes you think that?"

"I don't know. You're beautiful. And you work in a male-dominated field. I guess I thought the opportunities were out there, and you took them. That's what I was hoping you could teach me. The casual angle. Sex for fun."

Gabby took off walking again, forcing Leah to follow. "Here's the thing, Leah. I don't ascribe to the all-men-are-pigs view. It's simply not true. There are probably thousands of wonderful guys in Atlanta. I just haven't found one yet. One for me."

"But you're looking, right?" Leah wanted to hear the good and not the bad.

"There have been times," Gabby said, "when I've craved the comfort of another human being in my bed…in my life. I've tried, Leah. I've tried it both ways—the no-strings and the maybe-we-can-make-it-work."

"And?"

"I always end up disappointed. Even when the sex is good. Because deep down inside, I guess I'm more like you than I want to admit."

Leah hustled to keep up with her friend's longer stride. "Oh?"

Gabby walked faster now, her chin high, her gaze straight ahead. "I got my heart broken once a very long time ago. And I've never completely gotten over it. This isn't up for discussion. I want you to keep this between us. But I guess you could say I'm too picky. If I can't have the real thing, I don't want a tepid imitation. So yes, I cave and have sex a few times a year. For the warmth and the connection. But so far, it's never turned into anything more."

"Maybe some of the best men are intimidated by your looks and your brains, and they never put themselves out there."

Gabby snorted. "I'm pretty sure that's a lie women tell themselves to make excuses for why they're alone."

This was depressing as hell. Leah felt lost. "So where does that leave me with Lucas? What should I do?"

"Can you imagine the absolute worst thing that could happen? Theoretically?"

"Well, we live in a very small town. If we got serious and then it ended, life would be awkward."

Gabby shot her a derisive sideways glance, still walking swiftly. "Breakups happen every day in every town in America. You've got to do better than that."

They rounded a corner, and to Leah's relief, finally headed back toward the apartments. "It's confusing, I guess, but I feel so proud of what's happening at camp. I see myself growing and becoming the kind of person I've always wanted to be. I've even made some small inroads into changing my family's view of me."

"That's good, right?" Gabby said.

"Of course. But when I'm with Lucas," she said quietly, "I can see how he might become my whole world. He's the kind of man who stands out. Both in looks and in character. If I have sex with him on a regular basis, I'm afraid I'll lose my footing in the deep end. When we inevitably break up, I would be a mess."

"And then what? You'd wither away? Join a convent? Throw yourself off a bridge?"

"Of course not."

"Then go for it. Be with him. Wallow in sexual bliss. Camp Willow Pond is an amazing accomplishment on your part, but it's still a job."

"And love?"

"Love is never a certainty. Even when we think it is. Lucas may not be the man you'll grow old with, but he sounds like a fun guy and a valuable friend. Open yourself up. Have a good time. Heck, you might even eventually fall in love with him."

"And then what?"

Gabby slowed, bent from the waist, and put her hands on her ankles to stretch. "Then you'll know if one of life's big gambles paid off. But you won't be a coward. You won't be afraid to really live."

TWELVE

LEAH ENJOYED HER TIME WITH GABBY. THEY STAYED
up late watching classic rom-coms and eating popcorn. But
when the alarm went off Monday morning, they both had to
get ready for work. Gabby headed out first, of course. Leah's
appointment was later.

She lingered over a second cup of coffee and pondered what
Gabby had said last night. Could Leah really live in the mo-
ment? Not worry about the future? Could she have sex with
Lucas Carter and simply enjoy herself?

She liked to think so, but judging by past experiences, it
wouldn't be easy.

The day flew by. Her meetings both went very well. She felt
confident now about approaching the grant process. And she
had written a check for two vans that would be delivered mid-
week. Unfortunately, Gabby hadn't been able to take a half day
after all, but she promised to meet Leah for an early dinner.

In the meantime, Leah did some shopping. Her repertoire of

sexy underwear was not extensive enough for a long relation-ship. She wanted to impress Lucas.

Standing in a tiny dressing room wearing a black lace teddy made her heart race. She looked in the mirror and tried to imag-ine what Lucas saw when he looked at her. He promised never to lie to her. The test would be whether she could believe him.

She bought the sexy teddy and six sets of ridiculously ex-pensive and indulgent bra-and-panty combos. Seeing the rain-bow of colors folded into a fluffy nest of white tissue paper was a feast for the senses. She handed over her credit card without wincing. This was important. Her bank balance was healthy. She could afford to indulge.

Gabby met her for dinner at five thirty at a restaurant that had been around for years, one they both liked. Leah arrived first and secured a table. She had thought about inviting Cate to meet them, but there was something odd going on between her two friends, and she didn't want to ambush Gabby.

She waved when she saw Gabby come in, struck by her friend's easy elegance as she crossed the room. "How was work?" Leah asked when Gabby dropped her leather tote in a chair and sat down.

"Okay, I guess."

"You don't sound too sure."

"Well, it's a job. And I'm good at it. So I have nothing to complain about."

"But it's not your passion?"

Gabby shook her head, her smile wry. "Not everyone has the luxury of following their passions. You're lucky. Your aunt left you an inheritance that you're able to use for a wonderful cause, a project that brings personal satisfaction. I need to sup-port my mother. And myself, of course. I need a stable career."

"I get that. How *is* your mother?" Leah had met Gabby's emotionally fragile parent and liked her very much. Gabby was very protective of her mom.

"She's fine. I've tried a hundred times to get her to move to Atlanta with me, but she says Blossom Branch is more her speed. I think the city terrifies her."

"So you spend a lot of time on the road?"

"A couple of weekends a month. I have vacation days blocked off in August. She's always wanted to go to Disney World."

Leah snickered. "I can't imagine *you* at the happiest place on earth."

Gabby scowled. "I know how to have fun."

"Sure you do." Leah touched her friend's hand. Gabby knew Leah well enough to understand the kidding was in good fun. "You're a caring daughter and a wonderful person," Leah said. "But if I'm going to have sex for fun, I think you should, too."

Gabby shuddered theatrically. "I don't have time for that dance right now. Dating is brutal in the twenty-first century. I may get a better hold on my schedule and adopt a puppy. I never had a pet growing up, but I always wanted one."

"Or more likely, you'll keep going with the sixty-hour work weeks. Don't burn yourself out. You're young and healthy now, but stress can kill you."

"I know. I'm thinking about it, honest. Now let's talk about something more interesting. Has your hot fireman called or texted you?"

Leah grimaced. "Not a peep."

"Did you text him?"

"Are you kidding? I don't want to be that needy woman who has to know where her man is every second of the day."

"You said he's *not* your man."

"Well, you know what I mean."

"He might like to hear from you."

"What would I even say? *You were great in bed. Let's do it again?*"

Gabby laughed. "Men are straightforward creatures. He'd probably appreciate the clear signal."

★ ★ ★

All the way back to Blossom Branch, Leah thought about Gabby's words. Leah had never been one to push her way into a relationship. If Lucas was interested, he would call.

Or was that line of thinking hopelessly outdated?

Did she want to see him again? Yes.

When she was finally home and had unloaded everything from the car, it was impossible to walk into the bedroom and not see Lucas sprawled on her sheets. The memories made her face hot.

After thirty minutes of dithering, she grabbed her phone and pulled up his contact info. What was she supposed to say? Maybe light and breezy was the key.

Saturday night was fun.

That seemed abrupt. So she added more.

Hope your friend's wife and baby are okay.

She hit send and tossed the phone on the bed, not wanting to look at it. The feeling inside her gut was equal parts embarrassment and dread.

What if he was a one-and-done kind of man? What if he hadn't been all that impressed? What if he had already moved on?

Leah might have been nothing more than a notch in his fireman's belt. Did firemen even wear belts? Maybe they didn't need them because of those wide suspenders.

She stopped in front of the mirror, stared at herself, giggled, and got a little hysterical. Everything inside her said *pick up the phone.* Had he texted her back?

Who knew? She *wasn't* going to pick up the phone, and she *wasn't* going to obsess about this.

Instead, she took a shower, washed and dried her hair, and changed into light, summery cotton pajamas. Then she made herself a cup of her favorite herbal tea and settled in the den to watch something mindless and entertaining on Netflix. She was woefully behind on several of her favorite shows.

After two thirty-minute segments, she couldn't stand it any longer. She put her TV on pause, scooted back to the bedroom, and reached for her phone. The text icon had a tiny red numeral *one* beside it. Her heart pounded. It was probably Gabby making sure Leah got home okay.

She tapped, and there was Lucas's number with a terse message. Baby and mama fine. Working double shifts and trying to sleep between fires. Miss you, sunshine…

Suddenly, she felt guilty for not having checked on him sooner. Even if this new relationship was defined by fun and recreational sex, it was an equal partnership. She had to step up and be a confident woman.

She sent a follow-up message.

So sorry. Sounds rough. Sleep well.

That night, *she* slept soundly. Tuesday morning, she called Marisa and ordered two dozen club sandwiches and two dozen cinnamon buns to be delivered to the fire station just before noon. With her conscience appeased, she set about her day.

The camp was busy, even with the kids gone. A cleaning crew had descended on the sleeping cabins and was sanitizing bathrooms and putting fresh sheets on all the beds. Leah didn't have industrial laundry facilities on the property, so she was using a local service to supply linens. That system had worked well during the first camp session.

After the dormitories, the kitchen and dining hall would receive the same top-to-bottom attention.

She spent an hour going over her grocery order. The cooks

had tweaked the meal plans along the way, reducing quantities of some items and adding others.

After a lunch that consisted of nibbling a pack of cheese crackers along with an icy bottled Coke, Leah was soon on to the next item on her agenda. She and Jim and Peg had decided early in the summer that they needed kayaks and canoes, along with life jackets and other items. But though everything had been delivered before the end of the first session, storage was a problem.

Jeff Grainger was meeting her at one o'clock to give her an estimate on building a small, weatherproof shed down at the pond to house all the new equipment. Fortunately, he showed up right on time in his blue pickup truck. The back was loaded with raw lumber and other supplies.

He hopped out and gave her a grin. "Hey, Leah. I heard you survived the first session of camp." He shook her hand.

"How did you hear that?"

"From Luscious Lucas, of course."

"You know he hates that nickname, right?"

His grin expanded. "Yes, ma'am, I do."

Leah shook her head, laughing. "Some friend you are."

Jeff set to work right away. Leah showed him the spot by the pond where she thought they could build. Jeff suggested an area a bit farther away in case of flooding. She agreed, and Jeff began taking measurements and staking the outline of the new building to see if it met Leah's needs.

In an hour and a half, they were done. As they walked back up the low incline toward the main part of camp, Jeff pulled out his phone and consulted his calendar. "I can have my guys out here first thing Thursday morning. Does that work for you?"

"That would be perfect," Leah said. "Thanks."

When they reached Jeff's truck, he paused, his fingers on the door handle. His expression revealed awkwardness that surprised her. Jeff was a laid-back guy as far as she could tell.

He shrugged and sighed. "I know I asked you out when we

first met, but Lucas is clearly interested in you, so I'm good with that. I just wanted you to know there won't be anything weird on my end."

She smiled, liking him more and more. "I never thought there would be."

"But…" He trailed off, his discomfiture increasing.

"But what?" She was alarmed by his body language and his stuttering explanations.

Jeff's shrug was unhappy. "This may sound like sour grapes, but I need to warn you about Lucas. He's not like other guys."

Her smile was wry. "Meaning what?" She was pretty sure she knew where this was headed.

"He's one of my very best friends. We've known each other for fifteen years. He's a rock-solid buddy and a great human being."

"You still haven't gotten around to that *but*."

Jeff grimaced. "He's not the man for a long-term relationship."

Leah's stomach clenched. "I know," she said calmly. "He told me so. You're worried about nothing, but I appreciate the heads-up."

Still, Jeff didn't smile. "Women always think they can change a guy."

"Not me." She shook her head slowly. "You're trying to say that growing up in foster care for eighteen years messed with his head."

"That about sums it up."

Leah wrapped her arms around her waist, feeling vaguely guilty for discussing Lucas behind his back. "I understand your concern. Believe me. I've had a version of this conversation with myself over and over. Is it wise to get involved with a man who fights *demons*? Or is that too strong a word? Lucas always seems so positive and upbeat, it's almost hard to believe he has dark layers."

"Believe it," Jeff said bluntly. "One night about six years

ago when the two of us had too much to drink, he told me he doesn't want to search for answers about his family because he's scared of what he'll find." Jeff banged his fist on the hood of the truck. "Scared. Can you believe it? A man who will run into a burning building without flinching is terrified to confront his past."

"I can't even begin to understand," Leah said sadly. "I spend way too much time trying to prove myself to my family. Even now, it's clear they think this camp will fail. My brothers and parents make me nuts, but at least I *know* where all the skeletons are buried. Lucas is staring at a blank slate. From the time he was born."

Before Jeff could answer, they heard a car and both turned to watch Lucas's sleek sedan roll up the driveway.

Lucas stopped the car, got out, and shoved his hands in his pockets. "This looks cozy," he said. The bite in his words and the turbulent expression in his eyes told Leah he was in an edgy mood. Honestly, he looked exhausted, and no wonder.

Without overthinking it, she went to him, kissed his cheek, and smiled. "Do you two boys want to come up to the house for a cup of coffee?"

"Or a beer?" Lucas asked hopefully.

She shook her head. "Camp. Remember? We're a dry facility."

Jeff had been about to leave, but either he was willing to poke the tiger, or he was thirsty. "I could use some coffee," he said.

The three of them walked side by side with Leah in the middle. "Jeff's crew is going to build us a storage shed," she said. "For all our kayaks and water equipment. Plus anything else we might use."

It might have been her imagination, but Lucas's posture seemed to relax after her casual explanation. Inside the small house, the two men sprawled on opposite ends of the sofa while Leah measured out coffee and water and flipped a switch.

Jeff eyed his friend. "What have you been up to on a Tuesday?" he asked. "I thought you were taking time off this week."

Lucas shot Leah an unreadable look. "You didn't tell him?"

She shrugged. "It was a business meeting. Your name didn't come up." She uttered the little white lie smoothly. During the *business* part of the appointment, she and Jeff hadn't discussed Lucas at all.

As Leah poured three large mugs of coffee and gathered everything on a tray, Lucas yawned and explained. "I was *supposed* to have time off. But Ryker and Janie's baby came early. I'm covering for him, and damned if everything in Blossom Branch isn't burning down all at once."

"I hope you're exaggerating," Jeff said.

"Me, too," Leah said. She set the tray on the coffee table and watched as the men doctored their coffee. Jeff took his with cream and no sugar. Lucas skipped the cream but liked it sweet. She prepared her own drink and sat back in an armchair.

Lucas drained half his cup and yawned again. "We've had a big fire at the lumberyard, a smaller one in those storage units out on sixty-six, and two separate house fires after that. I've barely managed to string together a decent chunk of sleep at any one time. I'd kill for eight uninterrupted hours."

Without warning, his gaze clashed with Leah's. "The guys really appreciated all the food you sent to the station. I did, too. I'm sorry I haven't been very communicative. And to follow up on your earlier question, the baby's doing okay. He's spending a few days in the NICU, but the doc says he's healthy."

"I'm so glad."

Jeff finished his drink and set the mug on the tray. "I've gotta run. I'm bidding on two different projects for the elementary school. They want them done by August 15, so I hope they make up their minds soon."

When Jeff drove away, an awkward silence fell. Leah and

Lucas had come out on the porch to wave goodbye. Now they stood side by side.

Lucas turned and leaned back against a post, trusting the porch railing more than he should. The house needed TLC that Leah hadn't yet found time to arrange. "Was he hitting on you?" he asked quietly.

Leah sat down on the porch swing, moving it slowly with her foot. "Of course not," she said.

"You told me before that he asked you out."

"Yes. But that's in the past. Jeff understands you and I are…" She trailed off, feeling unexpectedly boxed in and uncomfortable.

Lucas's eyes narrowed, his gaze on her lips. "That you and I are what?" he asked, the words silky.

"Don't do this, Lucas." She was angry suddenly. She had no clue what they were doing together, and she wouldn't let him badger her. "I need to get back to town," she said. "You probably should get some sleep. You look like hell."

It wasn't entirely the truth. He was as gorgeous as usual. For some reason, the shadows under his eyes only made him more appealing.

When she stood, planning to go inside and grab her purse and keys before locking up, he straightened and caught her wrist. "I'm sorry, babe. I shouldn't take my lousy mood out on you. Let me buy you dinner," he said.

"No, thank you," she said, the words prim. "I have a couple of hours of work to do on my laptop. Grant writing. Boring stuff, but necessary."

He cupped the side of her face in one big hand. "God, I've missed you," he said quietly. "I've barely had time to think since I left your house Sunday morning, but the memories have been a splinter in my brain." He drew her close and rested his head on her shoulder. "Let me go home with you. I promise not to be grumpy."

She could handle his pissy mood by moving on with her life and ignoring him. But if he was going to be sweet and vulnerable, she was lost. How could she keep an emotional distance between them when she wanted to take care of him and support him in the tough times of his job?

As she gazed out across camp, seeing the rolling fields in the distance and imagining the next set of problems and challenges that would arrive Sunday evening, she knew it was stupid to waste what little time she had with Lucas.

With a deep sigh of surrender, she wrapped her arms around his waist, absorbing his warmth and vitality. She inhaled and exhaled, searching for an answer.

Could she indulge in the wicked, delicious treat that was Lucas Carter and yet keep her heart intact?

She lifted her hand and stroked his hair lightly. "Yes," she said. "You can come home with me."

Leah watched in her rearview mirror as Lucas followed her back into town. They had squabbled over leaving a car at camp. Lucas wanted her beside him in *his* vehicle. Leah had insisted that wasn't a good idea. In the end, she had prevailed. But now, she felt like she was being stalked by a big, hungry lion.

Once again, they both parked in the relative privacy of her carport out back. He followed her into the house. She was glad she had left the AC running and that she had made up her bed. "Why don't you stretch out on the sofa and take a nap?" she said. "I'll come up with a dinner plan."

Lucas curled his fingers into her ponytail and pulled her close, nuzzling her nose with his. "I don't care about dinner," he said gruffly. "I'd like a repeat invitation into that sexy, romantic bedroom of yours."

Her gaze widened, trying to decide if he was kidding. She pulled back so she could see his face. "You're talking about sex? It's the middle of the afternoon, Lucas." She knew her squeaky voice probably made her sound like an uptight virgin, but she wasn't used to abandoning responsibility in pursuit of sensual bliss.

His wicked grin made her knees wobble. "Lots of people have daytime sex, Leah. It's not a crime. Heck, I'm not even sure it's a sin."

Before she could come up with a snarky response, he settled his mouth over hers and worked his personal brand of sorcery. He played with her lips and her tongue while at the same time, his hands wandered. She was wearing a coral knit top and khaki shorts. Lucas slid a hand underneath her shirt and found her bra. Moments later, he fingered her nipple and stroked her breasts until she panted and squirmed against him.

"Lucas," she whispered.

He dragged her closer, letting her feel the full length of his erection. "I like how you say my name." He palmed her ass and ground his jean-clad sex against her belly. "Say it again."

His rough command made her hotter. She felt like she was in a dream. On any given day at any given moment, she was a competent, organized, productive member of society. But five minutes in Lucas Carter's arms, and all she could think about was climbing him like a fire pole and having her way with him.

He kissed her again. Their bodies were damp. He smelled like lime with a whiff of smoke. She wondered if pheromones were to blame for this insanity.

She rubbed her tongue across his bottom lip. "Did you bring condoms?" she asked, breathing hard.

His laughter tickled her ear. "I stashed some in the drawer beside your bed when you weren't looking."

"Good thinking," she croaked.

He backed her up against the nearest wall. "I want you more than my next breath," he said. "I want to slide in deep and feel you grip me tight. I want your legs around my waist and your beautiful breasts pressed against my chest. Does any of that sound appealing, my sweet Leah?"

She was almost beyond speech, awash in longing for this beautiful man and his incredibly honed masculine body. "All of it," she groaned. He licked her neck…bit her collarbone. Shivers raised gooseflesh on her arms. She unbuttoned the two shirt buttons she could reach. "I'm inviting you to my bedroom, Lucas. But hurry."

THIRTEEN

LUCAS SCOOPED LEAH INTO HIS ARMS, GRINNING when she gasped and curled an arm around his neck. As if he would drop such a precious burden. "Hallelujah," he panted. "I thought you'd never ask."

The bedroom door was partially open. He kicked it wide and told himself the dizziness he felt was from lack of sleep. As he stopped just inside, he inhaled sharply, filling his lungs with the clean, piquant scent that was uniquely Leah, a combination of her soap and shampoo and maybe a dollop of perfume.

He swallowed. "Am I rushing you?" he asked, the words feeling oddly formal as he uttered them.

The woman in his arms frowned. "Do I look like I'm being rushed?"

He glanced down at her. In his eagerness, he had left her shirt up around her neck. He hadn't even unfastened her bra. "Hard to say." He set her on her feet and finished removing her top and lacy bra. Now she was bare from the waist up.

Predictably, her cheeks turned pink.

He stepped back for a better view. "You remind me of a 1940s calendar girl. The ones all those lonely GIs fantasized about."

Leah frowned. "Calendar women had long, long legs."

"You promised to believe me when I give you compliments. I don't care how long your legs are, Leah. I'm talking about these." He cupped his hands beneath her full breasts. "Your body has this intense sexuality."

There was doubt in her eyes, but he didn't push the issue. Instead, he took off his clothes and tossed everything across the nearest chair. Leah's wide eyes and rapt expression as she studied his naked body deepened his arousal.

He liked the way she looked at him. As if she was fascinated and hungry and hesitant all at once. "Do you want me to strip you?" he asked quietly. "Or would you rather do the honors?" They had been moving at the speed of light since they entered the house, but now the pace slowed.

"I'll do it," she said. She'd left her sandals beside the front door. The graceful way she lowered her shorts and undies had him even harder. It was an erotic ballet, more alluring than ever because she had no clue what she did to him.

They stood six feet apart, maybe eight. Nothing between them but hushed anticipation and heavy air that seemed to spark and quiver and dance with emotion. "Tell me what you want, Leah."

She chewed her lip. "You mean positions?"

"Positions could be part of it." She was still skittish around him. He didn't know how to fix that. "Do you want to take the lead?"

"Oh, no." She shook her head firmly. "You're the expert here."

He frowned. "This is as new for me as it is for you. I don't automatically know what you like. I'm feeling my way. Learning your body. And you're doing the same with me. It's a level playing field. I'm not the teacher, and you're not the pupil. We're in this together. Do you understand what I'm saying?"

A small wistful smile lifted the corners of her mouth.

"What?" he said.

"That was beautiful, Lucas. Did you make it up on the spot or steal it from a movie? That speech, I mean."

She was so clearly skeptical, his fists curled at his sides. "Damn it, woman. I'm trying to be open and honest with you. Because I promised you that. I didn't steal anything. But if you're not going to believe the things I say, I might as well fuck you and get it over with." His neck was hot, and his jaw ached from clenching it so hard. She made him crazy—not always in a good way.

To his surprise, she closed the gap between them. When she was close enough for him to breathe the same air she breathed, she stopped and put both hands flat on his chest, fingers splayed. Her big brown eyes held a wealth of emotions as she looked up at him. "I'm sorry," she said. "I didn't mean to imply you were being less than honest. I'm just surprised at your eloquence, I suppose. You always know the right thing to say. I tend to second-guess myself or walk away from an encounter and two hours later come up with a pithy retort. I believe you, really I do."

He closed his eyes, trying to control his ragged breathing. "Then we're back to my original question. What do you want?"

She searched his face. Her hands petted him. "I don't *know* exactly what I want," she said. "But I'd like to start with kissing and touching and let it go from there."

When her fingernails raked his flat nipples, he hissed. It was like being hit with a jolt of electricity. Though that part of his body had never been particularly an erogenous zone for him, the way Leah did it—all sweet and artless—made him exponentially hotter.

"That's a great plan," he said, forcing the words from a tight throat. He took her wrists, kissed her once...hard...and drew her over to the bed. "Ladies first," he said.

Leah winced, or at least he thought she did. When she climbed onto the mattress, he had a million-dollar view. He joined her in a flash, wishing he could mount her and rid himself of this shaky, desperate feeling.

But he couldn't, of course. Not yet. She deserved a bit of finesse. A sexual courtship. A teasing, exciting journey to the ultimate goal.

He settled on his side with his head on his hand. The other hand was free to roam. He started with her navel. It was small and cute. Turns out, it was also ticklish. When he realized that, he grinned. "Some people like to be tickled," he said.

"Not me." She curled her fingers with his. "Can I ask you a serious question?"

He tensed. "I suppose."

She touched his forehead, traced his nose and his chin. Then she tested the stubble on his jaw and rubbed her thumb over his bottom lip. Each gentle caress sent him deeper into a haze of need. Again, she looked deep into his eyes. "How dangerous is what you do? I've worried about you this week."

He had expected something more personal. Not this. "It *can* be," he said, trying to be truthful without scaring her. "But we have excellent gear, and we train for many hours both before we get the job and then later for recertification."

"Have you ever been really frightened?"

How had they come to this with both of them naked? He realized she was trying to understand him. That made sense. Leah didn't give her trust and her body easily. He respected that.

"Once or twice," he admitted. "It's always soul-crushing to find dogs or cats who have succumbed to smoke inhalation. Breaks your heart. Because you know their human is going to be devastated."

"And the humans themselves?"

He didn't want to go there. But it was hard to hide. "I've had a couple of close calls," he admitted. "Both times the person was trapped with fire between them and me. But it turned out okay in the end." He glossed over the pounding panic and the stress of hearing someone cry out for help amid what must seem like literal hell to a layperson.

"Thank you for telling me," she said. "I've never been in a relationship with someone who has a dangerous job." She stroked his chest. "Please don't get hurt."

He brought her hand to his mouth and kissed her fingers. "I don't plan on it."

Leah sighed and scrunched up her nose. "I've ruined the mood, haven't I? I'm sorry, Lucas."

He leaned over to kiss her. "Quit apologizing. I'm not easily distracted, babe. We can pick up right where we left off. Have I told you how much I love your hair?" He winnowed his fingers through the tangled waves.

"I always wanted to be a blonde or a redhead," she said. "Brown is boring."

"Not even a little bit." He kissed a tender spot right under her ear. "Every bit of you is perfectly perfect. Leah Marks. The hidden gem of Blossom Branch. And she's all mine."

She swatted his shoulder. "A brown gem? Ew…"

"Have you ever heard of brown diamonds? They're real diamonds, just a little different from their bland, clear counterparts."

Her grin was wry. "Are you sure you don't have Irish ancestry in you somewhere? You have a gift for blarney, Chief Carter."

"I wouldn't know," he said lightly, trying not to let a throwaway comment dent his current contentment.

She stared at him. "Oh, Lucas. I didn't mean to be insensitive."

He shook his head slowly. "You weren't. It's merely an odd

fact, one part of me that's hidden away. It's not the end of the world."

Leah curled herself more tightly into his chest, her face hidden against his collarbone. "Can I tell you a secret?" she asked, her voice muffled.

"Sure."

"I've never been on top."

When she sneaked a look at his face, he tried not to react. "Okay."

"Well, my first boyfriend didn't like it, and later I was self-conscious about my boobs from that angle. So I never wanted to be."

"But you do now?"

She studied his face, her excited smile so adorable he might explode. "Yes, please."

"Kiss me first," he said.

When she reached up and set her lips against his, he felt something inside him shift and settle. Like tectonic plates maybe. A seismic movement that could bring disaster or create something bold and new.

He put a hand behind her head to keep her close. And then he kissed her lazily, drawing out the pleasure, spinning it into bright strands of gold that encircled them both. Without comment, he shifted onto his back. He was still hard. In fact, he had been achingly stiff for almost an hour now. It was beginning to seem like a normal state of affairs any time he was in touching distance of this woman.

Leah was on her knees beside him, an odd look on her face. "What?" he said, trying not to beg.

"Will you tell me if I do it wrong?"

He snorted, shaking his head. "It won't be wrong, babe. I swear. Grab one of those condoms and give it to me, please."

She did as he asked and watched as he tore it open and put it on. Then he reached between her legs and slid a finger through her sex, making sure she was ready for him. She made an odd little sound when his finger skated over a particular spot. Her eyes closed. Her chest rose and fell. Her sigh sent a shiver down his spine.

"Leah?"

"Hmm?" She was smiling, but her eyes were still closed.

"Look at me, angel. Please?"

When she opened her eyes and her gaze slammed into his, he knew beyond any doubt that she was as turned on as he was.

She scanned his body, nodded slowly as if she liked what she saw, and then she straddled his waist. "Hi," she said, blushing.

"Woman, you're hotter than the sun. Come and get me."

She lifted onto her knees and shimmied into position. The look of concentration on her face might have made him smile if he hadn't been stretched on a rack of shuddering anticipation. His whole body was rigid.

When she took him into her, he groaned. The feeling was indescribable. She was tight, so tight. His forehead was damp. His fingers dug into her butt.

But what threatened to drive him over the edge was the view of those beautiful pale breasts as they bounced ever so slightly. He wanted to bury his face between them, but he couldn't reach.

If he could have set the pace, he would have. But he was at the mercy of Leah's experimentation. Judging by the stunned expression on her face, she was a fan of this new experience. She moved so slowly at first, he nearly begged. But he bit back the words. This was her moment.

"This is nice," she said. Her ragged breathing and the flush of color that suffused her chest and face told him she was anything but calm.

"I don't know how long I can hold out," he said. "Just FYI. Don't want to disappointment you again."

Her smile was pure siren. Or maybe cat that ate the canary.

"Nobody is disappointing anybody today." She leaned forward and put her hands on his shoulders. "Would you lick my nipples?"

He nearly swallowed his tongue. "Anything for a lady." He found the closet one and sank his teeth into it, exerting the exact amount of pressure to make her go faster.

Her eyes got hazy. "The other, too," she pleaded. She moved her hips—up, down, and around—building the friction.

Teasing and pleasing Leah was so gratifying he managed to put the brakes on his own need. The little sounds she made when he tasted her made him feel invincible. He knew what women liked. But discovering what his Leah liked took things to another level. It was an irresistible challenge.

At last, she sat up and looked at him. Her bottom lip was puffy where he had sucked on it. Her pupils were dilated. The dark flush on her cheekbones told him she was totally into the moment.

"All good?" he asked softly.

She wrinkled her nose. "I love it. But I'm not sure I can come like this."

"Well," he said, weighing his words with care. "We can change and do it the traditional way. Or you could let me try something and see if it works."

"Something?" The word came out breathless.

He nodded. "But you have a part, too. You screw *me*. Take control. And I'll concentrate on *this*." He settled his thumb on her pleasure spot.

Leah sucked in a breath. "Got it."

Her compliance with his plan was enthusiastic and energetic. She set a rhythm of up and down, her body sheathing his in bliss. In fact, she was *so* energetic and talented at her job, Lucas lost his focus for a moment.

His body screamed at him to find that final burst of nirvana, but he set his jaw and focused on the woman he wanted to please. When he rotated his thumb with a light motion,

Leah gasped. He watched her face. When she settled hard on his erection, he added a bit more pressure.

Her eyes closed. She cried out his name.

Lucas felt her inner muscles flutter against his sex. Gripping her ass, he thrust wildly and came hard, blinded by the push to the end.

When he could breathe...and think, he found Leah draped over him like a seductive blanket, her face buried in his shoulder. He wasn't in any hurry to move. In fact, he felt oddly paralyzed. As if the encounter had zapped his circuitry.

He was at once uneasy and yet zoned out on physical bliss.

Why did sex with Leah Marks feel different?

Because he was uncomfortable examining that thought, he focused instead on the warm female body in his arms. He tapped her forehead. "Anybody in there?"

Leah mumbled something. Her hair covered her face. He brushed it aside, holding the silky mass in his hand. "Leah?"

She refused to look at him. "Close your eyes while I get up," she pleaded. "This isn't going to be an elegant dismount."

Lucas chuckled. "Not a perfect ten?"

"A six point five at best."

He grinned, loving the way her brain worked. "What if we roll, and *I'll* be the one to get up first?"

She lifted her head at last and nodded. "That would be much appreciated."

"No problem." He executed the maneuver and crawled out of bed, pausing to stretch. As he headed for the bathroom, buck naked, Leah pulled the covers to her chin. Big brown eyes followed his progress.

After he washed up and returned to the bedroom, he found her still mummified. "Here's your robe, Miss Priss. I *would* offer to turn my back while you put it on, but that's a little ridiculous, don't you think? I've seen everything there is to see."

She made a face at him. "Maybe so." But she pulled the robe

under the covers and wriggled her way into it. When she finally scooted to the side of the mattress and stood, he pulled her close and held her. "In case you wondered, that was amazing. At least for me. I hope you enjoyed yourself."

"You could say that." Her response was dry. She kissed his chin. "Give me ten minutes and I'll meet you in the living room."

"Yes, ma'am."

When she disappeared into the bathroom, Lucas got dressed and found himself pacing the confines of her modest house. It was hard not to remember meeting all her family. He knew Leah's brothers and parents had wondered about him. His intentions. His motives.

But that was the trouble. He wasn't used to being so involved in a woman's life. Already he had inserted himself at camp. Meeting her folks had happened because Lucas wrangled an invitation to dinner.

What did he want from Leah?

When she found him in the living room, she had changed into black leggings and a lemon-yellow linen top that was open and billowy over a white tank. She looked fresh and appealing, and his heart jerked in his chest.

He cleared his throat. "I know I said I'd buy you dinner, but I'm not really in a mood to go out. What if I grab some chicken breasts and grill them with yellow squash?"

"That sounds lovely. I need to make a couple of phone calls. I can be at your place in an hour if that works."

He frowned. "I thought you'd come with me. And maybe spend the night."

Leah folded her arms across her chest, giving him a stern schoolteacher look that revved his engines. "What time do you have to be at work in the morning?" she asked, her gaze daring him to lie.

"Six," he muttered. "But I don't need a lot of sleep."

"Well, I do," she said. "I'll come over for dinner. That seems reasonable."

"I've never been a fan of reasonable," he groused. He really didn't want to sleep alone tonight.

Leah's smile was sweet. "Get going," she said. "I'll be there soon. You want me to stop at the bakery for a macaroon pie?"

His mouth watered. "Definitely. But don't be too long. I might have withdrawal symptoms."

She lifted an eyebrow. "From waiting on pie?"

He smirked. "From being without you."

Leah took care of her two phone calls, but her attention was divided, partly because she was already anticipating the evening with Lucas. She was glad they weren't going to a restaurant. She liked being alone with him, even if it was dangerous.

Despite knowing he had to be at work at dawn, Lucas wanted to do a sleepover. The man was insatiable. Leah wasn't complaining though.

Thinking about the afternoon's activities made her restless. If Lucas's goal was to erase her insecurities when it came to sex, he was succeeding wildly. She barely recognized herself as that woman in the bedroom.

On top? What was she thinking?

Mostly that she wanted Lucas so badly her whole body trembled with need whenever he touched her. She felt safe in his arms. That was an incredible turn on. She'd been able to explore her fantasies without feeling stupid or awkward.

She was also coming to believe the man really did lust after her body. At the same time, her confidence was on the rise. Being with Lucas made her feel both strong and feminine. No negative thoughts about whether she was good enough. The way he related to her—both in bed and out—said he considered her an equal.

That was heady stuff for a girl who had spent most of her life as a mouse.

By the time she picked up their dessert and made it to Lucas's apartment, she was both excited and nervous. She knew this relationship wasn't long-term. How did she handle such intensity in the meantime? Wallowing in the moment was one choice. Maybe she could learn to compartmentalize the way men did. Separate Lucas and sex from her work at the camp and the rest of her life.

Boundaries. That's what she needed. Boundaries.

When she rang the bell and Lucas opened the door, all her sound reasoning flew out the window. He had changed into dark green cotton shorts. But other than that, he was mostly naked. Feet, legs, chest. She eyed him with a smile. "You look yummy."

He backed up to let her in. "It's hot as hell outside. I'm not sure grilling was the right choice, but everything is almost done."

"Go," she said, waving her hand. "Don't burn anything. I'm starving." They had worked off a lot of calories in her bed.

He paused for a quick kiss. "Back in a flash. You could pour the wine. And get the salad out of the fridge."

Leah found a glass for Lucas and poured the pinot noir. Then she filled another tumbler with ice and added water. She needed her wits about her.

When Lucas finally reappeared carrying a platter stacked high with food, she was waiting. He set the food on the counter. "Let me grab a shirt, and we'll eat," he said.

She put a hand on his chest, feeling his warm skin and taut chest. "Don't bother on my account."

His gaze narrowed. "A shirt would be safer."

"Seriously?" She rolled her eyes. "You think a shirt is going to keep either of us from temptation?"

"I didn't want to presume we were going to have sex again."

He stared at her intently. "You made it very clear you weren't going to spend the night."

She grinned at him, feeling happier than she had in a very long time. "I have it on good authority that daytime sex is perfectly acceptable."

His green eyes gleamed. His lips quirked as if he was trying not to laugh. "You are a brat."

"Me? Never?" She paused, relishing her new role as femme fatale. "How hungry are you," she asked, "on a scale of one to ten?"

He ran his thumb along her jaw. "Are we talking about sex or dinner?"

"Sex, I think."

"The chicken will get cold."

Leah took a deep breath. This was like diving into the deep end...an activity that had always been both terrifying and thrilling.

"I don't even care," she softly. "I want you. Dinner can wait."

FOURTEEN

THEY DID IT ON THE SOFA THIS TIME. IT WAS FAST AND furious and energizing. Leah didn't even have time to feel shy. When it was over, Lucas raised up on one elbow and stared at her. "Good grief. You're a sex maniac."

She felt her cheeks get hot. "No, I'm not," she muttered. "It's just that you're…" She trailed off.

"I'm what?"

Leah put her hand on his stubbly cheek. "You're wonderful," she said, risking honesty. "I've never met anyone exactly like you."

He seemed uncomfortable with her words. "I'm nothing special. You've just been hanging out with jerks."

Her stomach growled audibly.

His expression lightened. "I'd better resurrect our dinner before you pass out from hunger."

She nodded sheepishly. After all, she was the one who had

initiated *this* round of sex. Lucas had been surprised, but he hadn't complained one bit.

Once they were dressed, they nuked the food. It was tasty, though not as good as if it had come straight off the grill. Leah didn't mind, and she suspected Lucas didn't either.

She cleared her plate and then cut the dessert. "I'm stuffed, but this macaroon pie is famous in Blossom Branch."

"I may be new here," he said, "but I know that much."

When they were done, Leah carried their dishes to the counter while Lucas loaded the dishwasher. There was a messy, uneven stack of mail on the bar area. She straightened it and moved it to one side so nothing would get wet.

An official-looking envelope caught her eye. The return address was from New York State's Department of Health and Human Services. "What's this?" she asked, picking it up and studying it.

Lucas looked over his shoulder and froze. His gaze shuttered. "Nothing."

Leah frowned. "It doesn't look like nothing. It has your name handwritten on the envelope. Can't be junk mail. But you haven't opened it?"

His frown was dark. "No. And I won't. It's not important."

She was confused. "How do you know? It might be about your parents."

He shrugged, still not meeting her eyes. "Someone has been sending me those envelopes for three years now. There was a gap when I moved from Nashville to Blossom Branch, but they managed to find me again."

"What do the letters say?"

"Couldn't tell you. I've never opened one."

She stared at him open-mouthed. "Are you serious?"

His head came up, and his gaze iced over. "First of all, it's none of your business. And second of all—I. Don't. Care." He put a fist to his chest. "I am who I am. Me. I've built my life the way I want it."

Leah was horrified. "But you can't just ignore official government communications."

He scowled. "Sure I can. I'm not a rule follower like you, Leah. And I'm not one of your campers who needs to be *saved*."

"That's a low blow." She couldn't believe he was so angry with her. A level of anger that spoke of deep hurts in his past.

He shrugged. "You expect things to be tied up with a bow. But not everyone lives the way you do. Life is messy for most people. You and I are having fun, but if I'm not enough for you the way I am, then we can just forget it."

She gaped, stinging from his incendiary reaction. Yet thanks to her training in psychology, she recognized this storm was probably not focused on her at all. Something about that official letter had set him off. She kept her tone even, quiet. "But what if you need a kidney one day? And you've never responded to these letters? This might be your chance to finally get some answers. Your parents might be dead, but not all your people."

"I wouldn't take so much as a glass of water from anyone connected to my family. They abandoned me. I have no desire at all for any reunions, tender or otherwise."

She couldn't believe this was the same man who had made love to her beautifully twice today. Now he looked hard as ice, his demeanor cold and dismissive.

"What if *I* open it?" she said. "I'll skim it and see if it's important." She wanted so badly to help him.

Now, pure fury darkened his eyes. He stalked in her direction. "Give it to me."

Before she could react, he snatched the envelope from her hands, strode over to the corner of the living room where he had set up a small desk as an office, and thrust the piece of mail into a shredder.

The grinding noise was loud in the silent apartment.

When he turned around to face her, his expression was wiped clean. "I've made myself clear."

Leah nodded slowly as her heart cracked straight down the middle. "Yes, you have. It might help it we talk about this, Lucas." Even in the face of his anger, she had the confidence to know he needed her whether he admitted it or not.

"No, thanks." The words were calm but final.

She couldn't offer him support if he didn't want it. Her chest hurt and her throat was tight with unshed tears. "Then I think it's time for me to go."

His hands fisted at his sides. "So we're done?"

Was that vulnerability she saw in his masculine gaze? Or simply a desire to be left alone?

Her chin threatened to wobble. "I don't know. I suppose that's a tough question. We both have some thinking to do."

Later, she could hardly remember gathering her things and walking to her car. But there was one truth she couldn't escape. Lucas hadn't tried to stop her.

Crying wasn't even an option. She was stunned. Shocked.

Because her hands were shaking and she didn't trust her driving, she pulled over in a parking lot and tried to breathe. It was still early. Barely eight o'clock.

She took out her phone and found the contact she wanted. When the person on the other end answered, she swallowed hard. "Jeff. This is Leah Marks. Any chance you could meet me at the diner for a cup of coffee?"

Half an hour later, she sat across the table from the only person in Blossom Branch who really knew Lucas Carter. For five minutes, she poured out her heart, telling Jeff everything about the official letters and Lucas's stunning reaction. She also shared that she and Lucas had been getting close before today.

Not the intimate stuff, of course, though she was pretty sure Jeff read between the lines.

"I don't know what to do," she said, rubbing her eyes. They were gritty, as if she hadn't slept. But sadly, she was far too awake.

Jeff sat back in his chair and sighed. "I hate to say I told you so…"

"Then don't," she snapped. "You have to help me help him."

"This isn't a one-hour TV drama," Jeff said. "We're talking about a real man who suffered real emotional trauma."

"What do you think those letters are about?"

"I have no idea." Jeff shrugged. "But my boy Lucas is stubborn. If he says he doesn't want to know, then he really doesn't want to know."

Leah stared at him. "I don't like that."

"It's not up to us, though, is it?"

"No," she said. "I guess it's not. I think he may be done with me. I trespassed on private ground."

Jeff's wry gaze held sympathy. "We've all made relationship mistakes. It happens. For what it's worth, he's really hung up on you. Maybe he'll come around."

Remembering the look on Lucas's face made her shudder. "I don't think so. But I appreciate the pep talk." She summoned the waitress and paid for two coffees. "Thank you, Jeff. He's lucky to have you as a friend."

Jeff rolled to his feet and waited for Leah to join him. He patted her shoulder. "Give him time. Let the whole situation marinate. Who knows what will happen?"

Leah didn't have the luxury of wallowing in misery. Though her heart was heavy, and Lucas was never far from her mind, she had plenty of work to keep her busy. The gap between camp sessions had seemed long and full of promise, but it sped by in a flash.

Jeff's crew began building the shed by the pond on Thursday. The grocery deliveries started pouring in on Friday. Saturday, Jim showed up.

Leah met him by the kitchen, cocking her head and smiling. "You're twenty-four hours early," she said. "Did you miss this place?"

He chuckled. "I'll admit, I'm looking forward to a new crop of kids. The camp dynamic will be different this time."

"How so?"

"Because of the kids themselves. We may not have another Benjamin, but we'll have twenty more stories. Twenty more vulnerable souls."

"Now you're scaring me." Leah said it jokingly, but her words were true in part. It was a lot of responsibility not to screw up kids who were already fragile. She knew it was impossible to heal lifelong wounds in two weeks, but she wanted to do all she could. The students she had worked with at the alternative school when she was in college had broken her heart. So fierce and angry and sullen. It had taken almost the entire semester for them to trust her.

Jim walked with her to the boys' bunkhouse. "Everything smells clean," he said. "I like it. For some of our campers, that's a novelty by itself."

As they walked through, seeing the neatly made bunks and the spotless bathrooms, Leah knew she had to say something. "Jim…"

"Hmm?" He was distracted by the new hooks that had been installed near the showers.

Leah chewed her lip. "Don't count on Lucas for the fire safety thing this session."

Jim turned to face her. "Oh?"

"We had a difference of opinion, a pretty big argument." She grimaced. "I don't know if he'll be back."

Jim's gaze was measured, equal parts sympathy and curiosity. But he didn't push for details. "I'm sorry about that," he said lightly. "I liked him."

"Yeah. Me, too," Leah said.

She excused herself and walked up to the house. Other than a few phone calls, she felt ready for this session. Fully prepared. Loins girded. Mentally sharp.

Her personal life was another matter entirely.

After days of reflection—and replaying everything that had happened—she knew she owed Lucas an apology. Things had ended too abruptly. Though her words and actions in his apartment Tuesday night had been impulsive and not meant to cause harm, the end result had been the same. She had either hurt him or made him angry or both.

That was on her.

Confrontation had never been her strong suit. But she had learned that she could do hard things. Even if they weren't pleasant.

She sat down at the kitchen table and picked up her phone. Her fingers trembled and her palms were damp. In some ways, the possible severing of their fledgling romantic relationship was probably for the best. Lucas wasn't right for her. She wasn't right for him.

Though they were combustible in bed, they had no future.

But Leah grieved for the present.

Were her motives pure, even now? Was she contemplating an apology for her sake or his?

She missed him terribly.

Quickly, before she could change her mind, she composed a brief text and hit send.

I'm sorry Lucas. I stepped over a line. I shouldn't have pushed and pried.

Afterward, she stared at her phone screen, willing Lucas to answer. But there was nothing. Then—just as she had given up on hearing from him—her phone dinged.

It's possible I may have overreacted.

He followed the six words with a funny emoji.

Her heart leapt. Her fingers moved.

I hope we can still be friends.

She hit send before she could weigh her words. They were impulsive, but true.

Now, the lag in response time was longer. After all, the man was probably at work.

When Lucas's reply came, it took her breath.

With benefits???

The cheeky response both delighted and alarmed her.

She stared at her phone for long minutes, debating what to say. Was he seriously suggesting they pick up where they left off Tuesday night? Shouldn't they at least weigh the possibility that their sexual relationship was bound to lead to more eventual conflict? Could two such different people move forward without courting catastrophe? Or at the very least, a painful, inevitable separation?

Lucas was adamantly opposed to knowing anything about his family. He was a biological loner and he liked it that way. Leah, on the other hand, would always be surrounded by family—people she loved even when they made her mad or disappointed her.

It was impossible for her to imagine the kind of *unrooted* existence Lucas lived. He seemed to be happy, but even Jeff said his buddy struggled with darkness sometimes. As shocking as it had been, Leah knew she had seen a glimpse of Lucas's turbulent emotions concerning his past.

Because she didn't know what to say to Lucas's question,

she left his last text unanswered. Let him think she had gotten caught up in something at camp. Or was tied up on a phone call.

She would have to answer him eventually, but she needed time to weigh her options. With her emotions wistful and confused, she moved to the next thing on her list.

Sunday afternoon's camper arrival was pandemonium. Though Leah was less nervous than at the beginning of the first session, she still felt a flutter in her chest. Despite all efforts at organization, corralling twenty middle school kids was not an exact science.

She was struck by the physical range in this group. They were at an age where some had taken a growth spurt and others had not. A couple of the boys looked like full-grown men. A few of the tinier ones were dwarfed by girls who already had breasts and curvy hips.

After a very brief official greeting from herself and Jim and Peg, the schedule kicked into gear. An hour was allotted for unpacking and getting settled. Soon, the bell would ring for the evening meal.

She found Peg in the doorway to the girls' cabin. "I'm heading up to my place for half an hour," Leah said. "Call or text if you need me. I'll be back for dinner." Leah's role at Camp Willow Pond encompassed a little bit of everything. Supporting her staff. Keeping an eye out for problems. Working ahead on future camp sessions. Handling budgets and ordering and a million other details.

Peg smiled. Her gaze tracked her charges as they bounced around the room. "Will do. If we don't have a fire in the kitchen tonight, we'll already be ahead of the game."

Leah shuddered. "Don't even think about it. I'm hoping for low drama this session."

She strolled back up to the house, wondering if they really could make it through twelve days without a significant crisis.

As she rounded the corner, prepared to walk up her front steps, she came to a halt, her heart jumping into her throat.

Sprawled in a rocker was Lucas, looking just as luscious as his nickname implied. Jeans, a snug-fitting navy T-shirt. The same leather deck shoes.

He didn't smile when he saw her. His steady gaze was focused. Intense. A muscle in his jaw twitched. "I thought you were never going to show up," he said, the words a low rumble.

She swallowed hard and made herself ascend the steps until she stood in front of him. "I had no idea you were coming," she said. "I thought you knew camp started today."

"I knew," he said, the words terse.

"Then why are you here?" She kept her tone even, though she badly wanted to throw herself into his lap. Instead, she folded her arms around her waist.

He shrugged. "You never answered my last text."

"So that wasn't a rhetorical question?" she said, forcing a light tone. "Friends with benefits?"

"It was not." He rolled to his feet. "Are you mad at me?" he asked.

"No. Are you mad at *me*?"

"Not anymore." He glanced over his shoulder and back at her. "Can we go inside?"

Leah shivered. "Why?"

His eyes glittered. "Because I want to kiss you without an audience."

Her throat went dry. "Come in." She opened the door— which wasn't locked—and Lucas followed her into the house. She fancied she could feel his warm breath on the back of her neck.

In the small living room, she waited for her visitor to take a seat, but instead, he prowled. He didn't kiss her either.

She curled up in a deep armchair and waited.

Finally, he paused, standing at the window and looking out over camp. She had a feeling he wasn't seeing the view. After several minutes, he turned to face her. "I'm sorry I freaked out on you Tuesday night," he said. "I tell myself I've dealt with the past, but sometimes it slaps me in the face."

Leah swallowed, wondering how much that raw statement cost him. "I should never have touched your mail. I wasn't thinking. And it's not my business."

He winced. "If we're going to be lovers, it *is* your business. At least on some level."

Leah saw the muscles in his throat move as he swallowed. Despite his declaration about kissing her, he didn't seem particularly focused on that task. She twisted her hands. "It doesn't have to be. Not if you and I are casual."

He pulled a footstool in front of her chair and sat down so he was on eye level with her. "It occurred to me," he said slowly, "that our blowup Tuesday night might be a good excuse to call it quits. Before either of us gets in too deep."

Pain tightened her throat. "I had the same thought. So why are you here?"

He put his hands on her knees. She was wearing a denim skirt. His touch on her bare flesh burned. His thumbs caressed two sensitive spots on the inside of her legs.

"I couldn't give you up. Not yet."

That *not yet* tightened the knot in her belly. "You couldn't?"

"No. But I haven't been completely honest with you. And I think you deserve honesty."

"You told me you weren't a *minivan* or *making-babies* kind of man. I heard you loud and clear. It's okay, Lucas. I understand."

His expression was pained. "That's not the whole truth. The reason I don't do *permanent* is that I've never thought it was fair to a woman. My biological past is a blank slate. That's not what anyone wants for the father of their children."

"And the letter?" She brought it up again, knowing that any future they had, temporary or otherwise, was dependent on transparency.

The skin stretched tight across his cheekbones. "I've always been scared," he said quietly. "As much as I told myself I wanted answers, there was another part of me, a stronger part, that said to hell with the past. I am who I am. And I'm happy that way. But under those circumstances, I won't do marriage or fatherhood. That's *my* choice. I can't force it on anyone else."

"So where does that leave us?" She put her hands over his, feeling how warm he was, how strong.

Lucas flipped his hands palms up and curled his fingers with hers. "I think that's up to you, Leah."

She searched his face and saw nothing but uncertainty in his eyes, the same gut-wrenching uncertainty she felt. This man was going to break her heart. She knew it as well as she knew the sun would rise in the morning.

All the risks she had taken to start Camp Willow Pond paled in comparison to this moment. No matter how much confidence she had gained or how proud she was of her successes, to step out in faith—believing she and Lucas had something worth saving—was the riskiest venture of all.

Was she strong enough to see this through not knowing what waited at the other end of the road? Her stomach clenched. It had taken her a long time to get over Larry the turd. Not because he had been her soulmate. But because she had felt so foolish when it was all over. So naive and clueless and embarrassed.

That breakup had dented her emotional confidence badly.

She was a different woman now. Tougher. More resilient. Would the new Leah fare any better at recognizing what was real and what wasn't?

"We've wasted most of the week," she said. "And now camp has started again. You can't spend the night in this house, and I can't leave the property overnight."

"I understand. But you've said you can get away now and then during the afternoon or evening, right?"

"Yes. But what if those times are when you're working or

sleeping? What if we have to wait twelve more days to be with each other again?"

The ghost of a smile lifted the corners of his beautiful mouth. "I'll wait as long as it takes. Besides, I'm the boss. I have some flexibility. Whenever you want me, I'll do my best to be free."

She leaned forward and rested her forehead against his. "I want you now," she admitted. "But I have to make an appearance at dinner soon."

He cupped her face in his hands. "Then we'll make do with a kiss."

When he covered her mouth with his, something detonated deep in her gut. She had never known such intense passion, such desperate need. The kiss started out light and teasing for about five seconds, but quickly escalated. They devoured each other. Lucas dragged her out of the chair and into his lap—then onto the carpet. His big body covered hers.

"You make me doubt my sanity," he muttered. "All I can think about is having you. Naked. Willing. Available."

"I've missed you," she whispered. "So much."

Lucas nipped the side of her neck with sharp teeth. Suddenly, he cursed low under his breath and rolled away, stumbling to his feet and scraping his hands through his hair. The look of desperation on his face made her feel a little better about her own torment.

"I'm leaving," he said bluntly. "Call or text me when you know you can get away. I'm off Wednesday all day if that helps."

She scooted to her feet as well, smoothing her skirt self-consciously. "I'll see what I can do."

His hands fisted at his sides. "If this relationship isn't good for you, you can say so, Leah. I know I'm no bargain."

"Don't be absurd." She lifted her chin. "I care about you, Lucas. Whether you want me to or not. Spending time with you is important to me. I'll make it work."

He rolled his shoulders. "Should pleasure have to be work?" he asked wryly.

She stared at him, seeing the physical beauty, but even more than that the pure gold of the man he was. The honor. The humor. The dependability. He had endured so much, but life hadn't made him bitter or cruel.

"Important things in my life have usually involved effort or sacrifice," she said. "I love being with you, Lucas. In bed or out. You make me feel things no other man ever has. Whatever it takes, we'll find opportunities to be together. I promise you."

"This is about more than sex, Leah."

"Don't you think I know that?"

"I hope you do." His face reflected much of what she was feeling. Caution. Frustration. Confusion.

She glanced at her watch. "I'm sorry. They expect me down at the dining hall in ten minutes."

"I'm going," he said gruffly. "But I doubt I'll sleep tonight. I need you in my bed where I can hold you close."

Her smile was wistful. "We could have had that for five nights this week. Maybe it's a sign we should slow down."

"Not a chance, Leah. I want you like a man lost in the desert wants water."

"And when this fire between us burns out?" She was a grown woman. She knew the score.

"I can't predict the future," he said, his words uneven. "But I know what I want today and tomorrow. Is that enough?"

She nodded her head slowly. "I guess it will have to be. We'll take it one day at a time."

FIFTEEN

LUCAS ESCAPED LEAH'S HOUSE AND DROVE BACK INTO town, his stomach in knots. He wasn't accustomed to denying himself physical release. There was no other woman he wanted. Only Leah.

Standing so close to her, he hadn't even risked another kiss. He wasn't sure he had the strength to walk away. But tonight, he had no choice.

He'd known when he first met her that she was not going to pander to his whims. She lived a rich, fulfilling life without him. Earning her trust had been the first step.

This past Tuesday he had almost destroyed their connection beyond repair. He'd let old demons get the best of him. Those stupid letters. He couldn't get away from them. No matter how many he destroyed, they just kept coming.

He hadn't meant to hurt Leah. But he had. Remembering the look on her face when he shut her down so coldly made shame curl in his belly. Now he had another chance.

What terrified him even more than the persistent letters was the knowledge that he wanted what he couldn't have. Leah should belong to a man who could build a home with her. Watch her pregnant belly swell with new life. Plan a future together.

She shouldn't, couldn't belong to him. Because Lucas Carter belonged nowhere and to no one. No matter where he lived—Blossom Branch or the next town down the line—Lucas would always only be passing through.

For years he'd told himself he enjoyed the open road. With Leah at his side or in his bed, that lie no longer worked. He *wanted* to belong. But he could never undo the past, and he wouldn't ruin her future.

The emptiness in his home mocked him. It had never seemed unsatisfactory before now. This bland monthly rental suited him…or it had. Now, all he could think about was Leah's beautiful soft pink bedroom where she had let him know her intimately.

She'd had sex with him in his apartment, too. On the sofa. Crazy, hot, wonderful sex. Even now, the memories made him ache. When he was with her, he felt whole. Happy. Hopeful. The radiant light inside her almost banished the dark he carried.

Almost, but not quite.

He didn't know what to do. Leah deserved a man who was whole…and wholly committed to her. Lucas couldn't change who he was. He'd spent thirty-three years with nothing to tie him anywhere. It wasn't that he hadn't wanted anchors and roots. Anchors and roots had simply never been an option.

Because he felt like he was going to climb out of his skin, he changed into workout clothes and headed for the gym. He needed to push himself hard and long to outrun these feelings of doubt. Of hunger. Of dread.

Weights and the treadmill and punching bag were a start.

Three hours later when he finally made it back home, he

was exhausted but still in turmoil. His empty bed was nothing more than another place to miss Leah.

He couldn't let her get away. She belonged in his arms, warm and soft and sweetly sensual. He needed to tie her to him, to make sure she wouldn't leave. But how could he do that when he had nothing to offer in return?

The way he felt about his life with Leah in it was both intense and unique. He'd *never* wanted to be tied down. Why now? And why with her?

It occurred to him in one panicked moment that maybe he didn't want to answer those "whys" at all. It was far safer to leave his psyche unplumbed.

The status quo was his friend. Why mess with a good thing?

Monday morning, Leah was relieved when she realized they had made it through the first night of camp with no fires and no other commotion. Maybe this session would go more smoothly than the last one.

She felt guilty leaving camp and not telling Lucas. Still, this lunch date with Marisa had been on the books for a long time.

There were plenty of places to eat in Blossom Branch, but the Peach Crumble was always a favorite. She and Marisa had agreed to meet there at 11:45 a.m. to beat the lunch crowd. Leah hugged her friend when they both showed up at almost the same instant. The other woman was a little younger than Leah. They had bonded ever since meeting at the local library a year ago.

Marisa had been checking out exotic cookbooks. Leah's task that day was researching how to start a nonprofit. Now, they got together every six weeks or so.

When they were settled in a booth, Leah smiled. "I hope you've been enjoying your day off."

"If you call grocery shopping, paying bills, and vacuuming relaxing, then yes." Marisa wrinkled her nose. "I get so behind during the week."

"I know what you mean. Camp takes all my energy. I want to crash when I get home. But I did enjoy having my family over last weekend. Your food was a big hit."

"Enjoy?" Marisa raised an eyebrow. "The last time we talked, you were in a tizzy wanting to impress them all."

"True. But it turned out okay, I guess. I even admitted to my mother that I hadn't cooked everything."

"And?"

"She was decent about it. Told me she sometimes uses a caterer, and that I'll be a good cook, wife, and mother someday."

"Ouch. But at least it's over for now. I wish my parental obligations were so easily resolved."

After the waitress took their orders, Leah picked up the conversation. "What parental obligations?"

Marisa's expression was glum. "I don't know if I want to be a caterer anymore. But my parents sank a lot of money into my schooling. I can't let them down."

"I thought you had a scholarship."

"I did. Mom and Dad helped with housing expenses, though, and other things that weren't covered. They were thrilled when I came back to Blossom Branch and started my company."

"But?"

"It's not what I thought it would be. Your thing last week was a piece of cake. I love doing small dinner parties. It's the large corporate orders that are killing me. Assembly-line cooking is grueling."

"What do you want to do instead?"

"Honestly?" Marisa looked sheepish. "I think I'd enjoy baking cupcakes for my own kid's birthday party one day. Or catering a friend's bridal or baby shower. But that won't pay the bills, now, will it?"

When the food arrived, they tabled the serious talk. Marisa had lots of questions about camp. Leah had plenty of answers. They lingered until the restaurant began to clear out.

Finally, Leah circled back to the original topic. "Is it possible to pay them back?" she asked. "Erase the debt *and* the obligation?"

Marisa nodded slowly. "I could. It would take a fair amount of time. My profit is modest."

"Well, there's another way to go. My friend, Cate, lives in a ritzy section of Atlanta. I know she's mentioned a woman who will come to your house, prepare an entire meal, and take care of all the cleanup. Could you do something like that?"

"It would be expensive for the clients. The food and my time."

"Maybe so, but eating out is expensive. I imagine some families would love to splurge now and then. The thought of not having to go to a restaurant, not having to cook, and not having to clean up? I think people would jump at that."

Marisa nodded her head slowly. "You may be on to something. I'll prepare a few theoretical meals and run the numbers."

"It might be fun. You'd be with a different group of people every night. Hopefully interesting people..."

"I'll think about it," Marisa said. "It's not a bad idea."

"Well, while I'm meddling in your life, I have another question. Do you happen to know Jeff Grainger?"

Marisa blanched. Her eyes widened. "Why? Did he say I do?"

Leah was shocked. "Um, no. I've never mentioned you to him. But he's a nice guy and he's available. I thought you two might hit it off."

Marisa went paler still. "Nope. We dated once. It didn't work out." She stood hurriedly and slung her purse over her shoulder. The checks had already been paid. "I didn't realize how late it was," she said, sounding breathless. "This was fun, Leah, but I've got to run. We'll talk soon. Bye."

Before Leah could say a word, the younger woman was gone. How odd.

On the way back to camp, Leah was distracted. The Peach Crumble wasn't all that far from the fire station. Leah could have dropped by on some pretext. But the thought of seeing Lucas in his native environment was intimidating.

Besides, she didn't want to embarrass him. His crew already teased him.

Fortunately, she was immediately sucked back into the activities of camp. It wasn't until that night at bedtime that she spared a thought for what she would say to Lucas.

He was off all day Wednesday. Could she get away from camp for a few hours? The answer was yes. She grabbed her phone…

Why don't you come to camp for Wednesday lunch? Hot dogs and apple slices with homemade cookies. 😊 Afterward the kids have a couple of hours of pool time. I could go back to your apartment with you. Let me know if that works.

When she hit send, her face heated. Had she seriously just initiated a booty call? Ack. This whole dating thing was impossible. Lucas wanted her. She wanted him. But they couldn't spend all their time in bed. What did ordinary couples do?

For one thing, they didn't run a camp twenty-four seven. Or work twelve-hour shifts at the fire hall. Somehow, she and Lucas had to find their rhythm in this relationship. Whether or not they succeeded was anybody's guess.

Wednesday, it rained. Not a gentle shower, but a loud, stormy downpour. For adults, this was the worst time at camp. Most of the activities took place outdoors. Now, Camp Willow Pond had twenty active, disappointed kids to entertain.

Lucas showed up just before noon. Leah met him at his car, wearing a red rain slicker and holding a matching umbrella over her head. "I'm so sorry," she said, breathless and self-conscious. "When we have a rainy day, it's all hands on deck. I can't leave."

The twist of his beautiful, kissable lips was wry. "I suspected as much. I could do the fire safety thing today after lunch instead of Saturday like Jim and I had planned."

"Oh."

He cocked his head. "Oh, what?"

She swallowed. "I told him not to expect you, because you and I were…"

"Were what?" he asked quietly, his gaze stroking her like a physical caress.

"You know what I mean," she said, half cross with him and yet desperate to feel his arms around her.

He leaned under the umbrella and kissed her gently. "I do know, Leah. But you rise to the bait so beautifully." He moved closer. "If we tilt this thing the right way, nobody can see me do this." With one hand, he angled the umbrella so it covered them both—barely—but also blocked anyone's view. Not that it would have mattered. The rain was coming down in sheets. "Put your arms around my neck," he said.

"Okay." It never occurred to her to refuse. Not when the idea seemed so perfectly wonderful.

Lucas tugged her against him, close enough that she could feel his heart beating beneath her cheek. He kissed the top of her head. "I think I'm being punished for all my misdeeds," he said, with laughter in his voice.

She tilted her head to look up at him. Green-gold eyes sparkled beneath thick lashes. Water dripped off his nose and onto her cheek. "Then we're both being punished." She sucked in a breath, startled to realize that she was utterly and completely aroused by him. In the middle of the yard in broad daylight. Leah Marks. It boggled the mind. "Maybe you should go," she whispered. "This is torture."

He kissed her again, sliding his tongue between her lips and stroking hers. "It is," he agreed. "But it's my own dumb fault for wasting this week. We could have been together every night."

She grinned at him. "And sometimes in the middle of the

day. I have it on good authority that such things are perfectly acceptable."

Lucas's eyes darkened. He studied her face intently as if trying to decipher a secret code. "You make me ache," he said. "In every cell and bone. It's as if you're a fever, and I can't shake you."

Leah frowned. "That's not very flattering."

Her pique barely registered. He took her chin in his hand and kissed her again. Harder this time. More desperately. "Five minutes?" he asked, the words harsh and shaky.

She looked at him, dazed and confused. It wasn't as if she was punching a clock. "Not a second more," she whispered.

He took her by the hand and dragged her up the steps of her house. Leah fastened the dead bolt when they were inside. The moment she turned around, Lucas had her up against the wall with his hands under her damp shirt. He found her breasts and squeezed them through her lacy bra.

The groan he made sounded as if he was dying. "Take off your pants," he begged.

The fabric was wet from the knees down. It was a struggle. While she hopped on one foot, he found a condom in his pocket and unzipped his jeans.

Soon she was in his arms, and he was inside her and it felt like the whole world was a crazy whirl around them.

"Leah," he whispered. "I'm sorry. This isn't how I wanted it to happen."

She bit his bottom lip. "Then you shouldn't show up at my house looking hot and cute and sexy as hell."

"I put clean sheets on my bed," he complained.

"Poor baby." She cupped his cheek in one hand. "You have about ninety seconds left."

"Yes, ma'am." He sighed. "I wanted to impress you with my inventive foreplay."

Leah laughed, her heart turning over in her chest. "Next time, Luscious Lucas. Next time."

He shuddered and thrust hard until they both found what they wanted.

In the aftermath, Leah could hear her heart beating in her ears. "I can't believe we just did that."

He set her down carefully. "We're out of time, right?"

"Yes." She couldn't bear the thought of putting her wet pants back on, but on the off chance somebody remembered what she was wearing earlier, she did it anyway. When they were both decent, she kissed him and leaned into his warm, hard chest. "I'm glad you're here," she said softly. "Let's go eat."

Lucas was feeling shell-shocked and guilty. Leah was the kind of woman who deserved roses and romance. Not that she seemed to mind their wild coupling. In fact, the smug grin she gave him now and again said she was proud of herself.

He watched her as she worked the room. These kids had only arrived Sunday night, but already they responded to her. Smiles and hugs and laughter.

Lucas knew what that meant to a boy or girl who had come from difficult circumstances. They would be wary at first. Distrustful. But Leah's openness and genuine caring didn't let them stay in that negative space for long.

She was a nurturer. A fierce, loving presence. He wondered if this group of twenty kids had any idea how lucky they were to find themselves under her protective wings.

Even as the thought flitted across his mind, he realized why watching her disturbed him so. It was because he was seeing maternal devotion in action. Leah would be a wonderful mom one day. She was the kind of woman who should have three kids or four or maybe half a dozen. Her heart had plenty of room.

For a moment, Lucas allowed himself to grieve all he had missed. His childhood hadn't been bad. But there had been no one like Leah. No one who cared this deeply.

His foster families had ranged from kind and dependable to indifferent and lax. Never cruel. Never abusive.

But never like this. Never so generous with their love. Or maybe his foster families had come from their own difficult backgrounds. Maybe they had done the best they could—and with the best of motives.

By the time he was fourteen, he had quit asking himself *why?* Why had he been abandoned? Why had his parents said they would return? Why had they condemned him to never having a real family?

For the first time in years, those questions rattled through his brain.

Had his mother been anything like Leah or Peg? Had his father possessed Jim's quiet, sturdy strength? Where had his parents gone? Where were they now?

He thought of the envelope. The one he had shredded. Maybe a few of the answers were within reach. But honest to God, he couldn't bear the thought of being disappointed again.

Leah appeared at his side, her expression troubled. "Are you okay?" she asked, putting a soft hand on his arm and studying his face. "You look sad."

He shook off his mental funk. "Not sad," he lied. "Just hungry for that hot dog you promised me."

She laughed and urged him across the room to a small table for four. Jim and Peg had already finished their meal. The junior counselors had their own table.

"Sit down," Leah said. "I'll be back in a flash." She returned moments later balancing two earthenware plates and two plastic tumblers in her arms and hands. The camp had an industrial dishwasher. Everything was reusable.

Lucas relieved her of her burden. "This looks great," he said. "I haven't had a hot dog since the last Braves game."

"Our cooks try to strike a balance between nutrition and child-friendly choices. We'll even have steak one night, because that's a treat most of these kids wouldn't get at home. If you watch them over the course of camp, you realize they rarely leave any food on their plates. I think they eat it all because many of them have known true hunger."

He saw tears in her eyes. "Don't," he said. "You're doing a great thing here."

Her lips trembled. "It's only two weeks. That's like putting a tiny Band-Aid on a gaping wound. I can't alter the big picture."

"But you *are*," Lucas insisted. "When they go home, they'll remember this. And they'll have hope and purpose. Hope for the future and a determination to fight their way out of whatever hell they're living in. Believe me, I know."

"You told me your foster situations weren't terrible."

"That's true. But occasionally, a friend would invite me home after school. I saw what a real family looked like. A permanent family. A unit. Even though I had to go back to my temporary world, I remembered those peeks into normalcy. I focused on the idea that one day I might find my own permanence. A place where I didn't have to move every few weeks or months. A place where the scenery wasn't going to change again and again. Never underestimate the power of hope, Leah. It's what you're giving these kids."

She looked at him, her eyes still shiny with emotion. "Thank you," she said. "That means a lot."

Soon, the noise level in the room increased as lunch wound to a close. Jim came with a request. "Hey, Lucas. Leah said you wouldn't mind doing your fire safety gig right now instead of Saturday. I've looked at the radar. We should be able to swim in another hour. But I need to buy some time."

"Sure," Lucas said. "I don't have my gear, but I'll wing it."

Leah was feeling weirdly emotional. Camp Willow Pond was so very important to her. As was Lucas. Having those two worlds collide again and again was not entirely comfortable.

God willing, she would be running this camp long after Lucas exited her life. She didn't want him lodged in every memory and every corner of the property.

But he had been there from day one. What could she do?

When the last of the dishes were cleared, Jim quieted the room and introduced Lucas. Like last time, Lucas connected with the kids easily. Once he had covered the basics and answered questions, he threw in a few funny stories about being a fireman. The time he'd had to rescue someone's pet monkey from a telephone pole. And how his buddies at another fire station had pranked him by greasing the fire pole and making him fall on his ass.

The kids loved it.

Finally, Jim signaled for silence and announced that it was time to change and get ready for swim time. Cheers went up from almost everyone. During the first camp session, Leah had learned quickly that she would always have one or two campers who were scared of the water or self-conscious about wearing a swimsuit. The counselors had been trained in how to make kids in either situation feel more comfortable.

Outside, the air was thick and humid.

Lucas didn't touch her, not in such a public space, but his gaze was hot with intent. "Are we going to my apartment now?" he asked.

Before she could answer, movement caught her eye. A car. Coming up the driveway at a fast clip. The vehicle parked, and her brother Keith stepped out. When he waved, Leah turned to Lucas and sighed. "You may as well go home. I'll call you later."

"And we'll get together? For dinner? And whatever?"

She grinned at him. "I'll do my best. Besides, we've already…" She trailed off, waving her hand, feeling her cheeks get hot.

Lucas shook his head slowly, his expression turbulent. "Believe me, Leah. That was only an appetizer."

SIXTEEN

LEAH WATCHED LUCAS STRIDE AWAY...SAW HIM PAUSE briefly to say a word to Keith before climbing into his own car and disappearing down the drive.

Keith walked up and hugged her. "Hey, sis."

She returned the hug. "What are you doing here?"

"I fly back to Africa tomorrow."

"So soon?" She felt an ache of sadness at the thought of him being far, far away again. "You want to come up to the house for a drink?"

"Sure," he said. "No iced tea on the job in Africa. I'll miss this."

They sat across from each other at the kitchen table. "Are you happy?" she asked impulsively.

His gaze narrowed. "Completely. But what about you?"

"Me?" She gulped mentally.

"Yeah, you. First this Lucas person shows up at a family dinner. Now he's hanging out at camp. What's going on?"

She tilted her chin. "We're having fun, that's all."

Keith tipped his chair back on two legs and frowned. "That doesn't sound like the Leah I know."

"I'm headed toward thirty, Keith. I gave up on happily-ever-after a long time ago. Happy for now works. Besides, I've seen women parade in and out of your life for years. Double standard, you think?"

He winced at her sarcasm. "I suppose. But you're my baby sister. I'm supposed to look out for you. I don't want some gorgeous fireman with jock abs to hurt you."

"So you admit he's gorgeous?"

"Well, of course he is. In a rugged, take-no-prisoners way. That doesn't mean I want him toying with your affections."

"You've been watching too much Britbox on cable. Lucas and I understand each other. You have nothing to worry about." She paused. "Did you come here today to critique my love life, or is there something else on your mind?"

"I have an idea for camp," he said.

"Let's hear it."

"Well," he said, "when I was out here the other day, something struck me. You have a lot of land you're not using yet, even with the peach orchard. What would you think about starting a large garden next spring? Your campers could participate and learn valuable skills. Maybe they might even have a produce stand and share the profits to do things like buy movie tickets or special rewards. I don't know. Is it crazy?"

Leah stared at him. "I love that, Keith. Really, I do. But I wouldn't know where to start."

He smirked. "Luckily, you have a brother in the biz. You and I could spend the winter mapping out the idea. Figuring out what to plant and when. We can email and FaceTime. I'm sure you could hire somebody local to do the actual planting for you next year."

She exhaled as she paced, seeing the possibilities. "I'm surprised every day that this camp ever came to fruition. Now you're telling me we can do even more. It's a lot to take in. And all because of Aunt Trudie."

"No," Keith said firmly. "Because of *you*, Leah. Your inheritance might have financed this, but *you* had the vision and the passion. I'm proud of you, sis. You're doing a great thing here at camp. Mom and Dad were impressed when you brought us all out here, even if they didn't say the right things."

Leah wrapped her arms around his neck from behind. "It means a lot to hear you say that. Thank you."

He stood and faced her. "I think we've spent years ignoring and underestimating you. I'm as much to blame as any of the family. But you were our cute little plaything. The girl in frilly dresses who played with baby dolls. We three guys had no clue what to do with you."

"You loved me." She smiled. "That's what counts. I was a late bloomer. But now that I'm doing something important with my life, it's exciting."

"And your fireman?"

She shrugged, trying not to blush when she thought about what had happened in this very room right before lunch. "He's not *my* anything. By the time you make your next visit to the States, Lucas and I will probably be old history."

"Why would you say that?" The concern on his face was genuine.

"Lucas is not the marrying kind. He told me that from the beginning. We're good friends. That's all."

"I'm a guy, Leah. I saw the way he looked at you. The man wants more than milk and cookies. Surely you aren't that naive."

"And if he does?" She glared at her brother. "I'm entitled to a sex life."

Keith covered his ears. "Yes. Yes," he said. "But I don't want to hear about it."

Leah laughed. "I can't wait till you get married and have daughters. It will be fun watching you squirm."

"Maybe I'm like Lucas. Not the marrying kind." He hugged her. "I'll miss you, Leah. You know you can talk to me about anything. Even when I'm thousands of miles away. I care about what's happening in your life. Especially if this Lucas person tries to break your heart."

"Thank you," she said. "I appreciate it. But my heart is safe, I swear."

By the time she sent Keith on his way, Leah knew she had lied to him. Her heart wasn't safe at all. But she wasn't going to hide from her feelings. Even knowing what the future might hold, she was going to enjoy Lucas's company while it lasted.

When she checked in with Jim and Peg, she saw that the swim session was in full swing. Watching the kids laugh and bounce around in the water made her smile. It hit her suddenly that *she had done it*! In one crystalline moment of clarity, satisfaction wrapped her in a warm glow. Camp Willow Pond was a success. Everything she had hoped for and dreamed about was happening.

Would there be further challenges? Sure. But now she had the confidence to believe nothing was beyond her capabilities.

That assurance was an amazing feeling.

Peg was perched in a chair beside the lifeguard stand, watching the kids, as though the lifeguard's two eyes weren't enough. Jim hovered nearby, also on high alert. When he saw Leah, he waved.

She joined them, and they chatted briefly about a few alterations in the schedule. Then Jim smiled. "Everything is under control for now, boss," he said. "Why don't you cut out for a few hours? Peg and I can handle things." Peg nodded, never taking her eyes off the pool. "Yep. You've done a lot of work while the rest of us were taking an eight-day break. You need to breathe now and then."

Leah felt shaky, but she smiled. "Well, I might run into town, in that case. You'll call if you need me?"

"Of course." Jim shooed her away. "Have fun. We'll see you later."

Leah felt as if her plans were written on her face for all the world to see. Did anyone suspect? Or why would they care?

She excused herself and walked up the hill feeling a mix of emotions that denied explanation. She was far too old to be acting like a teenage girl with her first crush. What she and Lucas did in private was nobody's business.

But even saying the word *private* in her head made her blush.

In the house, she showered and dried her hair. She threw her damp jeans in the laundry room and kicked them, anything to let off some of the nervous energy that made her more jittery than three back-to-back cups of coffee.

Finally, she sent a text.

I can get away for a couple of hours. You want to eat an early dinner at the new Italian place?

She read the words three times and hit send. As far as she could tell, the message didn't sound like she was desperate to jump his bones.

His reply was prompt.

I'm used to eating at odd hours. I'll meet you there at 4:30. That leaves us plenty of time for...

He added a laughing emoji.

She covered her face with her hands. Impossible. The man was impossible.

Because it was a hot day, she wore a sundress. Not because

it made her waist look small and her legs long, but for practical reasons, she told herself. She was determined to convince Lucas she was calm and cool. *Not* in a sex-crazed tizzy.

When she parked at Mamma Mia's, hers and Lucas's were the only cars in the lot. Even the senior crowd was still at home. He met her just inside the door, wearing the same clothes he'd been wearing in the rain. His smile was gentle and sweet.

"Hey, sunshine. I've already asked for a table." He scanned the empty restaurant, laughing. "They said we could have our choice." He kissed her cheek. "You look beautiful."

"Thank you." Her hands were cold and clammy. She wasn't even sure she could eat. For one instant, she was mad at him. This was a huge deal to her, though for Lucas, she was just another woman. Another temporary woman.

Lucas wasn't stupid. When they were seated, he cocked his head and stared at her. "Something's wrong. Did your brother upset you?"

"Keith? No. He had an idea for creating a garden at camp next spring."

"Vegetables freak you out?"

"Stop," she hissed, trying to keep her voice low. "This isn't a joke. This is my life, my town. I'm not in the mood for comedy."

He sobered rapidly. "What's going on?"

Tears stung her eyes. It was mortifying to realize she was having what appeared to be an anxiety attack. "Nothing," she muttered.

The waitress brought menus and waters. Lucas smiled at the woman. "Give us a few minutes, please."

When they were alone again, he sighed. "Talk to me, Leah. I'm not a mind reader."

"I know that. I'm embarrassed."

"Why?" The single word was gentle.

"I'm in my twenties—not even my *early* twenties—but I

don't know how to handle a man like you. I don't know how to have this kind of relationship."

He stared at her. "There aren't any rules. We'll do whatever you want." He rubbed the back of his neck. "I though kissing each other in the rain was romantic. But maybe I misread the signals."

Leah glanced over her shoulder, making sure the server wasn't listening. "It wasn't the rain," she said, feeling her neck get hot. "It was the wall in my living room!"

"Ah." He sat back in his seat, his expression inscrutable. "I'm sorry," he said. "You could have said no. I understand what the word means."

She saw on his face that she had either hurt or insulted him. Both were bad. "Oh my gosh, Lucas. You know I was with you a hundred percent."

"Then what's the problem?" His question was quiet, measured.

"I'm not that woman," she said, the words shaking along with the rest of her body.

"I think you are. You're passionate and warm and sexy as hell."

"No one has ever described me that way before. And to be honest, I've never seen myself that way either."

"Maybe you've been hiding your true personality," he said. "Maybe your capacity for erotic pleasure scares you. So you pretend you're boring and ordinary, when you're not."

She stared at him, frustrated. "It's you," she said. "You turn me into someone I don't recognize."

"Are you saying you don't like her? The wild and wanton woman?"

It was a valid question. Did she? What she felt when Lucas made love to her was so incredibly exhilarating, it terrified her. Wasn't it safer to stay in her lane? "It's not that I don't like her," she said. "But I don't have a script for this. I feel dumb and awkward and out of my depth. I get that we're having fun and we aren't in it for the long haul."

"But?"

"I don't know what you expect from me," she said baldly.

He played with the butter knife beside his plate, his gaze on the table. Then he lifted his head. "Let's call a time-out," he said. "Dinner and conversation. After that, we can go back to my place and talk through this. Does that work for you?"

Relief flooded her chest. "Yes. I would like that."

Lucas hailed the waitress. They ordered lasagna for Lucas and chicken marsala for Leah. When the meal came, the portions were huge and delicious and tasted homemade.

Leah managed to eat a third of hers and asked for a box. Lucas ate more, but also requested a to-go container.

Probably because neither of them was in a hurry for the confrontation to come, they stayed at the table as other diners began to trickle in.

"So tell me more about you," Lucas said. "Tell me what it was like to be a kid growing up in Blossom Branch."

"It was pretty wonderful," she said, thinking back to simpler times. "The area was smaller then. Fewer transplants. But the core of town is still the same as it was. The quad. The gazebo. The shops around the rectangle. When we were little, we ate at the diner every Friday night. Then we would walk the streets and window-shop. In summer, we would pick peaches or buy them and make ice cream."

"And the friends I've heard you mention?"

"Gabby and Cate went to school with me at Blossom Branch Elementary. But back then, our families didn't socialize. Our parents may have crossed paths in the parking lot, but they didn't know each other really. Cate's father was ambitious and moved them to Atlanta when she was twelve or so. Her grandparents have always lived here, so she came back for summers year after year."

"What about the other one? You went to Atlanta to see her recently?"

"That would be Gabby. She was raised by a single mom. They lived very close to the edge financially. But Gabby is incredibly smart. She got scholarships and now has a great job in Atlanta. Finance stuff."

"So if you didn't spend a lot of time together outside of school, why are you so close?"

Leah smiled, reminiscing. "We all three ended up at the University of Georgia as freshmen. During orientation, we were so homesick and feeling a little lost. We bonded over our common childhoods. Cate was the one who made sure we joined a sorority. She took us under her wing. I was super shy. Gabby didn't initially feel comfortable with sorority life because of her background. We've been close ever since."

"And Blossom Branch?"

"It will always be our touchstone, I think. Gabby's mom is still here. And you know my parents are in Gainesville close by. There's something about this town, something almost magical. It may grow and change in some ways, but it preserves the best parts of the past. Family. Community. I can see myself living here forever, I think. Cate has even opened a business on the square."

He nodded, his expression hard to read.

While they waited for the check, Lucas tapped the laminated menu tucked between the salt and pepper shakers. "I guess not everyone jumps on board with the peach theme. Mamma Mia? Not entirely original."

"True. But how do you tie Italian food to peaches?"

"I'll have to think about that," he said, laughing.

The restaurant had begun to fill up, so it took some time to pay the check.

Soon, they were outside carrying their leftovers and feeling the humidity of a warm summer evening.

Leah turned to walk toward her car.

Lucas put a hand on her arm. "Let me drive," he said. "We can pick up your car later. Please."

She searched his face. "Okay." This meant she couldn't bolt if things got heated. But she trusted Lucas to honor her wishes when she said she had to go.

He put the containers of garlic-laden food in his trunk, then opened her door. She slid into her seat, taking in the smell of masculine driver and warm leather. It was an irresistible combo.

At Lucas's apartment, they stowed the food in the fridge and sat down in the living room. Leah's feelings of awkwardness returned. She might have made huge strides in her professional life, but on a personal note, she still lacked confidence. Maybe *she* was the problem. Maybe her lack of wide sexual experience made her an unsuitable partner for Luscious Lucas.

He took the seat across from her and bounced one knee, the only sign that he might be unsettled, too. At last, he sighed. "I care about you. A lot. And I'll admit, the attraction was there from the moment I met you. You tried to tell me you were too busy for a relationship, but I didn't listen."

"In the words of someone recently, I could have said no. But I didn't want to," Leah said. "I don't regret the things we've done. It's been an incredible experience."

He grimaced. "Am I about to get kicked to the curb? This sounds remarkably like a brush-off. Are we calling it quits?"

"I don't want to." The words hurt her throat. "But I also don't want to see you for brief moments that are only sex. The sex is great, don't get me wrong. But I like you as a friend, too. I don't know how to go forward in this relationship."

He stood abruptly and came to sit with her on the sofa, taking one of her hands between his and warming her fingers. His gaze was intent. "I know I can't give you what you need in the long term. Or maybe it's presumptuous of me to expect that you would want me in that way. But I promise you this…"

She saw muscles in his throat work. There wasn't a hint of lightheartedness or humor on his face. His expression was almost grim.

"What, Lucas? What do you promise me?"

He cleared his throat. "I promise that as long as we're together, you'll have *all* of me. Fully committed to you. I want more than your body. I want *you*."

The lump in her throat receded. Her stomach stopped its mad whirl of uncertainty. She believed him. He was being as honest as he knew how. No wedding rings. But no cheating. "I want you, too, Lucas. All in. All the way. I care about you. You make me smile and laugh and burn for you. So yes. I want this. I want you."

He exhaled sharply as if he really had been in fear of what her answer might be. "Thank God," he muttered. "That flirty sundress has tormented me for the last hour and a half. How soon do you have to be back at camp?"

"If we go pick up my car a little bit before eight, I can be back at camp for evening campfire. I'm speaking tonight about hopes and dreams. We don't do one every night, but tonight is one of them."

Lucas nodded. "We'll have you back on time, I swear."

"Thank you for understanding."

"My job is important to me, too," he said. "I won't dismiss yours."

She rubbed his knuckles. "If the serious part of the evening is over, could we adjourn to your bedroom and those clean sheets?"

He raised an eyebrow. "For the record, I'm *very* serious about sex with you, Leah Marks. It's all I could think about today. The quickie before lunch only made me want you more."

"It was pretty awesome," she admitted, wishing she could talk about this without blushing.

He cupped her hot cheek in one hand. "You're cute when

you're shy. But I love the fact that when we're intimate, you *forget* to be shy."

Wide-eyed, she looked up at him. "I do, don't I?"

His grin made her blush even more. "Oh yeah, babe. You're lightning in my arms."

She put her arms around his neck. "For the record, I know your guys call you Luscious Lucas, and for good reason, but I love your honor and your kindness—to me, to my camp kids... and the way you treat your crew like family. You're a special man."

For once, she'd had the last word.

His eyes darkened. He stood and scooped her into his arms. "Let's not waste time," he muttered. "I'm thinking three at least."

As he turned and eased her through the doorway to his bedroom, she croaked. "Three? Really?"

His masculine smile was filled with determination and hunger. "Yep."

When he set her on her feet beside the bed, she didn't have time to be shy. Lucas lowered her zipper, slid the dress down her body, and tossed it aside when she stepped out of it. Now, she stood naked in front of him, but for a tiny pair of teal undies. She hadn't bothered with a bra this afternoon.

Lucas wasn't smiling anymore. The breath sawed in and out of his lungs. His chest heaved. "I want you so much it scares me."

She wondered if he meant to say that. Again, the prospect of big, macho Lucas Carter being scared of anything seemed unlikely.

"You're still dressed," she pointed out. "Maybe I could help."

He stood perfectly still, his powerful frame rigid as she unbuttoned his soft cotton shirt and pulled it away. Then she worked at his belt buckle and unzipped his jeans. Snug, black cotton boxers did nothing to disguise the power of his erect sex.

She lost her nerve. "You can finish," she whispered.

When they were both down to a single item of clothing, he took her hand and dragged her onto the bed. His sheets smelled of sunshine and fabric softener. They were plain white. Soft. Welcoming.

Lucas came down beside her on his elbow. "Have I told you how much I love your breasts?" he asked.

It appeared to be a rhetorical question. Instead of waiting for an answer, he buried his face in her cleavage and sighed. When he brushed his fingertip over one nipple, Leah gasped. How had she never known she wanted to be touched like that?

She slid her fingers through his thick, silky hair, holding him to her. His hands were everywhere all at once, kindling fires, barely giving her a chance to breathe from one shuddery delight to the next.

By the time he shed his boxer briefs and took care of protection, she was desperate, needy. When he moved between her legs, she closed her eyes.

Lucas changed the script yet again. "Look at me, babe," he said. The words were a soft command undergirded with steel. Drunk on arousal, she lifted her lashes and stared at him. He was on his knees. A dark flush of color rode high on his cheekbones. He looked like a warrior about to enjoy the spoils of battle.

"Look at me," he said a second time. When he was sure he had her attention, he caressed her intimately through the thin fabric of her panties.

She moaned and instinctively pressed her thighs together.

Lucas's low laugh raised gooseflesh all over her body.

"You can't hide from me, Leah," he said. "I want all of you, body and soul."

It wasn't fair. Her heart wept. How could he demand her soul and not want forever?

But the time for rational thought was over.

He touched her again and again until a flash-fire orgasm

ripped through her body. While she arched blindly into the pleasure, he removed her last item of clothing and mounted her with a raw groan.

The sensation of being filled while she still quivered in the throes of her climax was almost unbearably intense. Despite their morning coupling, they moved together frantically, trying to get closer, and closer still.

Lucas rode her hard, his big body pressing her into the mattress. She inhaled his scent, felt his damp skin, heard his labored breathing.

And when he came hard, shouting her name, another small, less intense ripple of orgasm carried her with him all the way to the end.

Her skin cooled as the room grew dim. The sun would have dropped low by now. Night was on the way.

She wanted to spend it with him.

That certainty caught her off guard and left the bitter taste of regret.

Nothing about this relationship was going to be easy. She had known the timing was wrong. But she wanted him enough to ignore her doubts. That meant risking everything. It was scary, but the new Leah realized Lucas was worth a roll of the dice.

The man barely moved. Was he breathing? He was a deadweight holding her captive. When she tried to glance at the clock or her watch, he mumbled something and rolled onto his back.

Thankfully, it was only seven fifteen. She scooted from the bed, used the bathroom, and found her clothes and shoes. When she was dressed, she touched him on the shoulder. He had one arm slung over his face.

"I know," he said. His words were like sandpaper and gravel, all sulky and disgusted.

When he rolled to his feet, she had a front row seat to magnificence. He was still semi-aroused, and under her gaze, his erection flexed and rose.

"I'll wait in the living room," she said, averting her eyes.

"Good idea." His grumpy sarcasm made her smile.

She grabbed her leftovers from the fridge and perched on a chair, marveling that she had the power to make him respond like that. What did it mean? Random attraction? Plain ole horniness?

If there really were some matches that were meant to be, this wasn't one of them. Their long-term life goals were too different. But until their time ran out, she would be a fool to walk away.

Lucas had changed her world. He had shown her the power in *her* sexuality and in *their* compatibility. For the first time in her life, she was glad she was young and female and in need of sex. What if she had gone on living in her familiar rut? Would she have eventually settled for a tepid marriage with a man who was okay but not great?

Then again, maybe Lucas had ruined her for other men. That was a depressing thought.

When he came out of the bedroom, he was fully dressed. "Let's go," he said.

They didn't speak on the short drive to the restaurant. When Lucas pulled up beside her car, she hopped out. Then she leaned in the open passenger window and tried to smile. "Thank you for dinner," she said.

He snorted. "That's all?"

"Maybe *you* should thank me for the sex," she snapped.

"Nope. I was talking about the fact that you're gonna get in your car and drive away without another word. I'm not okay with that, Leah Marks. I need a few promises."

"Such as?"

"Daily phone calls. Until we can align our schedules again."

She nodded. "That's doable."

"I have night shift the next four days. So I'll be sleeping while you're running camp. Maybe a four o'clock call before I go back to work and you deal with dinner?"

"I'll try."

"Try hard," he said. "I need to hear your voice."

SEVENTEEN

LUCAS SAT MOTIONLESS BEHIND THE WHEEL AND watched Leah drive away until he could no longer see her car. Then he was forced to move his vehicle, because the parking lot was hopping and busy.

He couldn't go home yet. Instead, he drove out into the country. With his windows down, the scent of peaches filled the air. After only six months, he loved this place, this town of Blossom Branch. Which spelled trouble. His life only worked if he had the freedom to hit the road when the time came. He'd moved on dozens of times over the years. It was the only way he knew how to be.

Wanting permanence used to be a dream of his. But honestly, too many painful disappointments had taught him to keep his distance. To protect his heart. No long-term relationships with people *or* towns.

He didn't want to love Blossom Branch. He didn't want to love Leah Marks.

And he didn't. He honestly didn't. It was just that he and she had this incredible sexual connection. Though the night was pleasant, sweat dampened his brow.

Images of Leah in his bed played in his brain on an infinite loop.

He was so screwed. No woman had ever gotten to him this fast. No woman had ever elicited this degree of desperation in his gut.

When he returned home, he prowled the house. He needed to stay up until at least 4:00 or 5:00 a.m. so he could go to sleep deeply and wake up refreshed enough to make it through a twelve-hour rotation tomorrow night. This changing back and forth on shifts was never fun, but he knew how to do it. A couple of shots of whiskey might knock him out. That would be a last resort. He didn't want to wake up groggy.

As he walked through his apartment turning off lights and setting the AC on the frigid temperature that helped him relax, he thought of Leah in her bed at camp. Snoozing. Peaceful. In a few hours when Lucas finally went to sleep, Leah would just be getting her day started.

He showered and dried off, trying not to think about the fact that she had been naked in his bathroom, his bedroom. The images in his head were impossible to shake. The urge to get in his car and drive out to camp was strong. But he resisted. For him to show up in the middle of the night would be entirely inappropriate.

Leah owned the camp. She was in charge. He would never intentionally do anything to embarrass her.

At last, he decided he was calm enough and tired enough to conk out. He slid naked beneath the covers and told himself her scent wasn't on his pillows.

It was a lie.

She was everywhere…

The rest of the week dragged by. He did manage to speak to Leah each afternoon, but the conversations were rushed and ultimately unsatisfying. Adding to his unsettled mood was the fact that it was a slow time at the fire hall.

That was a positive thing, of course. Any firefighter knew that a big part of the job involved waiting. A quiet day meant no one was in danger.

These were the times when the crew washed the two trucks. Restocked equipment. Caught up with online training modules.

It was a good series of days. Only it wasn't.

Saturday night brought a reprieve. Sometimes when Lucas worked in the evenings, Jeff picked up sub sandwiches, brought them to the fire hall, and the two men sat outside at the picnic table to eat. It was especially nice this time of year.

Lucas was glad to see his buddy. He needed to talk about sports or current events or Jeff's business or *anything* besides women. Jeff popped the tab on a beer for himself. He'd brought a soft drink for the man on the clock.

"It's an awesome night," Jeff said. "Too bad we're not out on the lake fishing." Lake Lanier was a playground for water activities of all kinds.

Lucas nodded. "It's been ages. I'm not sure I remember how to bait a hook."

"At least you have a woman in your life," Jeff said. "I'm in the midst of a dry spell."

"Let's skip this subject." Lucas groaned inwardly. "I don't know how long things with Leah will last. She needs a guy who will settle down in Blossom Branch, somebody who wants a family."

Jeff eyed him curiously. "Somebody like me?"

For a moment, Lucas actually thought the top of his head was going to blow off. Something hot and dangerous roiled through his veins and sent his heart racing. "No," he said curtly, grinding his jaw. "Not like you at all."

"Then who? Leah Marks is a fantastic woman. Smart, cute, funny. When are you going to stop running, Lucas?"

Lucas bristled. "Who says I'm running? It was your idea for me to move to Blossom Branch."

"Yes, and from where I'm sitting, the job and the town have been a great fit for you. You're happy, right?"

"I'm too busy to think about it. What does that word even mean? Life is good. Isn't that enough?"

"Maybe." Jeff shrugged. "I've known you a long time. Usually, I can tell when you're restless, ready to move on. Am I getting those vibes now?"

Lucas jumped to his feet and wadded his trash into a ball. "I don't know. You tell me since you're such an expert on my life."

Jeff stood as well, his expression sober. "I don't want to see you lose out on something special. You're my friend. I'd like to have you around until we're old enough for rocking chairs."

That image was impossible for Lucas to imagine. He'd crisscrossed the country in the last decade. As a kid, he'd had no control over permanence, but the adult Lucas hadn't made a stab at it either.

Even he could see the irony.

Was it too late? Could he change his ways? The prospect was tantalizing.

Blossom Branch was everything he wanted when it came to a job and a community. And Leah was perfect for him.

Unfortunately, he wasn't who she needed. It would be irresponsible of him to father children with his blank background, and it was impossible to imagine her not giving birth to babies that carried her own DNA.

Adoption was always an option in his life. But is that the route Leah would want to go? It didn't make sense.

Even when he tried to imagine himself changing his spots, trying life a new way, he ran into the same old dead ends.

"I need to get back inside," he said.

Jeff nodded, his gaze resigned. "Sure. I'll see you around."

★ ★ ★

On Sunday morning, the atmosphere at Camp Willow Pond reached fever pitch. Today was the Fourth of July, and all the kids were giddy about a slate of special activities, especially the fireworks to come later that evening.

Leah found herself here, there, and everywhere, lending a hand whenever she was needed. Lunch was a hamburger cookout followed by fresh-cut watermelon. The kids were messy and loud, but there was no rain in the forecast, so that was a win.

She hadn't bothered to text Lucas because she knew he was sleeping. But around one o'clock, she finally sent him a note.

Would you like to come out to camp for fireworks tonight? Pizza at 6?

Never had she felt more torn. Professionally, her heart was full. This second session of camp had cemented her confidence. They'd had a few bumps in the road—one small broken bone, two spider bites, and a slew of bruises when two of the older boys got into a rolling-on-the-ground fistfight.

Still, camp was a success. The children were happy and involved, and they had responded well in the small groups. In fact, it had been amazing to see them open up and talk about the challenges in their lives.

Yet all the while, Leah missed Lucas fiercely.

When he finally responded to her text, it was a single word... Yes!

She smiled when she read it. It had been the better part of four days since she had seen him. Even surrounded by a crowd tonight, at least they would be together.

Blossom Branch always put on a spectacular fireworks display. Leah and Jim and Peg had discussed piling their charges into the new vans and taking them into town. But the crowds would make it hard to keep up with twenty kids, so that was a safety concern. Plus it would have meant a later than normal bedtime and cranky campers tomorrow.

In the end, Jim found a buddy of his who did pyrotechnics for a living and was willing to give Camp Willow Pond a great show at a discounted price.

The midafternoon block was swim time again. Leah slipped away to shower, wash her hair, and change into a fresh outfit for the evening. She chose stretchy black capris with white sneakers and a red, white, and blue shirt. Because of the heat and humidity, she pulled her hair into a high ponytail and tied it with a red scrunchie.

She realized the feeling in the pit of her stomach was nervous anticipation. This relationship with Lucas had developed against long odds. She didn't know his favorite color or which season he preferred. There hadn't been much of a getting-to-know-you phase.

But somehow, she *knew* him. And she liked to think he knew her, too.

Because Leah wanted to give the kitchen staff the holiday off to spend with their families, dinner had been ordered in advance from Peach-aria. The count had been difficult. Some middle school boys could probably consume an entire pizza.

So she erred on the side of plenty. She had ordered eighteen large pies spread between pepperoni, plain cheese, bacon, pineapple, and beef. Plus two medium veggies. Something for everybody.

The food was going to be delivered at six fifteen. Right now, half of the junior counselors were wrangling the kids in the cabins while the other half were helping Jim and Peg set up tables and cover them with red-checked tablecloths.

Lucas showed up before the pizza. He found Leah wrestling with rolling a large empty barrel.

He kissed her cheek, both of them conscious they were being

watched. "Let me," he said. "Move over. What are you doing anyway?"

She was flustered and hot. But she couldn't blame it all on the unwieldy barrel. "Between pizza and fireworks, we're going to have games. This is for the baseball toss. You can put it there by the fence, please."

He looked amazing. It felt as if they'd been apart four weeks and not four days. Lucas was wearing navy board shorts and a red T-shirt that said *Fire Safety Is No Joke!* His broad shoulders and flat belly might have made a lesser woman swoon. Leah didn't have time for such nonsense.

"I'm glad you're here," she said. And then, because she believed in honesty, she touched his arm ever so briefly. "I've really missed you."

He froze, letting the barrel thump to the ground, barely missing his toe. When he stared at her, she saw the muscles in his throat work as he swallowed. His sunglasses were tucked in his pocket. Which meant she could see the tiny squint lines beside his green and amber eyes. "I've missed you, too, Leah. A lot."

His gaze seared her. For a moment, everything around them faded away. Leah hadn't known until now that such a thing could happen. "I love this camp," she whispered. "But I wish we were alone."

"You have no idea." The gruff note in his voice made her shiver.

She shifted from one foot to the other. "You want to eat?"

"Sure."

As they walked across camp to where the tables were set up, Leah was very conscious of Lucas's hand resting on the small of her back. It was such a simple thing, but it made her feel special.

She smiled at him. "I'm so glad you didn't have to work tonight."

"Me, too." He grimaced. "But in the spirit of full disclosure, anything could happen. I *am* off the clock, but you never know.

People do all sorts of dumb things to themselves on the Fourth. I once had to rush a guy to the hospital because he had blown off two of his fingers. With fireworks. They found the fingers, and his surgery was successful, but it was gruesome at the time."

Leah's stomach wobbled. "You might want to save those stories until *after* dinner."

"Sorry." His grin was unrepentant.

Maybe if a woman was dating the fire chief, she had to have a strong constitution.

A few minutes later when the campers descended on the food, pandemonium reigned. Several of the boys paused to say hello to Lucas. A couple of the girls, too. The girls might have a tiny crush. Leah didn't blame them. Luscious Lucas stood out in the crowd.

Forty-five minutes later, the food was gone, and everything was back to normal. When Jim announced game time, a whoop went up from the campers. Only a couple of the kids looked apprehensive.

No one was forced to do anything. But each kid was encouraged to pick an activity. Some of the games were silly and easy. Some required athletic skill.

Lucas appeared at Leah's elbow. "I signed us up for the three-legged race," he said, looking proud of himself.

She gaped at him. "Are you kidding? We're nowhere near the same height. That would be a terrible match-up."

Something flickered in his gaze. He rolled his shoulders. "It might seem that way on the surface, but I think we can make it work."

Her stomach fluttered again, but in a good way this time. Surely he was talking about more than a middle school race. "If you think we can do it, I'm game."

"That's the spirit."

His broad smile lit a flame in her belly. A warm blaze that

meandered through her body until she had to fan herself. "It's hot tonight."

Lucas leaned down to whisper in her ear. "*You're* hot tonight, babe. Have I told you about my ponytail fantasies?"

"Stop that," she said, mortified...looking around to see if anyone could hear their conversation.

"I love making you blush." He chuckled.

Fortunately for Leah, she saw Jim and Peg corralling everyone into their areas.

The first activity was a raw egg race. One of the smallest, youngest girls won. She kept her eye on her spoon and the egg and hustled down her lane to the finish line while everyone else made huge messes in the grass.

Peg had ordered a wide variety of colorful ribbons, everything from traditional 1st/2nd/3rd place to participation prizes. Something so simple seemed like an unlikely reward, but the kids loved it.

The baseball toss was dominated by the guys. Then there were the dashes—fifty yards and a hundred. One of the junior counselors had constructed a sand pit for the standing broad jump.

Everybody wanted to be in the tug of war.

It was the perfect summer evening.

Leah watched the fireflies come out and felt the anticipation of waiting for fireworks. But first, she had to get through the last event.

Jim and three helpers came to each duo and tied two middle legs together snugly. As it turned out, to be fairly matched, this race had been reserved for the over-eighteen crowd. Leah felt self-conscious. Lucas was a good eight inches taller than she was. Now, they were pressed together from shoulder to hip.

It was an innocent event. Yet being this close to Lucas felt anything but innocent.

He slipped his arm around her shoulders. "Don't let go of

my waist," he said. "We're going to start out with our middle feet, got it?"

"Yes sir! Got it…" She was beginning to realize that her partner might be a tad competitive.

The white flag dropped, and they were off. Several things occurred to Leah in the first ten seconds. The ground was uneven. Lucas was a faster runner than she was. And all the campers had gathered along the sidelines to cheer their favorite partners.

"Faster," Lucas shouted.

They had set up a good rhythm, but she was too short. The logistics were off. Nevertheless, Lucas's determination urged her along. Out of the corner of her eye, she saw only one other pair close to them.

How long *was* this race? It felt like they had covered a mile already.

But then she saw the finish line. Her own competitive spirit kicked in. If Lucas wanted this win, she was going to give it to him.

They were three feet ahead of the nearest runners.

"We've got this, babe," Lucas said, jubilation in his words.

Sure enough, they crossed the finish line first. But their momentum carried them too far. Leah stepped on a loose rock and went down, taking Lucas with her. He rolled to keep from crushing her, and she landed on top of him, knocking the breath out of her lungs and whacking her head on his chin.

When the dust settled—literally—Leah was dazed. In the distance, she heard cheers.

Lucas groaned. "Quit wiggling, woman. You're giving me a boner."

She squeaked and buried her face in his shoulder. "Please tell me you're kidding."

"Wish I could."

Fortunately, Jim took pity on them. "Let me get you untied, boss."

Leah could swear she heard laughter in his voice, but she was afraid to look at him. When her leg was free and Jim walked away, she sneaked a peek at Lucas. "I'm going to get up now. Very slowly."

His face was flushed. His fingers tangled in her ponytail for a brief second. "When you do, see if you can distract everybody."

To be honest, she didn't really want to stand up. Except for her various bumps and bruises, she was enjoying her current situation. Unfortunately, the crowd was clamoring to give the fire chief and Miss Leah their first-place ribbons.

Leah got to her feet without inflicting further damage. "Somebody grab me a water," she called out, walking back toward the starting line and hugging the children who crowded around her.

A few minutes later, Lucas joined her. Peg pinned a blue ribbon on each of them. "Congratulations, you two."

Cheers went up, but soon the kids moved on to the next exciting moment. The fireworks were about to start.

Lucas bent his head and whispered in her ear. "You okay?"

She leaned her head on his arm briefly. "I should ask you that question. I wasn't the one on the bottom."

He played with her ponytail again. "You can be on top anytime, Leah. I like the view."

No one was paying any attention to them. The counselors were covering the kids in bug spray and spreading canvas tarps in the nearby field. Jim's friend had set up his firing station on the far side of the pond.

Leah linked her fingers with Lucas's, feeling the callouses on his palm, the hard masculine grip. "Thank you for coming tonight. It's more fun with you here."

He leaned down to kiss her. "I wouldn't have missed it."

It was dark now. Completely. When she kissed him back eagerly, the fragrant night gave them privacy. She heard him suck in a breath. Felt his hands settle on her butt and squeeze.

"This is torture," she said. "I want to be alone with you."

"But you can't leave tonight."

"And it wouldn't look right for you to stay."

He sighed. "This camp is like the cutest chastity belt ever."

She chuckled. "A little sexual frustration never killed anybody."

"A little? I've been needing you for days. I dream about you constantly."

Leah didn't know how to respond to that. Was he serious? Or was that hyperbole?

She heard him sigh. "You don't believe me, do you?" he asked.

"Well…"

"Never mind." He didn't sound upset. More resigned than anything. "Let's join the others."

Once everybody was settled, Leah and Lucas had a tarp all to themselves at the very back of the field. Not far enough away to fool around, but with a little margin of privacy. Besides, everyone was going to be looking at the sky.

Lucas pulled her against his side with her head resting on his arm. "This is nice. I don't usually get to watch fireworks. Last year in Nashville, we were literally putting out fires all night."

"I'm sorry we're missing the big show in town, but Jim says his friend is a pro."

That turned out to be an understatement. There was no warning before the first whoosh and boom sliced through the night. A sprawling arc of color painted the sky.

The kids went crazy, cheering and hollering.

"Wow," Leah said. "This is better than I expected."

"*I'm* impressed."

The booms came one after the other in quick succession followed by rainbow explosions. At times when the sky lit up, Leah could see the silhouettes of three men on the far side of the water moving quickly as they loaded more fireworks.

She rested her cheek against Lucas's chest, feeling his fingers play with her hair, caressing the back of her neck. It was a moment she would always remember. The beautiful patterns in the sky mirrored the emotions in her heart. If she could stay like this forever, she would.

Here on this tarp, in Lucas's arms, everything was perfect. There was nothing to keep them apart. No conflicts. No divergent opinions of what the future should be.

Pretending only worked for so long, though. She knew him well enough by now to understand that this momentary accord was fleeting. Lucas was who he was.

Like everything in life, the show finally ended.

In the hustle and bustle of gathering the ground cloths and shepherding the kids back to their cabins, Lucas stayed by her side.

Eventually, all was quiet. Leah and Lucas walked back up to her house on the knoll.

He stopped by his car and took her hand, lifting her fingers to his lips to kiss them. "It's important," he said, "that you know this is more to me than finding an easy lay. I'm not exactly sure *what* it is, but it's more than that."

"What if *I* want a quickie?"

He winced, squeezing her fingers till it hurt. "Don't tempt me."

Silence fell. Awkward and heavy.

"So what are you saying?"

"I'm working on a plan. I've arranged to be off for a few days starting next Friday afternoon. Ryker is back from parental leave, so I'm finally getting my break. What if I pick you up at the end of camp? We can spend some time at your place. Or mine. How does that sound?"

She sniffed. "It's a long time till Friday."

"We'll stay busy. It will go by fast."

"No, it won't."

He sighed. "No, it won't. But I'm trying to be positive."

Leah wrapped her arms around his waist. "I hate this plan, but I know you're right. Grabbing fifteen minutes here and there is not what I want."

He stroked the back of her hair. "Me either. And just so you know, by the time we're in bed together, I may not let you go for days."

"Is that supposed to be a threat?"

He groaned. "I have to go," he said. But he didn't move.

"I'm sorry this isn't easier."

"That's okay. I like a challenge."

EIGHTEEN

LEAH HAD NEVER KNOWN A WEEK TO CRAWL BY SO SLOWLY. Thankfully, camp demanded 90 percent of her attention. In a good way.

She had assumed before starting this venture that every session would be a carbon copy of the one before it. That she and Jim and Peg would simply repeat the schedule again and again with only minor tweaks.

But though the regimen of activities remained relatively static, it was the *campers* themselves who were different. Their unique personalities and specific needs changed the tenor of the days.

Leah should have anticipated that. After all, she'd been trained in psychology. But sometimes a person had to *live* a situation to truly understand it.

Sadly, that might mean she would never truly be able to understand Lucas's view of the world. How could she? Despite her struggles to make her family see her as a capable adult, her life had been stable and safe. He had grown up with uncertainty and vulnerability.

Thursday evening, she packed up her things and did some light cleaning. Her little abode was nothing special, but this home away from home had begun to feel comfortable. She and Lucas had agreed they would spend the weekend at her house in town. After that, they'd make a new plan.

The thought of spending an entire week with him excited and scared her. She loved being with Lucas. But what if too much togetherness spooked him? What if he decided their situation was getting too *domestic*?

Fortunately, she didn't have endless hours to obsess about the upcoming week.

The last day of camp was sunny, hot, and perfect. Even so, there were tears. Friendships had formed. Attachments made. These fragile kids loved Camp Willow Pond and were conflicted about going home.

The closing ceremonies elicited laughter and proud smiles. Peach ice cream sealed the deal.

At last, the buses were loaded. Goodbyes and hugs shared all around.

By four thirty, Leah was alone.

She hadn't expected Lucas to show up for the closing. He'd been sleeping during the day after a long overnight shift. When he woke up, he was supposed to text her.

It was odd to have the camp quiet and empty again. This was what it would look like during the other months of the year. Her next goal was to figure out some meaningful programing for the fall and spring.

There was time for everything…

She drove through the front gate, locked it, and headed into town. Her sweet brick bungalow welcomed her like an old friend. After finishing college and grad school, she had moved out of her parents' house completely and found an apartment in Atlanta where she had lived ever since. Maybe she had been hedging her bets, but at the end of April, she had decided at the last minute not to give up her lease. Who knew what the future would bring? Even so, she had been excited about moving into Aunt Trudie's carefully updated home.

This aging beauty was the first place that was all Leah's. She loved it.

She loved it even more when she found Blossom Branch's fire chief sprawled in her porch swing, using one foot to propel himself back and forth.

"Well, hey there," she said, feeling her heart stumble and jump. "I thought you might still be sleeping."

He shrugged. "I've been up since four. Had a few chores to do. A bag to pack." He paused. "I parked in back. Like you wanted."

She flushed. "Was it a quiet night at the station?"

He nodded. "Yep. How was the end of camp?"

"Great. I hated to see this group go."

"You said that about the last ones."

"True." She was having a hard time making the transition from business to pleasure. And she couldn't read Lucas's expression.

His body language seemed relaxed, but he wasn't exactly smiling. "What if we drive up to Atlanta for dinner?" he asked. "Somewhere fancy."

That had been his offer two weeks ago, but she'd turned him down because her family was coming.

She frowned. "I appreciate the offer, but you don't have to wine and dine me. We're both tired. Why don't we relax and order in?"

Finally, he stood. But still at a distance…and with his hands shoved in his pockets. "I don't ever want you to think I take you for granted, Leah. You deserve the best."

Her confidence in this relationship was growing. She went to him and curled her arms around his neck. When she rested her

cheek on his chest, his shirt smelled like him. Warm and wonderful. "I have the *best* right here." She reached up and kissed
him softly. "I sort of thought we'd spend the weekend in bed."

She felt the shudder that quaked through his big frame. His
arms tightened around her. "If that's an official invitation, I
accept."

He lifted her off her feet and kissed her roughly, his passionate impatience impossible to miss. She kissed him back, feeling a burst of exhilaration. Her entire body relaxed into his
embrace. She'd been waiting for this forever, it seemed. Now,
their time had come.

"Let's go inside," she whispered.

The house was stuffy, but not terrible. She turned on the
AC and the ceiling fans.

Lucas eyed her soberly, but his lips twitched. "We'd be cooler
naked."

"What a delightful idea."

She crooked her finger at him and fled to the bedroom,
knowing he would be on her heels. When he tackled her to
the bed, she was mostly undressed. Laughing, she admonished
him. "Naked was your idea. Get with it, Chief Carter."

"Gladly."

Watching him strip, clumsy in his rush, was both amusing
and arousing. He was sinew and bone, like anybody else. Cells
and skin and muscles.

But in Lucas's case, all the parts had been assembled into a
whole that was beautiful and powerful and aggressively male.
He had the kind of body an artist would love to paint. Or a
woman to explore.

When they were both bare and under the sheet, his hands
found her waist. "Tell me you missed me," he demanded.

"With every breath," she swore. "I thought about late-night
arson but only because I wanted a visit from the fire chief."

She felt his chuckle against her breasts. "I'm sure I could have asked the judge to go easy on you." He moved on top of her, but only to nibble her collarbone.

Leah shivered. His late-day stubble was dangerously sexy, not to mention the way it tickled her neck. "When do you have to work again?"

He ran his tongue along the slope of one breast, finding a nipple and lingering there. "Don't want to talk about work," he mumbled.

Between them, his arousal was impossible to miss.

"But I want to know," she insisted, gasping when he sank his teeth into her sensitive flesh. She arched her back as liquid pleasure turned her body taut.

Lucas lifted his head, eyes glittering. His pupils were wide and dark. "Next Friday. Now will you be quiet and let me kiss you?"

Friday? A whole week? She wanted to jump for joy. Since that wasn't an option, she ran both hands through his hair and tugged. "My mouth is up here, Mr. Fire Chief…in case you got lost."

His feral, unrepentant grin stole her breath. "Not lost, babe. Just enjoying the scenery along the way."

He kissed her then. Long and hard. Or maybe they kissed each other. It was hard to tell where one ended and the next began. Leah was so wrapped up in the way he tasted, the way he felt. He smelled of clean cotton and citrusy bodywash. The way he whispered her name in between kisses made her weak. She was drunk on the reality of wallowing in Lucas Carter's considerable expertise.

She didn't care if he outstripped her in age and sexual experience. Anything he wanted to show her, anything he wanted to do, she was game. When she whispered as much in his ear, his face turned red. "Don't say things like that," he pleaded.

"Why not?" She wriggled out from under him and sat up, grinning when his gaze settled on her breasts before moving to her face. "I thought you would be glad I was up for...*adventure*, or more than vanilla sex," she said. "Don't men like variety?"

"Oh, my sweet heaven." He sat up, too, and put his hands over his face. "You're going to kill me," he said, the words aggrieved. "I'm not eighteen anymore. I have to pace myself."

"We haven't even done anything yet," she pointed out. "Not that I'm complaining. You're a very good kisser."

He cupped her cheeks in two big warm hands. His eyes mesmerized her. The color and heat in his irises were beautiful. "What you call *vanilla* is about a thousand times more exciting than anything I've ever done with another woman. I don't need us to hang from the chandelier or catch pneumonia screwing in the rain. I want you right *here*. Right *now*. In this bed." He paused, sucked in a breath, and exhaled slowly. "It's everything, Leah."

For the first time since they met, she truly believed him. She felt the moment resonate in her gut. Shock, but a good kind of shock. For so long, she had felt alone. Disappointed by men more than once. Halfway convinced she would be single for the rest of her life.

And now, she had Lucas. Not indefinitely, but for now. It was an exhilarating realization. For whatever reason, her completely ordinary female anatomy was something he desired. Craved. She cocked her head and studied the expression on his face. No man was a good enough actor to fake that kind of desperate sincerity.

"Okay, then," she said, her body trembling. "I'm all yours."

Her words settled something in him. She saw it happen. His shoulders relaxed. His expression lightened. His playful personality returned. "Good." He coaxed her onto her stomach. "How do you feel about a back rub? You've had a hard week at camp."

She looked over her shoulder at him. "It wasn't bad." She closed her eyes and rested her face in her arms. "But I'm not going to turn down another Luscious Lucas massage."

His hands were magic. Just the right amount of pressure. "Relax, Leah. Let me pamper you."

Weirdly, he started at her feet and worked his way up her ankles and calves to her thighs. He didn't even try to trespass into forbidden territory. Her ass got a fair amount of attention. Then her spine and lower back. Her shoulders. And finally, he concentrated on her neck and her skull.

"So good," she murmured, her words slurred. "You should do this for a living." Then she thought about Lucas touching other women. "Never mind," she said quickly. "They need you for the job you're doing."

"All done," he said a few minutes later, his voice husky. When he finally helped her roll onto her back, he was kneeling beside her. His erection was firm and eager. As if it had been waiting a very long time.

Leah curled her fingers around him and stroked slowly. "I love touching you," she said. "Your body is beautiful."

He came down beside her, propping his head on his hand, his gaze rueful. "All for you, my sweet. Every night I've dreamed of having you at my mercy. Now that I do, I hardly know where to start."

Leah chuckled. "Oh, I think you do."

"Maybe so." He slid a hand between her thighs and touched her intimately. Her body was damp and ready for him. In fact, she ached.

"You're not the only one who dreamed," she said softly. "Whenever I couldn't sleep this past week, I imagined you inside me. On top of me. I didn't know I could feel like this. The craving is always there. Even when I'm working. It's like you've taken up residence inside my head. In my bed."

"Good," he said. "My plan is to make love to you on so many days and in so many ways that you can't breathe for wanting me."

She held his eyes as she stroked his thigh and caressed his

erection. "Works both ways, Lucas. I wouldn't mind seeing you beg."

His cheeks flushed. "I would do that. For you."

"I don't want to wait anymore," she said. "Time is precious." And it was. Her days with him were numbered, even if she didn't know how or when they would expire.

"Whatever you want, Leah."

He took her slowly, both of them enjoying the tight friction, the erotic push and pull. Had she forgotten already what it felt like to have him deep inside her, filling her, marking her as his?

It was more exquisitely pleasurable than she remembered. Maybe absence really did make the heart grow fonder.

He was demonstrating patience. But she wanted to make him snap.

She wanted desperation and wild heat.

When she wrapped her legs around him and linked her ankles, she was able to dig her heels into his back. "Harder," she begged. "I won't break."

Lucas was closer to the edge than she realized. He fisted one hand in her hair and shouted her name as he thrust wildly, giving them both what they needed.

Afterward, he slumped on top of her. "Holy hell. That was incredible."

Leah yawned. "Understatement."

They held each other in silence for long, warm, blissful moments. But mundane needs eventually pushed to the surface. "I don't have any food in the house," Leah said ruefully. "If we're going to do this all night, we may starve."

"Not on my watch. Get dressed, woman."

"I'm tired of pizza. And I think the diner is closed. The owner is on vacation this weekend."

He ran his thumb down her cheek. "How about burgers and shakes at Peachy-King?"

"Ugh. Do you know how unhealthy that is?"

"We worked off a lot of calories. Come on. We can pick up breakfast stuff on the way home."

Leah allowed herself to be persuaded. To be honest, once they were seated in a turquoise booth beneath an array of neon lights, the food wasn't half bad. Lucas devoured the triple decker special and a large chocolate shake. Leah settled for a kid's burger with cheese and an iced tea.

She grinned at him. "You've got ketchup on your chin."

He stared at her.

"What?" she said, alarmed. "Is mine worse?"

Lucas shook his head slowly, using the napkin she handed him. "Your face is perfect. No wonder the kids respond to you. Everything about you is real. And honest." He reached for her hand and curled her fingers into his palm, squeezing. "Thanks for letting me spend the weekend with you."

Her heart quivered. "Only the weekend? I was hoping for more."

She said it teasingly, but he took her words at face value. "Then more is what you'll get. But be careful. You might not get rid of me."

She knew he was kidding. She knew the rules. Even so, hope planted seeds in her heart. And hope was hard to root out.

Lucas leaned back in his seat eventually. "I'm stuffed."

"No wonder. You'll probably have nightmares."

"In your bed? No way." His smile was curiously sweet. Then his gaze shifted away before he spoke next. "So what will you do when camp is over?" he asked lightly.

"Oh." She hadn't expected that question. "Well, probably go back to Atlanta for the late fall and winter. I kept my apartment. I'll have potential donors to see and plans to make for next season. Most of my friends are in Atlanta. I'm still not sure I want to live in Blossom Branch permanently. I could probably make a fortune selling Aunt Trudie's house. If I invested the money well, my future would be set."

"Is that something you want to do?"

"Not really. I love it."

"So to be clear, you have three separate homes."

"At the moment."

"Wow. I'm not sure how I feel about that. I've never dated an heiress."

She winced inwardly. By admitting her good fortune out loud, she could hear his point. "Stop teasing me," she said. "I don't think of myself as rich. I'm trying to do something good with the money."

"And succeeding." His smile faded. "In spite of your many addresses, what would happen if you ever wanted to move in with me?"

She nearly choked on the last of her milkshake. "I doubt that's going to happen," she said firmly. "You have your world and I have mine. I don't think we should do anything crazy or impulsive."

"But you would consider selling that beautiful house?"

"Maybe. I don't know."

He shook his head slowly. "Enough serious talk. The nearest grocery store closes at nine. We'd better head over there if we want food for the morning."

They ended up buying freshly ground coffee, orange juice, cereal, and pastries.

Leah eyed the shopping cart. "You don't want bacon and eggs?"

He shook his head and lowered his voice. "I don't think either of us will have the energy to cook in the morning."

They were standing in the middle of the aisle. Not that there were many shoppers at this hour, but still.

She pretended to frown at him. "You can't say things like that in public. What if someone hears?"

He shrugged. "It's the weekend. Surely, we won't be the only couple spending Saturday and Sunday in bed."

Her lips twitched. "You're teasing me."

He kissed her forehead, smiling. "Maybe a little. I love the way your cheeks turn pink."

Back at the house, they put the groceries away and took turns in the shower. It really was too small for fooling around. Which was a shame now that Leah had an overnight guest.

It was after ten by the time she had unpacked and settled in. "You want to watch a movie?" she asked. Her awkward feelings and nerves had returned. She and Lucas had never actually *slept* together. In a way, that seemed more intimate than sex.

He must have picked up on her unease. His gentle smile was affectionate. "Would you be more comfortable if I went home, Leah? I can come back in the morning for breakfast, and we'll plan our day."

Her big, strong fireman was giving her an out...an escape route. That thing fire officials said everyone should have. But she didn't want him to go.

She swallowed, trying not to feel gauche and emotionally clumsy. "I don't want you to go," she admitted. "Really."

"But?" His grin was wry.

"But this is novel for me. And it seems like a big step. Especially for a relationship that's fairly new."

He took her hand and kissed it. "Do you snore?"

"I don't think so."

"And cover stealing?"

The way he rubbed his thumb over the back of her knuckles was not helping her concentrate. "How would I know? I sleep alone."

"You don't have to sleep alone tonight, Leah. If you'll have me."

His arms linked loosely around her waist. His gaze mesmerized her. It seemed to contain secrets. Things he wasn't saying.

"Spend the night with me," she said. "That's what I want."

His eyes blazed with a scorching heat. "Be sure."

"I'm sure."

They were standing in the hallway. Lucas backed her through the door into the bedroom. She thought they were headed for round two, but Lucas stopped beside the bed. He gathered her damp hair in his hands and wrapped his fingers in it, anchoring her head.

Then he kissed her long and slow until her knees wobbled, and her legs could barely hold her up. He nuzzled her nose with his, his breathing uneven. "I care about you, Leah. More than I have anyone else in my life. I know 'till death do us part' is what most women expect, but I never want to lie to you."

Even now he was making sure she understood the parameters. She did understand, but she didn't want to think about it every minute of every day.

For a moment, she flashed back to Cate's wedding. As a bridesmaid, Leah had been near the altar, right there in the thick of things. She remembered the pinch of envy she felt when the beautiful ceremony started and the horrified shock when Jason called it off.

People were complicated creatures, no two the same. Everyone was the product of all the hurts and troubles that had accumulated over decades of living. Until Camp Willow Pond, Leah herself had been a mouse of a person, always aware of being judged, always ultrasensitive to criticism.

Her new endeavor had given her a chance to toughen up, to grow and mature. Lucas's advent into her life had strengthened her in an entirely different way. She was falling in love with him. No doubt about that. But she was willing to be with him anyway, knowing that this experience was worth the heartache to come.

She slid a hand through his hair, relishing the feel of silky strands tangling between her fingers. "I know who I am, Lucas, and I know who *you* are. This time is ours. I want it more than anything. I don't need empty promises. All I need and want is you."

He nodded jerkily and began to undress her. It didn't take long. She'd put on a soft, white cotton T-shirt after her shower. He stripped it over her head and then slid her undies down her legs. When she climbed onto the mattress, he ditched his own T-shirt and boxers and followed her.

"Are you sleepy?" he asked, leaning over her with a light in his eyes that *looked* like love. Fortunately, Leah knew the difference.

She laughed softly. "Not *that* sleepy."

What happened next was so totally unfair she wanted to cry. Lucas made love to her the way she imagined a lover might on a wedding night…or the evening a soldier said goodbye before a long deployment. He gave her exquisite tenderness and endless pleasure.

There was no rush to the finish line this time. Only shivering increments of pleasurable sensation that built and built and built until she slid over the top into oblivion, all the while guarded and protected in his tight embrace.

They did sleep after that. She wanted to stay awake and absorb every wonderful minute. But she was exhausted. The last thing she remembered was Lucas spooning her and kissing the nape of her neck. "Good night, Leah," he whispered.

Lucas took her twice more during the night. How could he not? Her soft breasts and ass were the stuff of dreams. Having Leah naked and pressed up against him kept his arousal simmering throughout the hours until morning.

He should have been sleeping even though he had dozed all day Friday. The prior twelve-hour night shift had been long and demanding. Normally, going to bed at this hour wouldn't have been difficult.

Still, the situation didn't lend itself to slumber.

In the wee hours of the morning, he confronted his mental and emotional crisis. He might be falling in love with Leah Marks. That was a problem, a big problem. He knew it. And it hurt. He couldn't let it happen.

Perhaps he should never have let *any* of this happen. He had known the first day he met her that she was dangerous to him. He wasn't like other guys. His past made him broken and unfit to be a family man. No matter how much he cared for her, she needed somebody different with whom to build a future.

Jeff had been right about some things. Lucas did have a tendency to get itchy feet, to head out for new experiences. But in a definite *red-flag* moment, he understood that his usual restless mood hadn't materialized on the customary timetable.

If he left Blossom Branch, this time would be different. He wouldn't be running *to* something, he'd be running away. From sweet, passionate Leah. From unbearable temptation. From heartache, hers and his.

He couldn't stay much longer. It was too risky. Still, the thought of leaving was a punch to the gut. He loved Blossom Branch. He loved his job and his crew.

Staying here with Leah was a dangerous gamble, whether a week, a weekend, or even an hour.

He didn't know what to do...

NINETEEN

LEAH WOKE SLOWLY, HER BRAIN STIMULATED BY THE smell of coffee brewing.

She stretched and yawned, feeling a myriad of tiny aches in her body. Though there was no one around to witness her shocked awareness, she blushed, honestly stunned to remember the events that had happened during the night.

Lucas had been insatiable. She had given him everything—her body, her arousal, and though he didn't know it, her love. She'd held nothing back.

If she wanted him in her life, she had to show him that he was enough for her just the way he was. She didn't want Lucas to change. Maybe this would work if *she* changed what she was looking for. She *loved* him. That certainty filled her with delight and exultation.

Her dreams of happily-ever-after and a wedding ring were just that…dreams. Lucas was *real*. Their relationship was genuine and authentic.

Could she convince him that she wanted whatever he had to offer?

And if she did, maybe—

Stop. She shut down that line of thinking doggedly. She wasn't going to debate the future. Not right now when everything about this time with Lucas was perfection.

She found him sitting in the kitchen, wearing his navy T-shirt and boxers again and drinking coffee as he read the *New York Times* on his phone. He looked up when she walked in and gave her a smile that curled her toes. "There you are."

"Sorry. I should have been awake an hour ago." She wrapped her arms around him from behind and bent to trace his ear with her tongue. "Someone kept me up during the night." She snickered. "Or maybe you were the one who was *up.* It's hard to remember."

He laughed, a warm contented sound that filled her with joy. "Definitely hard. For a while there, I wondered if I needed to go to the emergency room. You know. Four hours and all that…"

"You're so bad." Leah pulled out a chair and sat beside him. She kissed his chin. "Admirable stamina, Mr. Fire Chief. Is that part of your fitness eval?"

He dragged her closer and slid his tongue against her lips, coaxing them apart. "Not that I can recall."

The kiss was better than coffee or chocolate croissants. But finally, she pulled back. "Bookmark that," she said. "I need caffeine and food."

The remainder of the day unfolded in a haze of bliss.

They made love so many times, Leah lost count. It was exhilarating and exhausting, even with breaks in between for Netflix or a quick two-mile run.

Around four, Lucas decided he wanted to talk about her house. "What else do you have to do?" he asked. "In terms of upkeep."

They were standing in her front yard. Huge rosebushes

bloomed in profusion around the porch. The neighbor boy who mowed her grass and trimmed the greenery was doing a great job while she was at camp.

"Not too much more," Leah said. "Though I think I may have to replace the gutters. They're old, and I want to buy that kind with the mesh guard on top. At the very least, I'm sure it's time to clean them out."

"Let me take a look," Lucas said.

Despite her protests, he dragged an extension ladder out of her carport and propped it against the front of the house. Her heart tightened when she watched him climb up quickly with no apparent fear. "Be careful," she called out.

He glanced down at her, laughing. "You know this is what I do for a living, right? I think I can safely handle a ladder."

"Maybe so, but accidents happen. How bad are the gutters?"

He scooped a pile of muck into his hand and tossed it down. "Pretty bad. And you're right. With so many mature trees in this neighborhood, the covered gutters would save you a lot of headache. If you do it soon, you could skip the cleaning-out phase."

"True."

When he was back on the ground, he washed his hands with the hose and dried them on his shorts. "Good news is, the roof seems to be in great shape."

"I think it's only seven or eight years old," she said.

"Anything else you want me to take a look at?"

Leah frowned. "You're not here to work. This is supposed to be a fun and relaxing weekend."

He tapped her nose. "I *am* having fun. I love old houses. In fact, if I ever get tired of being a fireman, I've thought about buying a couple of run-down houses and flipping them. It's hard work, but I enjoy stuff like that."

Her heart stumbled. "You've thought about giving up the

fire hall? Does Jeff know?" What really bothered her was the idea that Lucas might move on.

Lucas stared at her. "I don't tell Jeff my every waking thought. But yeah. I might have mentioned it to him. The market is hot right now. Plenty of opportunities out there."

Leah didn't say much after that. Had he deliberately introduced the topic to hint that he was free to roam?

She knew that. She didn't need a reminder.

Eventually, they decided to walk to the Peach Pit for dinner. It was a long way, but the evening was beautiful and the humidity low.

They bypassed the hamburger menu and ordered grilled chicken sandwiches with garden salads. As a reward for their smart food choices, Lucas declared they could treat themselves with brownies for dessert.

Afterward, they danced. But only to the slow songs. Leah rested her head on Lucas's shoulder and tried to memorize the moment. All their problems still existed. She and Lucas were no more suited tonight than on the day she met him. Why was he with her now if he didn't care? Her heart refused to give up on him...on them. Surely she could change. Hearth and home and forever were meaningless without Lucas.

That night, they showered together laughing and teasing and nearly falling out of the crowded tub. They ended up with water all over the floor of the bathroom.

A repentant Lucas sopped it up with towels and insisted on loading the washing machine. "You told me it wouldn't work, but I didn't listen."

She grinned at him. "It was fun to try."

They picked a movie together and cuddled on the sofa. Twenty minutes in, Lucas had her naked and under him.

"We'll lose track of the plot," she said breathlessly.

He surged deep, making her body clench with longing. "I'll make it up to you."

★ ★ ★

Sunday morning, they both slept in. Lucas was snoring when Leah slipped out of bed for a quick trip to the bathroom. When she returned, she paused to enjoy the sight of him under her covers. How many more times like this would they have?

She had two more camp sessions to get through. Would Lucas tire of waiting for her? And what happened at the end of the summer?

All day, her doubts troubled her, stealing some of the joy from this time with him. She knew it was dumb. Why ruin the present? Still, there was nothing she could do to wipe out the uncertainties that plagued her.

Before dinner, she surveyed her fridge. The groceries they had bought over the weekend were dwindling. "I wish I had a grill," she said. "It's too hot to turn on the oven."

Lucas nuzzled her neck. "Then let's go to my place. We can do steaks again or pork chops. Corn on the cob. Anything you want."

Her mouth watered. "Sounds perfect. Besides, I think we should feed your fish, poor things."

They stopped by the store and picked up what they needed on the way. While Lucas fired up the grill, Leah made iced tea and put together a fruit salad for dessert, with her grandmother's special dipping sauce. The calories in the sauce probably negated the health benefits of the fruit, but the cream cheese mixture was a crowd-pleaser.

They ate outside on Lucas's small porch. He had a tiny three-foot-wide metal table with two matching chairs. It was crowded but cozy.

"This is all amazing," Leah said. "You're a great chef."

"You don't have to flatter me, woman. I'm already your devoted sexual slave."

"No, you're not," she said. "If anything, I'm under *your* spell."

His smile was warm and intimate. "Let's agree that we're both into each other."

"Yes," she said softly. "Yes, we are."

That pesky hope surfaced again.

By the time they finished their meal and cleaned up, it was almost seven. Lucas caught her staring at him, anticipating the night ahead. When she turned pink, he laughed out loud. "I like the way you're thinking. Let's get out of here."

Before they could make a move in that direction, a knock sounded at the door.

Leah raised an eyebrow. "Are you expecting company?"

He rolled his eyes. "Probably the guy next door in 2B wanting to borrow milk. I'll get rid of him."

But when Lucas opened the front door, the man standing there was not a neighbor. He was pleasant looking in a medium kind of way. Not too tall, not too short. Sandy-colored thinning hair. Midforties. Large-frame glasses. A slight paunch.

He smiled. "Lucas Carter?"

Lucas nodded slowly. "Yes."

"Well, I think I'm your cousin." The man stopped. "No, I *know* I'm your cousin. From Pennsylvania. My name is Ed Carter. I've been looking for you almost two years now. May I come in? I have a lot to tell you."

Leah could see the rigid way Lucas held himself. His posture was braced. She knew he wanted to say *no* and slam the door. But he didn't have it in him to be so rude. Maybe if he'd been alone. But not with Leah watching.

He shot her a frustrated glance.

She touched his hand. "He's gone to a lot of trouble and come a long way. Shouldn't you hear him out?"

"You're okay with letting a stranger in?"

"I didn't think of that," Leah said.

The man held out a driver's license. "I mean you no harm, I swear."

Lucas glanced at the license, mumbled something under his breath and sighed. He addressed Ed with an expressionless stare.

"Sure. But make it quick, please. My friend Leah and I have somewhere to be."

The *somewhere* was only her house, but maybe Lucas needed the excuse.

Ed Carter sat down in an armchair. Lucas took his spot beside Leah on the sofa. But he left a good two feet between them.

Silence reigned for thirty seconds…then sixty.

When Leah realized Lucas wasn't going to make this encounter easy, she managed a smile for their visitor. "Mr. Carter, Lucas is right. Our time is limited. Why don't you jump right in?"

At her side, Lucas sat stony-faced. She wasn't entirely sure he realized Leah had said anything.

Ed nodded slowly. "I understand." He set a fat file folder on the coffee table. "My aunt became interested in genealogy about eight or nine years ago. She took courses, pursued training, documented my relatives—hers, too, of course—and produced elaborate family trees. Had them rendered in color by an artist. The finished products are impressive. But once she was done, I suppose the *itch* was still there. She began branching out, pardon the pun." He laughed quietly at his own joke.

Leah sighed inwardly. Lucas sat with his arms folded across his chest. "How does this affect Lucas?" she asked.

"I'm getting there."

She suspected Ed Carter liked the drama of the situation. "Sorry," she said. "Go ahead."

"When Aunt Judy began researching other arms of the family, she discovered a very sad story. In Barstow, Pennsylvania, there was a segment of the Carter family that supported themselves in a farming community. They established a *house* church, if you will. Incredibly strict. Sober. One of the teenage boys, Landon, got his girlfriend pregnant. Her name was Erin. Now, my aunt didn't discover all these details in a linear fashion. What I'm telling you was uncovered a bit at a time."

Because Lucas said nothing, Leah leaned forward, fascinated, despite Lucas's apparent disinterest. "So the teenagers were in trouble."

"They would have been," Ed said, "but they ran away. Over the state line into New York. Erin must have been almost five months pregnant when they left. That's judging from the dates on various documents. They lied about their ages—they were only seventeen. I'm not sure how they paid for necessities. Worked fast food maybe. Slept in their car. It was spring. When the baby was born, he was a healthy boy."

Leah thought she understood where the story was going, but Lucas's expression hadn't changed, and Ed seemed uneasy now. "So they took the child home?" she asked.

"Unfortunately, no." Ed grimaced. "The young couple knew there was going to be hell to pay when they returned to Barstow, but they were out of money and out of luck. Their families would know they conceived a child out of wedlock, even if they eventually had a courthouse wedding. Landon and Erin were certain they would be cast out. But they needed the support of their families to get established and thus be able to care for their son."

"What did they do?" Leah was emotionally invested in the story now. And she had a sick feeling she wasn't going to like the ending.

"They left their baby boy on the steps of a large church beside the building that housed the New York State foster care system. *Temporarily.* My aunt found scans of a handwritten note indicating that as soon as it was possible, the young parents were planning to return and retrieve their son."

"And did they?"

Ed didn't answer the question. "Landon and Erin admitted to their families they had married in New York. They were urged to have another ceremony within the religious community of which they were a part. There's a record of that union, also. Eventually, the group would have helped build a small house for the newlyweds on the farm. In the meantime, Landon and Erin found a tiny public housing apartment in town. They both got jobs and began saving their money."

"For their son," Leah said.

"Exactly. On the books in New York, there are a string of notes and communications from the young couple outlining what they were doing and promising to come and get their son before he turned three. I'm not sure why that was the target date. Maybe they were hoping their parents would become less rigid in their stance."

"Surely the grandparents would have been delighted to know they had a grandchild," Leah said.

"Perhaps not. The culture there had very clear rules. Not much gray area."

"So when the baby turned three, what happened?"

Ed twisted his hands in his lap, visibly upset. He shot a glance at Lucas, but Lucas was unmoving. "There was a carbon monoxide leak in the apartment. Both young people were deceased. The city of Barstow agreed to a financial settlement with the family."

Tears filled Leah's eyes. "How dreadful."

"Yes."

"And the baby?" *The baby who might be Lucas?*

Ed was sober. "The only people who knew about the baby were Landon and Erin. No one else realized there was an heir to be claimed."

For the first time, Lucas spoke. His expression was tumultuous. "And what about the foster care people? Wouldn't they have known something was up?"

"Indeed. But even in the later notes, Erin and Landon had given false last names, not wanting to be found out. The only reason my aunt was able to piece together the story was that she stumbled across the birth record from the hospital. That document was correct. And to be clear, *Carter* really is your last name, even though the note from your parents said it was your middle name."

Leah was incensed. "But wouldn't the social services people have followed up when they quit getting notes from the baby's parents?"

"You can guess what the system is like," Ed said. "Overburdened. Understaffed. There was an employee at the time who had five such situations to unravel. But he was terminated for calling in sick too many times. Somebody dropped the ball. Five children who should have been eligible for adoption were never identified as such."

Lucas was ashen now, his eyes burning with emotion. "So you're saying the baby boy was me? How could you possibly know the end of that story?"

Ed shook his head slowly. "When my aunt's research intersected finally with the State of New York's foster care system, she found another piece of the puzzle. Two doctoral students had worked on a dissertation following twenty older, *nonadoptable* children through various foster care homes over a fifteen-year period. Their project uncovered the derelict employee, the five boys and girls who should have gone to permanent families, and the wrong that was never righted."

Leah frowned. "That's it?"

"No." Ed shook his head. "Four of those five children, all adults now, of course, filed a joint lawsuit, including the one defendant who could not be located. The State eventually awarded each of the five a significant amount in damages." He gazed at Lucas ruefully. "It was only with their help that I was able to find you. They've been sending you correspondence, it seems, but with no reply."

Leah winced inwardly, remembering the shredding incident. She couldn't bring herself to look at Lucas. What was he thinking?

Lucas stood abruptly. "Thank you for your trouble," he said, the words formal. "I don't want the money. They can divide it among the others."

Ed rose to his feet, too, his expression troubled. "I'm not here about the money. I wanted you to know you have family. All your immediate kin are deceased, but you have cousins. Lots and lots of cousins, in fact. They'll be eager to meet you."

"I don't anticipate traveling to Pennsylvania, but thank you for your time."

Ed hesitated, clearly choosing his words. "That folder is for you. Copies of everything my aunt uncovered. I can only imagine this is an utter shock. I'm so sorry for what happened to you. It was a terrible situation. I'm glad your life turned out well in spite of the tragedy."

Somehow, Leah knew Lucas needed to end this bizarre meeting. She stepped in front of him and held out her hand to their visitor. "Thank you, Ed, for coming all this way. I'm sure when Lucas has had time to process all this information, he may check back with you." She physically edged the man toward the door. "Tell your aunt we're grateful. Take care now…"

When the door finally shut, she locked it and turned to face the man who meant everything to her. "How are you doing?" she asked quietly.

Lucas was no longer the person she had spent the weekend with. Only the shell of a man remained. His eyes were blank. The pallor lingered.

He shrugged. "Nothing is different. I told you before. I made the life I wanted."

"But you—"

He held out a hand, silencing her. "You're pleased," he said flatly. "Pleased to know my DNA is no longer a mystery."

"That's not true," she protested. "If I was comforted at all by what Ed had to say, it was because you finally have answers. Those answers are sad and tragic, but at least you know. Doesn't that change things for you?"

"I don't want to talk about this," he said, the words blunt.

Leah took a deep breath, refusing to be angry at his reaction. He needed her. She couldn't let her feelings get in the way. "Maybe we should go back to my house now."

His nod was jerky. "Yeah."

She wasn't completely comfortable having him drive in his condition, but the distance wasn't far, and she couldn't see herself asking for his keys. Instead, she grabbed her purse and waited by the door as he made sure the grill was cool and turned out the lights.

There wasn't a single safe topic she could think of to lighten the mood in the car.

Instead of using the carport out back, Lucas parked right in front of Leah's house. She decided on the spot not to make a big deal about it. Lots of people had seen them together tonight in town. The fire chief was dating a daughter of Blossom Branch. So what? She needed to quit worrying about other people's opinions. She was a grown woman.

Inside, she walked toward the kitchen. "I'll make some popcorn," she said. "Why don't you find us something to watch?"

Lucas didn't say anything. That worried her.

She knew he was in shock. How could she help him?

When she eventually carried the bowls of popcorn into the small living room, she saw Lucas standing in the foyer by the front door. His overnight bag sat as his feet.

"Good night," he said.

Her jaw and her stomach dropped. "Where are you going? Why are you leaving? I want to spend time with you. Not just sex. Any kind of time. This has been a hard day. Let me take care of you."

He jerked visibly when she said that last thing. "I don't need *anyone* to take care of me." The blunt words were like bullets aimed at her heart. There was no affection in his gaze. No sexual hunger. No nothing.

She was traversing a minefield without protective armor. "Stay for a bit," she coaxed. "We don't have to talk about serious stuff. Let yourself breathe. Everything will be okay, I promise."

Finally, the veil fell from his eyes, and for a split second, she saw the depth of his anguish. But it was gone quickly. He straightened his shoulders. "I think we're done, Leah," he said, the words flat. "We both knew this was temporary. I've enjoyed our time together, but you and I are too different."

"We're not," she said, fighting for her life...for *their* life. "If you want to ignore everything that happened this evening, I'm fine with that."

His smile was chilling. "But that's just it. You won't be. You'll pick and cajole and suggest and push. You know the truth now, and you'll want me to have a tender reunion with all those relatives Ed mentioned."

Her throat hurt. "I won't. Not if it's impossible for you." Was he right about her inclinations? Maybe. But she had done her best to give up a fantasy of the life she wanted. She had risked her peace of mind...risked everything...to make a life with Lucas. And she'd been proud of her personal growth.

Deciding she could live without guarantees for the future was one thing, but she couldn't accept a partner who was closed off. How could he shut her out?

She understood that he was hurt. But he was hurting *her* with his reaction to this trauma. "Talk to me," she begged. "Let me help."

"Find somebody else," Lucas said. She saw his throat work as he swallowed. "Somebody like Jeff. Somebody without all the skeletons in his past."

"Everybody has skeletons," she said. "Yours aren't so bad."

"It's over, Leah. You and I were an aberration. I enjoyed being on my own before, and I'll enjoy it again. I don't need a woman in my life. I don't need you."

TWENTY

THE PAIN WAS STAGGERING. WHEN THE DOOR CLOSED behind Lucas and he drove away, Leah collapsed on the sofa and sobbed. Damn Ed Carter and his truth bombs. It wasn't fair. Just when she and Lucas were connecting on such a beautifully intimate level. How could she have done anything differently?

Six hours ago, she had been the happiest woman in Blossom Branch. Now, she had nothing. What worried her even more than her own heartbreak was that Lucas was alone. Alone and dealing with serious emotional trauma.

He was a mature, well-adjusted man. But the information he'd been given tonight was like a radioactive explosion. The effects would linger indefinitely.

When she finally stopped crying, her eyes were swollen and her face blotchy. Her vanity wasn't important. She needed to go to him.

Standing in the foyer with her keys in her hand, she stopped and hung her head. Hurt and confusion made her chest ache. Lucas wanted to be alone. He had broken off their relationship.

No matter how much she thought he *needed* her, Lucas had made his decision. He chose to be on his own. She could confront him. Tell him he was wrong. But feelings were feelings. They weren't always rational.

After a sleepless night, she called Cate and begged for asylum.

The drive to Atlanta Monday morning was a blur. When Cate opened the door, Leah fell into her arms and bawled. She'd thought her crying jag was over. Apparently not.

Cate took charge of the situation. She tucked Leah into a comfy spot in the den and brought her a cup of Earl Grey tea and imported Scottish biscuits. Plus a brand-new box of tissues.

Leah managed a wobbly smile. "Am I interrupting anything important?"

"Harry is upstairs working. I told him not to bother us. I had a dental appointment at one, but I've already called and put it off. I'm all yours." Her gaze gentled. "Tell me what happened, hon."

"Well, you won't be meeting Lucas after all."

"Why not?"

"He dumped me." The tears started again. Leah was so tired of crying, but she couldn't stop.

Cate scooted over beside her on the sofa and wrapped her arms around Leah. "Easy, my love. Just talk to me. Tell me what happened."

Leah let herself be comforted. She felt shaky and lost and sick to her stomach. Being here with Cate was saving her life. "It's hard to explain," she said.

"We've got all day."

Leah inhaled a ragged breath. "I'm in love with him," she said. "And I decided I loved him enough to take whatever he can give. We spent an incredible weekend getting closer and closer, but then…" Tears welled in her eyes and rolled down her cheeks.

"Then what, Leah?"

Leah told her about the visit from Ed Carter, the incredibly convoluted story of Lucas's family, and finally, Lucas's reaction.

When she was finally done, Leah blew her nose again. "What do you think I should do?" she asked. "As an impartial by-stander?"

Cate winced. "I don't think you want to hear this, but the answer is nothing. You can't do anything, Leah."

Leah sucked in a startled breath. She'd been counting on Cate to fix things. That's what Cate did. "What do you mean nothing?"

Cate rubbed Leah's back. "You can't be his shrink *and* his lover. Besides, people spend literally their whole lives dealing with this kind of crap. Lucas hasn't even had twenty-four hours. The man has some serious shit to process. To find out that your parents *didn't* abandon you but that they're dead? And that you could have been adopted into a loving family, but were robbed of that chance? How does anybody wrap their head around that?"

"I know." Leah shredded the tissue between her fingers. "He looked crushed, Cate. Destroyed. And angry, too."

"Well, of course he did. What happened last night was a kind of death. Whatever stories he's been telling himself over the years to deal with his painful past have been completely up-ended. The people he was mad at are no longer the villains. And even if they were, they're gone. A stern bunch of relatives. A gas leak in a substandard apartment. An incompetent employee at social services. It's a lot. There's no outlet for his feelings."

"So he simply keeps them all in? Is that it? The emotional fallout will kill him, Cate. He'll run, any day now. To a new town and a new set of strangers. I think he's been running from his past for his entire adult life. If he runs far enough and fast enough, no one will know what happened to him. Not even his buddy Jeff. I'll never see him again."

If she had been expecting a pep talk, she didn't get one.

Cate's expression was miserable. "I don't want to say this, but yes. That might be the outcome. No one can work through all that trauma but Lucas. To be honest, he may *never* deal with it. Avoidance is a powerful anesthetic. His hurt runs so deep, he may be damaged forever. Be honest, Leah. Could you live with a man like that? Would you want to?"

Leah stared at her, processing the question. She thought she had come so far. That she had been willing to settle for an uncertain future. But did she want a man who was so terribly broken? It would mean no marriage. No family of her own. Nothing but a relationship based on sexual compatibility and one-sided love.

Did she love him?

Oh, yes. She did. Or else what happened wouldn't hurt so much.

"I don't know," Leah said. "This thing with Lucas has happened so fast. But now I can't imagine my life without him. He's made me see myself in a different light, and I like that woman. I have more confidence. More ability to reach for what I want."

Truthfully, she *had* been hoping he would change. Her subconscious was a sneaky bitch. Despite telling herself she would take whatever he could give, somewhere deep down, she had envisioned a day—

Nope…she wasn't going there. "I do love him," she said. "I can't *not* love him."

Cate grimaced. "I figured you'd say that. I can hear in your voice how you feel. And if that's the case, you only have one real option."

"And that is?"

"Give him time. You'll have to wait, no matter how long."

"And if he leaves town?"

"That will be your answer."

★ ★ ★

Cate took Leah to Key West for three nights. They invited Gabby, of course, but it was on too short notice for her to get away. The hotel was luxurious and the town delightful, but Leah had to force herself to relax and have fun.

She wasn't entirely successful.

Cate must have known the truth, but she didn't push. And neither of them mentioned Lucas. Occasionally, Leah glanced at her phone to see if she had missed any texts, but there was nothing. In her heart, she had known there wouldn't be…

Despite her heartbreak, playing hooky felt self-indulgent. There were tasks she should have been addressing at camp. Nothing that couldn't wait, though.

So she allowed Cate to pamper her. Cate even insisted on Leah having her own room so if she needed quiet to be with her thoughts, she could be at peace.

Cate and Harry were incredibly generous with their resources.

The second evening after dinner, Leah holed up in her room and called Gabby for a long talk to fill her in. Gabby's response was kind.

"I'm so sorry, sweetie. I know how much you invested in this guy. And how much he got to you. But don't give up on him."

Leah sighed. "I'm not giving up on him. It's just that I don't see this situation having a happy ending for him or for me. Cate thinks I have to give him space…and time."

Gabby laughed. "Well, as usual, Cate is right, but don't tell her I said that." She sobered. "I doubt this is the kind of thing he can get over in a day or a week or even a month. The news has to have shaken his foundations."

"I know. Even when we first met and he told me about growing up in foster care, it was hard for me to imagine what his childhood was like. But with this new information—well…" She paused, her throat tight. "It's just so terribly unfair."

"It is," Gabby agreed. "But at the risk of sounding like a fortune cookie, life isn't fair. You know that. Every one of your precious campers knows that."

"It sucks," Leah said. Her voice wobbled. She hoped Gabby didn't notice.

"What if I try to come down for the first weekend of the next session? I'd like to see the camp in action."

"I would love that."

"Then it's a date."

Five minutes later when Leah ended the call, she stared at her cell phone, willing one tiny green icon to change. But of course, it didn't.

To send long texts to Lucas would be an invasion of his privacy...an intrusion on the time he needed to come to terms with what Ed had revealed.

Suddenly, she had an idea. This hotel was fancy enough to have its own stationery. She tugged open the single drawer in the writing desk, and sure enough, there was a slim leather folio with three sheets of heavy-stock paper and three matching envelopes.

An old-fashioned letter would be just the thing. Personal, but distant. Lucas could read it, toss it, or do whatever. But at least he would know she was thinking about him.

After fifteen minutes of composing sentences in her head, she pulled a favorite pen from her purse and began writing...

Dear Lucas,
I'm so sorry about the way things ended between us. But I am most sorry that you had to hear such distressing news. When I think of your young, struggling parents, my heart breaks. For them *and* for you.

I understand that this situation and this new information is something you and you alone must handle and process. Even if you decide *not* to deal with it, I respect and support your choices.

This was not how I wanted our relationship to end, though I think we always knew there was an expiration date. Mostly, I am worried about you. Please let Jeff or a professional or whoever support you. This is not a time to bear your burdens alone.

In the coming days and weeks, I won't call or text you. If you would like to talk, you'll have to make contact. Not because I am upset or angry, but because the situation is painful for you and difficult for me to fully understand.

I care about you deeply and want the best for your life.

Please know I miss you terribly and will always be grateful for the time we had together.

Fondly,

Leah

She reread the note three times before folding it carefully and tucking it in the envelope. When she licked the flap and sealed it, a tear splotched the paper. She dried it with the hem of her shirt and put the letter on the TV. She would mail it from the front desk in the morning.

Already, she knew the nights were going to be the hardest. Too much time to think. Too much opportunity to remember what it was like to sleep in a bed with a large, warm, fascinating man who made her feel things that seemed impossible.

Lucas had shown her that she was a person with worth. No matter that her family might still treat her like the helpless youngest, she knew the truth. Establishing Camp Willow Pond and at the same time falling into a relationship with Lucas had given her strength and purpose. She felt confident and capable.

Sadly, now that she knew Lucas almost as well as she knew herself, she was helpless to be who he needed. If it were up to her, she would stand at his side, supporting him, nurturing him.

But Lucas walked alone. By choice. By habit. Maybe by necessity.

She feared she had lost him forever.

If that was the outcome, she still couldn't regret their time together. He had taught her so much about what it meant to love deeply. He had made her appreciate her sexuality. Despite the pain she felt now, Lucas had changed her irrevocably.

She loved him. Maybe she always would...

On the last full afternoon in Key West, Leah and Cate spent the afternoon by the pool. The day was hot and breezy. They both had books to read, but they mostly dozed and enjoyed a fruity drink or two.

Leah had one more thing to say, to *ask* really. But it seemed awfully personal, even between the dearest of friends. So she had put it off until now.

Desperation drove her, though. That and the fear that she would never recover.

"Cate," she said.

"Hmm?"

The other woman wore a tiny gold bikini that flattered her beautiful, tanned body. Her golden hair. Her beauty queen looks. Leah had always felt like a very ordinary duckling in Cate's presence. Not ugly, but not in the same league.

Lucas's lovemaking had erased many of those mental comparisons. He had made her believe in the unbelievable. That a man like Luscious Lucas could fall for someone who had often felt invisible growing up...

"Cate?" She said it again because she suspected her friend was mostly asleep.

"I'm awake." Cate lowered the back of her lounge chair a few inches and turned on her side in Leah's direction. "What is it?"

Leah stared out at the pool, unseeing, then back at her companion. "Is this how it felt? When Jason called off the wedding?"

"Oh, sweetie." Cate removed her sunglasses. A tiny frown

furrowed the space between her brows. "I understand what you're asking me. You're devastated. Incredibly hurt. So yes, in one way, the pain was hard for me to bear. But the two situations aren't really the same."

"Because you didn't love Jason like you love Harry?"

"That's part of it. Jason was right to call off the wedding. His timing sucked, but he saved us from making a terrible mistake. After some serious soul-searching, I could see that. When the wedding didn't happen, I was humiliated and embarrassed, and I didn't know what my future was going to look like. But ultimately, I wasn't heartbroken."

"I see."

"But there was something worse."

"What could be worse than getting dumped in front of twelve hundred people?"

"I fell in love with Harry. And I had no clue he cared about me. I thought he saw me as young and selfish and immature. When we finally understood each other, it was the most incredible time of my life."

"But then he thought you wanted to go back to Jason, and he broke up with you."

Cate nodded soberly. "Yes. So to answer your question, my wedding fiasco didn't feel the same as what you're experiencing, but almost losing Harry did. Even so, you're facing a difficult road to reconciliation. From what you've told me, Lucas has been shaped by secrets and lack of information."

"I know. He told me once that the past didn't matter to him. That he had created the life he wanted. I've never known him to show self-pity or make excuses. He's honorable and generous and strong in mind and body."

"And he thinks the only way he can keep that life afloat is not to let the past intrude."

"I think so."

Cate chewed her lip.

"What?" Leah asked. "What do you want to say?"

"I think I stand by my original advice. You have no choice but to wait. Wait for him to come to you. If he loves you—and it sounds like there's a good chance he does—he's eventually going to find his way back."

"I'm not sure about that. He thinks he's not good enough for me. That I deserve a *normal* guy. It's so stupid, and we argued about it, but the man is stubborn."

"Love is powerful," Cate said. "If you're the first woman he has truly loved, he may not understand the price he'll pay to turn his back on you. The situation isn't hopeless, Leah. But you'll have to be strong. Don't give up on him."

"I don't *want* to give up on him, but I hate doing nothing."

"Sometimes patience is the only defense we have when life knocks us down. Camp will keep you busy. Give Lucas time. Come the end of summer, everything may fall into place."

Leah appreciated Cate's counsel and advice. But Cate hadn't seen Lucas's face when he left Leah's house the night after Ed Carter's visit. Leah couldn't *unsee* it. She had awful dreams. Her lack of sleep took a toll.

Leah finished the break she was supposed to spend with Lucas and then welcomed her third set of campers on the eighteenth. Gabby spent a night at camp. That was one bright spot, but a vicious heat wave rocked Georgia during the last half of the month. Her counselors were getting tired, despite the time off. Tempers were short. Two of the college-age staff quit. Even so, that session was a success except for a short-lived stomach virus that went through the girls' cabin.

Leah worked harder than ever, trying to outrun the pain. Session three finally ended. Not once had she heard from Lucas. One evening at the grocery store, she saw Jeff Grainger at a distance, but she couldn't bring herself to approach him and ask about Lucas. That, like so many other things she wanted to do, seemed like an invasion of privacy.

Who knew if Lucas had even shared what happened in his life with his good friend?

Between the third and fourth sessions of camp, Cate and Harry finally had their wedding reception. Gabby and Leah went together as each other's plus-one. The intimate evening was held in a luxurious venue outside of Atlanta.

What had once been a working farm now served as a lovely event center. The cavernous barn was fully air-conditioned, and its rough timbers were strung with fairy lights and white netting. Cate and Harry were so obviously crazy in love, it made Leah's heart ache.

She was happy for them, so happy. But the joyous occasion made the turmoil in her own love life even harder to bear. Gabby put an arm around Leah's waist at one point. "How are you holding up, sweetie?"

Leah managed a smile. "I'm good."

"Do you know if he got your note?"

Leah had told her about mailing the letter to Lucas from Key West and then waiting, hoping. "I have no idea," she said. "If he did, he never responded."

"Have you tried setting anything on fire?" Gabby joked. "Seems like he would have to show up."

"Don't think it hasn't crossed my mind."

The evening seemed to last forever. Even though it was nice to see college friends and Cate's family, Leah was exhausted and dispirited. She had to climb out of this dark hole, but she didn't know how.

Lucas had *felt* like her soulmate. Clearly, she had confused sexual compatibility with love. Didn't people without a lot of intimate experience do that more often than those who had more experience, like Lucas?

At nine, Gabby appeared at her side. "I think we've stayed

long enough to be polite. We've both talked to Cate and Harry. The band is about to gear up for dancing. I was thinking you and I might slip out."

Leah nodded in relief. "Yes, please."

In the car, she found two pain relievers in her purse, washed them down with bottled water, and leaned her seat back.

Gabby kept one hand on the wheel but reached out briefly to squeeze Leah's fingers. "Talk to me, sweetie. I'm worried about you."

"I'm worried about me, too," Leah said, trying to be funny and failing miserably. "I don't think I can get past this unless I see Lucas at least once and talk things out. Even if it ends more badly than before, at least I'll know I tried."

"Okay," Gabby said slowly. "But when?"

"I thought I would wait until my fourth camp session is over. It will be the middle of August by then. More than a month since Lucas and I last saw each other."

"Is there a fifth session?"

"No. Most school systems start around the fifteenth to the twentieth, so we couldn't work it out."

"Do you know what you'll say?"

"I have no idea. Maybe I'll just wing it. Or better yet, write out a script. I'll probably be too nervous to be coherent otherwise."

"In that case, promise me something."

Leah stared at her friend whose attention was focused on the road ahead as they left the farm. "Promise you what?"

"Spend some time thinking about what you'll do if Lucas shuts the door in your face. Don't pin all your hopes on a grand reconciliation. Set the bar low. If things go well, you'll be thrilled. But if the meeting is disastrous, at least you'll be prepared."

Was that how Gabby approached men? If so, it was no wonder she hadn't found anyone.

Leah didn't *want* to consider the possibility that Lucas might shut her down. She clung to hope stubbornly, even if all evidence to the contrary told her Gabby was right.

"I'll try," she muttered. In her heart, she knew she was setting herself up for a major fall. Gabby's plan might have merit, but Leah was an all-in kind of woman.

She would take one more shot at convincing Lucas he was the man for her. If she failed, she would pick herself up somehow.

Her family had doubted Leah could pull off creating Camp Willow Pond. She had planned and worked and schemed and prayed and finally succeeded at something so very important to so many people.

Her professional endeavors were on track.

She had found strength and confidence in her personal life, too. It hadn't always been easy, but she had grown and changed in her relationship with Lucas. The woman she was now understood risk.

Her career in shepherding the camp was a home run.

Somehow, confronting Lucas one last time promised to be exponentially more difficult.

TWENTY-ONE

LEAH NEEDED TO BUY NEW CLOTHES, BUT IT WOULD have to wait until camp was over. Quite unintentionally, she had dropped that stubborn fifteen pounds and five more besides.

Food had lost all appeal. Between the heat and losing Lucas and the unimaginative camp meals, she made it through most days on an apple and a couple of protein bars.

Peg pulled her aside one afternoon. "Are you okay, Leah? I know it's not PC to mention a woman's weight, but I'm almost old enough to be your mother. I worry about you. Running this camp is a huge responsibility."

"It's the heat," Leah said, giving her half the truth. "And some stress, too, I suppose. I'm fine, really."

"If you say so." Peg seemed unconvinced. "I know you'll rest when this last session is over, but you need to take care of yourself in the meantime."

Leah grinned. "Yes, ma'am."

Jim and Peg obviously knew Lucas hadn't been back to camp

for the fire safety sessions. He'd sent one of his guys, though, to fill the gap.

Nothing was going to fill the bigger gap. Not for Leah.

On the very last day of camp for the summer, she was surprisingly emotional. These eighty kids had been her test case. She had learned so much from them, and she hoped and prayed that in return she had offered what they needed to survive and thrive at home.

She lingered for two days after everyone was gone. Cleaning crews came and went. One of Jeff's teams had driven out to talk about winterizing the dining hall and the two cabins. Leah wanted to have retreats in the fall and spring…maybe winter, too.

Oddly, Jeff didn't show up, but maybe he was busy finishing up projects at one of the local schools before classes began.

At last, Leah cleaned the small house that had been her camp home, made sure everything was in order, and locked it up. Afterward, she drove down the camp drive, stopped, got out, and swung the large metal gate across to lock that, too.

This segment of her life was over for now. There would be more camps and more campers, but the time had come to straighten out the wrinkles in her personal life.

Returning to town and her beautiful brick house with the roses and the white columns was bittersweet. She had hardly been here at all since Lucas walked out on her. It was painful to remember the hours they had spent together, in bed and otherwise.

It was time to get past that. She had decided to give up her apartment in Atlanta. She should have done it sooner. Aunt Trudie's home was Leah's home now, a refuge, a permanent base in Blossom Branch. Though things had gone sideways with Lucas, Leah had to reclaim this space as her own.

Remembering how he had looked sprawled in her bed was not productive.

Earlier, she had told Gabby she was going to see Lucas. That she had to find closure or some kind of resolution. But every time she picked up the phone to text him, she lost her nerve.

Equally impossible was the notion of simply showing up at his apartment.

To be honest, she didn't know for sure that he hadn't left town.

In desperation, she began cruising past the fire hall once a day. On day six, she finally got lucky. Lucas and Jeff were sitting outside at a picnic table eating.

She didn't slow down. Thankfully, they weren't paying attention to the flow of traffic. She slid by them without incident and drove home.

Her stomach flipped and flopped. Lucas hadn't run after all. He was still here.

What did it mean? Was he happy enough in Blossom Branch to stay indefinitely? Had Jeff been a sounding board for his buddy? Was Lucas okay with things now?

One possibility disturbed her more than any. What if Lucas had processed all he learned from Ed's visit and moved on? What if he simply didn't need or want Leah in his life anymore?

Her old insecurities reared up to taunt her. But she stared them down.

Lucas *had* cared about her deeply. If he was choosing to be alone, it was because he was clinging to the ridiculous notion that he wasn't a good match for her.

She didn't know what to do next.

One day turned into two, four, and six. A week went by. Then another.

Her cowardice began to disgust her. She was better than this.

Cate and Gabby had both encouraged her to *wait*…to give Lucas time. And Leah had. But the time for waiting was over.

She decided to invite him to her house for a Labor Day picnic lunch.

The Friday before, she realized that dragging her feet meant he might already have plans. She told herself she would text him Saturday morning. Without fail.

But she never got the chance.

Friday evening at ten thirty, someone rang her doorbell insistently. Loudly. When she looked out, she saw Jeff Grainger.

She swung open the door, alarmed. "Jeff? What's up?"

His expression was grim. "Lucas was injured in a house fire earlier tonight."

Her stomach clenched. "Burned?"

"No, thank God. But the second story of the house collapsed unexpectedly. A wall fell on him. Knocked his helmet loose. Cut his head. Gave him a bad concussion. His men pulled him out. He's at the hospital. I thought you would want to know."

Tears stung her eyes. "Thank you," she whispered. "I'll meet you there."

"You can ride with me if you want."

"Yes, please."

She grabbed shoes and keys and her purse. Jeff drove fast. Did that mean Lucas was worse than he was telling her?

At the hospital, they rode the elevator in silence. Jeff had punched the button for the ICU floor.

When they stepped out, she grabbed his arm. "Wait. Tell me how he is."

"The concussion is bad. They're monitoring him. If he's stable, and he behaves himself, he might get moved to a regular room tomorrow."

"Okay." She realized she was trembling, her breathing ragged. "I'm ready."

It was far past visiting hours, but maybe the fire chief merited special rules. Jeff paused in the doorway to cubicle three and spoke softly. "Lucas. I've brought Leah." Jeff grimaced at her. "He's been a little confused."

The man in the bed spoke. "I'm not confused."

The words were grumpy and hoarse. But it *sounded* like Lucas. He had white gauze wrapped around his head. Monitors beeped and whooshed. The man Leah loved was attached to an IV pole and other machines.

She approached the bed. Lucas's eyes had drifted shut again as if it was too much effort to hold them open. She wrapped her fingers around the hand that wasn't hooked up with tape and wires. "It's me. Leah. How are you feeling?"

He didn't open his eyes this time, but his face twisted. "My head hurts like hell. They won't give me any medicine."

Jeff shook his head and whispered. "They're giving him *something*, but not the good stuff yet, not until they make sure he doesn't have a skull fracture. The scan results should be back soon."

Leah pulled a chair close to the bed and sat down, still holding Lucas's hand. His skin was warm, and his fingers gripped hers. Surely that was a good sign.

"Rest," she said. "I'll be here when you wake up."

"We need to talk," he said, the words slightly slurred. "But not here. Not like this. They won't even let me go pee. When I'm home. Promise me."

The effort to talk visibly strained his stamina.

"I don't have to promise," she said, the words tart. "I'll be the one staying here with you at the hospital. I'll be the one taking you home when you're released. And I'll be the one looking after you at your apartment. If you have a problem with that, you can discuss it with hospital administration."

One eye opened. Then the other. Lucas stared at Jeff and managed to raise an eyebrow. "*You* did this to me?"

Jeff shrugged, grinning. "What can I say?" He smiled at Leah. "Do you need me to bring your car over here?"

She shook her head. "No. I won't be going anywhere until he does."

Jeff moved closer to the bed. He squeezed Lucas's shoulder.

"Thanks for not dying, buddy. I would have had that weighing on my conscience since I convinced you to come here and take the job."

Now Lucas barely managed the ghost of a smile. "Glad to oblige," he whispered.

Leah followed Jeff into the hall. "May I ask you a question?" she said. "Before you go?"

He nodded. "Sure."

She searched his face. "Why did you come to my house? Why did you tell me about the accident?"

His gaze was sober and perfectly clear. "Because he asked me to, Leah. He put your name and mine on all the HIPA paperwork, and he only asked for you."

The night crawled by. Leah didn't care. She was with Lucas again, and she would stay here indefinitely if necessary.

Sometime before midnight a doctor came by. He looked tired, but he gave Leah a thumbs-up. "No skull fractures. Chief Carter has a hard head. I've asked the nurse to bring him something stronger for the pain. They'll check on him frequently tonight. If all goes well, I'll move him to a room tomorrow afternoon. Let them know if he mentions nausea."

"Do I need to wake him on a schedule?"

"No. That's an old wives' tale. Get some rest while you can. That chair folds out. The staff will bring you a pillow and blanket whenever you ask."

The tightness in her chest eased a little. She'd been so scared when she saw Lucas. All that bold, strong masculinity bandaged and confined. It didn't seem right.

Whatever the nurse put in the IV calmed Lucas almost immediately. His grip on Leah's hand released, and his breathing deepened.

She used the bathroom, wiped her face with a damp cloth, and prepared to settle in for the night. In hindsight, she should have packed a small bag, but she hadn't known she was going to stay until she saw Lucas hurt and in that hospital bed.

The foldout chair was on the side of the room where it wouldn't be in the way when medical personnel came in to do what they had to do. When Leah curled up beneath the thin blanket and punched the pillow into a comfortable shape, she felt a wave of fatigue. The surge of adrenaline that had sustained her was gone.

For a couple of hours, she drifted in and out. ICU wasn't a particularly quiet place. She wanted to be close enough to touch the man in the bed, but that wasn't practical. So she rested and waited for morning.

Sometime around 5:00 a.m. his pain meds started wearing off. She woke to the realization that Lucas was restless. Moving around in the bed. Groaning.

After pressing the button to summon the nurse, Leah took his hand again. "Easy, love. You're okay. Would you like a sip of water?"

He opened his eyes, but his gaze was unfocused. "Am I dreaming?" he asked, the words raspy.

"No," she said quietly. "You're not dreaming." She raised the head of the bed and picked up the plastic tumbler with the bendy straw. Carefully, she offered it to him and waited while he drank.

"That's good," he mumbled.

The nurse was there by now. She added meds to the IV. "Sleep, Chief Carter. You'll feel better tomorrow."

He fought the effects of the medicine, turning his head to look at Leah. "I'm sorry."

She didn't know what he meant, and it didn't matter. His pupils were still dilated, and he was so clearly in pain. She put her hand on his forehead, stroking back his hair. "Close your eyes, Lucas. Rest…"

Apparently, stubborn men were no different even when concussed. Saturday was a very long day punctuated with meals of Jell-O and beef broth and plenty of sulky displeasure from the man who wanted a burger and fries.

Sunday morning, Lucas cajoled the doctor into releasing him completely instead of stepping down to a regular room.

Leah was horrified. "He shouldn't go home yet, should he?"

A different doctor, this one female, rolled her eyes. "Can you make him behave?"

"Honestly, I don't know."

She chuckled. "Well, he's gonna do nothing but raise hell if we don't let him out. I've checked the blood work. All his vitals are stable. As long as he won't be alone, I have no problem releasing him."

"If you're sure."

Lucas insisted on calling Jeff. When Leah protested, Lucas glared. "It's Sunday. We won't be disturbing him. Besides, I'm not having you dress me."

The man was irritable and grouchy, which must mean he was improving.

"Fine," Leah said, trying not to let exhaustion and frustration make her snap at him. "In that case, I'm going down to the cafeteria to grab breakfast. I'm starving."

He called her name, but she kept on walking. Lucas Carter could learn some manners.

When she finally went back upstairs, he was fully dressed and sitting in a wheelchair. Jeff sighed with relief when he saw her. "They just brought all the paperwork. We're out of here."

They were accompanied, of course, by an orderly who pushed the wheelchair. Between the hospital employee and Jeff, they managed to tuck Lucas into the passenger seat of Lucas's car. Jeff's truck wouldn't have worked. She could see by Lucas's expression that he wanted to shrug off the help, but he cooperated meekly.

When they were all in and Jeff had the AC cranked up, he

put the car in Reverse, not looking at either of his passengers. "Where am I taking him?" When Lucas was silent, Jeff's eyes met Leah's in the rearview mirror.

She shrugged. "Wherever he wants to go."

Jeff turned sideways. "Lucas?"

Lucas stared out the side window. "Her house," he said gruffly.

Leah swallowed. "In that case, I need groceries."

"And I'll need to swing by my place and pack a bag," Lucas said.

Jeff's expression never changed. "Then we'll drop you, Leah, at the market near his apartment. I'll help him grab a few things, and we'll come back to pick you up."

"Okay." She didn't know what else to say. She was honestly shocked that Lucas wasn't trying to hide anything from Jeff. Did that mean the two men had talked seriously?

After a month of nothing—more than a month, actually—suddenly Lucas wanted to stay with her? What did it mean?

An hour later, all the chores were accomplished. Lucas was fading fast. Though he was pale, and his forehead was damp, he insisted on walking inside under his own power. Stupid man.

Jeff followed him as far as the sofa. He glared at his friend. "For God's sake. Lie down before you pass out."

Lucas didn't say a word. He stretched out on Leah's couch and closed his eyes.

Leah and Jeff ignored him while they conferred in the kitchen.

Jeff shook his head slowly. "You'll call me if you need help? Or if he gets worse?"

"Of course." She smiled. "My friend Marisa is dropping off a chicken casserole later today. You're welcome to join us for dinner."

His gaze shifted. "Um, no. But thanks for the invite. I should get going."

Leah felt panicky suddenly. "Why did Lucas decide to come here? After everything that's happened? I don't know what he wants from me."

Suddenly, Jeff's gaze was mischievous. "Oh, I think you do. He's had a rough time. Go easy on him, will you? I know it hasn't been pleasant, but our boy is worth the trouble."

"I hope you're right."

Suddenly, Jeff was gone, and Leah was alone with her injured guest and a whole lot of questions.

Because Lucas appeared to be asleep, she showered for the first time in almost forty-eight hours and changed into clean undies and a soft cotton sundress in shades of green. She didn't bother with a bra. Once she twisted her wet hair into a knot on the back of her head, she knew it would dry eventually and come out wavy.

When she returned to the living room, Lucas was sitting up, his head in his hands.

"Would you like me to get you some medicine?" she asked quietly.

He straightened, his gaze widening as he took in her bare legs and perfectly respectable, comfy dress. Maybe he also noticed she had lost weight. "Not yet. I need a clear head for this."

She frowned. "For what?"

"Come sit with me," he said.

In the past he would have teased her with a sexy comment. Or suggested any number of naughty activities.

Now, she couldn't read him. "Would you like a snack?" He'd eaten lunch before they left the hospital.

"I don't care about food. And I swear I don't need a nurse. Please, Leah. I want to talk to you." His beautiful green and gold eyes seemed to be telegraphing a message, but she was afraid to read anything into it. Not when they had parted so abruptly.

She should be angry with him. Furious, probably, at his complete silence over the last several weeks. But she was so grateful he was alive, that emotion trumped everything else.

After a moment's hesitation, she joined him on the sofa, but at the opposite end. "So talk," she said bluntly. "You haven't been too chatty recently, so you'll pardon me if I'm surprised."

"I deserve that."

She folded her arms across her chest, trying not to throw herself into his lap.

When she didn't say anything else, he sighed. "Thank you for the letter you sent me. It was very generous of you." He reached in the pocket of his jeans and pulled out a twice folded envelope. "I've carried it with me everywhere for weeks."

"I wasn't even sure you read it," she said, her throat tight.

"I read every word. And I was ashamed. Because you have such a beautiful empathetic heart, and I treated you so badly."

"You had a terrible shock. I understood." She paused. "Or I tried to. I'm sorry about your parents."

"Thank you," he said quietly. "I spent so many years hating them, and turns out, they were nothing more than dumb horny kids who had a string of bad luck. It's almost been a relief to know I can let them rest in peace."

"And all the rest of the story?"

"Don't be mad," he said, "but Jeff went with me to Pennsylvania."

"Jeff," she said flatly. "Not me."

He held out his hands. "You were busy with camp. I needed to get my life straightened out. I didn't want you dragged into my family drama in case everything blew up."

"And did it?"

He exhaled, his fists resting loosely on his thighs. "No. Honestly, it was great. Awkward, but great. Ed arranged two different family meals. The Carters are nice people. I'll keep in touch, but they're a long way away and my life is busy."

"True." Her heart ached. Apparently, the point of this conversation was for Lucas to clear his conscience. He wanted to make amends. "I'm glad things worked out," she said.

Lucas stared at her. "I was a mess for days...weeks. Probably shouldn't have been working in that condition. But I put my head down and kept going."

"It was a lot to take in."

"Yeah." He stared at her as if waiting for something. Finally, he continued. "When that wall fell on me during the fire Friday, there was a split second before everything went black. All I could think about was that I was going to die without ever telling you I loved you."

"You love me." She parroted the words. Not a question. Simply a statement. One she wasn't sure she could believe.

His gaze pinned hers, refusing to let her look away. "I love you."

"Okay." It was a dumb thing to say, but her insides were a jumble of pain and fear and hope.

Lucas moved closer on the sofa. "You're still angry," he said. "I get that."

"No," she said sharply. "I don't think you do. Lucas..." She trailed off, unable to see how they could meet on two such different paths.

"What, babe?" He took one of her hands, but she pulled away. Touching him was impossible. All she had ever wanted was in arm's reach, but she was terribly afraid it was a mirage.

When he put a hand to his temple, she didn't know if he was making a play for sympathy or if he really had a headache.

"I think we should table this conversation until you're better," she said.

She tried to stand up, but he grabbed her wrist. "No," he said, sounding half-desperate and half-macho, bossy male. "Say what you need to say."

"It's a long list," she muttered wryly.

His jaw tightened. "I can handle it."

Leah gnawed her lip, trying to decide where to start. "I've changed, Lucas. After two plus decades of standing on the sidelines, now I know I'm good enough exactly the way I am. You told me that often, but I had to be the one to believe and change. I'm worthy of being desired. Being with you made me glad I'm a woman. For the first time, I reveled in my femininity. And it was wonderful. Heck, when you and I went toe-to-toe with my family, and I risked being honest about a few things, they finally began to see me as more than a mouse of a daughter and a sister."

He winced. "I hear a *but* coming somewhere."

"Exactly. You didn't practice what you preach. Because of how you grew up, you decided you were somehow broken. Not good enough. And because of that, you made a unilateral decision *not* to marry. *Not* to have kids. *Not* to love me. *That's* why I'm angry," she said. Tears welled in her eyes, but she didn't let them fall.

Lucas swallowed. "Okay."

Leah was shaking. "I get that you know your DNA now, and I'm happy for you. But if it wasn't for that knowledge and your recent near-death experience, you wouldn't be here with me today. You didn't believe in us before, and that hurts, damn it."

His expression changed. The light returned to his eyes. "That's not true," he said urgently. "I can prove it."

"How?"

TWENTY-TWO

LEAH WATCHED AS LUCAS HURRIEDLY REACHED DOWN into the duffel bag Jeff had dropped beside the sofa. When he sat up, he was holding a small red box. "I bought this a month and a half ago," he said. "You can check the date on the receipt. I had big plans for that week you and I were spending together. Big plans before you had to go back to camp. But then Ed came and..."

He trailed off, grimacing.

Still, he held the box.

"So that's for me?" she asked.

"Yes." He nodded, smiling at her in a way the old Lucas used to. "Nobody else, babe. The first day I met you, something happened to me. You were sweet and sexy and soft but not a pushover, never that. You were determined and a hard worker and you cared so much about your campers and your staff. All I hoped was that one day you would care about me half as much."

"Lucas…" She whispered his name, feeling her heart crack and break and instantly mend and fuse the pieces into a new shape.

For the first time since she had known him, he looked self-conscious. Unsure of himself. He held out the box. "If you don't like it, we'll get something else," he said. "But it's yours, no matter what happens. You might think it's too soon. I do love you, though, and I'm sorry I never told you. I'm sorry I made you doubt that I cared. I do care, sweet Leah. I love you so much I was willing to do anything to have you."

She took the box. Her heart beat so loudly she was sure he must hear it. Slowly, she raised the lid. Inside was a diamond ring. White gold. Or maybe platinum. A spectacular, fit-for-a-beauty-queen solitaire. Easily two carats. On a fireman's salary.

Holy heck. She was literally speechless.

Finally, she caught her breath. "Will you put it on me?" she asked, the words wobbly and quiet.

Lucas stared at her, green-amber eyes narrowed. "That depends. Do you want to keep it? Do you want to keep *me*?"

She was startled to realize he didn't know what she was thinking. He couldn't see the anguish she had experienced when he walked out of this house. Couldn't understand the fear when she heard he was hurt. The relief when he asked to come home with her.

"Oh, Lucas." She set the box on the coffee table and threw herself into his arms, wrapping herself around him until they were almost as close as two people could get. "I love you," she said. "I've loved you forever, it seems. How could I not? You're the perfect man for me."

Her wet cheek pressed against his. The big, brawny fire chief might have shed a tear or two as well. They clung together like lone survivors after a catastrophe.

Lucas stroked her back, nuzzled her neck, whispered words that only lovers used.

She couldn't seem to stop shaking. All the weeks of grieving and not knowing had weighed her down. Now joy replaced the aching sadness, and she was dizzy with relief.

At last, they pulled back to look at each other. She touched the white gauze on his head. "Are you really okay?"

His smile dazzled her. "Never better. And for the record, I plan to show you just how good I am as soon as I get you undressed."

She jumped to her feet, horrified. "Are you kidding me? I might accidentally kill you. The top of your head could literally explode. No sex until the doctor clears you on Tuesday afternoon." That was when Lucas's follow-up visit was scheduled.

"Spoilsport," he grumbled. But when she looked beyond the sexy teasing, she could see his pallor and the tension in his jaw that said he was in pain.

"Come to my room," she said. "Let's get you tucked in the bed, and I'll snuggle with you."

"Will we be naked?" he asked hopefully.

"Do you think that's wise?"

She was teasing him, but he took the question at face value. He stood slowly and pulled her close. "I want you naked and warm in my arms," he said, the words ragged. "Even if it *is* torture. God, I've missed you, Leah."

He kissed her then—long and slow and perfectly.

Somebody moaned. Leah, maybe. Or him. She wrapped her arms around his neck, careful not to bump his head. "I've missed you, too," she whispered. They were both trembling. "I hope this isn't a dream," she said. "If it is, I don't want to wake up."

Lucas rested his forehead against hers. "It's no dream. If I didn't have a knife stuck in the back of my skull, I'd rock your world."

"Big talk for a man with twelve stitches. C'mon. Let's get you comfortable."

When he stripped down to his underwear in her bedroom, she had to give herself a stern lecture. The man was hard-bodied and beautifully male, but he deserved to get well before she attacked him. The female ICU nurses had probably fought over who got to give him his sponge bath.

Lucas noticed the grin she tried to smother.

He lifted an eyebrow. "What's so funny?"

"I was laughing at myself," she said. "For luring Luscious Lucas into my bed knowing I can't have you. What a waste."

"You're a smart-ass, aren't you?" he said. "But you hide it well."

She ditched her dress, kept her panties, and crawled under the covers. When he dragged her close, tangling their limbs and kissing her wildly, she put a hand to his chest. "I'm serious. No sex. So you might as well close your eyes and take a nap."

Neither of them had gotten much rest at the hospital.

"Fine," he said, pretending to sulk. Then he reared up on one elbow. "I'm trying not to be insulted that you forgot to bring the ring with us."

Her eyes widened. "Oh, shoot. I did. Do you want me to go get it?"

He rubbed her butt, sighing. "You have a great ass. Nah. We'll deal with the ring later. Right now, holding you is all I need."

She cupped his cheek in her hand. "Ditto."

"Oh, and one more thing…" Now he looked sheepish.

"What?"

"You know how I didn't want the settlement money from the lawsuit?"

"I remember."

"Well, I changed my mind. But I asked them to make the check out to Camp Willow Pond. It's a lot of cash, Leah. You can use it for anything. Scholarships. New cabins. Whatever you think is best."

She couldn't help the tears that spilled over now. "That's a lovely gesture, an incredible gift."

He shrugged, his gaze guarded. "Well, I decided if the money could help some of your camp kids, then maybe those eighteen years I spent *not* being adopted would be worth something."

Her heart clenched hard. "I don't even know what to say except that I love you. Besides, those eighteen years made you the man you are."

"I guess so." He seemed surprised, as if he'd never thought of it that way.

When she snuggled down beside him, he stroked her hair. "In case the ring didn't make things clear, I'm asking you to marry me, Leah Marks."

She smiled against his chest. "And I'm saying yes. Yes, yes, and yes. Now, close your eyes and dream about Tuesday night."

He sighed. "It's going to be a great night, isn't it?"

Leah exhaled, burrowing closer to the man she loved, feeling peace steal over her. Peace wrapped in giddy happiness. "It's going to be a great *life*," she said. "And if you decide to flip houses instead of putting out fires, I'm definitely on board with that."

"I'll think about it," he promised. "But this concussion brought me back to you, so it was all worth it."

"There were easier ways to get my attention."

"Maybe." He dragged a finger across the tip of her breast, making her shudder. "Are you sure about the no-sex thing?" he asked, stroking and plumping her sensitive flesh until she wanted to break every rule she had made.

Fire streaked through her veins. The man did know his stuff. "I'm sure. Relax, my love. I'll be here when you wake up… and every day after that."

She realized he was already half-asleep.

"Love you, babe," he said, the words slurred.

"And I love you, too."

As she heard his steady breathing and felt his big body relax, she smiled up at the ceiling, hoping Aunt Trudie approved. Blossom Branch had brought Leah so much. A home. A purpose. And now the man who would walk by her side through good times and bad.

It didn't get any better than that...

★ ★ ★ ★ ★

*Look for the next Blossom Branch novel,
coming soon from* USA TODAY
bestselling author Janice Maynard!

MAYBE
MY
BABY

MAYBE
MY
BABY

ONE

GINNY BLACK WAS PREGNANT. POSSIBLY. PROBABLY.
There was a line on the white plastic stick in her pocket, and
she'd felt nauseated when she got up this morning.

The pregnancy test was wrapped in a Kleenex. She'd been
rechecking it every half hour, hoping the line would disappear.

So far, no luck.

To be honest, the nausea might have been from worrying
about the pregnancy test…and the fact that she was neither
married nor in a committed relationship.

She and Donovan had been introduced by mutual friends.
They'd been dating for nine months and sleeping together for
four of those. But it was a casual thing. Nobody had made any
promises.

Meanwhile, Ginny was losing it. Her nerves were frazzled.
A woman was entitled—right? This was the kind of life moment that called for a shot of hard liquor. Only Ginny wasn't

a drinker, and if she was pregnant, drowning her sorrows in alcohol was no longer an option.

It wasn't that she didn't like babies. From her limited experience, they seemed cute and cuddly. But she was not at a point where motherhood was advisable.

Didn't matter. The line on the stick was dark and impossible to miss.

Swallowing her understandable panic, she managed a smile for the next group of customers who entered the store. Peaches and Cream was Ginny's baby right now. As the only ice cream shop in Blossom Branch, Georgia, her fledgling business did well.

She was going into her fourth year. So far, she was breaking even. This endeavor would never make her rich, but ice cream made people happy, and Ginny liked doing that for her customers.

When she was alone again, she came out from behind the counter and paced. Her little shop included three small Victorian-style tables painted white. The matching chairs sported red velvet cushions.

She had hung four large oval mirrors with gilt frames, two on either wall, to make the space seem larger. The layout worked, especially because most people took their ice cream outside to eat while they walked or sat in the town square. The "square" was really a quad…two city blocks spliced together with a large, beautiful gazebo.

With big mirrors around the walls of her shop, it was hard not to see the look on her face. Given her strawberry blond hair, she had the usual fair-skinned coloring, but she was paler than normal. She sometimes wore a red-and-white-striped ball cap that matched the awning outside and carried out the theme of the store, but today it had made her head hurt.

She could use a haircut. Her natural curls tended to resemble a lion's mane if she let them get much past chin length.

A baby. A baby. What would Donovan say when she told him?

Even thinking about that conversation brought back the nausea. He had used protection every time, though condoms weren't 100 percent effective. Ginny had tried the pill years ago, but it had messed with her system.

Because she was not what a doctor would describe as *sexually active*—at least not until Donovan—the no-pill situation hadn't been an issue. Clearly, she had underestimated the danger.

Fortunately, the remainder of the day was very busy. She scooped cones and made milkshakes and cleaned up messes. All the while, she felt *aware* of her belly. Could she possibly be pregnant? It didn't seem real.

When she closed and locked the door at five thirty, she couldn't wait to get home. Her apartment wasn't fancy, but it suited her. Close to work…and affordable. At twenty-seven, almost twenty-eight, Ginny was proud of what she had accomplished in life.

Her parents were solidly middle-class. They had saved for years so their only daughter could go to the college of her choice. Her older brother, Richard, had chosen Georgia Tech. He was a chemical engineer with a great job, a wife, and a toddler, all in Atlanta.

Ginny had enrolled at Savannah College of Art and Design. Her major was illustration, which accounted for the colorful blackboard drawings on the back wall behind the counter at the ice cream shop. She had also taken electives in jewelry making, furniture design, and advertising. But without her leaving Blossom Branch, her choices were limited, especially since she had decided not to pursue a teaching certification in art.

Blossom Branch suited her, though. She didn't want to leave. The slow-paced, friendly little town would always be home. She felt grounded here. Content. Happy.

Most weeks, she was satisfied with the popular business she had established. Other moments, she chafed at scooping ice cream all day—and wondered about other creative possibilities that might offer more freedom. The *freedom* thing seemed a heck of a lot more relevant now. Nothing in college had prepared her for being a solo business owner with a baby on the way.

As she walked around the building to the tiny alley where her car was parked, she reached for calm. Ginny's parents still lived in Blossom Branch. She saw them frequently, though she hadn't gone as far as introducing them to Donovan yet. They would be thrilled to have another grandchild on the way, though possibly not so thrilled that their *baby girl* was pregnant and unwed. Ginny could already imagine the looks on their faces when she told them.

Blossom Branch was a small town that had embraced progress and change in many ways, but some social norms stayed stuck in the past.

Just as she unlocked her car, her phone dinged. It was Donovan…

Want to go to the new Marvel movie tonight?

She smiled wistfully. The invitation was so *him*. The guy wasn't a fan of superhero flicks, but he knew Ginny was. Hence the invitation.

Any other night she would have jumped at the offer. But the thought of sitting through a two-hour movie without talking made her antsy. She had to tell Donovan the truth…right?

That's what a mature, responsible woman would do.

Or maybe she should wait a few days and pee on a dozen more sticks. To be sure.

She hesitated for a long time before answering the text. Finally, she responded…

Long day. I'm beat. What if I pick up barbecue and bring it over to your house?

Donovan's reply was immediate.

You're speaking my language. Sounds great. 7PM?

Her chest fluttered with anxiety. Should she blurt out the truth before or after dinner? Was there an instruction manual for this? An ebook online?

Her fingers trembled…

See you then.

At home she took a quick shower and changed. Normally, she would have gone with leggings and a cute top. But tonight, she needed to pull out the big guns. It was still hot and muggy. She picked out a teal sundress with a flirty skirt and paired it with flats.

Her hair never cooperated. Especially with summer humidity. Donovan claimed to like the wild curls, and she believed him…but for now, she pulled the whole mess up in a high ponytail. Immediately, she felt cooler.

On the way across town, she practiced her speech. Nothing sounded right. How could she break the news gently to Donovan when *she* was freaking out?

The line at the drive-through was short. She picked up pork plates with all the trimmings and added a couple of the store's homemade brownies. When she put the bags in the passenger seat, the strong food smell made her stomach flop unpleasantly.

She rolled down her windows and told herself she wasn't going to puke.

As she turned onto Donovan's street, she looked ahead to his now-familiar house. The charming structure was one of the older homes in Blossom Branch. It had been built in the 1920s and renovated several times over the years. Donovan had bought it in run-down condition five years ago and spruced it up.

The brick bungalow with the wraparound porch and white

trim sat on a nice lot with an apple tree and a fenced-in back-yard, where Donovan's beagle, Sam, played happily.

Ginny took deep breaths and tried to find her composure. Honestly, this was the most difficult situation she had faced since losing two grandparents in three months when she was a senior in high school.

She got out of the car on legs that trembled. After grabbing her purse and the food bags, she locked the car and made her way up the concrete walk to the porch. Three shallow steps. One beautiful oak door. Two heartbeats to find the key he had given her a month ago.

Suddenly, she was inside. The familiar surroundings calmed the panic in her chest. Donovan was the kind of man who liked things to be neat but wasn't tight-assed about it. His home was comfortable and beautiful in equal measures.

Ginny left everything in the kitchen and went in search of her lover. She knew where to look. His workshop was connected to the back of the house by a covered breezeway. For a decade now, he had been producing handmade furniture for a wide variety of customers, particularly the wealthy ones who lived in Atlanta and maintained vacation homes in Blossom Branch.

She opened the door quietly, and there he stood, Donovan Mason. Boyfriend extraordinaire. His tall body was strong and broad shouldered. Not an ounce of fat on him anywhere. His streaky blond hair was longish and wavy. Everything about his looks and his temperament appealed to her.

He didn't hear her enter. With earbuds in and his music no doubt blasting, he was lost in a bubble of creative energy.

Today, he was working on what would become the top of a massive dining room table. For days now, he had planed the wood, sanded, and planed some more. Watching him make love to a rough board and turn it into something beautiful never grew old.

Ginny had been standing in this very workshop the first time she knew she was falling for him. He'd been rubbing linseed oil into the top of a hope chest, his big, long-fingered hands gentle and firm.

Even now, watching him work made Ginny dizzy with longing. She possessed intimate firsthand knowledge of those talented hands.

He must have sensed he was being watched. His head lifted, he turned off the music, and his face lit up with pleasure. "Hey, Sunshine. How long have you been standing there?"

His smile warmed some of the numb places in her chest. "Not long," she said.

"Hang on." He gave the wood one last glance before picking up a rag and wiping his hands. "This one's going to be a beauty. The family has eight kids. Can you imagine? They told me it's important they all be able to sit around the table together."

"Nice," Ginny said. And it *was* nice. But her mind was on other things.

Donovan crossed the room and caught her up in a bear hug. Because of him, she would always find the smell of sawdust arousing. He kissed her lazily, letting her know exactly how glad he was to see her.

She was breathless when he finally set her on her feet.

"I missed you today," he said. "And you look amazing by the way. I love that dress." He toyed with one of the spaghetti straps.

His fingers on her collarbone sent little tingles all over her body. "You knew where I was. We texted half a dozen times."

He rubbed his thumb across her cheek. "Not the same as having you here in the flesh."

The way he said the word *flesh* made her think about breaking a few rules…or throwing caution to the wind.

But if she was going to be a *mother*—her stomach clenched— she had to be sensible.

They walked into the house together. Donovan lifted his

head and sniffed the air. "Ah, good barbecue. Nothing smells more delicious." He turned and gave her one of those grins that weakened her knees. "Nothing except the curve of your neck when you're all damp and satisfied after I—"

She held up a hand, stopping him midsentence. "I get it. Hold that thought," she said. "We don't want to eat cold food."

Donovan nibbled her nape. "I have a microwave," he muttered. "In case you want to do anything *before* dinner."

A hard shiver quaked through her body. How did he do that? One touch of his lips and she melted.

She turned in his embrace and curled her arms around his neck. "Do you ever behave?"

His brown eyes sparkled with humor. "Where's the fun in that?"

"I missed you, too," she said.

"Nice to know." He sighed dramatically. "Okay. If I can't tempt you with anything else, I'll sublimate my urges with meat and potatoes."

Together, they set out the food. Donovan's kitchen cabinets were works of art—original to the house. But he had taken them off the wall, stripped half a dozen layers of paint, and refinished the wood to its true beauty.

The magnitude of that job stunned Ginny. He had tackled the project long before she met him. But seeing the final product told her he was a man who would follow through on his goals.

Still, raising a kid for eighteen years was a long way from woodworking. One job you could walk away from at the end of the day. The other, not so much.

The meal was unusually silent. Donovan wasn't one for chatter, and Ginny kept rehearsing her speech in her head.

She was eating her last bites of potato salad and hush puppies when he finished his beer and sat back in his seat. "I think I have a solution to your problem," he said. The fingers of his left hand drummed on the table.

The piece of food lodged in her throat. "My problem?" she croaked. *There is no way he could know about the pee stick. I only found out hours ago...*

Donovan gave her a puzzled look. "Your lease? The rent increase?"

She took a long swig of her soft drink and tried to breathe. "Oh, that. What did you have in mind?"

For the first time it occurred to her that her dinner companion seemed the tiniest bit nervous. He hid it well, but the signs were there. "The thing is," he said slowly, "you like the current location of your ice cream shop, and you love the building itself and the way it's right in the middle of the action on the town square."

"Yes."

"And you don't really want to relocate."

"True."

"So, your basic struggle is how to balance your budget and still absorb the hit from your landlord raising the rent."

"I know all that, Donovan. I've spent the last two weeks making lists of pros and cons about moving."

He cleared throat. "I was thinking that—"

A wave of nausea had Ginny on her feet. "Excuse me," she said. "I'll be right back." She made a dash to the bathroom and threw up everything she had just eaten. *Oh, God. It's true. I'm pregnant.*

She found a washcloth, wet it, and wiped her face. She was so pale, her freckles stood out. The dark circles under her eyes were the product of a sleepless night. If she didn't get her act together, Donovan was going to *guess* the truth before she ever had a chance to tell him.

After a minute of deep breathing, she returned to the kitchen. He was at the sink rinsing out the plastic barbecue containers to ready them for the recycle bin.

He stopped what he was doing and dried his hands. "You

okay, Sunshine?" He cupped her face in his hands and stared at her in concern.

Ginny grimaced. "I think the stress is getting to me."

"Poor baby." He folded her in his arms. She leaned into him, absorbing his quiet strength. Donovan was intensely masculine. But unlike a few guys she had dated, he didn't see caring and compassion as a weakness. That was astonishing to Ginny and completely disarming.

She had grown up in an extended family where the males fought good-naturedly to best each other in hunting and fishing and dirt bike racing. Everything was a competition.

Donovan had none of those traits. What had drawn her to him in the beginning was his absolute self-confidence and his wicked sense of humor. It didn't hurt that he was gorgeous and sexy.

In addition to his beautiful brown eyes, he had hair that fascinated her. The blond waves streaked with a darker caramel shade were nothing like hers. Before meeting Donovan, she had never cared for long hair on a man. But his chin-length mane, always tucked behind his ears—except when they were having sex—suited his looks and personality.

She didn't know if the longer length was a personal preference or simply a sign of the fact that he was too busy for frequent haircuts. But she loved running her hands through the thick, soft layers.

Finally, she stepped back from his embrace. She was swamped with guilt for no good reason. Maybe it was the fact that she was unable to blurt out two simple words. *I'm pregnant.* How hard was that to say?

Still, there had been two of them in that bed whenever this happened.

Wrapping her arms around her waist, she leaned against the fridge. "So what's this big idea you have that will solve all my problems?"

Donovan chuckled. "Not all your problems. Just the rent situation."

"Okay. Let's hear it."

He cocked his head and stared at her so intently her nipples tightened beneath the thin fabric of her bra. "I think you should move in with me."

TWO

WHEN GINNY OPENED HER EYES, SHE WAS LYING ON the kitchen floor. The usually unflappable Donovan knelt over her, white-faced, with a panicked expression.

She winced and put a hand to her head. "What happened?"

"You fainted." The two words sounded like an accusation. "Good Lord, Ginny. You need to see a doctor. This can't be normal."

"Let me sit up."

He put his hand on her shoulder. "Not yet. You caught the side of your face on the corner of the table when you went down."

"I'm fine," she muttered. Embarrassment heated her throat and cheeks.

Donovan stroked a lock of hair away from her forehead. It had escaped her ponytail. "Is the thought of living with me really that scary?"

His tone was humorous, but in his eyes she saw a flicker of hurt. "Of course not," she said. "I was surprised, that's all."

"Surprised? Really?" His jaw jutted. "I suppose I should apologize for spooking you. Clearly, we aren't on the same page about this relationship."

"That's not true," she said. But the words weren't convincing even to her own ears. "I want to get up."

She could tell he didn't like it, but he helped her to her feet and put her in a chair. "Don't move. I'm getting ice for that goose egg."

Ginny didn't *want* to move. She didn't want to do anything at all. Pitfalls in every direction. That's what she faced. And no clue how to navigate them.

She watched him dampen a dishcloth and wrap it around three ice cubes. Gently, he pressed the makeshift ice bag to the side of her face.

"I can hold it now," she said. Having him so close made it hard to think clearly. *Move in with me*, he had said. Wasn't that kind of earth-shattering news? Or was it no big deal to him?

Clearly, she couldn't answer *his* question without divulging her own change in circumstances.

Donovan took the seat across the table and stared at her, his jaw tight. "You want to tell me what's going on? I know you're stressed, but I've never seen you like this. It's scaring me, Sunshine." His half smile held only a fraction of its usual wattage.

Ginny was a wreck. Emotionally and in every other way. Donovan had asked her to move in with him. That was huge. Forty-eight hours ago, she would have been over the moon. Now she didn't know what to feel.

"It's been a hard couple of weeks," she said quietly. "Would you mind if we had a do-over? Tomorrow is Saturday. Why don't I make dinner and you come over around six? We can talk about this."

He was still. Watchful. His brain clearly operating on high speed as he tried to process all the things she wasn't saying.

Finally, he sighed. "It's okay to tell me you don't want to move in. I'm a grown man. I can handle a little rejection."

"I'm *not* rejecting you," she said, the words urgent. "But I don't think I'm up for sex right now, so it's best if I go home."

Storms flashed in his eyes. "Maybe you have the wrong opinion of me, Ginny. I'm not with you just for the sex. I want *you*. All of you. Does that include intimacy? Of course it does. But I thought the two of us were building something special."

She swallowed hard. He was breaking her heart into a million tiny pieces. "I did, too." Tears welled in her eyes and rolled down her cheeks. From Donovan's standpoint, everything had been going great. What was he going to say when Ginny revealed the truth? "I should go," she said. "I'm tired."

"I'll drive you. I can walk back," he insisted. "It's only a couple of miles, and it's a nice night."

She stood, managing a smile. "Don't be silly. I can drive myself. But thanks."

Donovan stood as well and took her in his arms. He held her carefully as if afraid she might break. "I'm sorry I upset you, Sunshine." He kissed her forehead. "Everything will be okay, I swear. You'll figure out the lease stuff, and you and I can keep the status quo."

It wasn't what she wanted, but she didn't have the strength to handle this conversation right now.

He walked her to her car, opened the door, and tucked her inside. Then he leaned an arm on top of the door instead of closing it. "I'd feel better if you'd let me drive you," he said, his tone troubled.

She smiled up at him. "You said it yourself. It's only a couple of miles. Don't worry about me. I'll feel better in the morning."

Ginny did *not* feel better in the morning. She lurched out of bed at six, dashed to the bathroom, and retched miserably. Then she sat on the floor beside the toilet and cried.

Thankfully, it was her Saturday to be off. She had a wonderful assistant manager, plus a part-time employee, who handled things beautifully whenever Ginny was away.

Even when the tears stopped, a sense of impending doom hung over her like an invisible cloud.

Donovan was the best thing that had ever happened to her. But how many couples got together because of a pregnancy and then didn't go the distance? She and Donovan hadn't even said *I love you* yet, though she had expected those words soon. Maybe that was supposed to have been part of the *move-in-with-me* invitation. Maybe if she hadn't passed out, he might have been ready to go on record with the big *L* word.

Instead, Ginny had created a huge scene, and she had hurt the man who was so very dear to her.

She *wanted* to know he loved her. But she didn't want him to feel trapped.

Clearly, there was no need to buy more expensive pregnancy tests. She would make an appointment with her ob-gyn, but the truth was staring her in the face. She was pregnant.

Donovan had been out of town for a few days last month. When he came home, they had indulged in wonderful reunion sex. That meant she probably knew when this baby was conceived.

Even now, sick and queasy, she found it hard to accept.

The only way she could get through the day was to compartmentalize. She made herself some hot tea and sipped it while eating saltines.

When she thought her stomach was under control, she dressed and went to the market. It would be dumb to attempt a fancy dinner given her iffy mental and physical state. Fortunately, Donovan loved her vegetable beef soup. It wasn't exactly a summer menu, but if she threw together some biscuits to go with it, he would be a happy man. Plus, she could make the soup early and have it simmering during the afternoon.

The day crawled by. At one point, she took out the letter from her landlord and read it for the twentieth time. The rent hadn't gone up in several years. Real estate on the town square was at a premium. She could understand the landlord's point. But that didn't make her situation any easier.

At four o'clock she put together the dry ingredients for her granny's biscuits. Then she turned the soup to low and took a thirty-minute nap. The aroma emanating from the pot on the stove was usually tantalizing. Today, it filled the apartment, threatening to make her ill.

When her alarm went off at four thirty, she groaned and put a pillow over her head. Why had she invited him to dinner? She didn't even know how or what she was going to say.

She made herself get up and splash water on her face. No cute sundress tonight. Stretchy leggings and a yellow tank top were comfortable and flattering. It was the best she could do.

The soup was perfect when she checked on it. And the smell didn't make her queasy anymore. All good on that front. She opened a bottle of wine, poured herself half a glass, and then froze after she took the first sip. *No wine, Ginny.* Good grief. How much else was going to change overnight?

When the doorbell rang at 5:45 p.m., she was mostly prepared. All she had to do was pop the biscuits in the oven a few minutes before they were ready to eat.

Donovan stood on her doorstep holding a sheaf of yellow roses. He grinned at her. "Hey, Sunshine. These are for you."

She stared down at the bouquet in bemusement as she backed up to let him enter. "What's the occasion?"

"Our first date was nine months ago tonight."

"Oh. I guess it was." She was embarrassed that she hadn't remembered, but honestly, she had bigger fish to fry. "Let me get a vase."

"How are you feeling?"

"Fine," she muttered.

As she rummaged under the sink, Donovan lifted the lid on the pot. "Hot damn. I love this soup."

Ginny straightened. "I know it's a million degrees outside, but I turned the AC down. You don't mind, do you?"

He put his arms around her from behind and squeezed. "Are you kidding? Your soup and biscuits? I'd eat those if it was a hundred and twenty and we were camping in Death Valley."

She leaned back against his chest, feeling the wave of comfort roll over her. Something about Donovan always made her feel safe and protected. She'd had a wonderful childhood. Nothing about her life was dark or bad. But he offered a steady, masculine presence in her life she hadn't known she needed.

While the biscuits cooked, the two of them set the table and poured drinks. Donovan didn't blink when Ginny chose milk. He opted for the sweet tea that she always made fresh and kept in the fridge.

They chatted about nothing in particular as they ate. When Donovan was buttering one last biscuit, Ginny knew the time had come for some straight talk. "I was flattered and touched when you asked me to move in with you," she said quietly.

He looked up, his expression guarded. "But?"

She swirled the tines of her fork through the honey and butter residue on her bread plate. "But I need to work out a few things before I make a big step like that."

"I didn't know it was so complicated."

Maybe it wasn't before this week. "I have to decide if I want to keep operating the ice cream shop."

He sat back in his chair and frowned. "Seriously? I thought you loved Peaches and Cream."

"I do. But think about it. Moving in with you helps my bottom line for right now. Still, I'm guessing there will be more rent increases to come. There's not a lot of profit margin in ice cream. Maybe I need to do something that's more sustainable in the long run." *Something that isn't quite so demanding for a woman with a newborn.*

Donovan shrugged. "It's your call, of course. But do you suppose the landlord might be open to *selling* the building? If you could buy it, you could rent out the upstairs floor to a lawyer or somebody like that to help with the mortgage. And it would give you several tax breaks you don't have now as a renter."

"I'll think about it," she said.

After they cleaned up the kitchen, they ended up on the sofa in her tiny living room. Donovan propped his feet on the coffee table and Ginny curled into his side, feeling content...mostly.

Except that she still hadn't told him about the baby.

"May I ask you a personal question?" she said.

He chuckled, making his chest rumble beneath her cheek. "Ask away."

"What made you decide to settle in Blossom Branch?" He had told her about being an army brat and how his mom died when he was sixteen. In fact, he'd told her a lot about his childhood, but not so much about the later years.

Donovan didn't seem to mind her question. "When my dad was stationed at Fort Benning, I was almost out of high school. One weekend a buddy of mine brought me here with him to visit his grandparents. I guess I fell in love with Blossom Branch that very moment. It was the kind of idyllic place I had never experienced growing up. People here put down roots."

"That's true. What happened after high school?"

"I had a scholarship to play football at the University of Georgia. I was a running back. Decent, not great. But after a couple of years, I realized the classroom stuff was stifling me. I had lived in eight countries by then. Traveled the world. Seen things most of my classmates could only imagine. So I dropped out."

"I see."

"You don't approve?"

"That's not what I said. If anything, I admire you for knowing yourself that well."

"You give me too much credit, Sunshine. Anyway, I came here on a whim and met an old guy who had a shop down by the railroad tracks. A single-story concrete block building that had been there since the 1950s. He made furniture. Beautiful museum-quality stuff. I badgered him to give me a job, and he did."

"Doing what?"

"At first, he paid me minimum wage to do grunt work. But eventually, he started teaching me the trade. I loved it. The smells and the tactile pleasure of working with wood. Once he trusted me, I became his apprentice."

"And now here you are. With a waiting list a mile long."

"Job security, right?" He kissed the top of her head.

For the first time in several days, Ginny felt normal. Which meant she felt other things, too. Like a surge of need for the man who held her close.

She nuzzled her face in his soft cotton shirt. "We could adjourn to my bedroom," she said. "If you're in the mood."

Now he laughed out loud. He shifted her to an upright position and kissed her lightly, his eyes glinting with sensual intent. "I've told you, Ginny. Men are *always* in the mood."

"Right. Got it."

His amusement faded by the time they made it to the bedroom. Now they were both in a hurry, stripping down as they eyed each other hungrily.

Ginny's bed was far smaller than Donovan's, though it was here he had first made love to her. When they were naked, she crooked her finger. "It's been too long. You've been neglecting me."

"A thousand apologies," he panted as he tumbled them both onto the mattress and leaned over her on one elbow. "God, you're beautiful." He buried his face between her breasts and drove her wild with tiny nips of his teeth.

She hung on to his powerful shoulders, her fingernails digging in as he slid his hand between her legs and stroked her. His body was honed and tough—accustomed to hard physical labor. She tested the flat plane of his belly with her palm, caressed the erect length of his sex.

Donovan was beautiful, too. He was comfortable in his own skin. Ginny envied him that. She had always wanted to be something she wasn't—tall, tanned, bosomy.

Instead, she was pale and freckled and medium everything. She got lost in the crowd in high school and college. Though she wasn't shy now, she certainly had been back then. Opening her ice cream shop had given her confidence and taught her to interact with the public.

Donovan waved a hand in front of her face. "No zoning out during sex," he said. "Where did you go?"

She smiled wistfully. "I was just thinking how gorgeous you are and how lucky I am."

He rolled his eyes. "Everybody in town knows I'm the lucky one," he muttered. "I get to sleep with the ice cream lady."

When he paused what he was doing and stared down at her, she almost panicked. Could he tell? Could he see a difference in her body? Was it written on her face? Suddenly, she wanted to pull the sheet over them, even though the room was warm.

Donovan was perceptive, always had been since the moment they met. A slight frown furrowed his brow. "Ginny. I feel like I've lost you. We don't have to do this if you're not feeling okay."

Her eyes filled with tears. Stupid hormonal tears. "I'm great," she whispered.

She didn't think he was convinced, but he didn't challenge her. He shifted to one side only long enough to retrieve a condom and roll it on. Then he came back to her and settled between her thighs.

"I could take you like this a dozen times a day and it wouldn't be enough," he said. The somber expression in his eyes told her he wasn't joking.

"Me, too," she said. "You make me happy, Donovan. I never knew I could feel this way about a man. I never have before."

Perhaps she should regret her honesty, but her lover groaned and surged inside her. "Good," he said. "Let's keep it that way."

Ginny had always heard pregnant women were insatiable. Perhaps it was true. She came twice, the orgasms like lightning strikes, and then her arousal built a third time, sweeter and even more satisfying.

When Donovan shuddered in her arms and buried his face in her neck, she held him tightly as if she could prevent the future from unraveling in a disaster of epic proportions.

Why couldn't life be simple? Meeting Donovan had made her feel as if she had won the lottery. He was hot and sexy and honorable and dependable. In fact, he was perfect daddy material.

But did he want to be?

That was the question.

She dozed in his arms, holding the time of reckoning at bay with nothing more than sheer will. As long as this moment never ended, life was perfect.

THREE

DONOVAN STRETCHED AND YAWNED. "I HATE TO SAY
it, Sunshine, but I've got to go home and get a few things ready
for tomorrow."

Sunday afternoons, Donovan met with clients at his place,
either delivering finished products or brainstorming with new
customers about what they wanted. When Ginny asked him
once why he gave up part of his weekend, he said it was because working families shouldn't have to take a day off when
he could be flexible.

Ginny had seen him interact with his adoring public. His
charisma and gentle charm were as much of a draw as his stunning creations.

"I understand," she said. Her own business was closed on
Sundays and Mondays. Tourist traffic was slow, and locals knew
to come later in the week. "I have a million things to do, too."

He leaned on his elbow and played with a lock of her hair.
"Like deciding whether to take me up on my offer?"

"It's not up to you to rescue me."

"Did you ever think *you* might be rescuing *me*?" he said. His tone was light, but in his eyes, she saw a different message. Was it possible the man who had spent so many years as a rolling stone was looking for permanence in his personal life? He'd made that choice in choosing a home. He had planted himself in Blossom Branch.

Did he see Ginny as his partner long-term?

As much as she wanted to say *yes, a thousand times yes*, it wasn't only Donovan she had to consider now. There was also the baby.

"Don't give up on me," she said. "I'll figure things out."

He pulled her to her feet and pressed her bare body to his, cupping her butt in his two big hands. "I'd do anything in the world for you, Sunshine. All you have to do is ask."

The naked hug almost derailed Donovan's plan to go home. But he and Ginny resisted temptation and scooped up their clothes.

After they were both dressed, she walked him to the kitchen. "Let me give you some soup for your lunch tomorrow." She squatted and found a plastic bowl and lid in a bottom cabinet. When she tried to stand too quickly, the room spun dizzily, and her stomach heaved. With her back to Donovan, she braced her hands on the edge of the counter, hoping he didn't notice anything amiss.

She puttered at the sink and in a drawer. After a minute, maybe two, she was finally able to turn around. "Here you go. I put biscuits in a separate container."

"You spoil me," he said.

When he smiled like that, his eyes crinkled at the corners. Would her baby be a boy who looked like Donovan? Big brown eyes and a grin that melted female hearts? If so, Ginny was doomed.

"I know how you get when you're working," she said. "Eating peanut butter out of the jar. You need real food."

He caught her wrist and reeled her in for a goodbye hug. "Yes, ma'am," he said, before proceeding to destroy her with a kiss that made her heart race and ache. After a few moments, he stepped back, a look of hunger on his face. They both knew how easy it would be to tumble back in bed.

"Bye," she said softly, wanting him to stay so badly it hurt.

His wicked smile disappeared, replaced by an inscrutable look. "Remember, I have that trade show Monday and Tuesday in Atlanta."

"Oh, right." Her heart sank. "I almost forgot."

"Dinner Wednesday night?"

"I'd love to…"

This time, he really did walk to the front door. But as he opened it and stepped onto her small porch, he turned back. "Call me. Text me. I know you have a lot going on. I'm here for you, Ginny."

Tears prickled in her throat and eyes. "Thanks," she said, the word almost inaudible.

And then he was gone.

Her morning sickness was regrettably unpredictable. And it was not limited to the dawn hours. She spent most of Sunday and Monday reading in bed and trying not to barf.

True to his word, Donovan kept in touch. Sometimes he sent silly memes via text. Sometimes a short cheer-up message in the vein of *everything will work out*. He was giving her space and yet being supportive. What more could she want in a man or the father of her child?

At some point on Monday, it occurred to her she was probably not going to be able to make it through an eight-hour shift at the ice cream shop. She felt like such a failure. Clearly, she was not going to be one of those super-capable pregnant women who kept their careers going right up until the hour their little one popped out.

Her assistant manager, Myrna, was not only an employee and coworker, but she was also a friend. So when Ginny called her sheepishly on Monday afternoon and asked if Myrna could drop by for an hour, she didn't even question it.

When the doorbell rang, Ginny had just spent half an hour hunched over the toilet. She hadn't dared even glance in the mirror. She had a good idea what she must look like.

But maybe Ginny underestimated her appearance, because when she opened the door and Myrna stood there, the other woman's eyes widened. "Good Lord," she said, her eyebrows shooting up in alarm. "What's wrong?"

"Don't worry," Ginny said glumly. "I'm not contagious."

When they were seated in the living room, Myrna stared at her. The other woman was in her early forties. She and her husband, Jim, had moved to Blossom Branch when they got married almost twenty years ago.

Myrna finally broke the silence. "Talk to me, hon. No offense, but you look like crap."

"No surprise to me." Ginny shredded the tissue in her hands. "I have a secret, and no one knows. But *you* need to know because of the shop. And I have to ask you not to tell anybody."

Myrna frowned. "Of course. You can talk to me about anything."

Ginny scrubbed her hands over her face. "I'm pregnant."

"Holy hell."

"Yeah."

The older woman eyed her sharply. "Morning sickness?"

"Oh, yes. And then some. I can't work if I'm dashing to the bathroom every fifteen minutes. The health department would love that."

"I can cover the extra hours," Myrna said. "Don't you worry."

"But we're so busy late in the week," Ginny wailed. "It takes three of us."

"I'll draft Jim. To be honest, he's just quit his job, so it would be good for him to get out of the house."

"What happened?" Jim was a delivery driver for one of the big shipping companies.

"They had two guys walk out, but corporate wouldn't approve any new hires. It was already a hard job with long hours. Now Jim and the other employees are being asked to do the impossible. So, Jim quit."

"Are you okay with it?"

"Oh, sure. We're pretty frugal. We've saved a fair amount over the years. Let us do this for you, Ginny. It's not charity, you know. We'll be drawing two paychecks."

"What you're doing is saving my life."

Myrna smiled gently. "So why am I the only person who knows about this? What about Donovan?"

That simple question—plus all the hormones—was enough to send a newly pregnant woman into a crying fit. When the sobbing and sniffling finally dwindled, Ginny told Myrna everything. About the rent increase and the moving-in offer from Donovan and not wanting to trap a man who hadn't said *I love you* yet and how Ginny wasn't even sure she wanted to sell ice cream anymore. But how could she be unemployed and pregnant and dump all that on a guy who didn't deserve to have his life upended?

Myrna snorted. "Don't kid yourself, Ginny. That baby didn't get in there by way of immaculate conception. Donovan bears responsibility, too."

"I suppose."

"Look, honey. You're sick and shocked and hormonal. Give yourself a break. It sounds like you have some big decisions to make. Promise me you won't worry about Peaches and Cream. You can trust me to keep things going."

Ginny smiled weakly. "I know I can. That's why I'm so lucky to have you."

"Why haven't you talked to your parents?"

"Because Donovan doesn't know yet. Besides, my mother is like a bloodhound when it comes to ferreting out secrets. I can't go over there until I've dealt with my unraveling life."

Myrna paused, her expression odd. "Do you *want* this baby?"

For a moment, Ginny was startled. That was one question she hadn't asked herself. But the answer came to her in a heartbeat. "I do," she said slowly. "The timing could hardly be worse. Who knows how Donovan is going to react? But yes. I want the baby. I hope I don't suck at this motherhood thing."

"You won't," Myrna said. "Besides, if all the old wives' tales are true, bad morning sickness indicates a healthy pregnancy."

Ginny scowled. "Oh, goody."

Myrna had the audacity to laugh in the face of Ginny's misery. "So when do you tell the new papa-to-be?"

"He's in Atlanta today and tomorrow. I guess it will have to be Wednesday night."

"Do you need anything?"

"No, but thank you. I'm hoping after a week or two I'll feel better."

"I don't want to be an alarmist, but for some people the nausea doesn't go away after the first trimester. Have you seen a doctor yet?"

"I made an appointment for tomorrow with an obstetrician in Gainesville. I know there's a women's clinic here in Blossom Branch, but I needed more privacy under the circumstances."

"Makes sense."

Ginny chewed her bottom lip, wanting to beg Myrna not to leave. But that was stupid. "You know how I can be sort of a control freak?"

Myrna grinned. "I've noticed on occasion."

"It's all falling apart. And there's nothing I can do." Panic fluttered in her chest like a hundred butterflies trying to escape at once.

"Make one of your famous lists," Myrna said. "Take it one day at a time, one decision at a time. You'll be fine, Ginny. I know you. Maybe this pregnancy has come out of the blue and knocked the feet out from under you, but you'll adjust. And I predict Donovan will be thrilled."

Ginny wrinkled her nose. "Thrilled?"

"Okay. Maybe *receptive* is the word. Or *pleased*."

"I hope you're right. Thank you for coming over. It means a lot."

Ginny didn't make it to the doctor on Tuesday. By midmorning, she had thrown up so many times, she was weak and shaky and a little bit scared about how bad she felt. She managed to call and reschedule her appointment, but otherwise, she curled up on her bed in a ball of misery.

If she hadn't been such a chicken Friday night or even Saturday, she would have already told Donovan and he would be here to help her. Knowing him, he might have canceled his Atlanta event.

That would have made her feel awful.

Later in the afternoon, Myrna left Jim in charge at the store just long enough to drop by with Sprite and Popsicles and home-made chicken soup from the diner. "You've got to eat something, honey. You're pale as death."

"I'm trying, believe me."

"You should call Donovan."

"He'll be home tonight. I'll talk to him tomorrow."

Myrna's smile was gentle. "The truth won't get any easier by postponing it. Ask him to come over this evening."

"He'll be tired. I'd rather have him in a good mood."

"Donovan is always in a good mood," Myrna said.

"Maybe."

"I've got to get back to the store. Jim is great, but he needs a good boss."

Ginny managed a laugh. "I can only imagine, poor man."

When she was alone again, Ginny paced from one end of her small home to the other. All other considerations aside, she would have to move somewhere more suitable before she gave birth. Her apartment was up two flights of steps. With all the necessary baby paraphernalia, that would be a nightmare.

She fixed herself a cup of the soup Myrna had brought and sat down at the kitchen table with a glass of lemon-lime soft drink. If she ate very, very slowly, this might work.

One bite stayed down. Then another.

Earlier, Ginny had set a notepad and pen on the table along with a medium-sized cardboard box that held some of her most prized possessions. Now she jotted a few things on the list. *Order baby books. Tell Mom and Dad I'm pregnant. Look for new apartment?* That last one was a question only because she might end up at Donovan's house. He even had a tiny guest room that could be converted into a nursery.

But Donovan had asked *Ginny* to move in, not Ginny and company.

She decided to wait a few minutes before trying more soup. Because the list was proving to be a challenge, she pushed it aside. Instead, she opened the box. In it were all her jewelry-making tools. Several kinds of pliers, a specialized saw, the disk punch, her practice material. Plenty of wire, mostly copper and sterling silver, but a bit of real gold.

After she set it all out on the table, she opened the red satin bag and carefully removed the necklace inside. The small sterling silver links were hand hammered. Suspended at the base of the twenty-inch chain was a single fire opal set in the same silver.

Ginny looped the necklace around her neck and fastened it. When she picked up the mirror, she saw the opal nestled against her plain navy T-shirt, right at the top of her breastbone.

She fingered the stunning stone, remembering the day she

had finished her project. The professor and her classmates had showered her with compliments, but Ginny had doubted. She had doubted her abilities, her technical skills, her originality.

So when she graduated, she returned to Blossom Branch and put all of these things away in a box on a high shelf in her closet.

It was ironic, really. Ginny was the one with the fancy, expensive degree. But Donovan, though he had dropped out of college, was the one who had found his calling and plunged into furniture making with enthusiasm and confidence.

Ginny hadn't believed in herself. And she wasn't sure why.

She hadn't given up art entirely. Her chalk drawings on the back wall of the ice cream shop were both personally challenging and entertaining to her customers. But the jewelry making—the real passion of her heart—had seemed like a foolish dream. She couldn't possibly make a living creating rings and necklaces and bracelets.

Could she?

So many thoughts swirled in her head. The prospect of decisions. Tough ones. But she realized that the absolute most important task facing her was to keep herself and her baby healthy.

She gathered up all her tools and packed them back in the box. Then she tackled the soup again. It was cooler now, almost too cold. But the taste was perfect.

After she finished half the bowl, she made herself stop. If her stomach cooperated, she could have the rest later.

It was six o'clock when her doorbell rang, an odd time for a visitor.

Something told her she knew who was on the other side. Her insides started to shake. After checking the peephole, she opened the door.

Donovan stood with his hands in the pockets of dress khakis, hair ruffled by the afternoon breeze, shoulders straining the seams of a button-down shirt in a dark-blue-and-green plaid. This was his version of work casual.

"Hey, Sunshine," he said. "May I come in?"

Ginny had thought she had at least another twenty-four hours before this stressful confrontation. Panic strangled her. Little yellow spots danced in her line of vision.

This time, Donovan saw what was about to happen. He scooped her up in his arms, kicked the front door shut with one foot, and carried her to the bedroom. When he set her down gently on the bed, his expression was a cross between concern and frustration.

"You were going to faint again, weren't you?" he said.

Ginny wrinkled her nose, not quite able to look at him. "Maybe."

He picked up her hand and stroked her palm with two fingers. "Talk to me."

When she turned her head and let her gaze meet his, she was struck by the worry in his thick-lashed brown eyes and the way his whole body was tensed as if braced for bad news.

She sucked in a deep breath. "I'm pregnant, Donovan."

He blinked, turned white, and squeezed her hand hard. "Oh, thank God."

"Excuse me?"

"I thought you were dying."

FOUR

GINNY DIDN'T KNOW WHETHER TO LAUGH OR CRY. "I'M pregnant. Did you get that? A baby, Donovan."

"But we used protection every—"

She held up her hand. "I know we did. It's those pesky percentages on the back of the box."

His expression was hard to read now as he ran his eyes from her head to her toes. "Are you sure?"

She reached into the drawer of her bedside table and retrieved the collection of plastic sticks she had accumulated, then scattered them on the comforter beside her. "Five out of five experts agree. It's positive."

"Have you seen a doctor?"

"I had an appointment today. But I was too sick to go. Had to reschedule for Friday."

Donovan winced. "Ah, hell, baby. I'm so sorry. I should have been here to take you." He sat against the headboard and pulled her into his arms, cuddling her against his broad chest. "How long have you known?"

"Since Friday when I brought barbecue to your house." Ginny paused and circled back to his earlier statement. "Why would you think I'm dying?"

He kissed the top of her head. "For one, your face is the color of skim milk. And your skinny jeans are hanging off your hip bones. Plus, you have this scary-as-hell habit of passing out like a rag doll."

"Sorry," she muttered. "It hasn't been a walk in the park for me either."

"What did you do about the ice cream shop?"

"Myrna and her husband are taking over in the short-term."

She felt a slight tension in Donovan's body even now. As if he wasn't quite sure of himself or the situation. *Join the club,* she thought bleakly.

He stroked her hair. "Have you been throwing up *every* morning? How many times?"

"I've lost count. And it's not just morning. Pretty much all day until right about now. Though if you try cooking something like collard greens or liver and onions, all bets are off."

"My poor sweetheart."

She let herself be comforted. It made her feel less alone amid this storm of uncertainty that had swallowed up her life.

Donovan sighed. "I'm taking you home with me tonight, so don't argue. You don't even have to pack a bag. I'll do it."

Maybe on another day Ginny would have protested his high-handed pronouncement. But she was so grateful not to face another night alone, she didn't even make a token protest.

Her lover was very efficient. And he took direction well. After he found her suitcase in the closet, he lifted an eyebrow. "Tell me what you want."

"Undies and bras in top drawer. T-shirt and shorts in the next one. I have a pair of black pants and a turquoise top in the closet. My toiletry bag is hanging on the back of the bathroom door. All you need to add is my toothpaste and toothbrush."

Her makeup, what there was of it, stayed in her purse.

Donovan moved around her small apartment quietly. Ginny pulled the quilt over her legs and dozed in a state of semiconsciousness. Multiple trips to the bathroom in the early morning hours had disrupted her sleep.

When Donovan roused her, half an hour had passed. "I'll put this stuff in the car and come back for you."

"Will you get the chicken soup and soft drinks out of the fridge? And a big box of soda crackers in the pantry?"

"Of course." He touched her arm. "I'll be right back."

She fell asleep again. When Donovan woke her this time, the worried look was back in his eyes. "Should we take you to a walk-in clinic?"

"No. I'm only sleepy because I was up so much in the wee hours. I'm fine, Donovan. Honestly."

She could tell he wasn't convinced. The crazy man wanted to carry her down two flights of stairs. But Ginny was adamant. "I can do this."

Despite her protests, by the time they made it back to Donovan's house, she was almost too tired to take a shower. But she also wanted to be clean. While her host unloaded his own luggage from the car, Ginny showered and changed into a pair of soft cotton sleep shorts and a T-shirt.

When Donovan found her in the bedroom, his expression sharpened, his eyes flashing a sensual heat she recognized. "I do love the sight of you in my bed, Sunshine." He stopped, an arrested look on his face. "Is this why you acted so weird when I suggested moving in with me? Because of the pregnancy?"

She raised up on one elbow. "Well, duh. I couldn't very well say yes when you didn't know the whole truth. I was just getting used to the idea myself. Besides, I..."

He sat down on the edge of the bed. "Besides, what?"

Ginny chewed her bottom lip. "I didn't want you to feel trapped into anything."

"Silly woman." The description was delivered with such a look of affection, it was hard to be insulted. He sobered. "Are you okay, Gin? Mentally, I mean. Do you want this pregnancy? This baby?"

She exhaled, staring past him at a painting on the wall. It was her work. A night scene of a mountain and a tree and a crescent moon done in oils. She had given it to him on his birthday a few months ago. Donovan had gotten choked up when he opened it.

Ginny had been touched by his genuine pleasure.

"If you had asked me even six weeks ago if I wanted to have a baby," she said, "I would have told you absolutely not. At least not right now. But it's weird, Donovan. At first, I was completely panicked—and I guess I still am—but once it slowly began to seem real, my whole worldview changed. I'm growing an actual human being. How is that even possible?" Her throat tightened, and tears spilled over her lashes.

He caught one on his fingertip. Then he leaned down and kissed her. "You have a few days' head start on me getting used to the idea," he said, "but I'm catching up. Babies are magical gifts. Not easy. Never that. But nothing worth having comes without effort. It's going to be okay, Sunshine, I swear. I'll be by your side every step of the way."

Her jaw wobbled. "Thank you."

He rolled to his feet and stared down at her. "Do you want a small snack?"

She shuddered. "No."

"Do you want to watch a movie?"

"I probably will, but I'm sure you need to catch up on work, especially since you've been away a couple of days. Go. Do whatever you would normally do on a night like this. I'm comfy, I swear."

"So you'll be okay if I hang out in the shop for a little while? I have my phone in my pocket."

"I won't even miss you."

Ginny fell asleep at some point during the evening. She roused only briefly when a warm, damp, yummy-smelling Donovan climbed into bed and spooned her. It felt amazing.

The next time she awoke, it wasn't so pleasant. She bolted out of bed and barely made it to the bathroom. How was it possible to throw up when she had hardly eaten anything?

Behind her, the hall light clicked on. She should have been embarrassed for Donovan to see her like this. But having him awake and keeping watch comforted her in ways she couldn't even explain.

She was sick twice more in the span of fifteen minutes. Then things seemed to settle down.

Through it all, Donovan held her hair back and crouched beside her. When it was over, he wiped her face with a wet cloth and, when she asked, found her toothbrush. The peppermint toothpaste almost made her sick again, but she took deep breaths and willed the nausea into submission.

"What time is it?" she whispered.

"Almost six."

Donovan scooped her up and cradled her in his arms as he took her back to bed.

She rested her cheek against his chest. "You can't carry me every time I get sick."

"Of course I can."

She was asleep almost instantly. But the peace lasted for only an hour before she was back in the bathroom. And again. And again.

By midmorning, Donovan was beside himself. "This can't wait until Friday, damn it. Give me the doctor's phone number."

Ginny had to agree. How much of this could her body take?

As she drifted in and out, she could hear Donovan in the

other room using a voice that was new to her. It was authoritative and demanding, though scrupulously polite.

The next time he walked into the bedroom, she struggled to sit up. "What did they say?"

"We're going at two thirty today."

Ginny burst into tears.

Donovan sat down and pulled her close, his expression frantic. "What's wrong? Tell me."

She swallowed back a wave of nausea. "I'm just so relieved."

He petted her until she fell asleep.

When she roused after that, the clock said two hours had passed. "Donovan," she called weakly.

He was in the room instantly. "What is it?"

"I think I should try the crackers and Sprite now."

"Are you sure?"

"No. But I need to eat and drink. I know that much."

Instead of asking her to sit at the kitchen table, Donovan brought everything to the bedroom. He watched like a hawk as she nibbled one saltine and barely sipped her drink.

They sat in silence to see what would happen. While they waited, Donovan picked up the opal necklace. She had put it on the dresser before her shower. "What's this?" he asked. "It's beautiful."

"I made it," she said. "For my senior project. I had a minor in jewelry making."

Donovan frowned. "You never told me that."

"I know. I thought you might wonder why I opened an ice cream parlor instead of a jewelry store."

He smiled. "It does raise the question." He examined the necklace even more closely. "This is exquisite, Gin. I've been to a lot of high-end craft exhibitions over the years. This is right up there with some of the best."

"Do you really think so?"

"I do." He frowned. "What made you doubt your talent?"

"*Everybody* at SCAD was talented. I was just one more kid who wanted to create art. When I graduated and came home, the old man who ran the ice cream shop was retiring. Something told me that's what I should do. I'm not sure why. Maybe because it seemed like a sure thing. Unlike jewelry making. My parents helped me buy out the business, and I've been doing it ever since." She glanced at the clock. "I think I can try another cracker."

Donovan handed her one. "Here's hoping."

It stayed down. For the moment.

She managed a smile, wanting to erase that look from his face. "This seems to be the pattern. I probably should get dressed, shouldn't I?"

Donovan glanced at his watch. "You've got time. Don't rush it."

Thankfully, her stomach cooperated. The only problem now was how weak she was from not eating.

Because she wanted to get ready on her own, she had Donovan lay out everything on the bed, including the black pants and turquoise top. He was prepared to dress her like a child. She could see it on his face. But a woman needed some shred of dignity, even in this unorthodox situation.

He took *his* clothes to another room, but when he returned, his jaw was grim. "Yell if you feel faint. And don't stand up, damn it."

Ginny managed a smile. "You didn't used to cuss this much."

His lips quirked. "Well, you didn't used to be pregnant."

They made it to the doctor's office with ten minutes to spare. Donovan insisted on holding her arm as they walked inside. His intense regard was sweet but overwhelming.

Because Ginny was a new patient, there were reams of paperwork to fill out. Finally, they called her back.

She glanced at Donovan, feeling as hesitant and unsure as a middle-school girl. "Do you want to come with me?"

His expression softened. "Yes, Sunshine. Yes, I do."

The nurse bustled through the usual routine of blood pressure, temperature, and medications. "The doctor will be in shortly," she said. "Put on this gown. The sheet drapes over your lap."

Without asking, Donovan disappeared briefly while Ginny changed out of her clothes. She sent him a text to come back in when she was ready.

Not surprisingly, *shortly* was a euphemism for almost an hour. Ginny slept on the exam table. Donovan leaned his head against the wall and napped in an uncomfortable chair.

With little fanfare, the doctor eventually entered the room and introduced herself. She was late fiftyish and no-nonsense.

As the doc prepared to do the initial assessment, Ginny felt her face flush. She gazed at Donovan pleadingly. "Would you mind stepping into the hall during the pelvic exam?"

His eyes might have bugged out a tiny bit. "Sure," he croaked.

The doctor did what she had to do and scooted back from the table. "Would you like me to bring your partner back in?"

"Yes. Please."

Ginny was modestly covered when Donovan returned. He took his original chair. The doctor addressed Ginny. "We're looking at a due date of late April. But tell me about this nausea."

"It starts at 5:30 or 6 in the morning and lasts on and off until late afternoon. At that point I can usually get a few bites down if I take it slowly. Same with drinking."

The doctor picked up the pages Ginny had filled out. "Because you're a new patient, I don't have any benchmarks. How much weight do you think you've lost?"

"Six pounds. Maybe seven."

"Over what period of time?"

"A week."

"Hmmm…"

The doctor laid the chart aside. "I think for now, you're not in the danger zone, though I know this is very unpleasant. My nurse will give you some information about over-the-counter vitamin B6 and ginger. Both of those help with nausea. You'll have to force yourself to eat and drink in the late afternoon and evening if that's the only time you can keep food down. But if your condition worsens—if you get dehydrated and your electrolytes go haywire—we'll have to consider admitting you to the hospital."

"I understand," Ginny said, chastened.

The doctor moved her attention to Donovan. "I need you to be the point person on this. Get her anything and everything to eat or drink that sounds appealing. When her nausea finally improves, we'll start her on prenatal vitamins."

Donovan nodded. "Yes, ma'am."

"And if you see her becoming listless or unresponsive, call my office immediately."

"Got it."

Ginny could tell that Donovan was freaking out a little bit.

The doctor stood. "You're very healthy. This pregnancy should proceed normally despite the morning sickness. For some women it abates after week twelve or thirteen, but don't pin your hopes on that. It's possible you'll have to manage the nausea long-term. But remember, it can only last nine months."

"Right." Ginny winced. "Fingers crossed."

"Do you have any questions for me before I go?"

Ginny felt her face heat, but she wanted Donovan to hear from a professional. "What about sex? Either now or later?"

The physician's somber expression morphed into amusement. "Young lady, when and if you feel like having intercourse, go for it. It's healthy for you, and the baby is perfectly safe."

When Ginny shot a sideways glance at Donovan, his usually calm face was beet red.

As the doctor left, Donovan sprang to his feet. "Are you feeling okay at the moment?" he asked.

"Yes."

"Then I'll meet you in the waiting room."

FIVE

HE WAS GONE SO QUICKLY GINNY BARELY HAD TIME to blink. She scooted down off the table and retrieved her clothes. No sudden movements. If taking things slow and easy helped the nausea, she could do that.

On the way home, they drove through the pizza place to get food for Donovan. He put the box in the trunk so Ginny wouldn't have to smell it. Her plan was to eat more of the chicken soup and crackers.

But she also knew she and Donovan needed to have a serious talk. If that could only happen in the evening hours, then tonight was her opportunity.

He was worried his meal would bother her. Ginny shook her head. "To be honest, it smells wonderful. But I'm not going to push my luck," she said hastily.

Donovan insisted on tidying the kitchen. Ginny lay down on the sofa in the living room and closed her eyes. When he joined her fifteen minutes later, she sat up. "I have some things to say," she said.

His grin was faint. "Maybe I do, too. But you first."

Ginny bit her lip, searching for the right words. "You asked me to move in with you before you found out about the baby. It occurs to me that this new information might change things for you."

"It doesn't," he said bluntly.

"I hate feeling helpless," she said. And she hated the tears that came so readily.

Donovan pulled her into his arms, cuddling her against his side. He kissed her temple. "I don't know what it's like to be pregnant. But I do have a fair amount of experience with being uprooted and feeling disoriented. It takes time, Sunshine. But you'll find your balance. We both will."

There was one question she wanted to ask, but it unnerved her. She asked it anyway. "How many times have you lived with a woman?"

He shifted so he could see her face. "Zero," he said. "Zilch. Nada. You're the first."

Her eyes widened. "Seriously?"

His crooked grin was rueful. "Yep. So when you didn't jump at my invitation, it was a punch in the gut."

She placed her hand, palm flat, on his washboard abdomen. "I'm sorry. I wanted to say yes more than anything. It seems unfair to you, though."

Donovan caught her chin in his hand and stared into her eyes. "I counted backward. I think I know the night we made the baby."

"I had the same thought," she confessed.

"There were two of us in that bed, Sunshine. You're not dumping anything on me. Are we clear on that?" His stern look was convincing.

Her throat was tight. "Yes."

"We'll make do the rest of this week. Saturday I'll get boxes and pack up your apartment. Your job will be to sit and watch and boss me around."

Ginny badly wanted to ask him outright if he loved her. But she was afraid of the answer. Maybe the roommate thing was just an arrangement for frequent, convenient sex.

"You should go work," she said. "I can entertain myself."

"I thought that was *my* job." He grinned, waggling his eyebrows with exaggerated lust. "*Entertaining* you is one of my favorite activities."

"Very funny." His reference to sex relieved her. She didn't want her current situation to interfere with their physical relationship.

He kissed her long and slow, rekindling the need that made her want him badly. "I'll *entertain* you night and day, Ginny. But only after we get you in better shape."

"I'm not feeling sick right now," she protested.

"But you've had a tough day, a tough week. I'm a grown man. I can wait."

"What if I can't?" she said, aggrieved that he apparently had more self-control than she did.

"Patience, little mama."

Thursday and Friday followed a pattern. Ginny was sick every morning, multiple times. But the B6 and the ginger did seem to help, even if only a little.

Once her stomach settled and she fell back asleep, Donovan headed to his workshop. He came in to check on her every hour, and he brought her food and drink—as much as she could tolerate. In the evenings, Donovan continued working while Ginny watched Netflix or looked at baby stuff online. More importantly, she spoke with Myrna about keeping tabs on the ice cream shop for the immediate future. Aside from that, Ginny made sketches of a series of jewelry designs that had popped into her head.

Saturday afternoon, they went to her apartment. After a difficult early morning, she felt weak and shaky, but less nauseated than before.

She had rented the apartment furnished, so Donovan's job wasn't onerous. There were a few boxes that would go into storage in his attic, but other than that, he had all her important personal things packed in three hours.

Ginny sat in the bedroom and wondered if she was doing the right thing.

When Donovan joined her and flopped down on the bed, eyes closed, she brushed the hair from his forehead. "You're a miracle worker," she said. "Remind me to always call you when I'm packing."

He opened one eye and glared at her. "This is your last move for a long, long time, Sunshine. Don't get any ideas."

"I have some news," she said quietly.

He sat up and yawned. "Oh?"

"Myrna and her husband have offered to buy the ice cream business from me."

Suddenly, he looked far more alert. "I didn't know that was a possibility."

"It wasn't. Until yesterday. But I need the money. I'm not moving in with you and becoming a financial burden. Besides, I thought I might use the months before the baby comes to work on my jewelry. The materials are pricey. I could start building an inventory of pieces and continue even after the baby is born. Then at some point, I could think about opening a small boutique. Or instead, maybe sell my things on consignment at Just Peachy."

Donovan absorbed her fast-talking, nervous explanation and nodded slowly. "I'm on board if that's what you *want* to do. But

I have money, Sunshine. An embarrassing amount of it, in fact. I want to take care of you and the baby."

Ginny frowned. "Are we about to have our first big fight?"

He sighed. "I can't fight with a ghost. That's what you look like right now. A beautiful, fragile spirit. Money is not an issue, Ginny. I could afford to buy the Peaches and Cream building from your landlord. What's important to me is your happiness."

"If you're going to say sweet things like that, I can't fight with you at all. You don't play fair."

He grinned. "All part of my evil plan."

Ginny leaned forward and kissed him desperately. She honestly didn't care if he had money. This man was her future, the father of her baby. Her eyes pricked with tears. The two of them were rushing into something that *could have* unfolded organically, romantically.

Instead, Ginny was unable to work right now. Donovan was seeing her at her absolute worst. And even though his words about caring for her could possibly mean marriage or at least something long-term, neither of them had been brave enough to say the actual words, *I love you*, out loud.

In a split second, Donovan took control of the kiss. His tongue teased hers. His strong arms wrapped around her and pulled her on top of him as he sprawled on his back a second time. The apartment had been hot when they first arrived. Ginny had changed into a thin cotton sundress to cool down.

Now her wardrobe choice made for easy access.

Donovan stroked her intimately, pressing between her legs against her bikini undies until she squirmed and gasped. "Take me," she whispered. "Or maybe I'll take you…"

She saw his inner struggle written on his face. "I don't want to make you feel worse," he said.

"Sleeping with you every night has been wonderful, but right now, I want more. I want all of you, Donovan."

"You're sure?"

"I'm sure."

"If you start to feel sick, we'll stop," he insisted, his expression torn between lust and indecision.

Ginny unzipped his pants and helped shimmy them to his knees. Suddenly, slow wasn't working for her. She found his erection and fisted it. "I need you inside me."

Donovan froze, his expression arrested.

"What is it?" she cried, alarmed by his odd body language.

"We don't need a condom," he croaked. "I've never once made love to you without one."

Her face flushed. Her breasts tightened. Desire—hot and greedy—poured through her veins. "Show me," she said.

Desperation made them clumsy. Instead of undressing, Ginny straddled his waist. Donovan shoved her underwear out of the way and filled her with one forceful thrust. "Oh, damn," he groaned. "This is incredible."

It was incredible and beautiful and desperate.

Ginny felt wild and free. Donovan gripped her ass. They moved as one. She was panting. They both were.

Donovan tried to slow down, but they were feeling the sting of a weeklong sexual fast. When he thumbed her most sensitive spot, she cried out and fell into a wave of pleasure that went on and on in endless ripples.

"Sunshine…" Dylan groaned out his pet name for her and arched his back, filling her with his powerful surge as he found release. She slumped onto his broad, warm chest, her head beneath his chin.

In the silence that followed, she could hear his ragged breathing. Outside on the street, cars went by. Ginny had a hard time catching her breath. She was elated and terrified and everything in between.

Eventually, they both got up. There wasn't much talking as they adjusted their clothes. Donovan finished carrying boxes to the car. They had ridden in his ten-year-old pickup truck, the one he used to transport wood and make deliveries.

Ginny ran a comb through her hair and used the bathroom. Then she sat in the living room and waited.

When Donovan climbed the steps again and came inside, he was hot and sweaty. She grimaced. "I feel bad making you do all this."

"You didn't *make* me do anything," he said, shaking his head. "I think I'll come back for your TV and the coffee maker. I'd rather put those in the car. Are you sure about this supper idea?"

She had suggested a meal at Peach Crumble. "I didn't think about leaving my stuff unattended."

"If we park the truck at the curb where we can keep an eye on things, I'm sure it will be fine. But I was really talking about your stomach."

"Oh." She grimaced. "I'm just so tired of staying in bed and eating crackers. Surely there's something I can try."

"It's your call." But his expression showed his doubt.

Fortunately, Ginny fared well. She ordered a plain grilled chicken breast with a side of applesauce and hot tea. Though she only managed to eat a third of the chicken, the food stayed down.

As Donovan enjoyed a slice of German chocolate cake for dessert, Ginny brooded. "I have to tell my parents about the baby soon."

"You don't want to?"

She shrugged. "They'll probably think I'm too young to be starting a family. My mom was thirty-five when she had me. She believes in women pursuing solid careers."

"I can go with you," he said. "For moral support."

Ginny couldn't quite meet his eyes. "Thanks. But I think it will be better if I go on my own this first time."

As soon as the words left her mouth, she knew it was the wrong thing to say.

His eyes flashed and his mouth tightened. "Are you ashamed of me? Or of the baby?"

"It's not that…"

But maybe it was exactly that. She didn't want to tell her parents this was an accidental pregnancy with a man who had given no promises to her and vice versa.

They made the short trip home in silence. Donovan carried in her bags and boxes. "I cleaned out two drawers in the dresser," he said. "And I moved most of my closet stuff across the hall. I don't want you to overdo it unpacking."

She sat down on the bed, feeling those damn tears clog her throat. "It can wait until tomorrow. I think I'll read or watch TV." She glanced at her watch. "At least you can get several hours of work in before bedtime. I know today jacked up your schedule."

Donovan cursed beneath his breath. She was so shocked, she clenched her fists. "What?" she asked. "What did I say?"

He shoved his hands in his pockets and stared at her with a laser gaze that laid bare every one of her insecurities. "*You* are my schedule right now, Ginny. You and this baby. Having you here is *not* an inconvenience. So please quit acting like an unwanted guest. Will you do that for me?"

She had never seen him lose his temper. She bit down hard on her lower lip to keep it from trembling. "Yes."

He stared at her for another interminable collection of seconds. Then he turned on his heel and disappeared.

She collapsed backward on the bed. All the breath left her body.

Living with Donovan wasn't going to work unless she was honest with him about her feelings. How would he respond if she told him she loved him? Would her admission make their situation better or worse? For the next hour, she huddled in bed with the covers pulled to her chin and tried to find the courage and the words she needed.

★ ★ ★

At nine o'clock she knew she couldn't go to bed alone. Not without trying to clear the air between her and Donovan. Dinner had stayed down, but her stomach was queasy.

When she stepped out onto the breezeway, she discovered that the summer night had cooled considerably. Tree frogs made a racket nearby. The neighbor's dog barked at unseen possums or skunks.

Ginny tiptoed barefoot to Donovan's workshop and quietly opened the door.

He noticed her immediately. No music tonight. He tossed a small tarp over the table and came in her direction. "What's wrong?" he asked sharply. "Are you okay?"

She held up both hands. "Stand down, soldier. This is a social visit."

His posture relaxed. "I thought you'd be asleep by now."

"I probably will be soon." She saw the huge piece of wood that was going to be a dining room table. "You're not working on that?" He'd said it was already overdue.

"No."

That was it. No explanation.

She inhaled sharply. "I'm sorry this has happened, Donovan. It would have been fun just to move in with you and enjoy playing around. Now, everything is…" She trailed off, not sure how to describe what she was feeling.

He closed the distance between them and took her hands in his. "There's something I haven't been honest about, Sunshine."

Ginny tensed, the nausea returning. "Oh?"

One of his shoulders lifted and fell. A look of self-derision painted his face. "I don't know why this has been hard to say."

Tremors made her legs wobbly. Was he going to offer her money? Or buy her a house nearby where she and the baby would be close but not underfoot?

"Go ahead," she said. "I'd rather you be completely honest with me than try to protect my feelings."

His chest rose and fell as he inhaled and let out a whooshed breath, maybe buying time. "I'm in love with you, Ginny. Head over heels. Till death do us part. The whole enchilada."

"Don't say *enchilada*," she whispered, and then everything went black.

When she came to, Donovan was cussing like a sailor and chafing her hands. They were both on the dusty floor of the workshop, she in his lap.

"Did I faint again?" she asked.

"Yes." He scowled. "I think I can handle fatherhood, but this pregnancy may be the death of me."

She held his hand to her face. "I love you, too, Donovan. And not just because you knocked me up."

His lips twitched. "Out of curiosity, why did you think I asked you to move in?"

"Convenient booty calls? And because I can cook? Maybe I'll be able to again when the smell of anything and everything doesn't make me want to puke."

He rubbed his thumb over her bottom lip, grinning when she nipped him with her teeth. "We live two miles apart," he said. "The booty was already convenient. And *I* know how to cook, too. I've just been letting you do it because I thought you liked feeding me."

Her eyes widened. "Are you serious?"

"My dad was a great cook. He taught me how. Lasagna. Beef Stroganoff. Fried-bologna sandwiches."

Ginny's stomach heaved. She put a hand over her mouth. "Stop. Stop. Stop. We can compare culinary notes later." When she thought the danger had passed, she levered herself upright and leaned into him. "Help me stand up, will you?"

Donovan did as she asked, but he hovered. "Take it easy, Sunshine." He smiled. "Do you know why I call you that?"

She shrugged. "I always assumed it was my hair."

"Could be. But mostly it's the way you make me feel. Like the sun is shining all the time, warming me even on the dreariest days. I adore you, Ginny. You're going to be a fabulous mother."

"Don't make me cry." She sniffed. Then she cocked her head. "Why aren't you working on the big dining room table? What's under that tarp?"

His smile changed, became guarded. "It was going to be a surprise, but maybe this will convince you I'm in it for the long haul."

With her hand clasped in one of his, he took two steps and flipped back the heavy canvas. Beneath it was a collection of wood, some pieces already cut. Cherry. Gorgeous grain. This time, there was nothing she could do about the tears that welled up and rolled down her cheeks. She looked up at him. Saw the love in his eyes. The cautious hope. "You're making a crib?" she said, the words shaky with emotion.

He nodded, picking up one of the narrow pieces that would eventually be a side slat. "Yeah. And if we're smart, we'll use it more than once. 'Cause you know I don't like to waste stuff."

She chuckled through her astonishment, incredulous that her passion for him could grow and grow and feel even more perfect.

"I love you so very much, Donovan Mason." She leaned her head against his arm. "We're going to be okay, aren't we?"

He turned her toward him and bent his head, finding her lips with his.

The kiss sizzled all the way down to her toes. "Better than okay, my dearest Ginny. We're going to have the best shotgun wedding there ever was, and we're going to live happily ever after. You can bet on it…"

★ ★ ★ ★ ★